THEIR LAST FULL MEASURE

(A Learning Experience, Book VI)

CHRISTOPHER G. NUTTALL

A VERY BRIEF RECAP

In the very near future, a handful of military veterans in the USA were abducted by an alien starship. Unluckily for their would-be captors—the Horde, a race of interstellar scavengers—the humans rapidly managed to break free and gain control of the starship. Steve Stuart, a rancher who had been growing more and more disillusioned with the government, saw opportunity—the starship could serve as the base for a new civilisation, the Solar Union.

Despite some small problems with planet-bound governments, the Solarians—as they would eventually be called—started to both recruit settlers for the new state *and* distribute alien-grade technology on Earth. After defeating a series of Horde ships that attempted to recapture their starship and attack Earth, the Solar Union was firmly in place.

This was, of course, unknown to the rest of the galaxy. To them, Earth wasn't even a microstate. This suited the Solarians just fine. Humans could and did travel beyond the solar system—as traders, mercenaries or even simple explorers—but no one wanted to attract the Galactics to Earth. The Solarians were already making improvements to GalTech that could not fail to alarm the major alien powers, particularly the Tokomak, the undisputed masters of the known galaxy.

Fifty years after Contact, the veil of secrecy fell. Humanity's involvement in a series of brushfire wars at the edge of known space could no longer be hidden, nor could elements of advanced technology. In response, the Tokomak dispatched a massive fleet to Sol with the intention of blasting Earth to cinders. Unknown to the Tokomak, the Solar Navy had *just* enough advanced technology to stand off the alien fleet and smash it. The follow-up attacks shattered the Tokomak grip on the nearby sectors, freeing hundreds of planets from their influence. Humanity had suddenly become a major regional power. A number of naval bases were rapidly established, both to extend human influence and protect human trade.

This had unfortunate effects on Earth. The expansion of the Solar Union—and its willingness to insist that anyone who wanted to emigrate, *could*—accidentally accelerated the social decline pervading civilisation. Europe, America and many other countries fell into civil war, something that caused considerable concern in orbit. One faction within the Solar Union wanted to intervene, others—feeling no loyalty to Earth—believed it was better to let Earthers handle their own affairs.

Captain-Commodore Hoshiko Sashimi Stuart—the granddaughter of Steve Stuart—accidentally stepped into a political minefield when she insisted that Earth should be left alone. Her family's political enemies were quick to use it against them. Accordingly, she was placed in command of a cruiser squadron and dispatched to the Martina Sector, where she would be well out of the public eye. However, she quickly discovered that the Druavroks—a powerful alien race—were bent on a campaign of genocide against their neighbours, including a number of human settlers. Allying herself with other threatened races, Hoshiko led a campaign that broke the Druavroks and laid the groundwork for a human-led federation—a Grand Alliance.

Unfortunately for humanity—and everyone else—the Tokomak had other ideas. Neola, the Tokomak who had commanded the fleet that died at Earth, managed to take control of the Tokomak Empire and prepare her people for a far more serious war. Her first step, after ensuring that the immense fleets were brought back online, was to attempt to lure a human starship—*Odyssey*—into a trap. Although humanity fell for what was presented, to them, as an olive branch from one of the oldest known races, the crew of *Odyssey* were able to escape and find their way back to the nearest safe port. In their wake, however, an ultimatum was sent. Humanity could surrender, or be mercilessly hunted down and exterminated.

This could not be borne.

Realising that the Tokomak would have to take their ships through a gravity point bottleneck at Apsidal, the Solar Union sent a massive fleet under Admiral Stuart to occupy the system and stand off the enemy forces. Unfortunately, Empress Neola followed the same line of reasoning and deployed her own fleet to pin the human ships against the gravity point. She was not, however, able to plan for the combination of advanced technology and sheer nerve, which allowed her human opponents to counter her and do immense damage to her fleet. Cutting her losses, Neola fled home... only to discover that she had been unseated, that half the known galaxy was on the verge of outright rebellion and, for the first time in a hundred thousand years, the Tokomak faced a devastating defeat...

PROLOGUE

It would have made Empress Neola laugh, if it wasn't so...*ironic.*

She had rebelled, the first junior officer—by the standards of her people—to rebel in thousands of years. She had led an almost effortless coup against the old ones, the ancients too doddering and old to realise that someone *could* overthrow them...only to discover, after the twin disasters of Apsidal and N-Gann, that someone had overthrown her in turn. They hadn't stripped her of power, they hadn't banished her to a retirement world nicely out of the way, but they had limited her power. The omnipotence she'd claimed was gone.

Although I was never quite omnipotent, she reflected, sourly. Sure, she'd been the absolute ruler of the Tokomak Empire, but...there had been limits. The humans and their pathetic Galactic Alliance hadn't surrendered, when faced with the prospect of clashing with the greatest military machine in the known galaxy. *The universe didn't bend to my will.*

She studied the handful of faces around the table, knowing her position was weaker than before. Once, she could have snapped her long fingers and everyone would have leapt to obey. Now...it was a popularity contest, where the soldiers and spacers decided for themselves who they'd follow, who they'd obey. Neola shuddered. She understood the importance of ensuring competence at the top—it was why she'd launched her coup—but soldiers and spacers shouldn't decide for themselves which orders they'd follow. At best, there would be long delays as they tried to argue out the pros and cons of each set of orders: at worst, there would be absolute anarchy. It was no way to run a government, let alone a war. And she knew they simply didn't have time to iron out the kinks before the humans set Tokomak Prime itself on fire.

And they know I lost the last campaign, she thought. *They're not inclined to listen to me.*

A human would have gritted her teeth. Neola was too practiced to reveal her emotions that openly, but anger and despair gnawed at her gut. It wasn't a complete disaster—she'd argued, time and time again—but hardly anyone believed her. Cold logic was no substitute for the shock of hundreds of thousands of lives, *important* lives, being expended on a gravity point assault. No one in the room cared one whit for the lesser races who served the Tokomak as sepoys, expendable cannon fodder, but the Tokomak spacers themselves? *They* were important. The Tokomak hadn't suffered such losses in living memory. And, given there were Tokomak who were literally thousands of years old, that was a very long time indeed.

"We expect you to behave yourself, Empress," Coordinator Hakav said. "And to listen to our advice."

You could just have taken power for yourself, Neola thought, coldly. It spoke of either rectitude or moral cowardice. She didn't care which. *Instead, you content yourself with giving advice.*

She wanted to laugh. Or cry. The youngsters often affected the manner of the old…but they didn't need to, not any longer. They were calling the shots. Now. And yet, they didn't have the courage to overthrow her completely. They had to know she was dangerous. Neola had overthrown ancients who'd held their posts for longer than most of them had been alive, sheer longevity giving them a legitimacy the youngsters lacked. She'd kill them all if she got a chance and they had to know it. But they'd merely hampered her. That was a mistake.

Unless they don't want to risk another round of infighting, she reminded herself. *We could lose the war with the humans while scrabbling amongst ourselves.*

She nodded, curtly, and directed their attention to the holographic display. "There is no point in lying to ourselves," she said. Let them think of her as fettered, for the moment. She'd regain what she'd lost in time. "We are not our servants, who need reassurance. We can accept that the situation is grim. The humans have scored a major victory."

"We have never lost a fleet base before," Admiral Kyan said.

"No." Neola conceded the point without rancour. "But we have many—*many*—fleet bases."

She spoke calmly, hiding her irritation as much as she could. "The humans have successfully prevented us from launching a major invasion of their sector. Right now, our fleets would have to proceed through FTL, a journey that would take decades. The human outposts blocking the gravity point chains have to be dislodged before we could mount an invasion in a reasonable space of time. We will be required to launch a series of gravity point assaults before we could even *think* about bringing our muscle to bear on Earth.

"However, we have other problems. The loss of a major fleet base"—she nodded to the admiral—"has...unsettled... our allies. Many of them are rethinking their stance in the light of new developments. Others are looking back to the days of their independence and wondering what, if anything, they can do while we're distracted. And while we are still strong enough to take out our allies if there is no other choice, they could produce a distraction at the worst possible time. Right now, there is a human fleet within striking distance of the inner worlds. It may only be a matter of time before that fleet starts an advance to the core."

She allowed her words to hang in the air. "To Tokomak Prime itself."

There was a long, chilling pause. She smiled inwardly, despite the seriousness of the situation. They'd never really considered just how easily a strength could become a weakness, if the balance of power shifted even slightly. The Tokomak had banned their servants from fortifying the gravity points, both to ensure free navigation and to make it difficult for anyone to stop their fleets from teaching any rebellious systems a lesson. Now, with a major enemy fleet pressing against the inner worlds themselves, the gravity points were terrifyingly undefended. Neola had started a fortification program, hastily repurposing planetary defence platforms and constructing floating fortresses from scratch, but she was uncomfortably aware the program would take time. Time she didn't have. The humans moved so quickly that they'd often managed to surprise even *her*.

And they've also managed to improve upon the technology they stole, she mused, sourly. The Tokomak had thought they'd taken technology as far as it could go. The humans had proved them wrong. In hindsight, it had been a convenient lie … a lie that had been believed, eventually even by the people who'd propagated it in the first place. Neola knew she'd pulled off some tactical innovations—she'd caught the humans by surprise, once or twice—but her people were ill-prepared to engage in a technological arms race. *Sooner or later, they'll come up with something that renders our giant reserve fleet nothing more than scrap metal.*

She shuddered again. The Tokomak had built literally *millions* of warships over thousands of years. They'd built so many ships they couldn't hope to man them, even if they gave every last one of their race a uniform and assigned him to a ship. The fleet had been held in reserve, the largest hammer in the known galaxy. The cost of keeping it even marginally operable had been staggering, even to them. But now, the fleet was only of limited value. The programs to bring the ships out of mothballs, crew them and deploy them to the front might not be completed in time to keep the humans from developing a whole new weapons system. And then the reserve fleet might become worse than useless.

"Time is not on our side," she said, calmly. She altered the display. "This is what I intend to do."

She outlined her plan, grimly aware that it was really nothing more than a more urgent version of her *previous* plan. She'd assumed she could secure Apsidal and open the way to Earth without much ado, forcing the humans to stand in defence of their homeworld rather than raiding the inner worlds themselves. She'd assumed...but those assumptions had died in fire, along with hundreds of thousands of Tokomak spacers. She hadn't bothered to calculate how many of their subjects had died—no one had cared enough to ask—but she knew *their* deaths were in the millions. And yet, she needed to demand much more from their client races. They'd all have to stand in defence of civilisation itself.

And yet, they're starting to wonder if we can be beaten, Neola thought. *And that makes them unreliable.*

She cursed the gerontocrats under her breath, savagely. The humans had an expression—Old Farts—that fitted them perfectly. They'd been so keen to make it clear that the Tokomak had never suffered even the slightest loss—not in recorded history, anyway—that losing even a single ship was a major disaster. And she'd lost *thousands* of ships. It was only a black eye—she had hundreds of thousands of ships coming online—but it looked bad. The public perception was that the Tokomak were losing. And the mere fact they had to consider public perception was itself a sign that things were going wrong...

"This could be the end," she warned. "The humans are at our gates. But we do have a preponderance of firepower and mobile units. If we can find the time to bring the rest of the fleet online—if—we can end this threat once and for all."

"*If,*" Coordinator Hakav repeated.

"*If,*" Neola agreed. "The galaxy has changed beyond measure in the last few years. We can no longer allow ourselves the delusion that we are unbeatable. We cannot afford to keep believing our own lies. We must adapt when change sweeps over us. Or die."

She let out a long breath. She was young, although by human standards she would be on the verge of death. And yet, even *she* had trouble grasping what might lie ahead. She'd been so used to the limits of everything from technology to politics, and to the concept of those limits being inflexible, that she had trouble imagining what might happen if they changed. The

Tokomak saw themselves as the undisputed and unchallengeable masters of the known universe. It rarely occurred to them—it *had* rarely occurred to them—that their dominance was not a natural law. The universe didn't guarantee them anything.

But it doesn't guarantee the humans anything either, she reminded herself, firmly. *They're strong, but they're not unbeatable. We can still reclaim the galaxy for ourselves.*

Sure, her thoughts answered, as the discussion continued to rage. *And what sort of galaxy will we pass down to our children?*

CHAPTER ONE

Hameeda's eyes snapped open.

For a moment, wrapped in the darkness, she was unsure of where she was or what she was doing. She'd been dreaming...she wasn't sure *what* she'd been dreaming, but it had troubled her on a level she couldn't express. There'd been shadows in her dreams...she shook her head as the cabin lights came on, illuminating a chamber that was surprisingly large and luxurious for such a small warship. But then, she was trapped in the LinkShip until the day she died. The designers had known they'd better make it comfortable.

She rubbed her forehead and sat up, trying to recover the dream. It bugged her, more than she cared to admit. She'd rarely dreamed since joining the navy...but then, she supposed, she'd often been too tired to do anything more than throw herself on her bunk at the end of her shift and sleep until the *next* shift began. Even now, with a small army of automatic helpers at her beck and call, she still got tired. Her body was in the peak of health, and would remain that way until she died, but she could still get mentally tired. And there was no one who could take her place.

Hameeda sighed, then reached out through her implants to touch the local processor. The LinkShip was surrounded by the featureless darkness of FTL, effectively alone within the folded universe. Her long-range sensors

1

had picked up the occasional hint of other starships passing through FTL, but none of them had come close enough to exchange greetings. They might have been hundreds of light years away, given how gravity waves propagated within FTL. There was no way to be entirely certain of anything unless they came a great deal closer. A status display appeared in front of her and she studied it. She was definitely alone on the ship.

Perhaps I should have asked for a companion, she thought, ruefully. *Or a sexbot.*

She snorted at the thought—she'd tried a sexbot when she'd reached her majority, only to discover that even the most humanoid robot wasn't human—and swung her legs over the side of the bed. The floor grew warm under her naked feet. Hameeda didn't bother to check her appearance in the mirror, let alone don her uniform, as she paced down the corridor and onto the bridge. She felt a twinge of the old disappointment as she stepped through the airlock—the chamber was really nothing more than a single command chair, surrounded by holographic displays she rarely used—and then pushed it aside. One day, all starships would be controlled by direct neural links and complex command bridges would be a thing of the past. She rather suspected that would be a long time in the future. A normal bridge might be less efficient, but it *looked* better.

Her lips quirked as she sat down, the neural links activating automatically. Her awareness expanded, twinning itself time and time again with the starship's processor nodes. She took a long breath as a string of status reports fell into her head, each assessed by her intellectual-shadow and classed as non-urgent. There was no reason to be concerned about anything, the network said. She checked anyway, just to be sure. The LinkShip was in perfect shape. It was more than ready to carry out the mission.

Hameeda nodded to herself, then checked the FTL drive. The LinkShip was rocketing towards Yunnan, a major Tokomak fleet base a few hundred light years from N-Gann. If Solar Intelligence was correct—and Hameeda took everything the spooks said with a grain of salt—the Tokomak were massing ships there, preparing for … *something*. Hameeda's tactical computers offered a number of possibilities, listed in order of probability. They could launch a counterstroke at N-Gann, despite the presence of two-thirds of the Solar Navy; they could withdraw the ships to block a thrust towards Tokomak Prime; they might even be bracing themselves for a revolution, for a whole *string* of revolutions. Hameeda had read the reports from the inner worlds. There were literally *hundreds* of alien races that hated the Tokomak, but were too scared to rebel. That might have changed, now the Tokomak had taken a black eye. Their servants might be wondering if they could launch a successful revolt against their masters...

And they'd better pray they could get away with it, if they did, Hameeda told herself. *The Tokomak won't hesitate to burn entire planets to ash if that's what they have to do to stop the rebels.*

She shuddered. She'd grown up in the Solar Union—she'd never set foot on Earth—but she'd heard the tales. Her grandmother had been born in the most barbaric region of the planet, a place that was up against some pretty stiff competition. She'd been aware, from birth until she'd escaped to space, that the strong did what they liked and the weak suffered what they must. Hameeda had found it hard to believe, when she'd listened to her grandmother's stories of near-permanent starvation, warlords, religious fanatics and raving misogynists who hated and feared women. She believed it now. The Tokomak would do whatever it took to keep themselves in power, fearful of what would happen if—when—they lost it. They and their human enemies weren't *that* different.

A timer appeared in her vision, counting down the final seconds. Hameeda checked her weapons and shields again, bracing herself for the worst. The FTL baffles were *supposed* to keep the enemy from detecting a ship in FTL, but the Tokomak might be wise to that trick by now. They were unimaginative, not stupid. And they *were* the ones who'd developed FTL travel. The Solar Navy's officers had spent years wondering just what, if anything, the Tokomak might have kept back for themselves. They didn't *have* to share everything with their allies. Why should they?

There might be an ambush lying in wait for me, she mused. *Or they might be preparing to yank me out of FTL early and pound the hell out of me.*

The timer reached *zero.* The LinkShip hummed out of FTL. Hameeda allowed herself a sigh of relief as the near-space sensors drew a blank, then started to deploy a handful of passive sensor platforms. A torrent of information rushed into her sensor processors as the LinkShip coasted towards the planet, daring the local sensors to detect her. Hameeda snorted to herself, half-wishing she could kick whoever had issued her orders. She could have gotten a *lot* closer without any real risk of detection if she'd remained hidden under cloak, but the analysts wanted to know when—if—the locals spotted her when she wasn't trying to hide. It wouldn't be long. They might not have seen her coming—the lack of a welcoming committee suggested the locals hadn't worked out how to track her yet—but they'd detect her drive emissions soon enough. She rather suspected it was too much to hope that some automated sensor would decide she *couldn't* be there and dismiss her as nothing more than a sensor glitch. There was a war on. The Tokomak would probably investigate any sensor contacts that appeared on their screens.

We could use that against them, she thought, wryly. *A few hundred fake contacts and they'd be ready to ignore an entire battle fleet bearing down on them.*

She put the thought to one side as more and more data flowed into the sensors. Yunnan had been populated by spacefaring races for thousands of years and it showed. Four rocky worlds, three of them heavily developed; two gas giants, both surrounded by cloudscoops and hundreds of industrial nodes. Her eyes narrowed as she recalled the history datafiles, the ones that stated the Tokomak had raised the natives from the mud and given them the keys to the stars. Reading between the lines of flattery so cloying that even the most narcissistic human in existence would vomit in disgust, it was clear the Tokomak had enslaved the natives after discovering their world and its three gravity points. They might have the stars, but only as passengers on someone else's ships. Their worlds were no longer theirs. And they might—just—want to rebel.

Her lips tightened as her sensors picked out the signs of new construction around the gravity points. The Tokomak were hastily fortifying them, although she wasn't sure who they thought they were fortifying them *against*. Admiral Stuart *could* take her fleet from N-Gann to Yunnan if she wished, but she'd prefer to take the long way through FTL rather than exhaust her fleet in punching through the gravity points. The fortresses would be expensive white elephants if Yunnan itself was attacked. They'd be unable to cover the planet *and* the gravity points. She shook her head, mentally. There might be other problems. The Harmonies were only three jumps away and *they* had a powerful fleet. They might be allies, as far as the Tokomak were concerned, but...given a chance, who knew what they'd do?

The Tokomak probably don't know, she thought. *And that might be why they're building the fortresses.*

A flash of red light flared across her vision. The enemy had pinged her, active sensors sweeping her hull. She watched, feeling a twinge of amusement, as their entire defence network flash-woke. Her sensors drank it all in, noting the position of everything from active sensor platforms to orbital fortresses guarding the planets and their industrial nodes from enemy attack. The Tokomak hadn't skimped on the defences, as a handful of enemy cruisers left orbit and barrelled straight for her. They'd clearly had some reason to fear attack.

And they might have been right, she thought. *They just didn't expect it to come from us.*

She watched the cruisers draw near, then kicked her drives into high gear. The cruisers swept their sensors across her time and time again, the universal signal ordering the unlucky recipient to stop or be fired upon. Hameeda wondered if they actually *expected* her to stop or if they were mindlessly following orders that had been written thousands of years before humans had discovered fire. She swept closer, bracing herself for the moment they took the gloves off and opened fire. They'd have a solid lock on her hull, with or without active sensors. They might not give her any warning before they opened fire...

There! She sensed the flicker and threw the LinkShip into an evasive pattern, sweeping through a set of manoeuvres that would have been impossible for anything larger than a gunboat ten years ago. A handful of shots rocketed through where she'd been, missing her cleanly. She smirked as she darted near a cruiser, trying to dare the ship to fire…knowing that if she missed, she might just hit one of her fellows. The Tokomak ships could take a few hits, but would they take the chance? She snorted as the enemy held their fire, then she altered course and headed directly towards Yunnan itself. The enemy ships were left eating her dust. They changed their course, following her, but it was too late. The only way they'd ever get back into weapons range was if she *let* them.

The planet grew larger as she zoomed towards it. The enemy panicked, hundreds of freighters leaving orbit and dropping into FTL without even bothering to boost themselves into high orbit first. There'd be some trouble over *that* when the unlucky crews returned, she was sure. Human bureaucrats were mindless fools—she'd met too many, even in the Solar Union—but Tokomak bureaucrats were worse. The freighter crews would probably be stripped of their licences when the dust settled, if they were lucky. Who knew? Perhaps they'd make their way to N-Gann and join the Galactic Alliance instead. They would be welcome.

She watched, grimly, as the planetary defences brought more and more weapons on line. The orbital battlestations would be a major threat if she got too close, while—oddly—the giant ring surrounding the planet was studded with tactical sensors too. She frowned, wondering if the ring had weapons mounted too. That was odd—the Galactics were normally careful not to do anything that might make the rings targets—but there *was* a war on. Perhaps they'd decided to gamble their human opponents wouldn't risk an accidental genocide by destroying the ring and bombarding the planet with debris. Or maybe they simply didn't care.

They have to care, Hameeda thought. The alternative was unthinkable. *The population below isn't expendable.*

She accessed her communications array and uploaded a handful of commands into the system as she swept into firing range. The enemy CO was an idiot, as he opened fire the moment she flew into range...*extreme* range. A full-sized battleship could have evaded his missiles, let alone the nimble LinkShip. Hameeda was tempted to hold her position and let him empty his magazines, if he was stupid enough to oblige her. But the risks were too great. A lucky hit—or an antimatter warhead—might do real damage. She had no illusions. The LinkShip was too small to soak up damage and keep going. If she lost her shields, she was doomed.

The barrage of missiles grew stronger as she darted closer to the planet, evading them with almost effortless ease. She wondered, idly, if *someone* was screaming at the CO to stop wasting missiles, to stop throwing warheads around too close to the ring for comfort. A single nuclear warhead might not do *much* damage to a structure that literally surrounded an entire planet, but why take chances? She evaded another spread of missiles, then dropped below the ring. Thankfully, if there *were* any weapons on the ring, they held their fire. Either they didn't exist, or whoever was in charge was smarter...

They could hardly be stupider, she thought. She opened the communications array, searching for enemy nodes. Here, so close to the planet, they couldn't keep her from hacking the system without shutting down the entire network. The Tokomak system wasn't badly designed, but it had its flaws. And humanity had had plenty of time to learn to take advantage of each and every one of them. *And now...*

She uploaded the hacking package, sending it into every communications node within reach. The message would spread rapidly, using codes they'd hacked from other Tokomak systems to stay ahead of any mass-wiping programs. It wouldn't last forever, she'd been warned, but it would take them weeks to get rid of it...weeks while the message, the call to war and revolution, would be seen by millions. If only a tiny percentage of them rose against their masters, the Tokomak would have a *real* fight on their hands. Who knew how much of their productive capability would be *lost* if they had to suppress a hundred revolts?

And how many of their servants and slaves will be butchered to keep the revolt from spreading, she thought, sourly. The Tokomak had always reacted badly to any challenge, particularly from the younger races. *We could be doing the wrong thing here.*

She put the thought away as new alerts flashed up in front of her. The enemy were launching gunboats, hoping they could chase her out of low orbit and back into missile range. She smiled, resisting the temptation to force them to play cat and mouse for the next few hours. It would be entertaining, but she couldn't risk being hit. Not here. She'd completed her mission and now it was time to run. She altered course and dove towards the ring, flying into a giant starship repair yard. A transport ship, large enough to carry a hundred LinkShips within its hull, was drifting within the yard, open to space. Hameeda flew right *through* it, resisting the urge to fire off a handful of missiles at the repair facilities. It would hamper them—slightly—if they lost the yard, but the risk was unthinkable. She wasn't prepared to risk genocide. Not now. Not ever.

The enemy commander opened fire as she climbed into high orbit, his missiles sprinting towards her. She cancelled her drives, coming to an abrupt stop, then dropped a handful of decoys before vanishing into FTL. The combination of sensor static and gravity baffles *should* keep them from realising what she'd done... she shook her head as she rocketed away from the system, all too aware that she'd never know. They might think they'd destroyed her. They might tell everyone they'd destroyed her. They might not even know they were lying. They might genuinely *believe* they'd destroyed her.

But no one will believe them, she thought. *They've lied so often that they won't be believed even if they honestly think they're telling the truth.*

She put the thought aside as she waited long enough to be sure she was clear, then slipped her mind out of the network and fell back into her own body. The experience wasn't so disorienting now, thankfully... she wiped sweat from her brow, her stomach grumbling angrily as it reminded her she hadn't eaten anything for hours. She disconnected herself from the chair and stood, feeling her legs wobble threateningly. She'd have to force herself to exercise, during the flight to her next target. There were limits to what a combination of genetic modification and nanotech helpers could do.

Not that it matters, she thought, as she headed to the galley. She couldn't be bothered to cook, but there were plenty of food patterns stored within the processor. *If we lose this war, there won't be anything of us left. And our opponents won't hesitate to commit genocide.*

CHAPTER TWO

There was an unfortunate truth of growing up a Stuart, Hoshiko had discovered a long time ago, that it was very hard to convince *anyone*, let alone everyone, that you'd earned something on your own merits. The Solar Union had no formal aristocracy, but anyone who could claim descent from the original Founders had to deal with both the advantages and disadvantages of having such illustrious relatives. And the simple fact that most of them were still alive and politically powerful made it even *harder* to defeat the charges of nepotism that were hurled about when one of their descendants reached a position of power.

It was an ironic point, Hoshiko had always considered. She was hardly the black sheep of the family, not in any *real* sense, but she *had* openly disagreed with some of her illustrious relatives. She wouldn't have been reassigned to Antarctica—in reality, the Martina Sector—if she hadn't pissed off a bunch of powerful people. Openly disagreeing with the family was a capital crime, in the eyes of some of the oldsters. It never seemed to occur to them that the younger generation didn't share their emotional attachments and saw no reason to shed blood and treasure for the sake of a world that had been driven into the dirt by its inhabitants. She didn't regret what she'd done, but there were times when she wished the family wasn't so rigid. The younger generation was growing larger all the time.

She held herself at parade rest as the teleporter pad lit up, a beam of light materialising in front of her and condensing into the form of a man. Steve Stuart—Grandpa Steve, to her—looked utterly unchanged, his age frozen at roughly thirty years old. The oldsters didn't care for the fads of the younger generation—they didn't swap sexes or colour themselves like rainbows—but they had hang-ups of their own. Steve looked old enough to be mature and yet young enough to be handsome. It was hard for some of his peers to believe he was really in his second century. He looked no older than Hoshiko herself.

"Grandpa." Hoshiko saluted, even though—technically—her grandfather was neither in the military nor a government official. "Welcome to N-Gann."

"Hoshiko," Steve said. He stepped off the pad and embraced her. "It's good to see you again."

Hoshiko nodded as she hugged him back. He'd always been there for her, a friendly ear when she'd started to rebel against her parents and—later—when she'd openly quarrelled with the rest of her family. He hadn't agreed with her—he'd made that clear—but he'd respected her right to have an opinion. Hoshiko supposed that came with maturity. It was just a shame her parents weren't old enough to be trusted. She snorted at the thought. They were in their seventies and *she* was in her forties. The Solar Navy wasn't in the habit of giving fleet commands to *children*.

She let go of him and stepped back. They were very different. Steve was tall, muscular and blond, wearing a simple starship tunic that dated all the way back to the early days. She was tall, with long black hair, almond eyes and tinted skin. The older generation commented, sometimes, that Steve had married a woman from the other side of the world. The younger generation didn't care. Hoshiko and most of her family were boring, to them. They didn't even change their skin colour to ensure they stayed fashionable, let alone anything else. But then, being a Stuart brought responsibilities. Hoshiko would probably have been disowned if she'd refused to serve at least *one* term in the military.

"This is a remarkable ship," Steve said. "And human-built."

"From scratch," Hoshiko agreed. "And they've held up very well."

She indicated the hatch. "Would you care to accompany me?"

"It would be my pleasure," Steve said. "And thank you for not laying on any formal receptions."

"I'm afraid there will be a formal dinner later," Hoshiko told him. "My staff wanted a chance to meet you, of course. And I'm sure you wanted to meet them."

She smiled as she heard her grandfather snort. He'd always dreaded pressing the flesh. And yet, he was easily the *most* famous person in the entire solar system. His fame reached well beyond Earth and the Solar Union itself, the man who had turned an entire world on its head and given the human race the stars. *And* brought the hope of freedom to countless billions of aliens. He could do nothing else—he could die tomorrow—and he'd still be remembered as long as the human race endured.

This too is fleeting, Hoshiko reminded herself. *Sooner or later, everyone is forgotten.*

She felt cold as she led him down the corridor and into her cabin. The Tokomak Empire had endured for thousands of years—the Tokomak themselves had been spacefaring for far longer—and yet their entire existence was a mere eyeblink, on the scale of the entire universe. A million races could rise, flourish and fall in the time it took for the galaxy to complete one grand cycle. There were people who wondered why there weren't hundreds of ancient races around, each one a million years older than any *known* race. Some of their speculations were truly disturbing. If there was something out there that ate advanced races...

Or maybe they just travelled beyond the edge of the galaxy and vanished, Hoshiko thought, dryly. *We may never know.*

She opened the hatch, motioned for him to take a seat and headed to the drinks cabinet. "Can I get you anything?"

"Anything," Steve said. "I never had the time to develop expensive tastes."

Hoshiko smiled as she poured them both a generous glass of Scotch. It was surprisingly good, she'd been told, for Scotch that had never been anywhere near Scotland. The oldsters might place value on alcoholic drinks that had matured for years, but the youngsters thought they were silly. It was simplicity itself to program a food processor to turn out something that was effectively indistinguishable from the original. But then, she supposed rarity alone gave the drink value. There was a certain pleasure to be had in owning something expensive and showing off a little.

"I was hoping the government would send someone out here," she said, as she passed him a glass. "I wasn't expecting it to be you."

Steve laughed. "You couldn't lie to me when you were a little girl with a bow in her hair," he said. "What makes you think you can lie to me now?"

"The optimism of youth?" Hoshiko grinned. "What makes you think I'm lying to you?"

"I was a serving officer too," Steve said. "Back then, we had a *real* problem with micromanagement. The oafs in the Oval Office thought they could issue orders in real time and get away with it. Which they did. It was *us* who paid the price. Here…you'd be foolish to expect the government to either hold your hand or issue orders you could actually follow. By the time you got them…"

"The situation would have moved on," Hoshiko finished. It took six months for someone to travel from Earth to Apsidal, let alone N-Gann. It would take a year for her to request orders and receive them. By then, things really *would* have moved on. "And things are moving already."

She sat down, resting her drink on her lap. Command was a lonely place. She didn't have anyone she could confide in, let alone share her doubts and fears. Her subordinates had problems of their own. They didn't need to know hers. And…she shook her head. If she confessed her weaknesses, some of her subordinates would start to lose confidence in her and start second-guessing her at the worst possible time. Steve Stuart, the man who had given Earth the stars, was perhaps the only person who understood the weight resting on her shoulders. She could lose the war—and ensure the destruction of the entire human race—in an afternoon.

"We beat them," she said. She was sure Steve would have read the summary when he passed through Apsidal. She was pretty sure he'd have read the entire report, from the cold-blooded analysis of the engagements to the formal assessments and suggestions for future operations. He'd certainly had more than enough time. "But we haven't won the war. Not yet."

She keyed her terminal, projecting a holographic starchart. N-Gann, Apsidal and the stars between them glowed green, although she knew that could change at any moment. The Tokomak hadn't started raiding her supply lines yet, but it was just a matter of time before that changed. They were probably reading their own history books, assessing how their ancestors had forged the greatest empire the galaxy had ever known. Hoshiko had studied their texts, when she'd been preparing for her first deployment. The alien authors had been long-winded bores—they never used one word when a thousand would do—but they'd generally made good points. Their early campaigns provided insight into how they should run a war against the human race.

"We're on the edge of the inner worlds now," she said. A tingle ran down her spine. No invading fleet had so much as *dared* to slip so close to Tokomak Prime, even though there were still thousands of light years between N-Gann and the enemy homeworld. "But that weakens our ties to Sol even as it brings us into contact with more and more of their mobile units. They're probably reactivating even more of them as we speak."

She gritted her teeth. It didn't seem fair, somehow. On the face of it, the numbers were so badly against the human race that it wasn't even a contest. The Tokomak could afford to trade a hundred ships for each and every one of hers, including the gunboats, and come out ahead. Their fleets could march towards Earth, blowing hell out of every blocking force they encountered until time eventually ran out. She knew the situation wasn't *that* bad—the Tokomak couldn't even *begin* to man their entire fleet—but it was pretty damn bad. And she was alone, right on the end of a branch.

She had no doubt the enemy was already plotting how best to saw it off behind her.

"We've heard reports of mass conscriptions," she continued. "We know their allies are sending spacers…some more reluctantly than others. We know time is not on our side. We have the edge now, but that won't last."

"We're in the same position as Imperial Japan," Steve commented. "We have to win quickly or not at all."

Hoshiko nodded. She'd studied her ancestors. She still found it hard to believe that they'd risked war when the odds were so badly against them, although—as she'd dug into the geopolitical background, she'd started to realise that they'd faced the choice between fighting now or fighting later, perhaps under far worse conditions. She had no sympathy for Imperial Japan—it had been as fascistic as Nazi Germany—but she understood the problem facing its leaders. And Earth now faced a worse one. The Tokomak would happily spend centuries hunting down every last human, just to make sure the threat was crushed beyond all hope of recovery.

"And that means taking the war into enemy space," she said, calmly. "And *that* means we cannot wait for orders from Earth."

Steve lifted his eyebrows. "Explain?"

Hoshiko met his eyes evenly. She was sure he understood—he'd done the same when she really *had* been a little girl—but she knew he wanted to understand her reasoning. It was quite possible, as she'd been taught in school, for two people to reach the same conclusions from widely different starting points and radically different logic. And besides, Steve *hadn't* commanded anything larger than a small squadron. It was odd to realise that, in some ways, she had *more* experience than her grandfather. The thought gave her an odd sense of reassurance. She really wasn't a child any longer. She could stand up for herself.

"They're already working on their defences." Hoshiko indicated the display, showing worlds and gravity points that were being hastily fortified. "The longer we wait, the longer they'll have to block our advance and bring more and more ships of their own online. If we don't move soon, we may have to resign ourselves to eventual defeat. It may take decades for them to crush us, unless we come up with a *real* silver bullet, but crush us they will. And that will be the end."

She took a breath. "*Is* there a silver bullet?"

"Not yet." Steve didn't bother to dissemble. "Admirals Webster and White have come up with a number of improvements, some of which have been added to our weapons already, but nothing that *really* changes the game. They keep promising a war-winner...unfortunately for them, everyone's already read *Superiority*. We do think there are some promising lines of research that will turn the enemy fleet into nothing more than scrap metal, but..."

He shrugged. Hoshiko understood. "Don't hold your breath, then."

"Yes." Steve nodded. "Right now, we don't have much hope of *really* shifting the balance of power through new technology. Give us a century, and..."

Hoshiko nodded. She'd heard rumours, so highly-classified that even a fleet admiral only heard whispers, of a handful of colony ships being launched into unexplored regions of space well beyond enemy control. A human colony, so far from the Tokomak that they might never stumble across it, would make all kinds of advances as it fortified its position and built a whole new war fleet. She understood the potential of GalTech better than most. Given time, and unrestricted fabricators, a fleet could be built up in short order. And if they lost the war, the colony would—one day—return to the sector and extract revenge. Who knew? Maybe their tech would advance so far it would be a very short war.

Or maybe not, she thought. She hated the enemy, but she had to admit they'd been ingenious. The war had killed off much of the deadwood infesting the enemy high command, giving them a chance to promote younger and more capable commanders in their place. And, perhaps, galvanised their long-moribund research and development programs. Given time, who knew *what* they'd do. *They might advance too, after the war. We certainly showed them that technological advancement was still possible.*

"Then we have to take the offensive." Hoshiko studied the starchart thoughtfully. "Do you see any objections?"

Steve gave her a sharp look. "Are you asking for my support, or for my opposition?"

"Your insight." Hoshiko wished, just for a moment, that they weren't related. It would be easier for them to disagree if they weren't grandfather and grandchild. "And your advice."

"I would be far happier if we hadn't drawn their attention when we did," Steve said. "I always knew it was inevitable, after we started expanding outside our own system, but I'd hoped we'd have a few more decades. Their power was always hard to grasp. At some point, the numbers become just ... *statistics*."

He smiled, rather dryly. "But that's no help, is it?"

"No." Hoshiko indicated the starchart. "Do you have any objections?"

"I have a *lot* of objections," Steve said, bluntly. "I dare say there will be hundreds of critics who will blast you for risking everything on one throw of the dice, if you lose. Such people are like cockroaches. You just can't squash them. And ... yes, I can see a great many things that could go wrong. You can have those insights and welcome, in the hope that you can minimise the risks as much as possible. But Hoshiko..."

He took a breath. "None of those objections outweigh the risk of sitting on our bums and doing nothing. You said it yourself. Time is not on our side. We either take the offensive, and force them to react to us, or we concede eventual—certain—defeat. There's no prospect of being able to force them to stop, unless we really do come up with a silver bullet, and little prospect of blowing up their worlds and calling it a draw. And ... I like to think we're better than that."

"Survival comes first," Hoshiko said. She hated the idea of mass planetary bombardment, but she wouldn't hesitate to retaliate if the enemy started it. Retaliation—or the creditable threat of retaliation—was the only thing that might deter the Tokomak from hitting Earth with antimatter bombs. "If it's them or us..."

"Then you have to do whatever you can to ensure it really *isn't* them or us," Steve said. He kept his voice very cold. "Are those the sort of insights you wanted?"

"Yeah." Hoshiko had to smile. Steve had been a good grandfather, looking after the grandkids without ever really *spoiling* them. "I trust you'll be joining the conference?"

"If I must." Steve looked amused. "But won't that undermine your authority?"

"I have a bunch of very keen subordinates," Hoshiko said. "Half of them will take your presence as a sign to start an argument."

"Which is better than the alternative," Steve told her. "Believe me, insincere flattery isn't worth having. *Someone* has to play devil's advocate and point out that the emperor has no clothes. Not a safe place to be, not when I was your age, but important."

He smiled in memory. "Just as long as they remember they're the ones on the sharp end."

"Right now, we're *all* on the sharp end," Hoshiko said. She drained her glass and stood. "Coming?"

CHAPTER THREE

Hoshiko forced herself to ignore Steve's quiet gasp as she led him into the conference chamber. It *was* striking, particularly to a groundpounder, but he'd been in space for longer than she'd been alive. He should be used to immersive holographic environments by now, even ones that gave the impression they'd walked right through an airlock and into airless space. Her lips quirked at the thought. If they'd somehow jumped into space, they'd be dying by now. Their implants and genetic enhancements had their limits.

Although people have survived long periods of exposure to vacuum with the right equipment, she thought, as she took her place in the centre of the chamber. *Some of them weren't even permanently harmed by the experience.*

She pushed the thought aside as she studied the god's eye view in front of her. The fleet itself, positioned close enough to the gravity point to reinforce the defences without sacrificing the ability to move rapidly to the defence of N-Gann itself; the planet, with its cluster of improvised defences and industrial nodes that had been reconfigured to support her fleet; the hundreds of freighters moving in and out of the system, carrying word of the war and enemy defeats back to their homeworld. She knew some of them might not be friendly—their sensor records would give the enemy insight into her defences—but there was nothing she could do about it.

They didn't have time to search every ship that wanted to visit N-Gann. Some of her officers had suggested closing the system, banning everything that wasn't human, but she'd overruled them. The Galactic economy was already a mess. They didn't need more reasons to hate humanity.

"It never fails to awe me," Steve said, quietly. He was studying the giant ring orbiting N-Gann. "They built on such a scale and then...they just lost the urge to keep going."

Hoshiko shrugged. The Tokomak were a planet-bound race. They might have lived and worked in space for longer than humanity had known how to use fire, but they still kept the mindset of their ancestors. They still thought there were limits. Hoshiko and her generation, on the other hand, wouldn't live on a planet if they were paid. The limits that kept ground-pounders...*grounded* simply didn't exist in space, where there was endless living space, unlimited resources and vast sources of energy. The Solar Union didn't need *planets*. It just needed asteroids, technology and a willingness to work. They'd be building rings of their own soon, if they didn't move straight to Dyson Spheres. She'd seen the plans drawn up by idealists, for the days after the war. A Dyson Sphere would be something *new*. No one, not even the Tokomak, had tried to enclose an entire sun.

"I guess they never realised the limits had vanished," she said, quietly. "And there are humans who have the same problem."

"It's an old problem." Steve shot her a sharp look. "Too much conservatism and you end up with stagnation, decline and eventual defeat. Too much progressivism and you end up with chaos, decline and eventual defeat. The trick is to find a way to balance them."

Hoshiko shrugged and returned her attention to the display as her senior officers started to flicker into view, her eyes studying the links between gravity points that led towards Tokomak Prime. The display felt a little condensed—in reality, the stars were nowhere near that close—but she understood. Control of a gravity point allowed someone to jump light years in a single bound, eliminating the distance between the two star systems. There was no need to worry about the stars and planets in the middle if you could just jump across them. She supposed that explained some of the oddities of galactic civilisation. Earth had remained largely unmolested for so long because the closest gravity point was fifty light years away. It was no wonder, to her, that the Tokomak hadn't bothered to fortify the points. As long as they'd possessed the biggest fleet in the known universe, there'd been no need.

Her lips twitched. *And now that's come back to bite them on the behind,* she thought, coldly. *I bet they regret it now.*

She cleared her throat as the last of the images blinked into existence, a handful of warning messages and security notifications scrolling through the air. Holographic conferences could be awkward at times, and there were lingering fears over security, but they had very definite advantages. If nothing else, she didn't have to assemble her senior officers on a single starship. The enemy would have to get *very* lucky to take out all the flag officers with a single hit, but she didn't feel like taking chances. War was dangerous enough without running crazy risks.

"You have all had a chance to review the latest reports," she said. "On one hand, we have received reinforcements from Sol. On the other, we have not received any real orders. The ships were dispatched well before we arrived at Apsidal, let alone captured, lost and recaptured the system. We remain bound to do as we see fit, within certain limits. And we must face certain unpleasant realities. The longer we stay here, tied to a handful of systems, the greater the chance of losing the war. They—our enemies—are already building up their defences.

"They are not going to talk to us. They've ignored the message drones we've sent, offering to discuss a truce. That may be lucky—delay works in their favour, not ours—but the blunt truth is that the war is going to be fought to a finish. Either we crush their ability to make war on us, by blasting our way to Tokomak Prime itself and *forcing* them to surrender, or we concede eventual defeat. There are no other options."

She paused. "Does anyone wish to dispute my assessment?"

There was a pause. No one spoke. Hoshiko wasn't surprised. Her senior officers were a mixed bag, from men and women who would follow her unquestioningly to people who feared her drive or simply wanted her position for themselves. But they were all experienced officers, people who knew the facts of life. Some would be more optimistic, others would be more pessimistic, but they'd all understand the realities. Their time was running out.

"We have no choice," she said, when it was clear no one was going to speak. "We must resume the offensive now, before they have a chance to recover and take the offensive themselves. Towards that"—she tapped her remote, altering the holographic display—"I have drawn up a handful of operational plans. My staff have refined them into basic concepts."

She smiled, rather grimly. Her staff had done a great deal more than merely *refine* them. They'd drawn up plans for actually putting her concepts into operation, putting together scenarios and simulations that suggested what might happen if one or more of the concepts were put into operation. Hoshiko dreaded staff work, but she appreciated it. The backbone of any interstellar war was logistics, which required careful planning. She dreaded to think what would happen if they outran their logistics and found themselves unable to either fight or retreat.

"There are three basic concepts," she continued. "Plan Donitz calls for the fleet to cruise around the inner worlds, blowing merry hell out of their defences and logistical support network. If we're lucky, it might even encourage some of the peons to rebel. The advantage of this plan is that we might avoid a decisive defeat, particularly if we split the fleet; the disadvantage is that we risk being defeated in detail, with each separate squadron being crushed by overwhelming force. And we won't be touching the core of their power.

"Plan Nimitz calls for a single solid thrust through the gravity point and straight towards Tokomak Prime. We wouldn't be messing around, not this time. We'd be driving on their homeworld and they'd know it. The advantage of this plan is that, if we win, we *win*. The war will be over.

The disadvantage is that they'd mass *everything* to meet us, which means we might lose most of the fleet for nothing. We'd be risking everything on one throw of the dice.

"Plan Wellington is a little more subtle. We'd split the fleet. One force would proceed through the gravity point, accompanied by sensor drones and everything else that might convince the enemy that we're actually running with Plan Nimitz. The other force, the main force, would creep *around* the enemy position and come at Tokomak Prime from an unexpected direction. At that point, the enemy would be caught between two fires. The advantage of this plan is that we'd have a shot at the enemy home-world, without giving them a convenient bottleneck they can use to stop us. The disadvantage is that the two fleets wouldn't be in close contact. Coordinating an assault on an interstellar scale is never easy."

She allowed herself a cold smile. "But that might be an advantage," she said. "They know the KISS principle as well as we do. They'd never expect us to risk a two-prong assault."

"They risked one themselves, at Apsidal," Admiral Rolf Hanker pointed out. "And they kicked our ass."

"They had more ships to play with," Hoshiko reminded him. "They still do."

She took a breath. "There are advantages and disadvantages to all three plans," she pointed out. There was no point in trying to deny it. "But I would prefer to go with Plan Wellington. It offers us the greatest chance of victory, mingled with the ability to concede defeat and fall back if it becomes clear that things *haven't* gone in our favour. And even if we fail"—her hands clenched, just for a second—"we'll give them one hell of a fright. We might even be able to do a *lot* of damage to their industrial base."

Admiral Teller frowned. "You've made up your mind?"

"Talk me out of it, if you can." Hoshiko hid her annoyance. She'd called a council of war to ensure she had their support, as well as their obedience. The price was that they were free to pick holes in the plan, if they could.

"Or would you rather we gave them time to pick themselves up and come at us with a very large fleet?"

"A *very* large fleet," Admiral Hanker said. "If they get even *half* of their ships online..."

"We've all seen the projections," Teller snapped. "If we risk everything, here, we...we risk everything."

"Yes." Hoshiko kept her voice even, somehow. "Might I remind you that our enemy is ruthless? They've already started pogroms against humans in their territory. It won't be long before they start crushing *everyone* who dares stand up to them. This is not a war that can be ended by a peace conference, with everyone agreeing to disagree."

She slipped into deliberate crudity to make her point. "We cannot bend over for them, in the knowledge that our submission brings our survival. They won't be content with crushing our independence and raping our bodies and souls until we can do no more than mouth platitudes...perhaps even come to believe them. They will *destroy* us, utterly. Every last man, woman and child will die. Defeat means the end of the fucking universe!"

There was dead silence. "We have to stay on the offensive," she warned. "And that means taking the fleet to Tokomak Prime and tearing the *guts* out of their empire once and for all."

She took a moment to gather herself. "Or would anyone like to dispute it? Does anyone think we can come to terms with them?"

"No." Steve's voice was very quiet, but it caught their attention. "I don't think anyone can dispute it."

"War to the knife, then," Hoshiko said. She knew it was going to be brutal. "And for that, we need Plan Wellington."

"We might be able to encourage the oppressed masses to rise," Teller pointed out. "If we take out the orbital defences..."

"It won't make that much difference," Hanker snapped. "If we captured their worlds intact, complete with their industrial bases, we will still be fucked. Given time, they can crush us effortlessly. The projections make that clear."

"Quite." Hoshiko nodded, curtly. "I would like to believe the oppressed masses will rise against their masters and tear out their throats. But we have no way of knowing when it will happen, if indeed it *will* happen. They may be waiting for us to liberate them. They may be waiting for us to slay their alien masters in their lair. Or they may be fearful of what *we* will do to them. The bottom line is that we cannot *rely* on triggering an uprising and, even if one did take place, it wouldn't help us. Not immediately."

She shuddered, envisioning alien battleships descending on rebellious worlds. The Tokomak wouldn't bother to land ground troops, not unless they had some reason to try to recover the worlds intact. They'd just bombard indiscriminately, slaughtering rebels and loyalists alike to deter other worlds from rising against them. Entire cities would be wiped out in an eyeblink, taking millions of lives with them. And Hoshiko wouldn't be able to retaliate, not for worlds that weren't part of the Galactic Alliance. That would open Earth and the other Alliance worlds to attack.

"There is something to be said for simplicity," Hanker said. He indicated the starchart with one hand. "Plan Nimitz ensures we can bring *all* of our firepower to bear against the target, without trying to be clever. Being *clever* is a good way to get one's butt kicked."

"It's a minimum of nine gravity points between N-Gann and Tokomak Prime," Hoshiko pointed out. "Twelve, if we go a slightly longer route. That's nine possible bottlenecks they can use to bleed us white, each of which will cost us dearly in ships, munitions and manpower. And they will know we're coming. They will have ample time to assemble a fleet to block us, if they don't already have fortifications in place. We have to assume they've learnt from their experiences. We did that to them in the lead up to the last set of battles."

"We would also not be risking losing contact between two prongs," Teller objected. "At best, it will take weeks to get a message from one prong to the other. At worst, we'd lose touch altogether."

"There's no way to avoid it," Hoshiko said. "Unless you have a long-range FTL communicator in your pocket..."

Teller snorted. "Admiral, I understand your point," he said. His voice was very calm. "But I also have to check you understand the dangers."

"War is *never* safe," Steve said. "When I was a young man, just going through basic training, there were people who believed they could eliminate risk entirely. Some of them believed they could use technology to make sure that the only people who died were the ones on the other side, our clear and irredeemable enemies. They believed they could somehow prevent innocent deaths and"—he shook his head—"they meant well, I believe, but they made wars worse. They kept us from applying overwhelming force until it was too late for a quick and decisive campaign.

"There are risks here, as there are everywhere. But the risk of losing becomes progressively greater, the longer we delay. We can either take action now or sit and wait to be hit. And we cannot *afford* to be hit. A single major defeat will be the end of us."

"Yes, sir," Hanker said.

Teller's eyes narrowed. "Is that your opinion as an officer in the navy, *sir*?"

Hoshiko felt a hot flash of anger. Steve showed no visible reaction. "It's an opinion born of fifteen years in the United States military, then my experiences in the Solar Union and the galaxy at large," he said, calmly. "Right now, we have the edge. If we delay, that edge will start to blunt. We've all read the reports. If they bring their entire fleet online, or rationalise their industrial production, we're finished. They will *bury* us in weapons that are qualitatively inferior to ours, but... there will be millions of them. And that, as the admiral said, will be the end of the world. We cannot back down. We either tear their throats out or get crushed."

"Yes, sir," Teller said, stiffly. "That said, we may not have the *power* to tear their throats out."

"Yes." Hoshiko schooled her face into immobility. It was Teller's *job* to voice his concerns, if he had them. And he had every reason to be irked at Steve's intervention. "But we have to move now."

She looked from face to face. "I estimate it will take us two weeks to integrate the newcomers and assemble the support fleet," she said. She had no idea how many of the locals would stay with them, once they launched the big offensive. "I intend to launch Plan Wellington. Before then, we will simulate all the possible outcomes and do our best to reduce the variables. It will not be easy, but...we have no choice. Earth is depending on us."

The holographic star charts vanished at her command. "We will allow them to think we're moving with Plan Nimitz," she added. "We won't take our security *too* seriously. They have to have spies watching us. Let them think we're going the easy way. Let them think that...until we appear in the worst possible place."

Teller smiled. "For them or for us?"

"We'll see." Hoshiko felt a flicker of anticipation. They were finally about to resume the offensive. The last few weeks had been spent refitting the fleet, integrating their alien allies and considering their options. Important, but boring. "Dismissed."

CHAPTER FOUR

Here we go, Hameeda thought, as the LinkShip dropped out of FTL. An alien system appeared in front of her, a handful of icons turning red as their active sensors came online and locked onto her hull. *Again.*

She smiled, rather coldly. She'd flown through four systems in the last week, buzzing a handful of enemy facilities, uploading her messages and generally making it clear that she could have done a great deal of damage if she'd wished. She had no doubt the message had been received, if only because of the ever-increasing enemy defences...all of which had been putting immense strain on their sensor arrays by ramping them up as much as possible. She hated to think how much stress they were putting on the crews, who were only flesh and blood. No military force could remain on alert indefinitely and hope to be in fighting trim when the alert finally came.

And they knew I was coming, this time, she thought. She'd flown in as close to a straight line as possible, cutting her flight time to the bare bone. The Tokomak were unimaginative, but even *they* could see the pattern. They had to know she was coming here. *And they're ready for me.*

She felt her smile grow wider as more and more enemy defences revealed themselves. The system—it had an alien name she couldn't even *begin* to pronounce—didn't have a ring, but it did have a handful of smaller orbital stations and defences. Her files informed her that the lack of a gravity point and other, more useful systems only a few short light years away, had kept the aliens from *really* developing the system. It was a little looser than most of the core worlds, with a surprising amount of racial equality... even between the Tokomak and their subject races. She was almost sorry it was on the list of targets. Perhaps, just perhaps, she didn't *have* to push things too far.

Another alert flashed up in front of her. The enemy communications network was down. Her eyes narrowed as her sensors probed the system, picking up only a tiny handful of signals and communications nodes... the latter so heavily encrypted that she *knew* they were military installations. The entire system seemed to have gone dark. She cursed under her breath as she realised what it meant. The defenders had shut down the entire system, rather than risk having her uploading the message into a hacked node. They'd risked all manner of death and destruction just to keep her from talking to them! It almost made her smile, even though it meant her mission was doomed. At least they were taking her seriously.

And they'll get copies of the message anyway, she thought. There would be copies fanning out from all the worlds she'd visited, no matter what the Tokomak tried to do about it. It was quite possible the message had already reached the new system. *And by trying to wipe it, they'll only harm their credibility further.*

She was tempted to jump back into FTL and vanish, conceding—for the moment—that there was no point in trying to slip further into the system. In hindsight, perhaps she should have sneaked into the system and hacked the datanet before announcing her presence. There was no way they could shut down the datanet indefinitely, not when everything from the local stock market to life support systems depended on it. The Tokomak had never heard of distributed computer networks, she'd been told. A centralised network was much easier to monitor, police and shut down. Smart resistance movements knew better than to rely on the enemy communications network.

And here I come, she thought, as she angled towards the alien ships. *Are you ready for me?*

The alien ships grew larger as she zoomed closer. They were old, even by Tokomak standards. They looked to have been passed through a dozen hands before finally winding up in a fifth-rank star system. They'd be good for intimidating smugglers and primitives, she thought, but it was clear they hadn't been refitted with modern weapons. They were little more than targets for a modern ship, even a simple destroyer. Hameeda was tempted to power up her weapons and put the ancient ships out of their misery. But it would be a waste of weapons she couldn't afford to squander.

She deployed a handful of drones instead, surrounding herself with a web of false sensor images. The enemy targeting locks slipped as they realised they were suddenly facing seven different targets, or one real target and six decoys. Their sensors weren't good enough to tell the difference, not even at close range. They'd have to engage *all* the possible targets ... Hameeda allowed herself a smile as she blazed forward, throwing her ship into a series of evasive manoeuvres as she finally entered weapons range. The enemy CO was a little *too* smart to be in command of such rustbuckets. He was careful to hold his fire until she got closer, rather than wasting missiles trying to hit her at extreme range. This far from the core, in such a low-priority system, she would be surprised if there were any missile production facilities. Her opponent might have to wait for months until he received replacements from the core worlds...

The enemy ships launched missiles, trying hard to coordinate their fire. Hameeda gleefully screwed with their targeting, deploying a handful of additional drones to ensure they didn't come *remotely* close to her. They didn't have antimatter warheads either ... she smirked, then evaded a missile that locked onto one of its fellows, destroying both of them in a single blinding flash. The enemy CO was good, but his tech really wasn't up to the job. She fought down the urge to open hailing frequencies and transmit an entire list of insults right across the system. Instead, she transmitted the message instead. *Someone* would be listening. Who knew? Maybe they'd record the message and upload it to the datanet when the system came back online.

She blazed through the enemy formation, feinted at the planet and turned away, aiming for deep space. The enemy might have had a chance to set an ambush, if they'd had the time to summon a more modern squadron, but they'd squandered it. She sent the message one final time, then drove onwards into the night. Behind her, the enemy ships turned and retreated towards the planet. She didn't want to know what might be going through their commander's head. The idealist in her hoped he wouldn't suffer for his failure. The cold-blooded part of her noted that he really *had* been disturbingly competent, compared to most of his fellows. If the enemy killed him, it would work out in humanity's favour...

This war will probably get him killed before too long anyway, she told herself. She didn't bother to cloak as she rocketed away from the planet. They'd already be on the verge of losing track of her, if they hadn't already lost her. *And that will be the end.*

A radio signal, surprisingly primitive, blinked up in her mind's eye. Someone was trying to *hail* her? She stared in astonishment, studying the line of code words and phrases that scrolled through the system. They were all positive, all *human*, but... she frowned, remembering just how popular human movies and television series had become amongst the younger Galactics. It was possible, just possible, that it was a trap. A very un-Tokomak trap, if it *was* a trap, but that alone would recommend it. The Tokomak knew she could evade any enemy fleet, as long as she saw it. A smaller ship might just get through her defences and into position to take a clear shot at her hull.

She frowned, reaching out through her sensors. A lone freighter drifted in space, almost completely powered down. There was no way in hell anyone on the planet, now falling behind her at a terrifying rate, would know it was there. She wasn't even sure they would have seen the freighter arrive. She hadn't picked up any major sensor arrays around the planet. And that meant...

If this is a trap, they would have had to put the freighter along my exit vector, she mused. It was possible that someone had guessed her exit vector, but... how would they have known where and when she'd drop into FTL. The trap would have failed completely if she'd vanished after escaping the planet. She wouldn't even have known it was *there. But if this isn't a trap... what is it?*

She opened a communications link, narrowing the beam to reduce the chance of eavesdroppers. It was unlikely there were any prowling around, but... the odds of encountering the freighter were very low too. She didn't care to calculate them. There was a pause, then a response. Audio only.

"This is Samuel Piece," the voice said. Her analysis software insisted it was a human voice, although that was meaningless. Deepfakes had been a problem for decades. The Tokomak wouldn't have any trouble faking a human voice, if it occurred to them to try. "I request that you pick myself and my comrades up before they catch us."

"This is Captain Hameeda," Hameeda said. Her computers blinked up a number of people with the same name, none of whom she knew personally. A couple had obscured files, suggesting they worked for Solar Intelligence. "Explain yourself."

There was no answer for a long moment, long enough for Hameeda to start to worry. She checked her FTL drive, ready to jump out and run at a moment's notice. If this was some kind of trap... she was sure she could get out before the jaws slammed closed. But she knew better than to take it for granted. If the freighter was crammed with antimatter, she was already inside the blast radius. And there would be no warning before the blast wave hit her.

"I admit you don't know us from Adam," Piece said, finally. "I have ID codes in my implants and..."

Hameeda frowned. Human slang was suggestive, although she knew it proved nothing too. A skilled xenospecialist could put a profile together and then... she closed her eyes for a long second, trying to think. If Piece was human, perhaps a deep-cover agent, she had to recover him. If not... she cursed. She'd have to put her ship and herself at risk, in a place where *no one* would ever know what had happened if things went wrong, or…or she'd never know if she'd done the right thing.

"I have four people with me," Piece continued. "They require asylum."

"Really." Hameeda made up her mind. "Power down your ship, then transfer yourselves to the escape pod and launch yourself into space. My drones will collect you. Or stay where you are."

"Understood." Piece didn't sound surprised. "We'll be out in a moment."

Hameeda gritted her teeth as she launched the drones. In hindsight, she should have requested a marine platoon or two before setting out to wreak havoc. She disliked the idea of company, at least for longer than a few days, but they'd have been very useful now. Instead, she had to watch through the drones as they powered their way towards the escape pod. Piece seemed to be following orders. She hoped that was a good sign.

The drones split up as they approached the pod, two heading to the pod itself and the others inspecting the freighter. Up close, it was so old that Hameeda was surprised the hull itself wasn't starting to decay. She hated to think just how many people had owned the ship before it reached its final pair of hands. The drones probed the airlock warily, then opened the hatch and slipped inside. The air was cooling rapidly—a handful of warning signs suggested there were tiny breaches in the hull—but the drones had no trouble picking human DNA out of the air. Hameeda allowed herself a moment of relief as the drones hacked the ship's datacore, then turned her attention to the escape pod. If it was a trap, it was a very odd one.

She peered through their sensors as they dragged the pod towards the LinkShip. Piece himself was a dark-skinned human male, his face scarred and pitted. Beside him were three aliens, fragile-looking green-skinned humanoids she didn't recognise. Piece had a handful of implants, including one that pinged a Solar Union IFF code at her when she scanned it. The other three were completely barren of tech. It looked as if they'd had implants, from the deep scans, but they'd been removed at one point.

The scans kept pulsing, breaking their bodies down to the submolecular level. Piece carried a pistol, seemingly of human design…a chemical weapon, rather than a phaser or blaster. The others carried a handful of tools, some of which were clearly designed to function as weapons with a little imagination. She scanned them carefully, then decided she was being silly. They didn't have anything *really* dangerous. She'd feared a backpack nuke or antimatter containment chamber. The only thing Piece would have had to do to take her out, if he'd had one of *those*, was simply turn it off.

Well, she thought. *It is either a very* weird *trap or they're innocents.*

She paused long enough to assess the live feed from the freighter's datacore—it was so old that she suspected it was rather unreliable, the starcharts so badly corrupted that it was impossible to trace the vessel's flight path—then made up her mind. "Remove all your tools and weapons and place them to one side," she ordered. "Prepare for teleport."

Piece made no objection, putting his gun to one side with casual ease. The others looked more reluctant and didn't seem inclined to obey until Piece pushed them into it. Hameeda felt a flicker of sympathy as she activated the teleporter, beaming the three aliens into a stasis chamber. Piece looked surprised, his expression suddenly freezing as he was teleported into a second chamber. Hameeda studied the matter feed through her sensors as they materialised, making very sure there were no surprises within their bodies. Her biosensors reported nothing, but that was meaningless. The Galactics were ancient. They'd invented the teleporters. They would presumably know how to circumvent them.

And the stasis fields worked perfectly, she mused. *They can wait there until I deal with them.*

She took one last look at the freighter, then recovered her drones and dropped into FTL. There was no hint that anyone on the planet was watching her—she was fairly sure they'd lost track of her—but she took evasive action anyway. She'd have to be more careful when she reached the next system, if Piece didn't convince her to cut her mission short and go elsewhere. He'd sought her out, perhaps deliberately. And that meant…what?

The hacked datacore files lay open in front of her. She cursed under her breath, wishing she could have a long chat with the engineer who maintained the piece of junk. The machine was so outdated that a pre-space human computer would be more capable, at least when it came to keeping the starship functional. It looked as if someone had systematically disabled a number of safety features, each one more important than the last. The Tokomak were very keen on safety—they worked so many safeguards into their starships that they actually impeded their operations—but they weren't completely wrong. Or misguided. She was mildly surprised the freighter hadn't exploded when it jumped into FTL.

Score one for the Tokomak, she thought, as she disconnected herself from the neural net and stood. She wanted to eat, but…she also wanted to talk to Piece. She ran his ID through her records and came up with a classified file, marked with the Solar Intelligence verification code. It was something of a relief. Whatever else she'd done, at least she hadn't wasted her time. *And I need to know what he's doing here.*

She ate quickly, taking something from the store rather than bothering to cook for herself, then headed into the shower. She'd have to wear *something* if she was coming face to face with a stranger. An alien might not notice—interspecies sex was rare, and flatly banned amongst the Galactics—but Piece would. She snorted at the thought as she checked the internal defences, just in case. Piece probably couldn't be conditioned to turn against the Solar Union -his implants would see to it—but there was no reason he couldn't be bribed or threatened into compliance. The Tokomak had a *lot* of collaborators. They could hardly be slouches when it came to finding out what someone wanted and offering it to them.

A deep-cover agent would know better, she told herself, flatly. *Right?*

She sighed as she dressed rapidly, the simple tunic feeling odd against her skin. She'd grown too used to walking around naked. Normally, she wouldn't care if anyone saw her, but right now…there were too many uncertainties, too many things she didn't know, for her to allow herself any distraction. She *had* to know what was going on before she committed herself to anything.

The LinkShip hummed around her, steadying her. She relaxed into its embrace, silently praising the designers. If she had to spend the rest of her life on a starship, this one would be more than enough. Who knew? After the war was over, if she survived, she could slip into unexplored space and seek out new life and new civilisations.

"To boldly go where no one has ever gone before," she quoted. "Apart from the people who already live there, of course."

Smiling, she headed to the stasis chambers.

CHAPTER FIVE

Up close, floating in the stasis field, Samuel Piece looked almost peaceful.

Hameeda studied him, both through her eyes and through a dozen different medical and security sensors. He was definitely human, to the ninth decimal place. His DNA spoke of an origin in the Solar Union, rather than Earth or one of the human colonies established by aliens who wanted their human slaves to breed. He was quite heavily enhanced, with both biological tweaks and implants. She was mildly impressed. He was almost as heavily implanted as herself.

And he'd be more so, if he wasn't trying to hide his implants, she mused. A GalTech scanner might miss most of Piece's augmentations, although Hameeda wouldn't have cared to bet her life on it. Perhaps one of his implants was designed to feed false readings back to the scanner. The Galactics took their tech for granted, but surely it would have occurred to them that their scanners could be fooled. As technology advanced, the technology to fool it advanced too. *But his implants don't seem to be messing with my scanners.*

She took a step back, then deactivated the stasis field with a thought. Piece staggered as the blue light vanished, looking around wildly as the tractor field caught him before he could hit the deck. To him, it must have seemed like an instant transfer from his ship to the stasis field. He'd known he was being teleported, but... Hameeda nodded to herself as he stood up. Piece clearly wasn't someone who could be stunned by a simple trick. He would have expected her to take precautions.

His eyes alighted on her, looking her up and down in a manner that slightly discomforted her. It wasn't sexual, as far as she could tell. His eyes didn't linger on her breasts. He was evaluating her as a potential threat. She braced herself, ready to snap the stasis field back into existence if he did anything dangerous. She had no qualms about keeping him in stasis and taking him back to N-Gann. Admiral Stuart could deal with him. Hameeda was *sure* she'd have the codes to unlock his implants, if there was no other choice. And the codes to confirm his identity.

Piece met her eyes. "This is a *human* ship?"

"I thought we'd already established that," Hameeda said, dryly. "What can I do for you?"

"Take me and my companions to higher authority, wherever that may be." Piece looked around, his eyes narrowing. "What *is* this ship?"

Hameeda frowned. "Classified," she said. He *was* sharp. The LinkShip was hardly a *conventional* ship. He'd picked up on that very quickly. "Come with me."

She turned and led him through to the gallery, grimly aware of his eyes following her. Piece would have to be an idiot to miss the absence of other crewmen. He knew the LinkShip was small, compared to most FTL ships, but not *that* small. She wondered, idly, what he made of it. It was standard procedure to quarantine strangers, isolating them from the rest of the crew in case they had bad intentions, but the LinkShip didn't really have the *space*. The majority of the hull was crammed with weapons, sensors and drives. There was enough room for *her*, and perhaps one or two more, but after that... they'd have to get *very* friendly.

"What would you like?" She waved him to a chair and turned to the drink processor. "I'm having tea."

"Tea would be fine, thanks." Piece sank into a chair, looking more relaxed. "Where is the fleet now?"

"N-Gann." Hameeda was surprised he didn't already know. Or perhaps it wasn't a surprise. The Tokomak hadn't been able to hide the fall of Apsidal and much of the Apsidal Chain, but they'd stayed mum about losing N-Gann. They'd *never* lost a fleet base, not in all their thousands of years of unquestioned dominance. The news broadcasts she'd picked up had carefully avoided mentioning anything about N-Gann. "They took the world a couple of months ago."

Piece looked up, sharply. "Really? I was told N-Gann was impregnable."

Hameeda smiled. "They did say that, didn't they? It must be very embarrassing for them."

She picked up the mugs and handed one of them to him. "And now we're on our way to N-Gann," she said, "I think you owe me an explanation. Who are you and what are you doing here?"

"I told you," Piece said. "I'm a deep cover agent on long-term assignment..."

"And you had the wit to flag me down," Hameeda said, curtly. "How did you even know where to meet me?"

"I didn't." Piece grinned at her. "It was a stroke of luck."

"Really," Hameeda said, drawing out the word. "What happened?"

Piece straightened. "To cut a long story short, I was assigned to a freighter crew with orders to jump ship when we reached the twins, the Alphan Stars. My mission was to make contact with dissidents there and see what, if any, support we could offer them. The dissidents were very pleased to see me, for obvious reasons, and we forged an alliance. They don't think much of our chances, I should add, but they know we're the only game in town."

Hameeda nodded, slowly. "And how much of the story are you leaving out?"

"Just the details no one wants to know," Piece said. "I'll have to put them in my report, of course, but... right now, no one wants to hear them. Anyway... I was helping them to establish communications networks by piggybacking signals on the enemy communications systems and setting up operative cells for direct action. It wasn't easy, as most of the dissidents hate each other almost as much as they hate the Tokomak, but…we were getting somewhere when we heard the war had turned hot. Again."

"Again," Hameeda echoed.

"It was hard to be sure," Piece said. "The Tokomak managed to blank out a great many reports before they reached us. They're still pretty much in control of everything, corewards, and they're cracking down hard. The dissidents lost a lot of cells after their enemies started peering into everything. The rest had to go deeper underground. There's a lot—and I mean a *lot*—of people who'd turn on the Tokomak in an instant, if they thought they could win, but right now the Tokomak look to be in control."

He took a sip of his tea. "My friends and I thought it might be a good idea to contact the fleet and request help," he said. "We set out, intending to travel to Apsidal. It wasn't easy. We had to take the long way 'round. We were planning to swap ships here"—he jerked a finger at the bulkhead—"when you entered the system. I decided it might be easier to contact you and request a ride. Thank you."

Hameeda smiled. "You're welcome. Who are your companions?"

"Three representatives from the Alphan Twins," Piece said. "They're here to make the case for military support."

"I see." Hameeda activated the holographic projector and displayed a starchart. The Alphan Twins were close to Tokomak Prime, linked to the enemy stars by a single gravity point chain. She was mildly surprised the dissidents had managed to escape. The system had been enemy territory for so long that they probably no longer remembered being independent. "I can't make that decision."

"I know." Piece studied the starchart with hungry eyes. "But I figure that whoever's in command of the fleet *can*."

"Quite." Hameeda shot him a sharp look. "Why do they think they can win?"

Piece gave her a grim smile. "Technically, the system is owned and controlled—not *ruled*, controlled—by the Tokomak. Practically, the vast majority of the population consists of their servitors, entire races they've enslaved and put to work for them. They hate their masters with a passion...hell, even the Galactics who live there hate their rulers. The entire system has been a tinder box for *centuries*. Really...I'm not even sure the Tokomak are breaking even. Oppression and repression *costs*."

Hameeda laughed, then sobered. "And they can't reform because that would unleash forces that might destroy them."

"Right now, I don't think they can *imagine* having to reform." Piece shrugged. "There was some hope that the new Empress would change things...youth at the helm, they said, although the Empress is older than any living human. But there's a war on and...I don't expect things to change in a hurry, if they ever do. They've already started slaughtering human slaves and cyborg soldiers."

"Yeah." Hameeda had never met a cyborg, but she'd heard the stories. The aliens had practically brain-burned them into monsters, unleashing them against their targets and then snapping the leash back as soon as the battle was over. They'd been grotesque parodies of the worst humanity had to offer, practically revelling in atrocities that would have made Hitler, Stalin, and Bin Laden blanch. "They *really* intend to destroy us, don't they?"

"I think they won't be happy until every last human is dead," Piece said. "They were offering rewards for anyone who turned in a human for the extermination chambers, big rewards. I thought it might be better to leave before someone turned me in for the thirty pieces of silver."

Hameeda allowed herself a moment of respect. Piece had lived and worked within enemy reach. If they'd known he was there, they could have taken him. And then...she knew herself to be brave, but it was easy to be brave when the worst thing that could happen was a quick and painless death. Piece would have been brain-burned if he'd been caught, his mind destroyed by alien mental probes or his own implants. She wasn't entirely sure how seriously to take his claims—she knew he could be mistaken—but if he was right...she sent a mental command to the drives, ordering them to increase speed. The sooner they reached N-Gann, the better.

"They'll do everything in their power to restore the *status quo*," Piece said. "I think their next target will be their allies, the Galactics. Once they have all their ships online, once Earth is a blackened cinder and the Solar Union nothing more than space dust, they'll turn on the Galactics. They'll crush them all, knock them back to pre-space levels; they'll impose controls that will make Earth's worst police state look like the Solar Union. And I don't want to know what they'll do to the servitor races. Genocide, perhaps. They just can't be trusted."

"They'll destroy their economy," Hameeda protested. "They couldn't survive without cheap labour."

"I imagine they'll bring more and more automation online," Piece said, darkly. "It isn't as if they don't have the tech. They just built their empire on slave labour because they needed scapegoats for the Galactics to sneer at. And they could dispose of most of them without *really* upsetting their economy. I dare say they've already started putting together plans for mass genocide."

Hameeda didn't want to think about it. Slaughtering an entire race…it was a crime on a scale so big that she couldn't even *begin* to grasp it. Hitler had killed well over six million people, directly or indirectly; the Tokomak would kill billions or trillions of people just to secure their position forever. They'd bathe the entire galaxy in blood. She couldn't imagine they'd wipe out *everyone*—even *they* had their limits—but they could easily force the survivors to hide or flee for the Rim. And the Tokomak would come after them…

She shuddered. "And then…what?"

"I have no idea." Piece shrugged. "They'll probably go back to contemplating their own navels. It isn't as if they have the drive to succeed any longer. Without the war, without the need to police tens of trillions of subjects, they might just start to decay again. Or…who knows? Maybe they'll change so much they'll look back and realise they committed the worst set of crimes in the history of the entire galaxy."

"Which won't be any consolation to the souls of the dead," Hameeda said, more sharply than she'd intended. "How could they even *begin* to atone for such a crime?"

She stared down at her hands. Humans didn't live *that* long, not compared to the Galactics. The humans who were responsible for ordering and carrying out an endless stream of atrocities were dead. There was nothing to be gained by punishing their descendants. But the Tokomak were practically immortal. Their children, a hundred thousand years in the future, might start to ask their elders and betters why they'd committed such crimes. And what answer could their elders give? They'd have none.

No, she corrected herself. *They'd tell their children that they had a choice between committing genocide and being the victims of genocide. And they'd rewrite the history books to make that true.*

She shook her head. "We'll be at N-Gann within the week," she said. "You can tell Admiral Stuart your story. She'll decide what to do about it."

"A week?" Piece looked surprised. "How fast *is* this ship?"

"Classified," Hameeda said. She snorted. Given a starchart, Piece could make an *excellent* guess at the LinkShip's speed. Admiral Stuart would probably tell him to keep his guesses to himself. The Galactics hadn't realised—yet—that there were ways to coax more speed out of a stardrive, if one removed the safety interlocks. If she was lucky, they never would. "And keep that to yourself, please."

"My lips are sealed," Piece assured her. "But you do realise, don't you, that my companions will *notice*?"

"Yeah." Hameeda shrugged. "I think that will be the admiral's problem."

She finished her drink and placed the mug in the washer. "I've had the servos make up a bed for you, in the spare room," she said. It was designed to be reconfigured into anything from a secondary bedroom to an emergency cargo hold. "But you can go back into stasis if you like."

"I have a report to write, if you'll give me access to a terminal," Piece said. "And I could do with some decompression."

"There's a full-scale entertainment suite down the corridor," Hameeda said. "Feel free to use it, however you like."

"A holodeck?" Piece blinked in surprise. "What sort of ship *is* this?"

"Classified," Hameeda said, dryly. "Speaking of which, don't try to access the datacore directly. It'll take any unauthorised access as a hacking attempt and respond violently. You really *don't* want to have it pushing back at you."

"I know the rules," Piece said. "And I wouldn't *dream* of hacking a datacore when the ship was in flight."

"You might spend the rest of your life in a detention cell, assuming you survived the experience," Hameeda warned. She had no reason to think Piece would be so stupid, but she'd known enough operatives to realise the danger. Better to warn him off now than spend hours, afterwards, scraping his brains off the deck. "Just use the standard user interface and everything will be fine."

"Understood." Piece gave her a mischievous smile. "How many people are on this ship?"

"Classified," Hameeda said. "Realistically speaking, you won't see anyone else until we reach N-Gann."

And you can draw whatever conclusions you like from that, she added, silently. She didn't really want to admit she was the *only* crewmember, although Piece might already have deduced it for himself. *You'll be off this ship in a week or so anyway.*

She stood. "I'll show you to your cabin," she said. "And you can write your report while we're in transit."

"Thanks," Piece said. "I'm very glad you came by."

Hameeda nodded, then led him down the corridor to the spare room. The servos had done a good job, hastily installing everything from a simple bed to a tiny washroom. It was smaller than her cabin, but still larger than the average living compartment on a cruiser. There was *just* enough room to swing a cat. Piece glanced into the washroom and whistled, appreciatively. Hameeda concealed her amusement with an effort. After spending so long in alien environments, using washrooms designed for all kinds of alien races, even a simple shower and toilet designed specifically for humans looked like the height of luxury. She allowed her eyes to wander up and down his back, noting the muscles and the signs of a stressful life. She'd heard stories about deep-cover agents. Some of them went so far as to disguise themselves as aliens. Her lips quirked at the thought. It couldn't be easy. Who knew what would happen if the aliens caught a fake?

The Tokomak would probably be horrified, she mused. It was possible, in theory, to change race through nanotech. It wouldn't be easy, nothing like as easy as gender or skin colour, but it could be done. *How would they justify their supremacy if everyone could be a Tokomak?*

"There's no regular routine on this ship," she told him, putting the thought aside for later consideration. "If you want something to eat or drink, just go to the gallery and ask the processors. Ditto for clothes and supplies. Or use the onboard communications network to call me. Don't try to explore. This whole ship is..."

"Classified," Piece said, quickly. "I do know the score."

"I know," Hameeda said. They shared a smile. "We'll be at N-Gann very soon."

"I was expecting the trip to take another month, at least." Piece shrugged. "There were rumours of chokepoints being closed, of entire fleets going missing...right now, a week sounds like a miracle. We can be there and back before they notice we're gone."

"I hope you're right," Hameeda said. "And that the Admiral listens to you."

And that this doesn't get a lot of innocent people killed for nothing, her thoughts added. *The Tokomak won't hesitate to crack down hard if they get even a sniff of rebellion.*

CHAPTER SIX

"An interesting report," Hoshiko said, once Samuel Piece and his allies had been shown out of her ready room. "What do *you* make of it, Grandpa?"

Steve Stuart sat up from where he'd been half-lying on the sofa. "I think we should treat it with extreme caution," he said. "I also think *you're* the one who has to make the final call."

"Gee, thanks," Hoshiko said, dryly. "As if I didn't already know that."

"Good thing I reminded you, then," Steve said. He grinned at her, resting his hands on his knees. "I suppose the real question, therefore, is if we should try to take advantage of it or not."

Hoshiko scowled. She'd listened, very carefully, to the alien pitch. The dissidents believed they could rise against the Tokomak, taking and holding their worlds—their entire binary star system—long enough for her fleet to come to the rescue. Indeed, with a little help, their position might become practically impregnable. But, at the same time, it would disrupt *her* plans if she sent aid to the Alphan Twins...and, if she failed to get help to the aliens in time, the Tokomak would slaughter them. And yet...

She allowed her scowl to deepen as she considered the possibilities. A rebellion on the Twins, combined with one prong of her fleet moving *towards* the Twins, would pose a threat the Tokomak could not afford to ignore. They would *have* to send ships to the Twins, giving her a chance to stick a knife in their backs. But the timing would be a nightmare and … she shuddered, all too aware of how many people might die because she couldn't get help to them in time. The hell of it was that cold logic insisted she *should* send enough help to inspire a revolution, even if she couldn't save it from being crushed. Their deaths might buy her time to win the war.

And lose my soul, she reflected. She knew she might have to launch a planetary bombardment, if human worlds were scorched clean of life by the aliens, but … she wanted to postpone that decision as long as possible. It was *inhuman* to consider mass slaughter as a viable military tactic. *What would it cost us, in the long run, if we encouraged the dissidents to rise and then left them to die?*

"You have several options," Steve said. "You can send help, but encourage them to put off the rebellion until our ships actually enter the system. This lets us make use of the uprising, without running the risk of watching helplessly as they get slaughtered. You can send help and encourage them to rise now, which will distract the enemy at the price of getting untold millions of people killed. Or you can do nothing, aware that the dissidents might rise at any moment anyway…"

Hoshiko glared at him. "Do you have anything *useful* to say?"

"Yes." Steve met her eyes, earnestly. "There's no *perfect* answer. Not here. And you may not be in control of events anyway. War is a democracy…"

"And the enemy always gets a vote," Hoshiko finished. "And not just the enemy, either. Our prospective friends and allies always get a vote too."

She sat back at her desk, silently running through the calculations. It would take roughly a month, according to the analysts, to get a sizable force to the Twins. That hadn't been a problem a day ago, when there had been no reason to think there was a time limit. Indeed, she'd planned for Force One to take its time. The Tokomak wouldn't be drawn out of place if they didn't have time to notice the advancing fleet and take countermeasures. She'd planned to do everything short of ringing up the enemy commander and personally telling him she was on the way. But now…

"It's never easy to make such a call," Steve said. "You should start by giving up any thought of *controlling* what's to come."

Hoshiko gave him a sharp look. "What do you mean?"

"I had to work with…*allies*…in Afghanistan," Steve said. "Our commanders, who were literally on the other side of the world, thought our allies were bought and paid for. They thought they'd do as they were told. They couldn't have been more wrong. The allies had their own interests, their own reasons for joining us…if things changed, if we looked like bad allies or losers, they'd change sides in a heartbeat. It was maddening, but…to us, it was appalling. To them, it made a great deal of sense."

"How so?" Hoshiko cocked an eyebrow. "Weren't they like you?"

Steve shrugged. "An Afghan warlord was…still is, unfortunately…a big man because he has a band of fighters under his control. If they died, his power died with them. He didn't want to send them into intense battles because it might cost him everything. There wasn't any sort of bribe we could offer that would compete with self-interest. And then…we were supposed to turn a blind eye to their conduct, even when it reflected badly on us. We had to ignore filthy fucking paedophiles because it was politically incorrect to draw attention to it, which gave our enemies a field day…"

He shook his head, controlling his anger with a visible effort. "You have to bear in mind that their interests and yours won't always align. The good news is that they *know* what the Tokomak will do, when—if—they lose the war. That gives them an incentive to stick with you. The bad news is that you can't command them and, if you try, that will harden them against you too. They may jump at any point and…well, you might get the blame for not saving them."

"Fuck," Hoshiko said. Her people were an understanding people—Solarians knew it took time for messages to move from star to star, even without an alien blockade—but there were limits. She had political enemies back home, including—ironically—people who wanted to curry favour with her family. It wouldn't get them anywhere, but…it wouldn't matter.

"We might as well help them, then. But we'll have to make it clear that we can't rush to their aid."

"Unless you want to throw Plan Wellington out the airlock," Steve agreed. "And gamble everything on Plan Nimitz."

Hoshiko shook her head. She'd seen the simulations. Nothing could be taken for granted, of course, but…the bad guys won more often than they lost. It wasn't very reassuring. She tried to tell herself that the simulations were based on educated guesswork, but…she shook her head. It would be grossly irresponsible to bet everything on one throw of the dice. They'd have to go with Plan Wellington.

And if they rise ahead of time, they'll die, she thought. *And the rebels might die before we even know they need help.*

Her expression darkened. She'd reviewed the files on the Twins, hoping they'd help her make up her mind. From one point of view, the planned uprising would be almost effortless. From another, the uprising would be crushed before it ever became a major threat. She could see the logic…both sets of logic. Personally, she suspected the *reality* would be somewhere in the middle. The planetary administration might be riddled with holes, with all kinds of gaps in their security, but that didn't mean they could all be exploited at the same time. The KISS principle still applied. There were just too many things that could go wrong.

"Samuel Piece wanted an SF team to accompany him," she mused. "I'll ask the marines to recommend a good officer."

"One who has no problem with aliens," Steve reminded her. "He'll have to treat with them as equals."

Hoshiko snorted. The oldsters really *did* have problems with aliens, although she wasn't sure if they stemmed from the Bombardment of Earth or a simple awareness that they were no longer alone in the universe. Humanity's first encounter with alien life—the first *recorded* encounter— had been traumatic, but hardly as bad as some others. *Her* generation didn't have anything like so many hang-ups. Aliens were people. Different people, to be sure, with values that were very…well, *alien*, but *people* nonetheless.

Outside Earth, and some of the more isolated Cantons, outright racism was almost unknown.

"It won't be a problem," she assured him.

"I hope not," Steve said. "We sometimes came across as overbearing assholes and *we* had the advantage of dealing with fellow humans."

"No wonder you could never win those pointless wars," Hoshiko said, sweetly. "Why were you fighting them with one hand tied behind your back anyway?"

Steve gave her a warning look. "Back then, our…*government*"—the word was a curse—"was dominated by hereditary idiots, bureaucrats and people who believed that the only way to win wars was through politically-correct PR. They thought things could be perfect and when they weren't, which was inevitable, they blamed the people on the ground. And the hell of it was that the vast majority of the voters would have *understood* if their leaders had been open and honest about it. There's no such thing as perfection and *trying* to be perfect was worse than useless."

He smiled. "That's why I built the Solar Union to ensure that people with power had actual experience and responsibility. That's what made it work."

"And we're outgrowing you," Hoshiko said.

"It happens." Steve sat back on the sofa. "Kids grow up, even though parents like to pretend otherwise. And then they either learn from their parents or repeat their mistakes."

He sighed. "I'd like to go myself," he said. "And I do have a ship."

"I can't let you," Hoshiko said. "And I think you know it."

She winced at his expression, steeling herself to resist. She had no doubt her grandfather could accomplish the task—and *he* had no fear of aliens—but she was all too aware of the dangers of him falling into enemy hands. The Tokomak didn't know many humans—she had the nasty feeling that *she* was one of the humans they knew personally—but her grandfather had to be right on top of the list of humans they wanted to kill. There was literally *no one* else who had brought so much change to the galaxy in less than a century. She smiled, rather humourlessly. His only competitors for the title of 'most influential person in galactic history' were Tokomak. It was just something else for them to take personally.

"I understand," Steve said. "Do I get to accompany the fleet, at least?"

"Yeah." Hoshiko made a mental note to insist he stayed with her. Someone else might be too impressed by him and allow his reputation to override her common sense. "I'd be honoured to have you."

Steve stood. "I'll transfer a handful of my possessions to the ship, then," he said. "And thank you."

Hoshiko watched him go, wondering if she'd made a mistake. She didn't think he'd seek to undermine her command—he'd been very good about keeping his mouth shut when someone else was in the compartment, saving his advice for when they were alone—but she didn't want him to go into danger. And yet... he looked so *young*, no older than herself. It was hard to reconcile her awareness that he was in his second century with his appearance. He looked the sort of person she'd have no qualms about sending into danger.

We're all going into danger, she thought, as she altered the display. *Any of our ships could be hit and destroyed, even this one.*

She smiled, coldly, as the holographic fleet appeared in front of her, surrounded by a small galaxy of tactical icons. Her crews had worked like demons over the last week, hastily preparing both formations for deployment. They'd been some confusion over some of her orders, made worse by the simple fact she couldn't explain the reasoning behind them, but overall... they were well on their way to meeting the deadline. The aliens crewing their ships—a ragged fleet composed of captured warships and refitted freighters—were less ready, but it wouldn't matter. She'd planned operations on the assumption she and her crews would be fighting alone.

Her smile grew wider as she worked her way through the reports. A couple of her commanders looked to have played games with the readiness reports—she made a mental note to read them the riot act later—but otherwise, the fleet was about ready to go. The *real* problem lay in holding the system while the majority of the fleet was heading deeper into enemy space. If the Tokomak realised the system was suddenly undefended, who knew what they'd do? N-Gann wasn't *that* important, particularly now she'd rigged the fabricators to blow if there was a chance of them falling back into enemy hands, but a powerful enemy fleet could easily block Force One's line of retreat if it took control of the gravity point. And they wouldn't have to take the planet itself to be a major headache. Blocking communications between the two prongs would be more than enough.

And there really are too many things that can go wrong, Hoshiko thought. She understood the illusion of control better than she cared to admit, but it wasn't one she could allow herself. The enemy could *really* screw things up if she ordered her officers to wait for orders before counterattacking. *And if we lose contact...*

She snorted. The researchers had been promising a viable FTL communicator for decades. Literally. She wouldn't be surprised to discover that *Tokomak* researchers had been promising the same for centuries. Whoever cracked FTL communications would have a colossal advantage over everyone else, at least as long as it lasted. But she would have to fight her battles without it... knowing, all too well, that the enemy's communication loop was shorter than hers. It was vaguely possible they'd be able to take advantage of the enemy's lines of communication, but... she dismissed the thought. That was little more than whistling in the dark. Maybe it would work. Once. She couldn't rely on it.

We'll have to improvise, she thought. Thankfully, she was *good* at improvising combat tactics while under fire. The Tokomak would be hampered by their weaknesses... although she was grimly aware that they were learning too. *Let's hope we can keep our edge until the war is over.*

She opened her log and started to write out a set of formal orders for Admiral Teller. He'd command Force One. There were more aggressive officers, but... for once, she wanted someone who *wouldn't* always have an eye open for a chance to push the offensive. The enemy would need time to realise what was heading in their direction and do something about it. She hoped they'd take the bait. The hell of it, she told herself, was that a rebellion would make the bait almost irresistible. And yet, if the rebellion failed...

There's nothing you can do about it, she told herself, firmly. *All you can do is stack the deck as much as possible and hope for the best, while preparing for the worst.*

Her terminal bleeped. "Admiral, I've assigned Captain Douglas to your operation," General Edward Romford said. "He's on his way now."

"Have him report to me when he arrives," Hoshiko ordered. Captain Douglas would have as much freedom as she could give him, even to the point of allowing him to draw whatever he needed from the fleet's supplies. She was grimly aware she might be sending him to his death. The thought had never bothered her before, but... she shook her head. She'd never sent someone into a possible trap, knowing they were practically naked and defenceless. But she couldn't see any way to avoid it. "I'll brief him personally."

"He did good work planetside," Romford assured her. "And he played a major role in setting up the provisional government."

"I know." Hoshiko rather suspected the provisional government wouldn't last, but... she wouldn't mind, as long as it lasted just long *enough*. "This mission is going to be harder."

"I'll make time for him and his squad to meet their romantic partners, then," Romford joked. "A shame there's no real shore leave..."

Hoshiko laughed. N-Gann had quite a few shore leave facilities, but most of them had been destroyed in the fighting. The remainder hadn't been configured for humans. The Galactics were depressingly *boring*, by human standards. They didn't drink, they didn't eat to excess, they didn't watch movies or have sex or... they didn't even have *porn*. It reminded her of a joke about a man who lived a healthy—and boring—life. Why would he *want* to live for so long?

"We'll just have to make our own entertainment," she said, dryly. It wasn't as if they didn't have a few distractions. Senior officers would turn a blind eye, as long as it didn't impede operational efficiency. "And we can play when the war is over."

CHAPTER SEVEN

Captain Martin Luther Douglas, Special Forces Recon, started awake as the shuttle moved into teleport range of SUS *Defiant*. He'd been too keyed up to sleep properly, ever since he'd received orders to hand his duties over to his XO and report to *Defiant* as soon as humanly possible. In his experience, abrupt orders only came when he was in deep shit, when he was getting a new mission, or both. And he hadn't done anything that would deserve a bollocking from General Romford himself as far as he knew.

He rubbed his eyes, feeling bone-weary. He didn't mind action—he *thrived* on it—but the last week had been boring beyond words. He'd patrolled N-Gann, he'd helped to sort out disputes between different alien races that seemed to believe their independence would never be threatened again ....he'd made a difference, he thought, even though there was no way the provisional government could keep the lid on forever. N-Gann would have to hang together or hang separately and he had no idea which they'd choose. He almost wished he were back on Apsidal. The insurgency had been hell, but at least it hadn't been boring.

The intercom bleeped. "Teleport in one minute," it said. The voice was flat, atonal. "Prepare for transport."

Martin stood, grabbing his knapsack and pulling it on as the countdown headed remorselessly towards zero. He didn't have much with him, save for his service pistol, ammunition and terminal. Everything else could be found on the ship, if he was going to be posted there. He hoped not, even though Yolanda was on the ship. Shipboard duty was often boring. He'd earned his place in Special Forces Recon. He deserved to be pitting himself against the very best the enemy had to offer.

The shuttle's interior dissolved into blinding light. Martin resisted the urge to close his eyes, feeling a very primal fear as the light coalesced into a teleport bay. The younger generation of Solarians believed the teleport was normal, that it was safer than flying on a jumbo jet or riding a bus to school, but Martin had never believed it. He knew just how easy it was to jam, or scramble, a teleport signal. There were no shortage of horror stories about what happened when humans were accidentally merged with flies. The fact the stories were impossible had never stopped them from creeping him out.

"Martin!" Yolanda was standing by the control panel, smiling. "It's good to see you again."

Martin checked that his body was intact—a twitch he'd never managed to suppress—before stepping off the pad and hurrying towards her. Yolanda looked strange, by groundpounder standards. The part of her that was still firmly rooted on Earth wondered at her appearance, finding it hard to place her. The rest of him, the part that had seen all kinds of humans since leaving Earth behind, found it impossible to care. He wrapped his arms around her, enjoying the kiss. It was more than he'd had for weeks.

"I guess I'm not in trouble, then," he said, as he pulled back. "You wouldn't have greeted me otherwise…"

"I don't know," Yolanda said. She drew back, slightly, her lips twisting as if she wasn't sure of herself. "You might not be in trouble, but in trouble…if you see what I mean."

"I don't know what that means, but it sounds bad." Martin gave her another kiss, then let go of her. "The Admiral wants to see me personally?"

"I'm afraid so," Yolanda said. "And she was very close-lipped about what she wanted from you."

Martin frowned as she led him through the corridors. His orders normally came from General Romford or one of his staffers. It was a severe breach of military etiquette for Admiral Stuart to summon him directly, certainly not without laying the groundwork by having him assigned to her first. It wasn't *quite* as bad as issuing orders to the ship's crew directly, without clearing them with the captain, but it was still pretty bad. And the Admiral had gone and done it. Either General Rumford was fuming now or... or he'd recommended Martin personally. And that meant...?

He put the thought out of his mind as they reached the admiral's hatch. They'd come the long way around, without going through Officer Country or the CIC. He wondered if that was a good sign. There was little point in secrecy, as far as he knew. The system itself might be riddled with spies—they'd uncovered plenty of evidence that the Galactics were still keeping the system under surveillance—but *Defiant* was a human ship. There was no reason to believe they had a rat onboard.

Which doesn't mean there isn't one, he reminded himself. *The Galactics could afford to offer entire star systems in bribes, if they thought to do it.*

Yolanda glanced at him. "Good luck."

Martin opened his mouth, then closed it firmly as the hatch slid open. He stepped inside, torn between relief and fear that Yolanda was clearly not invited. Relief, because she wouldn't have to witness whatever it was; fear, because whatever was happening was clearly *very* secret. And that meant... he straightened to attention and saluted as he saw the admiral sitting behind her desk. She didn't waste time with power games. She returned the salute, then motioned him to take a chair. Martin sat, gingerly. This was *not* going to be good.

Admiral Stuart studied him, carefully. Martin studied her back, noting her tinted skin, almond eyes and very dark hair. She reminded him a little of Yolanda, although she was clearly a decade or two older. But then, it was hard to tell. Yolanda had maintained an almost girlish appearance for as long as he'd known her, for as long as she'd had access to nanotech; Admiral Stuart clearly saw advantage in appearing a little more mature.

Martin understood, better than he cared to admit. He'd grown up in a world where people took one look at the colour of his skin and crossed the road, rather than meet his eye. The Solar Union had long since outgrown human-on-human racism. There were alien races to hate now.

"I heard good things about you, on Apsidal and N-Gann," Admiral Stuart said. Her voice was clipped, very precise. And yet, there was a faint hint of the American South in her accent. "You worked well with the various rebel and resistance groups. They were very pleased with you."

"We had to work together or die, Admiral," Martin said. "I did what anyone would have done, in my place."

"Perhaps," Admiral Stuart said. "But the fact of the matter is that you did very well."

She keyed her terminal. A holographic image—a man, wearing a shapeless tunic—appeared in front of them. "Listen to this, carefully. I'll want your opinion afterwards."

Martin leaned forward as the man—a tagline identified him as Samuel Piece—spoke rapidly, but with consummate force. He didn't know anything about the worlds he talked about—he'd have to look them up, the moment he got out of the office—but the logic was unmistakable. A revolution in the enemy rear might *just* knock them off their high horse, once and for all. Martin doubted it would be *that* simple—Apsidal's resistance movements hadn't worked together very well—but it would certainly cause problems for the enemy. And who knew? A tiny little virus could bring a grown man to his knees…

The recording came to an end. "Your thoughts?"

"I don't know anything about the Twins," Martin said. He'd learnt the hard way to admit ignorance, rather than letting people think he knew what they were talking about. "But if he's right, the rebels would be in a good place to launch an uprising."

"Perhaps." Admiral Stuart dismissed the recording with a flick of her hand. "The real question, right now, is are you prepared to head into enemy space and support an uprising?"

Martin frowned. "On what timescale?"

"A month, perhaps two months," Admiral Stuart said. "Ideally, your uprising would start six weeks from today."

"Tricky," Martin said. "It isn't easy to time such an operation."

"So I've been told." Admiral Stuart didn't sound angry, merely amused. "Do you think you could provide support...?"

"Yes and no." Martin met her eyes. "I could take a team there and provide support, but—on the scale of such an operation—the support would be very minimal indeed. There is no way we could make *that* much of a dent in enemy operations. The vast majority of the operation would have to be carried out by the rebels themselves."

"But you would be a sign of our commitment," Admiral Stuart mused. She met his eyes. "The blunt truth is that I *couldn't* guarantee punching fleet support through to you in time to keep the enemy from reoccupying the orbitals. At best, you'd be fighting a full-scale insurgency. At worst, they'd nuke the entire planet and kill everyone, including you. I might not be able to extract you or *anyone*."

She let out a long breath. "It seems fairly clear that they're planning to rise, with or without us," she added. "Our help may tip the balance in their favour. But if we cannot get through to the Twins in time..."

"We all die," Martin said. "Admiral, I understand the risks."

He took a long breath, feeling his heart start to pound. He had no illusions about himself. He'd been warned, time and time again, that recon troopers were often marked as *expendable*. The missions had sounded exciting, when he'd sought new challenges. Now...it came home to him, violently, that he might be out on a limb, with someone behind him merrily sawing it off. Admiral Stuart would do everything in her power to get to him in time—she didn't have a reputation for abandoning people—but it might not be enough. And he might never go home.

"I'm glad you do," Admiral Stuart said, sympathetically. She sat back in her chair. "You can take an entire recon platoon with you. Under the circumstances"—her lips thinned, as if she'd bitten into something nasty—"you can have complete freedom in planning the operation. If you want to borrow the LinkShip to get there, you can ask. Just let me know before I start making other plans that involve it."

Martin nodded. He'd been briefed on the LinkShip project. Most of the details had been classified, of course, but he knew the ship could pass through a gravity point without being detected. It would have been a war-winner, before the Tokomak invented stardrive. Now, it was still one hell of an advantage…if the enemy hadn't realised what the humans had learnt to do. The last set of reports he'd read insisted the enemy had laid so many mines on the far side of the gravity point that someone could probably walk on them.

"Agent Piece is waiting for you in Briefing Room C," Admiral Stuart continued. "I expect you to remember that walls have ears, even here. If they figure out what you're doing, you'll be in trouble."

"I'll be dead," Martin corrected. He rose and saluted. "Thank you, Admiral."

Yolanda was waiting outside, looking as pale as always. "You alright?"

"In the words of Edmund Blackadder, another tempting opportunity to commit suicide beckons," Martin said. The quote would normally have made her smile. This time, she looked as if she was already weeping by his grave. He shuddered. If he died this time, there wouldn't be enough of him left to pick up with a pair of tweezers. "I have a meeting in Briefing Room C."

"Good luck," Yolanda said. "I'll take you there."

She led him through empty corridors and through a hatch that was not only locked but guarded by two marines. Martin wondered, dryly, if the admiral wanted to draw attention to Agent Piece or if she simply didn't trust him. Or maybe she just wanted to make damn sure that no one outside the handful of people in the know laid eyes on him. People would talk, unfortunately. And no one really knew what piece of information would allow the enemy to put the whole picture together.

"I'll see you tonight," Yolanda said, as the hatch opened. "Call me when you're done."

Martin nodded and stepped into the compartment. Agent Piece sat at a table, studying a file report. He rose as Martin entered, looking him up and down with practiced ease. Decent training, Martin noted absently. Piece looked sloppy, as if he was nothing more than a poser, but there was something about his movements that suggested his sloppiness was an act. Martin wondered if the aliens noticed—and, if they did notice, if they cared. They found human body language as hard to read as humans found theirs. He doubted there were many human-specific xenospecialists among the Tokomak.

"Agent," he said. "I'm Captain Douglas."

"Captain," Piece said. "Or should it be *Colonel*, here?"

"Here, it doesn't matter." Martin took a seat. "I heard the lecture you gave the admiral. I want to hear it again, from you."

Piece didn't look surprised at the request. Instead, he sat down and calmly recited the entire speech for a second time. Martin formulated questions and interrupted to ask them, giving Piece as little time as possible to think of answers. It wasn't that he didn't believe Piece was who he claimed to be—by now, Admiral Stuart and General Romford would have run his ID through the wringer—so much as he wanted to make sure he knew everything he could. He'd run into trouble, during exercises, by assuming he knew more than he did. If he did that during a *real* mission, he'd be dead and his team along with him.

"A small team isn't going to make that much of a difference," he said, finally. Piece seemed to have an answer for everything. Martin was curious to see how he'd answer that. "I know the movies make us into superhumans, who can leap tall buildings in a single bound and smash entire battleships with a single punch, but reality is rarely that obliging."

"No," Piece agreed. "On one hand, your team will be a sign to the dissidents that they're not alone. And, on the other, your team may come in handy."

"Really." Martin met his eyes. "And what's to stop the Galactic Overlords from simply vaporising every last planet in the system? Or merely scorching them clean of life?"

"The Twins are a vitally important part of the galactic economy," Piece said, evenly. "Their population is one of the most highly-trained and educated workforces in the core, the second or third largest in the galaxy. In addition, they are owned—owned outright—by the combines, the enemy's interstellar corporations. Their owners would not be pleased if their military saved the system by destroying it. The dissidents are effectively using themselves as human shields."

"I'm sure there's a flaw in that logic somewhere," Martin said. It was hard to keep the sarcasm out of his voice. "Will they be pointing guns at their own heads and threatening to shoot if the Tokomak don't go away?"

"No." There was a faint hint of irritation in his voice. "The point is, Captain, that they are limited in how they can react. If they blow up the entire system, they will blow up a sizable chunk of their own economy with it. And the knock-on effects will be serious. It will set their fleet refitting and mobilisation programs back *years*. They will have to try and take the system back *without* destroying it."

Martin considered it. "And a long-term insurgency will render the system useless anyway."

"Yes," Piece said.

"How can you be so cold?" Martin cocked his head. "How many of your allies are going to die when the fighting starts?"

Piece's face sagged. "It wasn't my plan, Captain. They're going to do it, with or without us. They understand the risks, they understand what's at stake, but...they want to die on their feet rather than live on their knees. Because that's what they're facing, right now. A system that is blatantly racist, that will not grant even the slightest glimmer of respect to the most useful workers...workers who could make the difference between saving the galactic economy and letting it continue to stagnate. They're *desperate.*

They're sick of living with the Sword of Damocles constantly hanging over their heads. They want to put an end to it."

Martin frowned. "Even if it costs them everything?"

"Even so." Piece looked at the table. "I won't pretend any of this is good, Captain. I won't pretend that millions of people—aliens, but still people—aren't about to die. All we can do is take advantage of it."

"Right." Martin sat down. "How do you plan to *get* there?"

"I've asked for a freighter to be modified for us," Piece said. "Assuming the codes still work, and they should, we shouldn't have any trouble getting there within three weeks. If they don't"—he smiled, coldly—"things may become slightly *problematic*."

"Slightly," Martin repeated. A freighter couldn't run or fight. If they ran into pirates, let alone an enemy warship, they'd be dead. "There are other options."

"So I've been told," Piece said. "But we also need to take supplies. I've had a bit of an idea."

Martin laughed. "Just a bit?"

"Just a bit," Piece said. He keyed his datapad, bringing up a holographic display. "But I was hoping you could help me flesh it out."

"As you wish," Martin said. He'd see what the plan was before he either started to improve it or vetoed it. "And then I'll have to call the rest of the team."

CHAPTER EIGHT

Martin couldn't sleep.

He lay next to Yolanda, feeling her curled against him. The last week had been hectic, starting with a detailed assessment of the captured databanks—he'd never been so glad the Tokomak were obsessive bureaucrats who listed *everything*—and continuing with training, preparing the modified freighter and readying the team for the mission. It was good to know that he could requisition anything he wanted, and he'd taken shameless advantage of it to make sure the team had everything it needed, but it wasn't enough. He knew he was going into danger. And he knew there was a very good chance he'd die, along with the rest of the team, thousands of light years from home.

Yolanda shifted against him, pressing against his warmth. Martin was tempted to wake her, to make love one final time before the alarm rang and he had to leave, but he resisted. Yolanda had a job to do too. And besides, they'd spent most of the evening making love. He smiled at the memory, then sobered. Who would have thought a black kid from whatever remained of the once-great United States of America would end up so far from home, fighting to defend the entire human race? He felt a pang of guilt for everyone he'd left behind, mingled with the grim awareness that they too could have left if they'd worked up the nerve. It was hard to leave *everything* behind, he admitted in the privacy of his own mind. He knew he wouldn't have left if he hadn't been certain he'd been on the short road to an early death. And yet, it had been harder than he'd expected to start the first leg on the journey to space.

He closed his eyes, silently contemplating all the things that could go wrong. They'd done their best to plan for everything, but they knew—all too well—that the slightest mistake could end in disaster. No plan ever survived contact with the enemy. The Tokomak were stodgy and unimaginative, but that didn't make them stupid. And, right now, they *had* to be cracking down hard right across their territory. An invading fleet was bad enough, but a string of uprisings had to be worse. If even a relative handful of their worlds exploded into rebellion, their empire was screwed. It would take so long to put down the revolts that humanity would have all the time it needed to build a whole new fleet and deploy weapons right out of the fertile dream of a science-fiction author. His lips quirked at the thought. *Someone* had honestly proposed building a Death Star. It *was* technically possible, just incredibly expensive. And vulnerable to a single enemy gunboat.

And we could build a million cruisers for the resources wasted in a single Death Star, he thought, dryly. He'd taken a course on grand concepts and practical realities during OCS, where his instructors had pointed out the flaws in a hundred brilliant ideas that—somehow—never worked so well in the field. *And the cruisers would probably be more useful.*

Yolanda stirred, her hand stroking his chest. Martin opened his eyes and saw her looking at him, her dark eyes worried. She knew everything, he guessed, although she wasn't—technically—on the list of people who had a need-to-know. Yolanda was Admiral Stuart's tactical aide. She'd probably done much of the legwork involved in getting Martin and his team the resources they needed. And she wasn't stupid. She might not know the exact details, but she could probably put together a very accurate picture.

"You'd better come back," she said, as her hand slipped downwards. "I don't want to lose you."

Martin nodded, although he knew there were no guarantees. That had been true in the ghetto and it was true in deep space. He'd learnt that the hard way. The cold equations would always claim their due, whatever happened. The slightest mistake—the slightest innocent mistake—could get people killed. One could take every imaginable precaution and *still* wind up dead. It didn't bother him. He'd lived on Earth. The environment might be safer, by and large, but the people were not. Solarians tended to be a more practical, and tolerant, breed.

He smiled as she clambered on top of him, pressing down. His hands rose to her breasts, stroking them gently. It had taken him longer than it should to realise the value of a single partner, one he knew—and knew him—intimately. They moved together, building towards a climax. He held her tightly as he came, pulling her down so they could kiss. He wanted to stay with her. He needed… but he knew he had to go. He glanced at the chronometer and swallowed a curse. There were only a few minutes left until the alarm rang.

"When we get home, I think I…"

Yolanda broke off. She knew—they both knew—that it was bad luck to talk about the future. There was no guarantee that either—or both—of them would survive. Yolanda was on a cruiser, the most heavily-protected ship in the fleet, but a lucky hit might destroy the ship with all hands. She might die… they both might die. Martin pressed his lips against her lightly, trying to say with his kisses what he couldn't say with his mouth. Afterwards, if there was an afterwards, they could have children. They'd talked about it, more than once. But the war had always got in the way.

The alarm rang. Martin allowed himself a quick fantasy of drawing his pistol and shooting the alarm, then reached out and silenced it with a tap of his hand. Yolanda rolled over, her pale skin glistening with sweat. Martin wanted her—his body was urgently reminding him that it would be months, at least, before he saw her again—but he ignored it. His team would make sarcastic remarks if he was late for deployment. And he hated to think what Admiral Stuart would say to his lover. Yolanda *was* the Admiral's tactical aide.

He stood and walked into the shower, turning on the water. Yolanda followed, pressing against him as he washed the sweat from their bodies. He kissed her again, then dried himself and donned his tunic. He thought he heard a sob from inside the washroom, but didn't dare look. Yolanda would never have forgiven him. Instead, he checked his appearance in the mirror. He looked like a soldier, a very dangerous man. Any human would have spotted him at once. Thankfully, the Tokomak weren't human. All humans looked alike to them. Martin would have been annoyed if he hadn't known humans had the same problem. The Tokomak really *did* look alike.

Yolanda stepped out of the washroom, a towel wrapped around her body. "You'd better go," she said. She'd never been good at dealing with partings. "I'll be here when you get back."

"And I will," Martin said, although he knew he could be wrong. It wasn't as if he was going to the shops for a carton of milk. "You'd better be here when I come back."

Yolanda smiled, wanly. "I'll be here," she said. "Goodbye."

Martin turned, feeling like a heel as he walked out. He'd be back...he promised himself he'd be back. His father had walked out on his mother shortly after she'd become pregnant, if she'd been telling the truth. He didn't know. He would have liked to have known his father, even though cold logic told him his father hadn't been a man to admire. What sort of bastard walked out on a pregnant woman? He shook his head, firmly. If he had kids, he was damned if he was leaving them to grow up alone. They'd have a father in their lives whether they liked it or not.

He reached the teleport compartment and spoke briefly to the operator, clearing a teleport path to *Hoyden*. The alien freighter was far too close to *Defiant* for comfort, even if her presence was masked by sensor decoys and ECM fields. He would have preferred to launch the operation from N-Gann itself, or even build up a data trail before altering course and heading for the Twins, but time was short. Besides, he admitted sourly, the more systems they passed through, the greater the chance someone would ask awkward questions. And if they did...

"Captain," Sergeant Butler said. He was a thickly-built man with a strong accent Martin had never been able to place. It was unusually thick, for someone who'd been born and raised in the Solar Union. "Welcome onboard."

Martin nodded, shortly. "Are we ready to depart on schedule?"

"We're just waiting for two men," Butler said. "Simmons is on his way. Haw-Haw has been a little delayed."

"We have time," Martin said. Haw-Haw—his real name was in the files, but Martin had never bothered to check—had a partner who'd been deployed to N-Gann. "If he isn't here in a couple of hours, though..."

He shrugged as he stepped off the pad. *Hoyden* had been designed by a committee for multispecies accommodation and it showed. The interior felt oddly out of proportion, as if a child had put the ship together out of plastic bricks. The hatches were alternatively too wide and too short. He shook his head, reminding himself that they could hardly use a human-designed freighter for the mission. *That* would definitely draw unwanted attention. There'd even been reports of human-designed ships being unceremoniously blown out of space when they tried to pass through the gravity points.

And if they realise what we're carrying, he thought glumly, *we're screwed.*

"Piece and his companions are in their cabins," Butler informed him. "They've been quite cooperative."

Martin nodded, although he did have his concerns. He had nothing against aliens, but he had a great deal against untrained amateurs interfering with his operations. Rumour had it that the Solar Marines had a very quiet ongoing operation on Earth, arming and training men who fought back against the madness engulfing the planet. Martin would have hated that role, as much as he hated the men who'd thrown Earth into the gutter. You just couldn't trust amateurs to play their part. They had hopes and dreams of their own. They were always a two-edged sword.

And we have to rely on them, he thought. *There's no other way to do it.*

"Once the stragglers are onboard, take us to our planned position," he ordered, putting the thought aside. "The flag will tell us when to move."

"Yes, sir," Butler said. "We'll be ready."

"And hope that we don't draw fire from the wrong side," Martin said. Accidents happened—he *knew* accidents happened, despite their best efforts—but it would still be embarrassing to be killed by his own side. A lone freighter, in a place where no freighter had any business being…it was all too likely that someone would draw the wrong conclusions and throw a missile at him. "That would be bad."

"Yes, sir," Butler said, with studied indifference. "That would be *very* bad."

• • •

"Can't sleep?"

Hoshiko looked up, sharply. Her grandfather was standing in the hatchway, his expression unreadable in the half-light. She beckoned him into the room with a single motion, then returned her attention to the holographic display. The fleet revolved around her, each and every ship ready for war. They were as ready as they'd ever be. They *had* to go soon or they'd start to degrade. No military force could remain at readiness indefinitely, no matter what politicians or armchair admirals claimed. And merely ramping up some of their sensors would hasten their demise.

"No." She tapped a switch, bringing the cabin lights up. "I keep thinking about the operation."

"And about how much relies on you?" Steve smiled at her, his young face oddly contrasting with his old eyes. "You wouldn't be the first person to worry."

"No." Hoshiko turned away from the display, trying not to think about the hundreds of ships under her command. "I feel like Jellico."

"The one man who could lose the war in a day, at Jutland," Steve said. He'd taught her military history. "What *about* him?"

"I was happier playing Beatty," Hoshiko admitted. "Beatty could have lost every ship under his command and it wouldn't have materially altered the balance of power. Not enough to allow Germany to win, anyway. Beatty could take chances Jellico couldn't afford to risk."

"Beatty also stabbed his commanding officer in the back, metaphorically speaking," Steve pointed out. He'd studied war for longer than she'd been alive. "He claimed he could have delivered a decisive victory, if he'd been in command of the Grand Fleet."

"It's a lot easier to carp and criticise when you're not the one with ultimate responsibility," Hoshiko countered. "Or the one who will be made a scapegoat if the battle is lost and the war lost with it."

"And you are happy to criticise your superiors?" Steve cocked an eyebrow. "Do you think that's good for morale?"

"It's never been easy to give feedback without criticism," Hoshiko said. "Or of coming across as an armchair critic, even if one isn't *intending* to put someone down."

She smiled. "And no commanding officer wants to hear his subordinates criticising her, even when she knows she needs it."

"One should always bow down to tyrants," Steve said. It sounded like a quote. "I speak as a tyrant, of course."

Hoshiko lifted her eyebrows. "Pardon?"

"Old joke," Steve said. "A king once asked his bards to explain the nature of courage to him. One of them dared suggest that courage lay in resisting tyrannical demands from one's monarch... or something along those lines. The king didn't see the funny side. Resistance is commendable as long as they're not resisting you."

"Oh." Hoshiko had to smile. "I can see his point."

She waved a hand at the display. "How did you cope? I mean... when you realised that everything was resting on *you*?"

"It took me a long time to *really* grasp it," Steve said. He sounded pensive. "You see, when I was a little boy..."

"Back when dinosaurs ruled the Earth," Hoshiko put in.

"That joke's older than *me*," Steve said. "Back when I was a little boy, which was a long time *after* the dinosaurs died out, there were no aliens. We were limited to a single world, which was both very small—thanks to the magic of radio and the internet—and very big. It could take literally *hours* to fly around the globe. There were no aliens. There was no sense, in our collective mindset, that there was anything beyond the sky. You really can't grasp just how ignorant most people were, back then. On one hand, our society depended on orbital satellites. On the other, there were idiots who called the space program a waste of money and wanted to keep pouring cash into black holes instead. We were *very* lucky it was the Horde that rediscovered Earth first, back then. Someone more competent could have fucked us up with both hands tied behind their backs.

"I didn't realise just how big our world had become, not at first. I didn't grasp the towering interstellar civilisation, not until…not until I started trading myself. I didn't realise the scale of the challenge facing us until it was too late. If I had, I might never have started. I might have given up without even *trying* to face the challenge."

"I find that hard to believe," Hoshiko said.

"You grew up in the Solar Union," Steve reminded her. "All of this"—he waved a hand at the bulkhead—"is normal to you. To us, it was an outside context problem. A lot of people on Old Earth never really recovered from discovering that we weren't alone in the universe. They just couldn't take it."

Hoshiko frowned. "Is there a point, Grandpa?"

"You're not Jellico or Beatty," Steve said. "You're not in the same position. Yes, a great deal *does* rest on you. But you have a good staff, good crewmen and good ships. You can't guarantee anything, of course, but you've done everything in your power to make sure you come out ahead."

"If Jellico had lost, Britain would have been invaded," Hoshiko said. "Germany would have won the war. It would have been a disaster. But it wouldn't have been the end of the human race."

"No," Steve agreed. "But you never know. Maybe things will change. The Tokomak might change. Or their servants might rise up against them.

Sometimes, all that is needed is proof that one's tormentors are *not* invincible. And you stopped a mighty fleet in its tracks."

"Sure," Hoshiko said, sardonically. "And maybe the horse will learn to sing."

"It might," Steve said. "You never know."

Hoshiko had to smile. "Thanks for the distraction, Grandpa."

Steve bowed. "You're welcome."

"And I really should kick you off the ship," Hoshiko pointed out. "If you die here..."

"I'm old enough to make that decision for myself," Steve countered. "And I started all this, a long time ago. I should be there to see it end. I sometimes wonder, you know, what would have happened if I'd turned the ship over to the government."

He shook his head. "But you know what? It doesn't matter. We play the cards we're dealt and do our best to rig the odds in our favour."

"Very profound, Grandpa," Hoshiko said. "Maybe I'll have it engraved on my tombstone."

"I want someone to write something sarcastic," Steve said. "But I fear they'll go for something polite instead."

He laughed, then sobered. "Go get some sleep, young lady. Mornings always come too soon."

CHAPTER NINE

Commodore Piling was surprised, deep inside, that she'd been left in command of the system defences. She was old—incredibly old, by human standards—and she really *should* have been removed, if only because she was too old to impress the new empress. Piling had no combat experience, little diplomatic experience…indeed, the simple fact she *hadn't* been promoted earlier, before the coup, spoke volumes. Perhaps the empress had too much to do to sack her personally, Piling thought, or perhaps she was simply rated as expendable. It was what *she* would have done.

She sat in her command chair and surveyed the tactical display with a grim feeling of bitter dissatisfaction. There was nothing particularly important about the Hellene System, save for the simple fact that it was part of a chain of gravity points leading from N-Gann to the Twins and through them to Tokomak Prime itself. The handful of inhabited planets had been denied the investment that had been given to N-Gann, ensuring that they were poorly developed and their defences were minimal. The planners had always assumed that N-Gann would cover the system, if they'd had the imagination to think that the system might ever be threatened at all. It had probably never crossed their mind that N-Gann would fall to an outside force.

The gravity point pulsed in the centre of the display, mocking her. Piling had done everything she could, from deploying thousands upon thousands of cheap mines to arming her freighters with missile pods in the hopes they might score a handful of hits before they were blown out of space, but she was grimly aware that her defences were flimsy. N-Gann had been heavily defended and the fleet base had fallen...intact, if some of the reports were to be believed. Her eyes shifted to the handful of planets within the system, almost entirely inhabited by servitors and outright slaves, their contracts owned by the big combines. She'd heard the rumblings of discontent, the growing awareness that their masters could be beaten. It was only a matter of time before the system exploded...

And the empress isn't rushing support up the chain either, Piling thought. She knew, intellectually, that the fleet had taken a beating, that thousands of ships had been lost, but she found it hard to believe. She'd watched hundreds of thousands of ships making their way down the chain, a force so vast it seemed impossible to believe it could lose. But it *had* lost and now...she hated to admit it, but the empress was right. She was expendable. *And it's only a matter of time before we lose.*

She turned her attention to the reports, but she couldn't force herself to read them. She'd risen in the ranks through a pathological obsession with bureaucracy, yet...something was wrong. Half the reports were so optimistic that it was clear the writers were either lying or delusional, the remainder were so pessimistic that it was difficult to tell just who was writing them. The paperwork that has sustained the empire was starting to collapse, more and more people writing lies into the official record...Piling wasn't *naive*. She knew the empire lied to its subjects. But it couldn't afford to start lying to *itself*...

An alarm rang. She jerked her head up, just in time to see a red icon materialise in the gravity point. The mines started gliding towards it, too late. The icon flashed, transforming into an expanding sphere as the anti-matter warhead detonated. More and more flooded the gravity point, each explosion wiping out hundreds of mines. The humans were clearing the gravity point by brute force, not even bothering to send recon probes or actual starships through the gap as they worked. She cursed savagely as her crews rushed to battle stations, bringing their weapons and sensors online. They just didn't have the time to do more than make a brief stand.

The surging energies seemed to still, just for a moment. Piling allowed herself a second of hope, even though she *knew* it was futile. Hundreds of thousands of mines had been wiped out, along with a pair of freighters that had been too close to the gravity point. She didn't have time to mourn their loss. More red icons were already appearing, human-made assault pods. She wondered, savagely, why her people had never thought of building jump-capable missile pods. The humans were insane! Their fantasists seemed to have spent *years* dreaming up ideas and tactics for weapons they hadn't possessed, weapons they would never have been able to build without help. And it had given them an edge.

"Order Force One to fire at will," she said. "Force Two is to remain in place..."

She felt her stomach churn as the assault pods opened fire, launching a wave of missiles in all directions. They *were* quick, damn it. Their targeting data had to be almost non-existent, yet—even as they moved—they were picking up targets and moving to attack. She traced the vectors as some of her freighters opened fire, trying to get their missiles off before they were blown out of space. It was unlikely they'd hit anything important. The humans were fighting smart, wearing down her defences before committing their warships to the engagement. She thought dark thoughts about the industrial might of N-Gann, a system that might as well be on the other side of the galaxy for all the good it would do her. The humans had probably put the giant fabricators to work, churning out hundreds of missiles and antimatter pods. They could just keep firing blind until her defences had been reduced to dust.

A new red icon appeared in the display. She ground her teeth in frustration as her sensors picked out the human destroyer. It was targeted instantly, a wave of missiles roaring towards it...her crews had done everything right, but it was still too late. The destroyer vanished, jumping back through the gravity point. Piling snapped orders, directing her uncloaked ships to alter position as quickly as possible. It wouldn't be long before the next wave of assault pods materialised ... she didn't even have time to finish the thought. The assault pods jumped through the gravity point, a handful intersecting and wiping themselves out of existence. The remainder opened fire as one.

That was quick, she thought. She'd heard rumours that the humans had made breakthroughs in computer technology, perhaps even produced a working AI, but she hadn't believed it. AIs were dangerous. Everyone knew it. But if the humans had made a breakthrough ... she swallowed, hard. They *had* to have found *some* way of collecting data and turning it into targeting information at terrifying speed. AIs or no AIs, they'd done it. Somehow. *We might be in some trouble.*

She tried to ignore the unpleasant feeling in her chest as her defences shattered, the remaining visible ships either falling back or being ruthlessly blown out of space. A couple dropped their shields and tried to surrender, something that would have been unthinkable two years ago, but the humans ignored them. She couldn't tell if the automated systems were incapable of recognising a surrender or if the humans simply wanted to commit a war crime. A handful of human ships materialised on the gravity point, bringing up their sensors and weapons with terrifying speed. This time, they took no fire. None of the forward defences had lasted long enough to greet them.

But they don't know about Force Two, she reminded herself, as the human ships started to move away from the gravity point. *They don't know we're lying in wait.*

Her hands moved over her console as the display continued to update. A steady stream of human warships began to appear, deploying so quickly that there was a serious risk of one ship interpenetrating another and destroying both ships. She hoped a few of them would, if only to convince the humans to slow down. She'd seen the reports, heard the horror stories passed down from a dozen battles, but she hadn't actually believed them. No Galactic race would ever take the risk. But the humans were barbarians. They took risks with their lives that no sane race would *ever* take. They seemed to consider *themselves* expendable.

The deployment continued, slowly but surely. A handful of ships dropped into FTL, rocketing towards the other gravity point or the planet itself; the remainder stayed near the first gravity point, watching and waiting as the assault force grew stronger. Piling forced herself to wait, knowing it was only a matter of time before the humans made their bid to seize the next gravity point. The planets were immaterial, as far as she was concerned. If the humans managed to take the gravity point, they could cut the entire system off from the rest of the empire and block all hope of reinforcement. And then…her lips thinned as she saw hundreds of freighters, the ones she hadn't managed to press into service, streaking away from the planet. Their commanders could read a tactical display as well as herself. They knew it was just a matter of time before they were locked out of the gravity point. They *had* to get through before it was too late or they'd face so many penalties they'd probably lose their licences to command starships.

And the combines won't give a damn, she thought. *Don't they know there's a war on?*

She leaned forward as the human ships started to move, powerful squadrons heading towards the other gravity point. They were taking their time, she noted; they could have moved a great deal faster if they wished. She frowned, wondering if it was some kind of trap. The humans didn't know she was waiting for them, did they? Or…she smiled, grimly, as she understood what she was seeing. The humans *wanted* the freighters to run. They *wanted* them to spread the word. They *wanted* the entire galaxy to see the Tokomak lose yet another system. And word would spread…

Piling reached for her console to issue orders, then shook her head. There was no hope of closing the gravity point, not in time to matter. The freighters would carry news of defeat…she hoped they'd carry news of a valiant last stand too. The humans were good, but they weren't gods. They'd be buried in starships and missiles, once the reserve fleets were online and the fabrication nodes were up to speed. And her battle here, as tiny as it was by the standards of previous engagements, would buy time. It was worth it.

She tapped a switch. "Prepare to engage," she ordered. Her ships had their drives and shields stepped down as much as possible. Thankfully, the human ships weren't trying to hide. The engagement would have become impossible if both sides were relying on passive sensors. "Fire when they reach the planned waypoint, unless they scan us first. If they do, fire at once."

Her heart started to race as the human ships drew closer. She'd planned the engagement carefully, running through hundreds of simulations, but it was all too clear the humans had never read the tactical manuals. Or, if they had, they hadn't paid any attention. Their tactics alone were crazy, by pre-war standards. Now... Piling had the odd feeling an era was dying, even if the war was won without further ado. She'd heard her junior officers openly discussing new tactics, as if they no longer trusted what they read in the manuals. They'd never get promotion with attitudes like that... no, *once* they would never have got promotion with those attitudes. Now, Piling wasn't so sure. The empress had thought outside the box. It was why she was empress.

And if I'd had that sort of imagination, she told herself, *perhaps I would be empress.*

She snorted and put the thought out of her head. She didn't have that sort of imagination. She'd never had the nerve—or the need—to think outside the box. And that was all there was to it. She would never have thought to launch a coup. She would certainly never have considered that a coup might succeed... the thought had been laughable.

She was sure no one was laughing now.

"Prepare to engage," she repeated. She knew she was nervous. She couldn't help herself. Whatever happened, she wasn't going to survive. She was old and yet she felt unready to die. A year or so ago, death would have been unthinkable. A year or so ago, the war itself would have been unthinkable. Who would have thought there was *anything* that could stand against the masters of the universe? "Prepare to..."

The display washed red. The human ships seemed to *jump*. Piling knew it was her imagination, but she clung to it anyway. She'd hoped the enemy would obligingly crawl into point-blank range before noticing her ships, yet... she'd given them a fright. And *her* ships were close enough to launch their missiles in sprint mode. The humans would have to either stand on the defensive or flee into FTL and they didn't have time to do either. She smiled, coldly, as the first missiles launched from her ships, their drives powering up in a desperate bid to generate gravity wells. It might *just* keep the humans from fleeing when they realised they'd walked into a trap.

She leaned forward as the human ships started to return fire. The cloaking devices had been rendered useless the moment her ships had launched their missiles, of course. The humans would have to be blind not to see where the missiles were coming from, blind and stupid to miss the obvious fact that there were invisible ships lurking under cloak. But their targeting was disturbingly accurate, accurate enough to make her wonder if they'd known she was there all along... she shook her head. They *really* weren't gods. If they'd known she was there, they would have opened fire while her ships were defenceless. She might not even have known what had hit her before it was too late.

Icons—human icons—flickered as her missiles started to explode. Their shields were tough—it was disconcerting to realise that a human cruiser had better shields than one of her battleships—but they weren't designed to take such a pounding. A vindictive sense of cold glee washed through her as a human cruiser vanished, followed rapidly by a pair of destroyers and a ship of indeterminate class. The losses were going to be uneven, in both senses of the word. She might lose her entire squadron, but the humans—proportionally—would suffer worse. The explosions pockmarking her ships would represent a net loss to the human fleet even if they killed her entire squadron.

Her ships brought up their drives and plunged forward, trying to narrow the range as much as possible. Piling had put her biggest ships in the vanguard, trying to ensure that they drew fire so her smaller ships could get into range. The humans seemed to be wise to the trick, but they could hardly ignore millions of tons of battleship trying to get into energy range. A low shudder ran though the CIC as her flagship took a hit, alerts flashing up to warn her the humans were using antimatter warheads. Piling wasn't surprised, but she *was* disconcerted. The humans—somehow—had managed to get a bigger than expected yield...

They must have found a way to compress antimatter safely, she thought, as she glanced at the sensor reports. It was hard to be sure—the antimatter blasts were disrupting everything—but the human missiles didn't *look* any larger than her own. And yet, compressed antimatter was very dangerous. It would be a hellish risk, whatever advantages it offered its users. Perhaps they'd found a way to produce miniature drives. It was theoretically possible, if one didn't mind the radiation surge. *They're quite happy to take risks if it gives them the edge.*

Another impact shook her ship as the range closed rapidly. The humans were blasting away with phasers and other energy weapons now, burning through her shields and cutting into her hulls. Her ships were doing the same, her smaller ships deliberately trying to ram the bigger enemy warships. Their losses would sting, but...Piling told herself, again and again, that her people would come out ahead. They could afford to take losses. Their human enemies could not. She smiled, coldly. She wouldn't be promoted—she wouldn't survive long enough—but she'd be remembered. She just hoped it was enough for her family. They would suffer if she was remembered poorly.

A human starship—a cruiser, she thought—exploded as her energy weapons tore through its hull. She noted a handful of lifepods, a couple mistaken for mines and picked off as the remains of her formation careened through the human ships. Her ship shook again and again, her crew fighting desperately to keep the damage under control a few minutes longer.

And yet, the damage was mounting up rapidly. She cursed as a console exploded, something that only happened when the damage was beyond control. Power surges within the vessel's control systems meant certain destruction. Her time was up...

They'll remember me, she thought, vindictively. The display blanked as the ship shook again and again. She wanted to run to the nearest lifepod, but she knew it was already too late. They'd been on a collision course before the drives had failed... she hoped they'd maintain enough speed to hit their target. *They'll remember me...*

And then the world went away in a flash of blinding light.

CHAPTER TEN

"The last of the enemy ships has been destroyed," Yolanda reported.

"Continue to deploy drones," Hoshiko ordered, keeping the annoyance out of her voice with an effort. The enemy commander had planned an ambush and pulled it off perfectly. Almost perfectly... she snorted, reminding herself the enemy wasn't stupid. Their commander, who was hopefully dead, had reasoned out a plan to hurt her deployment and succeeded magnificently. "And order Force One to advance to the gravity point."

She leaned back in her chair as the fleet picked up speed. The enemy ships—mainly freighters, as far as her sensors could tell—seemed intent on running for their lives. A handful had dropped into FTL and were fleeing, while the remainder were heading for the gravity point as if they feared she'd slam the door closed at any moment. And she would, given time. She could do it a great deal quicker, if she wished. They knew it. They'd probably be unsure why she *wasn't* slamming the door closed.

Which won't stop them taking advantage of it, she thought, feeling the time slowly ticking by. *Let them think I made a mistake.*

She forced herself to check the figures as the fleet crawled through space. The enemy hadn't had the time or the resources to mount a proper defence, although what they'd done had been bad enough. In some ways, it wasn't reassuring. The main body of the enemy fleet, the survivors of

N-Gann, had continued to flee. She would have preferred to bring them to battle before they could link up with reinforcements, let alone have time to start learning from their own mistakes. The Tokomak were inexperienced, but that was changing rapidly. A smart commander would start distributing experienced crewmembers around his fleet to ensure they had a chance to teach the inexperienced what to do.

And they gave us a bloody nose, she thought, sourly. A bloody nose was hardly fatal—she'd had her nose bloodied a few times in playground fights, when she'd been a great deal younger—but it was still a shock. *The next engagement will be harder.*

She glanced at Yolanda. "Inform Captain Douglas that he may deploy as planned," she ordered. She knew perfectly well that Yolanda and Douglas were in a relationship, but it didn't matter as long as they stayed professional while they were on duty. They weren't in the same chain of command. "And remind him he has a time limit."

"Aye, Admiral," Yolanda said.

Hoshiko scowled. The files stated there were no gravity point defences between N-Gann and the Twins. She was pretty sure the files were out of date. The Tokomak *had* to be doing everything they could to slow her down, assuming that she intended to drive on their homeworld with all the force she could muster. It was what *they* would have done. And if they happened to start searching *every* freighter that passed through the gravity point, Captain Douglas and his team were doomed. They wouldn't even have a chance to sell their lives dearly. She would have preferred to send them through FTL, but by the time they reached their destination the whole mission would be pointless. The war—win or lose—would be over.

She turned her attention to the display and watched as a steady stream of freighters headed for the gravity point and made transit. Captain Douglas should have plenty of cover amongst the rats leaving the sinking ship... she hoped, prayed, that he made it. The Tokomak shouldn't have *time* to start searching every ship, not when they had to scramble to get their defences in place. And yet, they were more mindlessly bureaucratic than the worst bureaucrats humanity had ever produced. They might start searching the ships because they didn't have the imagination to realise they had worse problems breathing down their necks.

Yolanda looked up. "Admiral, we're picking up a signal from the planet," she said. "There's an uprising. They want our help."

Which would be a ready-made excuse to leave the door open a little longer, if the enemy wasn't so unimaginative, Hoshiko thought. *They might start wondering why we were ignoring their tactical manuals.*

"Detach two squadrons and the LinkShip to the planet," she ordered, tersely. It would be enough firepower to make a difference, if luck was on their side. There were so many rats leaving the sinking ship that it was quite possible that there was *no one* in charge on the surface, certainly no one with the authority to order mass reprisals. "If the enemy defences are strong enough to stand them off, the rebels will just have to wait."

"Aye, Admiral." Yolanda hid it well, but she wasn't pleased. She was too young and idealistic to realise the rebels couldn't be supported, not until the operation was completed and the gravity point was firmly closed. Who knew? There could be an entire alien fleet lurking on the far side, just waiting for the humans to come into range before they sprang their trap. "I'm redeploying the units now."

"Good." Hoshiko studied the younger woman's back for a moment, then turned her attention back to the display. "Inform me when we're entering weapons range."

"Aye, Admiral."

• • •

Hameeda felt oddly like the angel of doom as she flew towards Hellene-II, even though none of the defenders—or the hundreds of freighters fleeing the planet—could see her. It looked as though the entire planet was being evacuated, hundreds of thousands of people running for their lives. She knew it was an illusion—there was little hope of evacuating an entire planet in the space of a few hours, even if the combined ships of every galactic power were pressed into service—but it lingered in her mind. She felt torn between guilt and an odd kind of relief. Whatever else happened, there would be no—or few—reprisals. The cycle of hatred might just be broken.

She monitored the planetary communications channels with a subsection of her neural network as the range closed, trying to get a handle on what was actually happening. It was hard to be sure—she didn't have any idea of what the planet had been like, before the gravity point had been taken and the revolution began—but it sounded as though the majority of the planetary industry and defences had fallen into revolutionary hands. Her onboard analysis programs suggested the communications networks were definitely in friendly hands, if only because they were filling space with their chatter. The Tokomak were definitely more dignified. Now, all the limiters seemed to have been removed.

The planet grew larger in her mind's eye, a single rocky orb surrounded by a hundred orbital stations of varying size. It was tiny, compared to N-Gann. There was no ring, no sense that—one day—the entire planet might be wrapped in sheet metal and lost forever. Her sensors noted that the atmosphere was thin, almost impossible to breathe without heavy genetic or technological enhancement. The files stated that a terraforming program had begun, but it had only ever been half-hearted. Reading between the lines, Hameeda suspected the combines hadn't wanted their workers—their slaves, to all intents and purposes—running away. It was an easy way to keep them in place without being brutally obvious.

Her tactical sensors updated sharply, picking out a handful of orbital weapons platforms firing on their fellows. A handful of possible scenarios appeared in her mind, suggesting that the Tokomak still controlled a number of platforms. It wasn't easy to be *sure* which platforms were friendly, for any meaning of the word. The Tokomak would fire on her without a second thought, if they saw her, but the rebels might *also* fire on her. They simply didn't have the ability to be *sure* she was friendly.

And they might think I'm not remotely friendly, she thought. *Just less hostile than the Tokomak themselves.*

She frowned as she considered her options. One side seemed to be controlled by an orbital battlestation, the other side seemed to be being steered from the ground. Given the somewhat haphazard conflict, she guessed the rebels had hacked the command network rather than taking physical control of the system. The bad guys were probably trying to undo the hacking and take back control, if they weren't already planning to flee the system. She felt a stab of sympathy, despite herself. The Tokomak on the battlestation were probably too low-ranking to flee. And they were doomed if the rebels won. The only thing they could do was sell their lives dearly.

Time for a gamble, she told herself. *And hope for the best.*

She opened a channel. "This is Captain Hameeda of the Solar Navy," she said. It was unlikely they knew her, but if they ran her voice through their processors they'd realise she was human. Or a pretty good fake. "If you stand down now, and surrender your positions when my ships arrive, you will be taken into custody and we will guarantee your safety. If you refuse, we will remove you with all necessary force."

There was a long pause. She waited, unsure what would happen. The Tokomak might take the lifeline she'd offered them, or they might think it was just a trick. God knew they had reason to fear human tricks. And the rebels wouldn't be pleased if she denied them their revenge, even if she prevented a mutual slaughter. She felt the seconds ticking away, her neural net drawing up attack plans. If the Tokomak refused to surrender, she'd have to take them out. Quickly. It wouldn't take them long to realise they could steer most of the orbital facilities into the planet's atmosphere, smashing the fragile biosphere beyond repair.

And forcing us to decide between saving as many lives as possible or continuing the advance, leaving the poor bastards to die, she thought, grimly. It wouldn't be humanity's *fault*—they wouldn't be the ones who started a genocide—but the Solar Union would probably get the blame anyway. *Look what you made us do.*

Her eyes narrowed as tactical sensors swept across her hull, leaving her feeling naked and exposed. Her skin crawled as the sensor lock hardened.

She found it hard not to flinch as the enemy battlestation opened fire, launching a full spread of missiles towards her. Their formation was painfully blunt. They might not be hoping for a direct hit, but they clearly thought they could catch her in their blast. She cursed whoever was in charge as she gunned the drive, sprinting *towards* the missiles with terrifying speed. Her ECM surrounded her like a shroud. They'd have very real problems locking onto her again.

But not enough problems, she thought, as she threw the LinkShip into an evasive pattern that left the missiles eating her dust. *They cannot be allowed to bombard the planet.*

She spiralled closer to the battlestation, bringing her hammers online. It was a waste—hammers were expensive, particularly the two stripped-down weapons that had been loaded onto her ship—but there was no choice. And yet…she ducked as the battlestation kept firing, spitting death towards her. Normally, she would have hurled the hammer at the enemy ship from a safe distance. Now, the risk of slamming the planet was too great. She'd be safer tossing antimatter warheads in the same general direction.

Two seconds, she thought, as she prepared herself. *Now!*

The drive twitched as the hammer dropped away, the missile's gravity well expanding rapidly. Hameeda felt the entire ship shudder as it struggled to compensate for the sudden change, remembering—again—why hammers were so rare. The Tokomak *did* have a defence, if they had time to use it. She launched her remaining drones, then yanked the ship away as the enemy locked onto the hammer. There was no point in engaging the missile with conventional weapons—the gravity well dragging the missile towards its target would eat energy blasts and missiles with equal aplomb—but an antimatter warhead *might* take out the missile itself. The Tokomak had done it before. They might even get lucky if they threw a nuke at it.

Hameeda counted down the seconds as the hammer picked up speed, the enemy defences struggling to stop it before it was too late. Theoretically, the missile could—eventually—reach the speed of light, or as close to it as made no difference. It didn't matter. The miniature black hole smashed through the battlestation's shields and tore through the hull. The blast was strong enough to take out the generator, snapping the black hole out of existence, but it was too late. The force of the impact—and the torrent of radiation—was enough to smash the entire station. Hameeda felt a moment of pity, mingled with angry contempt. They could have lived, if they'd had the wit to surrender. They could have gone home...

She blinked away tears as she swept through the orbitals, watching for other threats. The remaining industrial facilities were already signalling their surrender, now the battlestation was gone. Hameeda chose to believe they'd seen sense, as opposed to realising they were doomed... even *more* doomed. She sent them a short message, informing their crews the cruisers would take care of them, then pulled away from the planet. The rebels tried to contact her, but she ignored them. The cruisers—and the marines—would have to deal with them.

And then we'll have to go on, Hameeda thought. She knew her role in the greater scheme of things. It would begin once the system was secure, once Admiral Stuart handed command to Admiral Teller. *Then we'll see what we see.*

• • •

"Confirm that *Hoyden* has passed through the gravity point," Hoshiko ordered, as the fleet closed on its target. "Check twice, to be sure."

"Aye, Admiral." Yolanda worked her console. "They jumped through twenty minutes ago."

Hoshiko nodded. The timing wasn't perfect. It *couldn't* be perfect. There was simply no way to hide the freighter from enemy sensors. If they noticed that *Hoyden* had appeared from nowhere, if they realised the freighter hadn't fled any of the inhabited worlds, they might ask a few pointed questions. Her fleet had scattered drones around the system, deliberately trying to confuse the enemy with unbelievable reports, but there was always a risk in any deception operation. If people knew you were lying, even if they didn't know what you were lying *about*...

The easiest way to lie is to tell the truth, she reminded herself, *but do it in a way that makes sure you won't be believed.*

She scowled. The Tokomak wouldn't believe the reports of a million human cruisers advancing on the gravity point. They'd *know* those ships didn't exist, if only because they'd be smashing their way to Tokomak Prime if they *did*. And she had no idea what they'd make of giant cubes, flying saucers and police boxes prowling the system. They'd probably assume their sensors were being spoofed. And they'd be right. She hoped—prayed—that a single freighter, a perfectly normal freighter with an apparently non-human crew, would make it through without being detected.

"Then keep us moving," she ordered. It wouldn't have been *easy* to slow the fleet further, whatever happened. The Tokomak would wonder why she was letting so many freighters escape. She'd been bombarding the system with messages proclaiming the end of Tokomak hegemony, but...she shook her head. "What news from the planet?"

"The marines have landed and taken the Galactics into custody," Yolanda said. "The rebels want their heads."

"Preferably not attached to their bodies," Hoshiko guessed. Her grandfather had told her stories of countries that no longer existed, their governments swept away by the chaos washing over Earth. The oppressed didn't just want to be free. They wanted revenge. "Tell the CO to keep his distance. We don't *want* to commit any war crimes."

She sighed, inwardly. It was going to be impossible to prevent the rebels from slaughtering at will. They'd have to use force to protect the Galactics and the rebels would see them as enemies...she reminded herself that the marines had orders to hustle the Galactics onto the freighters and send them away, as quickly as possible. The Tokomak wouldn't be happy—the freighters were hardly luxury liners—but at least they'd be alive. And—hopefully—the rebels would calm down. Hoshiko didn't have *time* to get into a squabble over who had the right to kill a few thousand enemy civilians.

We can worry about the combines after the war, she told herself, grimly. *Right now, we have other problems.*

The gravity point seemed to shimmer in front of her as the fleet settled into blockade positions, keeping a wary distance from the gravity point itself. The Tokomak had never invented the assault pod for themselves, but they'd seen them in action and there was nothing particularly special about the technology. She had no doubt it was only a matter of time before they put them into mass production and started to use them against their inventors.

And the antimatter pods are even cheaper, she mused. *It wasn't as if we cared much about what they actually hit, as long as they hit something.*

"Deployment complete," Yolanda reported. The handful of enemy freighters that hadn't jumped in time were reversing course and fleeing into FTL, their commanders no doubt cursing the timing that had left them stuck in a suddenly-hostile star system. "The system appears to be secure."

"In space, at least." Hoshiko relaxed, slightly. The first stage of the operation was over, but she could still draw back. Soon, they'd be committed. "And now we wait."

CHAPTER ELEVEN

"Well," Butler said. "We'll find out soon."

Martin shot him a sharp look as *Hoyden* made her slow way towards the gravity point. The sensor display—civilian-grade sensors, pathetic by military standards—was blurring in and out as the computers struggled to cope with the fleet's ECM. It was a good thing Martin *knew* what was happening, or otherwise he might have panicked. The sadist who'd turned clips from old movies into sensor spoofs had to be laughing his ass off right now. Giant Borg cubes hacking their way through an entire fleet of fanciful starships were the stuff of nightmares. The Tokomak wouldn't believe what they saw.

Piece shrugged. "The codes are in order and the AI mask is in place," he said. "We're as ready as we'll ever be."

"Hah." Martin wasn't so sure. "And if we're wrong?"

"We die," Piece said, simply.

Martin scowled. He was no stranger to dangerous missions, but it was rare for him and a lone platoon to be *completely* behind enemy lines. There had always been *some* support on call, even if it consisted of a lone starship and a handful of weekend warriors. But now…the moment they transited, they would be on their own. And facing an alerted enemy that might *just* decide to inspect *everything* that came through the gravity point. Piece swore blind that his codes were valid—and Marine Intelligence seemed to agree—but Martin wasn't as confident they were right. The slightest mistake could land them in an entire universe of trouble.

He told himself, firmly, that there was no point in worrying about it. *Hoyden* couldn't run, if the enemy grew suspicious. There was no way to escape, if the shit hit the fan. There wasn't even any way to strike back at their foes before they were vaporised. There was honestly no point in worrying about it... he forced himself to relax as the gravity point came closer and closer, a steady stream of ships crossing the nexus and vanishing in flashes of light. The planners had had a point, he admitted, when they'd outlined the concept. *Hoyden* would just be one of hundreds of freighters running for their lives.

Unless they start wondering why the freighters were allowed *to run*, he thought. *They know we could have slammed the door closed almost as soon as we punched our way into the system.*

The timer bleeped once, announcing ten seconds to transit. Martin drew in a breath, trying not to think about the odds of interpenetrating with another starship. Normally, the odds of two starships colliding were very low, but that didn't hold true near a gravity point. One starship could wind up accidentally sharing the same space as another, utterly destroying both ships. There were no ships coming *into* the system, thankfully, but... he calmed himself, as best as he could, as the final seconds ticked away. The line of freighters knew the danger of sticking around to be killed. They'd be running from the gravity point as fast as they could.

"Transit in five," Butler said, coolly. "Four. Three... two... one..."

Space *twisted* around them. Martin gritted his teeth, feeling as if he'd been punched in the stomach without actually *having* been punched. For a long chilling moment, it felt as if he'd swallowed rocks or something worse, something far larger than he could hope to *fit* in his stomach. And then the feeling was gone, as if it had never been. He heard someone vomit behind him and deliberately didn't look to see who. Transit effects were dangerously unpredictable. He'd heard that even starship helmsmen sometimes covered their consoles with the contents of their stomachs.

"Transit complete," Butler said. "Passive sensor array coming online... now."

"Take us away from the gravity point, then start broadcasting our ID," Piece ordered. "We don't want to look like we're skulking around the system."

Martin glanced at the operative's back as he watched the display. Deliberately *announcing* their presence struck him as the very opposite of stealth, although he had to admit that Piece had a point. The mere act of trying not to be seen was indicative, suggesting that one had a very good reason not to want to be seen. A cloaked—or even masked—ship was up to something. The very act of broadcasting their ID would suggest they had nothing to hide.

And we're claiming to be Harmonies, he thought. The ancient race could give the Tokomak lessons in arrogance, even though they were very clearly subordinate. *They wouldn't sneak around even if it cost them everything.*

He watched the display light up, hundreds of icons flaring red before the processors managed to start cataloguing them. He'd been torn between installing a military-grade passive sensor suite and a civilian one, then reluctantly decided to go with the military equipment. There was no point in hampering themselves. If the Tokomak insisted on searching the ship, they were screwed anyway. And they wouldn't even know the passive sensors were there unless they *did* search the ship.

"They haven't had time to install a real defence," Piece mused. "That's a good thing."

"Really?" Butler snorted. "What do *you* call a real defence?"

Martin listened to the argument as he studied the display. The gravity point was surrounded by a cluster of mines, a handful of automated weapons platforms and a single monitoring station that was clearly of civilian design. It was hard to be sure, but it looked as if the station wouldn't stand up to a single nuclear warhead. There weren't even any mines on the gravity point itself, although *that* wasn't a surprise. The mines wouldn't be able to tell the difference between friendly starships and enemy transits. Martin had studied the tactical manuals. Gravity points simply *couldn't* be mined thoroughly unless one *knew* the only people who were likely to jump through were enemy ships.

His eyes narrowed as he spotted the lone enemy squadron holding position some distance from the gravity point. They were modern ships, by enemy standards, but... it was hard to be sure, of course, yet there seemed to be an air of *fear* surrounding them. Martin smiled, coldly. The Tokomak had been masters of the universe for so long that it was hard for them to wrap their heads around the concept that *someone* could beat them. A single squadron of their ships could trash any foe, if anyone was stupid enough to fight. And if they couldn't, the remainder of the fleet would make short work of anyone who dared fight back. Now...

"We're being pinged," Butler said. "They want to know who we are."

"Cheek," Piece commented. "As if we weren't telling them."

He tapped his console, triggering the basic AI overlay. Martin frowned as a holographic Harmony lodged an angry protest, demanding immediate clearance to proceed and threatening everything from formal complaints to legal action if the ship didn't receive her clearance *at once*. Piece had claimed that one could be either master or slave to the Galactics—and the key to convincing them to accept you as the master was to act like it—but Martin hadn't been convinced. If someone had talked to *him* like that, when he'd been inspecting starships for enemy agents, he'd have made damn sure to draw the inspection protocol out as long as possible. But he supposed it did make a certain kind of sense. There was no one as insecure as someone hanging just below the very top, powerful and yet aware that power could be snatched away at any moment. He'd seen it before, on Earth. The Harmonies *would* lodge angry protests because the alternative—that they might not have the power to browbeat someone into submission—was unthinkable.

Butler glanced at him. "How long do you think it'll take?"

The console bleeped. "We have clearance to proceed," Piece said. "I told you so."

"No one likes a gloater," Martin told him, dryly. "Do you think they would have taken longer during peacetime?"

"I doubt it." Piece shrugged. "Galactic society is rigorously stratified, in ways both subtle and gross. Gross in all senses of the word, I should add. The Harmonies normally have the right to go wherever they like, with neither transit fees nor inspections. It was why we copied their codes."

"It still sounds a little off," Butler commented. His hands danced over the console, setting course for the next gravity point. "You'd think they'd know better by now."

Piece grinned. "You'd think, wouldn't you?"

He sat back, resting his arms in his lap. "Think of the Galactics as religious fanatics. They'll cling to their religion, the doctrine of supremacy, even when cold-blooded analysis tells them it isn't true. The more they hear the truth, the more they reject it. They're just like us, in that way. They won't give up something they *should* give up because they think they should have it. The Harmonies cling to their favoured status and we can rely on them to make things difficult for the Tokomak, if the Tokomak violate it."

Martin lifted his eyebrows. "Even if the Tokomak are right?"

"Even so," Piece confirmed. "A bunch of enemy agents use Harmony codes to get through the gravity points? So what? That's not *really* important. What's important is keeping their ancient rights and privileges. They don't have space in their heads for anything else."

"It makes no sense," Butler grumbled. "How can a society *survive* with such a glaring blind spot?"

"Because it wasn't really a problem until the war actually started," Piece pointed out. "They didn't really care about fringe activities. A handful of smugglers plying their trade never really bothered them. No matter what they did, it never really upset the balance of power beyond easy repair. One of my tutors used to think it was deliberate, although that might be giving the Tokomak too much credit. The whole system might be a way of drawing rebellious souls into doing something rebellious that's actually harmless."

He stood. "I'm going to sleep," he said. "Wake me if you need me."

Martin watched him go, scowling at his back. Piece was an experienced agent—it hadn't been hard to check his credentials—but Martin detested relying on the stupidity of others. A plan that relied on the enemy being an idiot was doomed, in his experience. Sure, there were ways to use enemy tactics against them—and get inside their decision-making loop—but they could only go so far. And yet, it wasn't as if they were top of the enemy priority list at the moment. The hundreds of freighters scattering in all directions were merely the tip of the iceberg. For the first time in *ever*, an enemy fleet was within the Tokomak's borders.

Butler shrugged. "You want to stay on the bridge?"

"Someone has to," Martin said. Freighters didn't require a constant watch, unlike warships, but it went against the grain to leave the bridge *completely* unmanned. "You can wake the others in a few hours."

He shrugged. He'd sent the rest of the team to get some rest, knowing that it wouldn't matter if they were awake or fast asleep if the deployment was uncovered. They'd worked themselves hard over the last week, trying to prepare for every last possibility before they set out on their mission. And yet...he was glumly aware there were just too many things that could go wrong. He'd sooner be in the middle of a planetary invasion, wearing nothing more than his briefs. At least he'd be able to shoot back.

The display continued to update, a handful of icons fading as enemy asteroid settlements shut down their emissions and pretended to be worthless rocks. Martin didn't fault them. Hiding was their only protection, unless they had starships they could use to evacuate the settlements. A handful of freighters were heading out of the system, joining the fleeing throng from the previous system. Martin wondered, idly, where they thought they were going. Where *was* safe, these days? His lips twitched, remembering the handful of middle-class kids he'd met as a child. They'd been safe and secure in a way that had always ground at him, as if some invisible force was keeping them from the very bottom of society. The Galactics were worse. They'd been safe for so long that being attacked in their lair was almost beyond their imagination.

No, it was beyond their imagination, Martin corrected himself. The defences surrounding the gravity points had been thrown together in a tearing hurry. A more measured approach, with all the time in the universe, could have made the system impregnable. *And now they've come face to face with the bitter reality.*

The hours crawled by, one by one. Martin forced himself to get some rest, then return to the bridge in time for the next transit. The ID codes worked again, somewhat to his surprise. Each jump was taking them further and further from the fleet, from all hope of help if things went wrong…he shook his head as he watched the panic spreading through the system, heralded by the refugee freighters. The Tokomak really *did* have other problems. How long would it take for them to mount an effective defence?

They have a vast fleet at Tokomak Prime, he reminded himself. Sooner or later, the advancing human fleet would run into its alien counterpart. *And they have to make a stand a long time before we reach their homeworld.*

Piece returned to the bridge, looking amused. "I downloaded a local update, galactic-level," he said. "They're warning all ships to avoid a dozen sectors."

Butler coughed. "Are you sure they can't trace the download?"

"It's a free briefing for Galactics." Piece waved off his concern. "Point is, chaos is spreading."

Martin looked at the display, then frowned. He wasn't an expert in interstellar shipping patterns, few of which made logical sense as far as he could tell, but it was clear the affected sectors were some distance from the Twins. They weren't *that* important, not in the grand scheme of things. But if they were rebellious—if the Galactics were ready to *admit* they were rebellious—who knew where it would end? In fire? Or in freedom?

He watched the pattern grow as they crawled from system to system. The official news bulletins were bland, utterly uninformative. They sounded as if they'd been put together by someone who didn't have the slightest idea what was *real* news, except they were just a little *too* deliberate for him to believe it. No one could be *that* stupid unless they were under orders. The unofficial broadcasts, hints of messages routed through random communications nodes, all traces of their existences wiped as soon as they were detected, told a different story. The humans were coming, freedom was in the air...there were stories of everything from strikes and shutdowns to outright rebellions, too many to be put down. Martin had no idea how many of them could be taken seriously, if *any* of them could be taken seriously, but it hardly mattered. The times were changing. He wondered, deep inside, how the Tokomak would take it. Even *they* couldn't emerge unchanged, after fighting a war for survival. Surely...

"What happens if they crack down on the Twins?" Butler raised the issue, one evening. "And we can't get down to the surface?"

"There are contingency plans," Piece said, vaguely. He'd been spending a lot of time with his alien comrades, discussing the news reports. "It depends on what we find when we get there."

"How very reassuring," Butler said, sarcastically. "Don't you have *any* idea at all?"

"No, because I don't know how much we can rely on the news reports." Piece didn't sound angry, but Martin thought he was irritated. "If things haven't really changed, we should have no trouble getting down to the surface. If they have, we might have to make contact with the spacers instead. And that poses other problems."

"Quite." Martin didn't know the specifics, but he'd read the generalist reports. The Tokomak kept a wary eye on *all* space-based industries and settlements, particularly the ones owned and controlled by their subordinates. "We might be betrayed."

"Or worse." Piece shrugged. "There are bounties on human scalps, you know."

"We should start force-growing them," Butler said. "And see how many we can sell before they catch on."

Martin laughed, although it wasn't really funny. "They'd smell a rat, sooner or later."

"But they wouldn't *know*," Butler mock-protested. "They'd *have* to take it seriously."

"We don't want attention," Piece pointed out. "There aren't supposed to be any humans left, not on the Twins."

"Shit." Martin sobered. "What happened to them? The ones who were settled there, I mean?"

"Dead, if they're lucky." Piece shrugged. "The Tokomak *might* have transported them to another world, but I doubt it. They're much more likely to have killed them all."

"And if they have, we'll kill *them* all," Butler said. "We have to teach the bastards a lesson they'll never forget. Human lives don't come cheap."

Martin wanted to agree, but he held his tongue. The Tokomak would be much more likely to come to terms with humanity, and their former subordinates, if they thought they'd survive the peace. And yet, he wanted to pay them back in their own coin. He wasn't the only one, either. There would be uncounted and uncountable numbers of people, human and alien, who wanted to extract a little revenge. The war—so far—had been relatively civilised. It might not stay that way.

And it won't, when they get desperate, he told himself. The Tokomak *had* to be getting desperate. There was an entire fleet inside their borders, threatening to cut its way to their homeworld. *All hell will be out for noon.*

CHAPTER TWELVE

N-Gann looked different, Hoshiko thought, as she surveyed the holographic display. There weren't many visible differences, since the fleet had chopped its way into the system, but... it felt different. The provisional government had taken over the ring, the orbital facilities and what remained of the defences, swearing that every last person on the planet would sooner die on his feet—or whatever he had instead of feet—then live on his knees. Hoshiko wasn't so sure—the Tokomak could retake the system, if they committed a sizable fleet to the effort—but, for the moment, it didn't matter. Either they won the war, in which case N-Gann would have its independence, or they lost. If that happened...

She shook her head, telling herself not to be so pessimistic. The first part of the plan had worked perfectly. Admiral Teller was in position, ready to start smashing his way towards the Twins—and Tokomak Prime. Preliminary reports suggested there wasn't *much* in his way, although that would change quickly. Word was already spreading, rocketing down the chain at the speed of light—and FTL. The Tokomak would know he was on his way well before he challenged the *next* fleet base. And they'd have to react.

And in the meantime, we'll be moving around the edge of their empire, she thought, coldly. It would take time to reach their target, but—if they were lucky—they would get there without losing the advantage of surprise. And then...even if they failed, her most pessimistic calculations suggested they'd still be able to pull off the plan itself. *Even if we lose, we'll give them one hell of a fright.*

Her gaze slipped to the gravity point, where a dozen orbital weapons platforms and thousands of cheap, mass-produced mines were being pushed and prodded into position. They wouldn't last long, not against a determined assault, but they'd force the Tokomak to *work* if they wanted to punch into the system. It might just buy the provisional government more time for when the inevitable counterattack materialised. The Tokomak would *have* to retake the chain if they wanted to launch a thrust towards Earth...

She closed her eyes, cursing herself. Things had been a *lot* easier when she'd commanded a lone squadron, or even sat in a starship's command chair. There had only been a few hundred lives resting on her, not uncountable trillions. She knew what the Tokomak would do, if they won the war and restored order. Humanity wouldn't be the *only* race hurled into the fire. They'd slaughter billions to cow trillions...or maybe they'd just wipe out *every* last race, even their fellow Galactics. Hoshiko had signed off on black propaganda that suggested just that, but she hated to think it might be true. The slaughter would be beyond comprehension if they won.

Her intercom bleeped. "Admiral," Yolanda said. "Commander Khalid is reporting, as ordered."

"Ask him to remain in the outer office," Hoshiko said, opening her eyes. "I'll be along in a moment."

She tapped her console, turning off the holographic display. Her office snapped back into focus. She rubbed her eyes, trying not to look at the sofa. She'd slept there over the last few days, catching what little sleep she could while making frantic preparations for departure. Her grandfather had urged her to sleep in her own bed, but she couldn't. There was just too much to do. She'd promised herself a proper rest once the fleet was underway, having broken contact with prowling enemy pickets...

Her finger rested on the terminal. "Secure mode, *on*," she ordered. "Record, Level Ten."

There was a pause. "Secure mode engaged," the terminal said. The voice was cold, masculine. The feminine user overlay was gone. "Status check…working…done. Secure mode confirmed secure. Level Ten recording, standing by."

Hoshiko let out a long breath. "You will have seen the tactical concepts developed by my staff," she said. "It is my intention to proceed with Plan Wellington. I believe that Wellington offers the greatest chance for winning the war in a single campaign, for ensuring that the Tokomak either surrender or lose so badly that they will never be able to threaten us again. My staff and I have evaluated the risks and decided that we can proceed. Defeat remains a possible outcome, but…"

She paused, choosing her next words carefully. "I am aware that I am pushing my authority beyond its limit," she added. "I am aware that I am risking more than just myself and my fleet in committing us to Plan Wellington. However, our window of opportunity is slight and there simply isn't time to request and receive orders. We have to move now or not move at all. It is my considered judgement that we have to move now.

"I have consulted with others, but the final decision is mine and mine alone. I accept full responsibility for the consequences, whatever they happen to be. If it becomes necessary to disown and disavow me, or to put me in front of a court martial, I will accept your judgement without hesitation. I—and I alone—will bear the burden. Goodbye."

Hoshiko took her finger off the terminal. "Seal the recording, then cancel secure mode," she ordered. "And eject the datachip."

The terminal bleeped, ejecting the chip. Hoshiko picked it up, the fanciful side of her mind wondering why it felt so *light*. The weight of her words seemed to hang in the air. She knew she would be blamed, if things went wrong. She shook her head as she stood, knowing she was being foolish. If things went wrong, she would be dead or trapped in a POW camp. And the Solar Union would pay a price for her failure.

But I'll win them time, she thought, as she headed for the hatch. *There'll be enough time to build a new fleet, with newer weapons. And the Tokomak will never catch up with us.*

She stepped through the hatch, which hissed closed behind her. Commander Khalid was talking to Yolanda. He straightened up as he saw her, throwing a salute that was just a *little* sloppy. Courier boat commanders tended to be more than a little sloppy, if only because they rarely spent much time on *real* starships. Hoshiko found it hard to care. There simply weren't many volunteers for the job.

"Reporting as ordered, Admiral," Khalid said.

"Good." Hoshiko held out the chip. "You are to take this chip back to Sol, where you are to put it directly into Admiral Mongo Stuart's hands. No one else, and I mean *no one*, is to take possession of it unless Admiral Stuart has been replaced, in which case you are to pass it to his successor. In the event of your ship being boarded, the datachip is to be destroyed along with your datacores."

"Aye, Admiral," Khalid said. "I won't let you down."

"Very good." Hoshiko nodded, shortly. "Dismissed."

Khalid saluted, slightly snappier this time, then turned and left the compartment. He'd beam to his ship shortly before the fleet departed, heading back to Sol at speeds few other ships could match. Hoshiko told herself, firmly, that most of the chain was in human or allied hands. He'd have no trouble making it back. And...she felt oddly free, knowing she was committed. Whatever happened, it would be all on her. She'd reap the rewards of victory or the punishment of defeat.

And none of my officers will bear the blame, she told herself, although she knew it might be wishful thinking. She *was* pushing her authority further than it should go and everyone knew it. She could have been relieved of command, quite legitimately. Even her grandfather's quiet support had its limits. *They'll say my staff should have refused to follow orders...*

She sat in her command chair and studied the display. The fleet was in position, dozens of squadrons ready to head out in all directions. Half the ships were under cloak, flying so close to their uncloaked fellows that any watching eyes should have problems realising the ships hadn't been assigned to Admiral Teller. Teller had complained bitterly about the number of sensor decoys he'd have to deploy, as he began his march to the Twins and Tokomak Prime, but he'd understood the logic. Hoshiko didn't want the Tokomak considering *her* fleet a strategic threat. Let them think her a minor nuisance. The longer they believed she was merely raising hell, behind the lines, the longer it would take them to react when they discovered the truth.

"Admiral," Yolanda said. "The final units have checked in."

"Good." Hoshiko turned to her. "And our people on the ring?"

"The stay-behinds are in place," Yolanda said. "The remainder have returned to their ships."

Hoshiko nodded, curtly. She didn't want to leave anyone behind, but the provisional government needed help. She had to do whatever she could to support it, at least as long as it didn't impede her operations. She wondered, sourly, what would happen after the war, then told herself to worry about it after they actually *won*. Right now, they had to hang together to hang separately. They could worry about the future when it arrived.

"Then order the squadrons to depart, as planned," she said. "It's time to move."

"Aye, Admiral," Yolanda said.

Hoshiko smiled as the first squadrons dropped into FTL, heading out on vague courses that gave any watching eyes a number of potential destinations. The Tokomak would *know*, of course, that the ships could simply change course once they were beyond the range of any known detector, but...they'd have to warn all the possible targets. And the number of possible targets would rise rapidly, until it was completely impossible to warn—let alone defend—them all. And then...

Her smile grew wider as the second squadrons vanished, followed rapidly by the third. There would be a *lot* of potential targets, none of which would be remotely decisive. The Tokomak might be *pleased* she was wasting her ships and munitions on such targets, knowing she had little hope of resupply. Ships without missiles or spare parts could neither fly nor fight. She hoped they believed it for as long as possible, then forced herself to relax. She was committed. But, in truth, they'd been committed long before she'd been born.

"Admiral," Yolanda said. "Our squadron is ready to depart."

"My compliments to Captain Lifar," Hoshiko said formally, "and she has full permission to depart as planned."

She leaned back in her chair as the squadron jumped into FTL, racing away from the gravity point—and N-Gann—at many times the speed of light. It seemed impossible to believe that it would take years to return to Sol, or head to Tokomak Prime. A groundpounder would have found it impossible to comprehend the vast distances between the two stars. Even Hoshiko couldn't comprehend them, not really. She knew the figures and what they meant, but she didn't really *believe* them.

"We'll reach the waypoint in ninety minutes," Yolanda warned. "And the fleet should be reassembled..."

"I know." Hoshiko cut her off. "Don't worry about it."

She smiled, grimly. They'd planned it as best as they could, although there was no way to be *sure* they'd *truly* be out of detection range. The Harmonies had deployed a small fleet of pickets to track *Odyssey*, when she'd punched her way out of the trap and fled into interstellar space. The Tokomak could have done the same, if they'd realised she was trying to con them. There were just too many dangers ... she shook her head, irritated at herself. She'd done everything she could to minimise them. All she could do now was wait.

The display continued to update, assuring her that the fleet was alone. She knew better than to take that for granted. The warped nexus of space created by stardrive made it difficult to use sensors, even FTL sensors. A ship would have to be very close, matching the fleet's gravity harmonics perfectly, to be detected. The upside was that it made continued pursuit almost impossible. The downside was that it made it impossible to be sure that someone *wasn't* following them.

They'd have to get very lucky, she told herself. The fleet had scattered so many sensor platforms around the gravity point, back at N-Gann, that she'd been morbidly sure the enemy didn't have a hope of sneaking a cloaked ship into attack position. *But luck can favour the enemy too.*

She pulled up the tactical and readiness reports and forced herself to read them, cursing the irony that she had to worry about paperwork even as she launched the greatest offensive in human history. Paperwork was important, but she knew it couldn't become an end in itself or the Solar Union was doomed. Grandpa Steve had set up the military to ensure it avoided developing a permanent class of pen-pushers, mainly by rotating good officers in and out of staff positions so they had no chance to get lazy, yet... she shook her head. She had to keep careful track of everything, if only so she knew what she had to play with. Her subordinates were good, but she had to make the final call. Thankfully, they had a good idea of what was and wasn't important.

The drive hum changed, slightly. Hoshiko glanced at the status display. They were reducing speed, readying themselves for the drop back to normal space. Hoshiko braced herself for the transition, but—for once—it was surprisingly smooth. It probably helped they were light years from anywhere, floating in the middle of an interstellar wasteland. The display flickered, then picked up a handful of ships heading to the waypoint in FTL. The remainder of the fleet was still out of range.

A small cluster of icons appeared in front of her. "Admiral," Yolanda said. "The decoy fleet is in position."

"Order the crews to begin tethering the ships," Hoshiko said. She wished she had another LinkShip or two, but... she'd make do with what she had. It was just a shame they couldn't render the entire fleet stealthy. Being able to charge towards a target without setting off alarms right across the system would have been very helpful. It would change the face of warfare. "And keep me informed. I want to depart as soon as possible."

"Aye, Admiral." Yolanda looked confused. "We do have time...?"

"Not as much as we might like," Hoshiko said. She scowled at the trackless emptiness on the display. The entire enemy fleet—their active ships and reserve fleets—could be lurking out there and she'd never know about it, not until it was too late. Hundreds of thousands of ships were little more than grains of sand on the interstellar beach. "We don't know what might happen next."

She watched and waited as the remainder of the fleet assembled, hoping and praying that they'd escaped enemy scrutiny. The Tokomak disliked interstellar space, although she wasn't sure why. She certainly wasn't prepared to gamble her entire fleet on them not bothering to sow the entire region with pickets and sensor platforms. But the sheer size of interstellar space worked in their favour. Logically, the Tokomak couldn't be watching *everywhere*.

"The fleet is in position, Admiral," Yolanda said. "And the decoy ships are live."

"Then order the fleet to depart, as planned," Hoshiko ordered. "The recon ships are to go directly to the target, as planned. The remainder of the fleet will head to the second waypoint."

"Aye, Admiral," Yolanda said.

Hoshiko nodded as the fleet slid back into FTL. She'd planned their course carefully, ensuring they kept their distance from enemy systems. It would add another week to their journey, but it would minimise the chances of detection...she told herself, firmly, that it would suffice. There was no point in worrying about things she couldn't change. And hoping for an ambush to give her something else to focus on was just stupid.

She stood. "Inform me if there are any changes," she ordered. "I'll be in my cabin."

Yolanda nodded. "Aye, Admiral."

Hoshiko headed for the hatch and stepped through, schooling her face into impassivity. It *was* just possible that the Tokomak could mount an ambush, although...if they did, it would be a fairly clear sign that the plan had gone spectacularly wrong. The Tokomak would have to have known the details right from the start. She had no idea how they could have guessed the truth—she'd gone to considerable trouble to avoid sharing more than the bare minimum with her officers—but stranger things had happened. The Tokomak were the only known race to fight wars on such a large scale, at least until now. They'd spent longer thinking about them than humans had been experimenting with fire.

But they can't cover everywhere, she told herself, as she opened the hatch and walked into her cabin. The hatch hissed closed behind her. *They cannot be strong everywhere.*

She sighed as she undressed. It wasn't true. Given time, the Tokomak *could* be strong everywhere. They commanded such vast resources that only their own weaknesses kept them from winning the war overnight. They could deploy vast fleets to every possible target, build impregnable defences around every gravity point, even design and put new weapons into production on a scale humanity couldn't hope to match. Their entire empire was a monster suffocating the life out of the galaxy. It had to be stopped.

And if it can't be stopped now, she thought as she climbed into bed for the first time in weeks, *it will never be stopped at all.*

CHAPTER THIRTEEN

Hameeda braced herself as the LinkShip glided through the gravity point, her drives carefully—very carefully—baffling her gravity signature. The files stated that the enemy hadn't had time to fortify the gravity point, but the files hadn't been updated since the first Battle of Earth. Hameeda's briefers had made it very clear that they expected everything from a giant minefield to an entire fleet of enemy battleships, the former possibly positioned right on top of the gravity point. Sweat trickled down her back as the last of the gravity waves faded away. The LinkShip was very capable, but a single mine would be more than enough to blow her into atoms.

The display filled up rapidly as her passive sensors came online. A handful of mines were floating around the point, rather than actually emplaced on top of it. Hameeda wondered if the enemy expected to see more friendly ships jumping through the point, or—more likely—if they thought the human ships could clear the minefield simply by dumping a handful of antimatter pods into the enemy defences. There might be no point in laying a minefield that could be cleared instantly...she smiled as she inched away from the gravity point, watching carefully for stealthed mines. Thankfully, there were enough sensor pulses filling the area to spare her from having to activate her own sensors. *That* would have made detection certain.

Although they might have managed to miss me, she thought. *Their ships aren't in position to draw a bead on me without getting closer.*

She frowned, reminding herself that the previous enemy force had mounted an ambush and inflicted a considerable amount of damage despite their technological inferiority. The handful of battleships holding position near the defences might be just the tip of the iceberg, sacrificial lambs being deployed to lure the attackers into a false sense of security. She told herself that no navy could make such ploys indefinitely, that even the Tokomak themselves would be unable to cope with having their lives thrown away to bait a trap, but…it was hard to believe. Aliens were *alien*, not humans in funny clothes and funnier makeup. The Galactics didn't share a common biology, let alone a common culture. And it was easy, very easy, for them to do something that would leave a human scratching her head in bemusement. Why the *fuck* would they do something like…well, *whatever*?

Because it made perfect sense to them, Hameeda thought. There were a *lot* of alien races out there, from egg-layers and hermaphrodites to races that only had one intelligent gender and races that had a dozen *different* genders. Laws that made perfect sense to one race might be another race's belly laugh. *And they don't think remotely like us.*

She put the thought out of her mind as she slowly prowled around the gravity point, carefully watching for any traces of cloaked or powered-down ships. The system looked surprisingly empty, almost deserted. Her neural net pointed out the locations of a dozen asteroid settlements, all of which had gone dark. She guessed they'd been powered down in the hopes of avoiding detection, their populations either placed in stasis or surviving on reduced resources. She doubted it would make any difference. The asteroids simply weren't important in the short term. The planet itself wasn't that important either. It was a rocky wasteland that made pre-terraforming Mars or Venus look hospitable. Really, she was surprised the Tokomak had bothered to plant a colony. Perhaps they'd seen it as a convenient place to dump people they didn't like.

Or they just wanted to stake a claim to the system, she mused. *We're not that far from their core worlds, if one jumps through the gravity points.*

Her lips thinned as she completed her search pattern. There didn't seem to be *any* hidden defences, as far as she could tell. The ships were powered down so completely it would be impossible to flash-wake their systems in time, when Admiral Teller assaulted the system. And they had to know it. The ships probably didn't exist, unless…she assigned her subroutines to work out a handful of scenarios, but she already knew the answer. The Tokomak were choosing not to make a fight for the system.

Which is going to cost them, she thought, as she uploaded her sensor records onto a stealth drone and launched it towards the gravity point. *They're still going to look like losers even if they haven't lost anything worth fighting for.*

She held position near the gravity point, watching the drone as it followed a ballistic trajectory towards the twist in time and space. Admiral Webster's NGW program hadn't produced anything *really* new, if the last set of updates were accurate, but they *had* improved the basic gravity jump drive. It was a one-shot device, and expensive enough to give even the Solar Union pause, yet…if it worked, it would change the face of war. Again. She tensed, watching the drone slip out of her ken and vanish. If the enemy picked up the slightest hint of gravity emissions, they'd assume she was trying to sneak through the gravity point. And they'd start looking for her in earnest.

They'd be right, but for the wrong reasons, she thought, sourly. *It wouldn't make them any less right.*

She waited, silently counting the seconds. It was possible the enemy ships would simply ignore the gravity surge—the surge wouldn't have looked big enough for even a relatively small capital ship—but they knew humans had *some* way of transiting a gravity point without being detected. They *did* emit fluctuations from time to time—the boffins claimed that was how they'd been discovered in the first place—and normally they

110

were simply ignored...now? Now, she didn't know. They might be paying attention to a *lot* of things they would normally ignore.

It was nearly an hour before she decided the enemy weren't going to react and pulled the LinkShip away from the gravity point, gliding towards the only inhabited planet. The briefing notes hadn't made it look very appealing and the reality was worse, a poisonous atmosphere that would be unpleasantly lethal to almost all known races. Either the world was extremely unusual, she decided, or it had been heavily polluted at some point. The planet's natural atmosphere contained a lot of trace elements that suggested heavy industry and a complete lack of regard for the planet's biosphere. She considered it as the LinkShip drew closer, wondering if the Tokomak had turned the world into an experimental laboratory. They'd normally install dangerous and polluting machinery on an asteroid, which could be thrown into a star if they had to get rid of it, but perhaps they thought they needed a gravity well. She puzzled over it, the LinkShip carefully orbiting the planet at a safe distance. It would probably be worth taking a look at the planetary installations once they secured the system itself.

Assuming they leave them intact, Hameeda thought. If there was something deadly secret on the surface, the Tokomak wouldn't let it fall into human hands. *They've had plenty of time to start rigging self-destruct systems by now.*

She ordered the LinkShip to glide back into interplanetary space, then performed one final passive scan before disconnecting herself from the neural net and standing up. Her legs felt uncomfortably stiff, as if she'd been sitting there for hours. She smiled. She *had* been. A status display followed her as she limped down the corridor and into the gallery. The automated systems had already produced a cup of coffee and a hot bacon sandwich, dripping with butter. She stared at it blearily. It was funny how her parents and grandparents had never eaten pork, even though it wasn't *real* pork. They'd thrown away so much, when they'd fled to space, but not *that*...

It doesn't matter, she told herself. She took a bite, savouring the taste. Warm butter dripped to the deck. *Right now, all that matters is winning the war.*

She chewed her way through the sandwich and ordered another, knowing the processor would have crammed all the vitamins and nutritional support she needed into the food. In some ways, the taste didn't matter. Her distant ancestors wouldn't have known if they should condemn her for eating the sandwich or approve, on the grounds the bacon had never been anywhere near a *real* pig. But that was the true value of the Solar Union, she told herself. A citizen could pick and choose what she wanted to do, knowing that no one else could stop her. And she alone was accountable for her behaviour.

"I should have asked Sam to stay on the ship," she said. "It would have been nice."

She shivered. Her voice sounded odd in her ears, as if it wasn't quite *hers*. It was odd enough having her words played back to her, but now...she wondered, sourly, if she should ask for a permanent companion. There were people already talking about brain and brawn teams...she snorted. It would have to be someone she actually *liked*. She had no idea how she'd put up with someone she didn't like. Ask him to leave, probably. It wasn't as if *she* could leave. Even now, delinked from the net, she still felt as if she was rattling around inside her own body. She was mildly surprised she hadn't been permanently wired into the system. But then, there wouldn't have been much point.

Her lips twitched at the sour thought. She'd known Samuel Piece couldn't stay with her. Of *course* she'd known that. But it had been nice to have someone sharing her bed for a week...she shook her head in irritation. It wasn't as if it was *hard* finding partners in the Solar Union. The datanet ensured that people could meet other people for anything from a casual hook-up to a long-term affair, that people with odd tastes could meet people who *shared* those tastes. Hameeda wondered, idly, if LinkShip pilots would eventually count as their own fetish. It wasn't as if there were very many of them.

A low tone ran through the ship. Hameeda looked up as a red icon appeared on the holographic display. She tensed, before realising that it was just a freighter making its way into the system. Her sensors would continue to track it, just in case the freighter was towing something larger and nastier, but she doubted it posed any real threat. The ship's crew probably hadn't heard the next couple of systems had fallen. They were going to get a shock when they dropped out of FTL and saw the defences around the gravity point. She smiled coldly, wondering just what the defenders would say to them. They'd probably be told to return home and stay out of the firing line.

Unless the locals want to evacuate a few hundred people, Hameeda mused. She was surprised her sensors hadn't picked up more freighters or even interplanetary transports. Either they'd already fled or they simply hadn't been there. It wasn't as if the system attracted much notice. It was torn between being on the gravity point chain and being almost useless, the former ensuring the system wouldn't draw much attention from those who lived on the wrong side of the law. *The freighter might be seized as soon as it drops out of FTL*.

She made her way to her cabin and closed her eyes, drawing on her implants to get some sleep. She knew she'd regret it later—and she certainly shouldn't come to depend on it—but she had to rest before all hell broke loose. Her awareness seemed to flicker—it was hard to believe, somehow, that she'd actually *slept*—and she sat up, feeling as if she hadn't slept at all. If she hadn't known it was impossible, she would have thought the displays were playing tricks on her. Her body was insisting, loudly, that she hadn't slept at all. She didn't start to feel better until she'd taken a shower and dried herself thoroughly.

The display updated her as she ate her breakfast, swallowing cereal with coffee so strong it felt like acid. The enemy freighter had dropped out of FTL near the gravity point and vanished. It didn't *look* as if the ship had flown to the other gravity point in realspace...she guessed the ship had been seized, although it was impossible to be sure. It was *vaguely* possible the ship had transited, although it would have jumped right into Admiral

Teller's fleet. The poor bastards might have been blown away before they had a chance to explain themselves.

She checked the time again, then made her way back to the command centre. Her chair was calling to her. She sat down and pulled the helmet down, her mind expanding back into the neural net. She felt alive again...she gritted her teeth, remembering all the horror stories about virtual reality and direct brain stimulation. They weren't exaggerated, she reminded herself. She'd been through a dozen screenings to confirm she didn't have an addictive personality, but her counsellors had warned her that was no guarantee she *wouldn't* get addicted. The direct neural interface was more powerful than a simple teenage-friendly VR implant. It was hard to believe, sometimes, that the real world was actually *real*.

Which is probably why they didn't *hook me permanently into the ship*, she thought. It wasn't a pleasant thought, but one that had to be faced. *They wanted me to remain grounded.*

The LinkShip hummed into life. Hameeda performed one final passive sweep, then glided back towards the gravity point. A handful of extra energy signatures glowed in her mind's eye, the freighter and a number of smaller clusters. It looked as though they were bolting missile pods to the freighter's hull, turning it into a weapons platform that wouldn't—normally—stand a chance in hell of surviving more than a few seconds in a real battle. She guessed they were hoping to give themselves a little extra punch when Admiral Teller smashed his way into the system. Who knew? Golden BB hits *did* happen and the human ships would be appearing in a precisely-defined sphere. There would be no hope of a mobile battle, not near a gravity point. The first few seconds would be defined by who threw the most punches in a very short space of time.

But that isn't entirely true, any longer, she mused. The laws of war had changed—and were still changing. The Tokomak were playing catch-up in a universe that no longer bent to their every whim. *And they haven't yet realised it.*

She ran through a handful of simulations as she circled the gravity point, carefully logging the positions of every starship and weapons platform in the enemy formation. It was harder to see the mines, but it looked as if they hadn't had time to change positions. The enemy doctrine called for altering their positions every so often, yet...she smiled again. Right now, the enemy had other problems. They probably couldn't even produce new mines in the local fabricators. It was quite possible they hadn't been able to produce antimatter warheads for their mines.

And if they're just nukes, they can be taken out without detonating them, Hameeda thought, grimly. It was to be hoped, definitely. *They certainly don't look to be anything more than antimatter pods.*

Her orders appeared in front of her, insisting it was time to begin. Hameeda let out a breath, wishing she could trust Admiral Teller to have everything ready to *move* when he received her second drone. The orders made perfect sense, on paper, but she was uncomfortably aware that too much could go wrong. Better to test the theory *here*, Admiral Teller had said, than in some star system where the enemy had enough firepower to stop him if something *did* go wrong. And yet...she felt uncomfortably exposed, naked mentally as well as physically. She took one final look at the enemy positions, reminding herself that *she* wasn't in great danger. It was others who would pay the price for her mistakes.

The second drone glimmered in her mind's eye as she pushed it into space, using her automated systems to shove it along a ballistic trajectory. In theory, it should be less noticeable than a piece of space dust. The last one hadn't been detected, she reminded herself once again. Unless the enemy had decided to let the drone through...no, that made no sense. The enemy would have changed its deployments, at the very least, if it had any reason to think an attacking force knew *precisely* where to aim. And now...

She watched the drone as best as she could, trying to take a little reassurance from the simple fact *she* could barely track the drone, even though she knew precisely where to look. She kept watching, noting the moment it vanished. The tiny flicker of gravity emissions came a few seconds later, marking the jump. The enemy fleet didn't seem to react, even though it was the second such pulse in less than a day. Hameeda let out a long breath, then turned her attention to the work crews swarming the freighter. It was unlikely they would see her—she was too far away to be seen with the naked eye—but their emissions might accidentally reveal her presence. If the enemy got lucky... very lucky.

And now we wait, she thought. She was achingly aware of time passing. Each second felt like an hour. *I hope that Admiral Teller is on the ball.*

CHAPTER FOURTEEN

Admiral Colin Teller knew, without false modesty, that he lacked the killer instinct so highly prised by his fellows. They would charge into the very flames of hell itself for victory, heedless of the risks; they would expend hundreds of ships and thousands of lives for gains that might be largely meaningless. Fighting intensive battles for worthless tracts of interstellar waste or systems of little real value was pointless, in his opinion. It was better to pick and choose one's battles if it was at all possible, to make sure that tactical victory didn't lead to strategic defeat.

He stood in the CIC of SUS *Implacable* and studied the monitor, bracing himself. The tactic had looked good in simulators, but just about *every* tactic looked good in simulators. Colin had seen quite a few disastrous engagements wargamed thoroughly, only for reality to outdo their worst predictions. But he had to admit the concept was sound and, at worst, he could pull back and conduct a more conventional campaign. Admiral Stuart wouldn't be happy—she wanted him to grab the bastards by the neck and shake them—but he wasn't going to throw lives away if it could be avoided. A steady march towards Tokomak Prime would be just as alarming as a series of one-sided battles fought and won with new concepts and technologies.

Commander Karan Bridgewater glanced up from her console. "Admiral, the drone transited the gravity point," she said. "I'm downloading the targeting data now."

Colin nodded, curtly. The problem with mounting a full-fledged gravity point assault was that it was very difficult, almost impossible, to get solid data on the other side of the point without alerting the enemy. The Tokomak had never solved the problem, although they'd never *needed* to. They'd just funnelled hundreds of minor warships through the gravity points, clearing them with brute force. Humanity, with fewer ships and fewer expendable allies, had come up with a more elegant solution. The stealth drones—really nothing more than tiny jump drives mounted on a missile shell—were supposed to be the answer. He hoped the researchers were right, for once. In his experience, few concepts ever worked so well in real life as they did in the simulations.

The display lit up, showing an enemy force resting near the gravity point. Colin allowed himself a cold smile, even as he reminded himself not to get overconfident. The data was already a few minutes out of date. If the Tokomak had realised the drone had made transit, they'd be flash-waking their systems and altering position as quickly as possible. A timer appeared beside the enemy icons, counting the seconds as the computers tried to predict enemy positions. Colin knew not to trust the projections. The variables mounted up so rapidly, they quickly became nothing more than guesswork.

"Order the first wave of pods to launch," he said. There was no more time. "And ready the first squadron for the offensive."

"Aye, Admiral." Karan tapped her console. "Pods jumping…now."

Colin leaned forward as the green icons vanished through the gravity point. The Tokomak were famously conservative—it was regularly joked that they'd stolen the *wheel* off some long-gone alien race—but it still surprised him they'd never invented assault pods for themselves. There *had* been a time when they'd been competing with other races on even terms, hadn't there? They couldn't have deployed such vast fleets and accepted such huge losses before they'd become the undisputed masters of the universe. Maybe they'd quietly buried all traces of the technology once they'd invented the stardrive, he decided. They wouldn't want to give potential enemies anything that might be more of a threat to the Tokomak than the enemies themselves.

"The pods will be launching now," Karan said, quietly. "Admiral...?"

"Order the first squadrons to jump, as planned." Colin felt a stab of guilt he wasn't going with them. "And then move up the second units."

"Aye, Admiral."

. . .

Hameeda watched, feeling the urge to whoop in delight, as the first assault pods materialised on the gravity point and started to open fire. The missiles roared out, aimed straight at the enemy ships. Hameeda smiled coldly—the targeting wouldn't have been that accurate without the information she'd sneaked through the gravity point—and allowed her eyes to follow the missiles as they streaked through the minefield and fell on their targets. The Tokomak had had their automated servants on alert, ready to engage sudden threats, but their crews weren't ready. She felt her smile grow wider as missiles overwhelmed their shields and slammed into their hulls. The entire enemy squadron was wiped out before it had a chance to fire a single shot.

Take that, you bastards, she thought. The Tokomak had fought hundreds of one-sided battles in the past. It had never occurred to them that someone would find a way to do the same to them. *It's only going to get worse from here.*

She watched the first wave of human ships materialise on the gravity point, their weapons and sensors already scanning for targets. The mines started to move, gliding towards the human ships. They were rapidly blasted out of space before they got into attack range, the tiny explosions confirmation the enemy hadn't had time to produce hundreds of antimatter mines. Hameeda didn't think any of the attacking ships were as much as scratched as they punched through the remainder of the minefield and plunged into clear space. She hastily sent them her IFF, a reminder she was friendly. She didn't fear death, but being blown away by her own side would be *embarrassing.*

Her lips tightened as the second squadron arrived, slipping into a scanning formation as they circled the gravity point. Admiral Teller was moving with deliberate speed, rather than rushing his ships to the second gravity point. She understood the logic—the admiral wanted to be sure he wasn't going to be caught by surprise—but it seemed pointless. The Tokomak could have hid an entire fleet in interplanetary space, powered down and beyond detection unless the humans got very lucky. She didn't think so—they could have deployed a much more effective defence, if they'd had more ships and weapons to play with—but it was impossible to be sure. She allowed herself a flash of frustration. Admiral Teller should be moving faster. She was tempted to send him a message urging him to hurry up.

Which would probably get me shoved in front of a court martial board, she thought, wryly. *That* would be tricky, if she couldn't leave the LinkShip. They'd have to hold the inquest in her territory. *And he does want them to have time to notice.*

She sighed as she surveyed the entire system. A handful of messages were being beamed towards the second gravity point, but there were no more freighters making a run for it. The system seemed utterly quiet, almost dead. Even the planet was shutting down. She eyed the icon in her mind's eye warily, wondering just what was hidden on the planet. They'd have to find out, once the fighting was over. Who knew? A new weapon? A research program that couldn't be carried out somewhere safer, somewhere further from the front lines? It wasn't as if the Tokomak were short of options. They could have carried out the research on Tokomak Prime itself.

A third wave of ships materialised on the gravity point. She spotted *Implacable* amongst the fleet and scowled. Admiral Teller had finally arrived. She knew it was low of her to consider him a slowcoach, or perhaps a coward, but...she shook her head. Admiral Teller had nothing to prove, not to her. A man couldn't reach high rank in the Solar Navy without genuine combat experience. Admiral Mongo Stuart had set it up that way, citing his experiences with wet navies on Earth. Too many commanding officers who didn't know what they were doing had caused all sorts of problems, some utterly disastrous. Admiral Teller was slow, but he wasn't incompetent.

And we don't want to push them too hard, she mused. *Not yet.*

• • •

The system was barren, almost lifeless. The display showed a handful of asteroids settlements that seemed to have powered themselves down completely, settlements that would have been unnoticed if they hadn't been listed in the captured files. Colin wondered, absently, if the Tokomak hadn't realised they'd lost the files. It wasn't as if settlement data was highly classified, with strict orders for burning the files before they could be read. The data had been stored in unencrypted datacores...

He put the thought aside as more and more ships slid through the gravity point and fell into formation. The system had been invaded, but it hadn't been occupied. Not yet. Admiral Stuart's orders had left it up to him, the man on the spot, if he was to land occupation troops or not. Colin suspected it would be pointless to do more than a brief survey. The system was practically worthless, unable to pose a threat to his supply lines or support an invading enemy fleet that *might*. He wasn't even sure the system would be able to *survive* without outside help. The Tokomak might not have designed the system to be self-sufficient.

"They'll have gotten a good look at us," he said, slowly. It was impossible to be sure, but he was fairly certain the enemy would have gotten off a message before they'd been blown to hell. And there *would* be a picket, if not a bigger force, sitting on the second gravity point. "How much did they see?"

Karan looked up. "Unknown, sir."

Colin smiled—it had been a rhetorical question—then returned to his thoughts. If the enemy knew what had happened to their ships, what would they do? Tighten the defences on the next gravity point? Or ... or what? He didn't know, but he'd have to find out. Smashing through the next gravity point would open up all sorts of possibilities, forcing him to make some hard decisions. Not, he supposed, that they were the *really* hard decisions. He already knew where the fleet was going, unless they ran into something so hard they *had* to stop.

"Dispatch Force Two to seal the second gravity point," he ordered. He'd given the enemy *quite* enough time. They'd have to be extremely incompetent not to take advantage of it. And he didn't want them thinking too hard about *why* he'd given them the time. "Force Three is to remain on this gravity point until the remainder of the fleet is through."

He leaned back in his chair, silently bracing himself. "And Force One will proceed directly to the planet."

"Aye, Admiral."

Colin felt the drive shift as *Implacable* glided away from the gravity point and slipped into FTL, as if the fleet was trying to make up for lost time. The armchair admirals would bitch and moan about the delays, as if their hindsight was somehow superior to Colin's foresight. He supposed it was, but he didn't *have* hindsight. Not yet. He'd settle for surviving long enough—and keeping the fleet intact—so the critics could bore him to death with their accounts of what *they* would have done later. They never seemed to grasp that they had the advantage of knowing far more than the man on the spot, at the time...

He remained tense until the squadron dropped out of FTL and slid towards the planet. It was thoroughly unwelcoming, too inhospitable to serve as a penal colony. The LinkShip report had made it clear that the planet had an odd kind of biology—it wasn't as dead as Mars or Venus—but one that was largely incompatible with most known races. Colin was surprised—and suspicious—the Tokomak had ever bothered with the world. It wasn't as if they *needed* to establish a colony to stake their claim.

"The orbital defences are going live," Karan reported. "They're badly outdated."

"Looks that way," Colin agreed. "Take them out."

His eyes narrowed as more and more icons appeared on the display. There were no battlestations, no giant orbital weapons platforms or gunships...just a handful of automated platforms, barely capable of deterring a lone pirate or scavenger ship. The Tokomak had either never expected to be attacked or, more likely, had concluded there was nothing in the system worth taking. Or, perhaps, that mounting a hefty defence of a seemingly worthless world would be suspicious in itself. The planet—it didn't even have a name, merely a catalogue number—might be hiding in obscurity.

But they wouldn't put anything really *sensitive out here,* he mused. *A weapons research lab would be better kept in their home system.*

The enemy defences fired a handful of shots, all ineffective, before they were destroyed. Colin tapped commands into his console, dispatching marines to land on the various orbital and planetary installations and inspect them. The fleet broadcasted demands for surrender, promising good treatment to anyone who gave up without a fight, but there was no response. He wasn't sure if the facilities were abandoned or if the enemy simply refused to answer. Or if they could hear him at all. The biosphere was so charged that teleporting was almost impossible. But a communications signal really should get through...

"Admiral, Force Two is reporting that the gravity point has been secured," Karan said. "Commodore Fairbank is requesting permission to deploy recon probes."

Colin scowled. The problem the Tokomak had *never* solved, the problem that had kept them from deploying recon probes for themselves, was how to produce a miniature jump drive capable of two jumps in rapid succession. It took time to recharge, time that was normally never an issue for a jump-capable ship. But for recon probes, it gave the enemy a window of opportunity to destroy the probes before they could gather their data and return home. He would either have to expend hundreds of probes or...or what? There were no other options.

"Tell him to hold the probes back for now," he ordered, finally. The defences on the other side would be tougher, but...he'd have to deal with that when the time came. "And to prepare the antimatter pods for deployment."

"Aye, Admiral," Karan said.

Colin could hear the doubt in her voice. He didn't blame her. The recon probes were supposed to eliminate most of the problems with scouting gravity points, assuming they worked as their designers promised. But he didn't want to reveal the probes too soon, not when the enemy had had ample time to prepare their defences. The next system was going to be a far tougher nut to crack. And he was going to have to take it at a run.

We want them to see us as unstoppable, he reminded himself, sternly. *And we cannot afford to slow down.*

He watched as the marines reported from the orbital facilities, such as they were. The locals had surrendered without a fight, something that relieved him. He took no pleasure in slaughtering enemy combatants who couldn't do more than throw rocks at his ships, even if they refused to surrender. The facilities themselves were little more than basic production nodes, the smallest he'd seen outside primitive star systems. He wasn't surprised. The system couldn't support anything larger. No wonder they hadn't been able to prepare a proper defence.

"Order all but two ships to head to the second gravity point," he said. The planet was interesting, but he didn't have time to waste. He certainly couldn't attend to it personally. "I want to launch the next offensive as soon as we deploy the next assault pods."

"Aye, sir," Karan said. "The logistics ships are already on their way."

Colin kept his face expressionless as *Implacable* altered course and glided away from the planet, drives humming as they prepared for the jump into FTL. The brief engagement hadn't been particularly costly, although he knew they probably wouldn't be able to repeat it. Any halfway decent tactician who looked at the pattern would deduce the attackers had been able to secure hard targeting data before mounting their assault, even if they didn't know *how*. The Tokomak weren't stupid. They might not be able to match human ingenuity, not yet, but they had to have a wish-list of technology they'd like to invent too. Would they deduce the LinkShip? Or would they assume humans had found a way to produce *stealthed* recon drones? They were pretty much the Holy Grail.

And just as unreachable, he mused. He'd seen the reports. It was hard enough compressing a jump drive into a recon drive, let alone rendering it as stealthy as a LinkShip too. Colin had no doubt the problem would be solved, in time, but probably not soon enough to be helpful, let alone decisive. *And yet, if we can solve that problem, who knows what it will do?*

He put the thought aside. It wouldn't take long to deploy the next set of assault pods, then launch the assault. He'd smother the gravity point in missiles, even though his logistics chain wasn't as firm as he would have liked. N-Gann was churning out cheap assault pods, but they weren't as good as Solarian-designed units. He shook his head in quiet frustration. They'd have to do. The fleet was on the end of an unimaginably long supply line...

No wonder the Tokomak invested so much blood and treasure in their fleet bases, he mused to himself. *They knew how quickly they could lose control.*

"The marines are on the ground, sir," Karan reported. "They're advancing on the main facility now."

"Very good," Colin said. "Keep me informed."

CHAPTER FIFTEEN

Lieutenant Darryl Farnham kept as low as he could as the squad advanced towards the alien facility, feeling conspicuous in his armoured combat suit. The planet was a nightmare, environmental warnings blinking in his HUD every few seconds warning him not to even *think* of taking off his helmet. The entire planet seemed to be a sickly shade of yellow, from the yellowish clouds looming overhead to the puddles of sticky liquid he splashed through as they approached the alien base. He was all too aware that any contact with the atmosphere might prove fatal. The aliens had picked one hell of a place for a holiday home.

He scowled as the facility came into view, a cluster of domes built next to a single giant structure and a small landing pad. Perhaps it *was* a holiday home, or a set of biospheres…he frowned as he inched forward, keeping a wary eye out for threats. There were no visible defences, but that didn't mean they didn't exist. He kept his sensors jacked up as high as they would go, alerts blinking up for every flash of lightning high overhead. His eyes started to hurt, a mocking reminder that the environment was getting to him. Mars had been a far more *human* environment.

The rest of the squad followed him, weapons at the ready, as he slipped up to the airlock. It was giant, easily large enough to take a pair of tanks. There didn't seem to be any security precautions, although *that* wasn't a surprise. Galactic-designed airlocks tended to let people operate them manually, with or without access codes. Better to let someone into the airlock than risk having them die outside. Besides, it was unlikely they'd be able to get through the interior door. The system was designed to trap anyone who didn't have the right codes.

He pressed the button, opening the hatch. The interior was as bland and boring as any other airlock, lacking even a row of environmental suits. He supposed that shouldn't have been a surprise. A mere environmental suit would have melted, almost instantly, when it was exposed to the outer world. The squad followed him inside, constantly updating the orbiting fleet. Darryl was uncomfortably aware that they were expendable. It was unlikely there would be a second attempt to enter the complex, if the first one failed. The facility would merely be wiped off the planet by the orbiting starships and the purpose of the structure written off as an unsolved mystery.

The outer hatch closed behind them. Darryl couldn't help feeling trapped, even though there was plenty of room in the airlock. He pressed his hand against the inner hatch, but it remained resolutely closed. He shrugged, then tried to hack the airlock's control processor. It took longer than it should have for his suit to hack into the system, isolate it and then command it to run the cycle. The poisonous air was pumped out of the chamber before the inner hatch opened. Darryl kept his helmet on, even though the air was safe to breathe. Who knew what might be waiting for them?

He inched forward, his eyes flickering from side to side. The interior looked as boring as the airlock, stripped of every last hint of individuality. He glanced into a handful of rooms and saw signs the occupants had fled in a hurry, leaving behind everything from their personal possessions to a section of datachips, datapads and devices he didn't recognise. He marked them down for later attention—Admiral Teller would have to decide if it was worth deploying a Sensitive Site Exploitation team—and then stepped through the next airlock. His suit blinked a series of alerts, warning him the air was no longer entirely safe to breathe. And that meant...

His eyes widened as he looked around. He was in a giant room, a cross between a medical centre and a butcher's shop. A handful of tables were placed around the room, each one surrounded by clusters of machines he didn't recognise. And, on top of the tables, there were bodies. Human bodies. Alien bodies. They looked as if they'd been being dissected when the facility had been abandoned. Darryl was no stranger to horror, but his gorge rose helplessly. He had to swallow hard to keep from throwing up in his helmet.

"Sir..." Corporal Patron sounded as though he wanted to be sick too. "What the fuck were they *doing* here?"

"I don't know." Darryl clenched his teeth until they hurt, trying to keep himself calm. It was hard, almost impossible. One of the bodies looked to have been a child, although it was so badly mutilated he couldn't tell if it had once been human. Humans weren't the only race with red blood. "There'll be records somewhere. Find them!"

He forced himself to step back and survey the room with cold eyes. Twelve tables, each with a body... four clearly human. Two more that *might* have been human. And six that were definitely *not* human. What the hell had they been doing? And why... he wondered, grimly, if the whole display was a taunt, if they wanted to show off the horrors they were prepared to commit. Or, perhaps, if they'd thought they'd never be discovered. Darryl had seen terrorists who'd done just that, murdering bastards who'd turned into whimpering cowering beggars when confronted with justice. It was funny how they'd never realised they might not get away with it...

"We'll find out who you were," he promised the dead bodies, although he knew he might not be able to keep the promise. "And there will be justice."

• • •

"This is unbelievable," Colin said. The report was sickening. "They were trying to engineer control structures into human brains?"

128

"Yes, sir." Doctor Faith Roster sounded as stunned as Colin felt. "Basically, they took the precepts signed into law by the First Senate and threw them out the airlock. They were trying to make their victims naturally submissive to their commands, then devise a way to splice it into our genetic structure. They might even have come frighteningly close to success."

Colin frowned. "I suppose that explains why they were doing it *here*," he mused. "How close *did* they come?"

"I'm not sure," Faith admitted. "The concept of engineering control structures, effectively robbing someone of their free will, was banned years ago. It was decided by the Mariko Commission that such research would eventually be perverted, whatever we did. If I'd come across traces of this sort of research back home, I'd be obliged to report it. Here, of course..."

She shrugged, heavily. "I think they did come close to crafting proper control structures," she added, slowly. "But they didn't have any way of actually grafting them into us—or the other races—without massive surgical intervention. This is an order of magnitude more complex than basic gene-editing, Admiral. I think they saw it as a long-term project."

Colin raised his eyebrows. "You *think*?"

"They took the main datacore with them," Faith said. "We don't know for *sure* what they were doing. It's possible the research was entirely benevolent. And if you believe that, I have a lovely white house in Washington to sell you. A couple of careful owners...shame about the others."

"Quite," Colin said. "If they did deploy it...would it *get* us?"

"I don't think so," Faith said. "They'd never get it through the bioscanners. And if they did, somehow, our immune systems would handle it. But, given time, I imagine they could find ways to solve that problem."

"Given time," Colin mused. "Fuck. What *were* they thinking?"

Faith looked uncomfortable. "I imagine they wanted a bunch of slave races so enslaved they couldn't even *think* for themselves," she said. "That's where their research seemed to be going."

"Madness," Colin said.

"Yes, sir," Faith said. "If they're actually designing viruses that can cross species lines…"

Colin shuddered. "Madness," he repeated. "Draw up a complete report, then…we can decide what to do about the facility. It might have to be destroyed."

"Yes, sir," Faith said. "It might be…politically awkward if this got out."

"Quite." Colin snorted. "Let me worry about that, please."

Faith nodded, then left the office. Colin sat back in his chair, rubbing his eyes. Admiral Stuart would have handled it better, he was sure. No doubt there would be people complaining that he could have trapped the alien doctors if he'd acted faster, if he'd launched the offensive sooner…he shook his head in irritation. He hadn't known what lurked on the world, nor had he realised how much rested on his success. And…it was clear, at least to him, that the aliens hadn't come close *that* to a breakthrough. They hadn't created something that could instantly turn an entire race into willing slaves.

Sick, he thought. *What were they thinking?*

He keyed his console. "Karan, inform the fleet that we will begin the assault on schedule," he said. It was unusually fast, for him, but he wanted—needed—to try to trap the alien doctors in the next system. If he could get answers out of them…he wondered, sourly, what the government would say when they heard about the alien research. Would they order a genocidal response? "And I want to alter the later stages of the plan. We'll go with Theta-Three instead of Two."

"Aye, sir," Karan said. If she was surprised, it didn't show in her voice. "I'll see to it at once."

"And order the antimatter pods to be deployed as soon as the LinkShip is in place," Colin added. It would alert the enemy, but the enemy had to know the humans were coming soon anyway. "I want recon data as quickly as possible."

"Yes, sir."

...

Hameeda hadn't been told *precisely* what the marines had found on the planet, but she had monitored the fleet's communications network and she was perfectly capable of putting two and two together. The hasty deployment of a full SSE team, including a number of doctors and xenospecialists, suggested all sorts of possibilities...none of them good. Her simulators churned the data and tossed out a handful of the most likely, starting with a POW camp. She hoped that was the truth. The other options were worse.

She steered towards the gravity point, watching as the lead wave of antimatter pods crossed the event horizon and jumped to Mercado. The enemy would notice, of course—it was hard to miss an antimatter explosion—but hopefully it would clear the gravity point and create a window where she could sneak through without being detected. She tensed as the second wave vanished, keeping a wary eye on the timer. If she jumped too soon, or too late, the entire exercise would be worse than useless.

But they have to have found something really bad back there, she mused as the last seconds ticked down to zero. She'd known she'd be going to Mercado, once the last system was secured, but not so quickly. *Admiral Teller wouldn't have bumped up the schedule if he hadn't thought it was urgent.*

The LinkShip jumped into a maelstrom. Hameeda gritted her teeth, cursing under her breath as she angled away from the remnants of a flight of gunboats. The remains of a minefield were clearly visible on her sensors, so ragged she was *sure* they were antimatter warheads that had been consumed by a giant chain reaction. She smirked at the thought, then concentrated on putting some distance between herself and the enemy sensors. The platforms near the gravity point itself should have been blinded, she thought, but there was an entire enemy fleet some distance from the point. Her eyes narrowed. It was *quite* some distance from the point. She was damn sure the bastards had learnt from what had happened to the *last* fleet.

And they can jump into FTL and land on top of us the moment they see the real fleet transiting the gravity point, she mused. Someone on the other side was clearly thinking ahead. *Not bad tactics, all things considered.*

She kept her drives as low as she could as she crawled away from the gravity point, her passive sensors telling her things she hadn't wanted to know about the enemy defences. The sudden bombardment had done some damage, but much less than she'd hoped. There were more mines, lurking close to the point; others seemed to have been laid in ever-expanding circles, although she wasn't sure if that was any good. Mines grew progressively less and less useful the further they were laid from the gravity point. Someone could simply move *around* the field and avoid engagement, or clear it easily with railgun pellets. Beyond them, a handful of fortresses—they'd probably been towed from the inner worlds—maintained a wary watch on the gravity point. And, beyond them...

Her blood ran cold as she silently counted the alien ships. Seven entire squadrons of battleships, backed up by almost a thousand smaller ships. Mercado *was* a good place to make a stand—there were four gravity points in the system, all of which were vitally important to the galactic economy— but she wished the enemy had been less perceptive. They probably believed that the human ships would spread into the inner worlds if Mercado fell, even if they didn't head to Tokomak Prime itself. A combination of luck and judgement could tear the entire empire in half. If the human ships could be stopped, they had to be stopped here. The alternative was unthinkable for a race that believed it couldn't possibly lose.

Not good, she thought. The defences grew larger and larger. They didn't look *that* firm—the enemy formation looked ragged—but they had enough firepower that it probably wasn't going to matter. And they were on the alert, their active sensors ruthlessly quartering space for threats. She was grimly aware they might find her, if they looked directly at her. *They could force us to fight a real battle for* this *system.*

She spread her sensors wide, studying the live feed. The entire system was alive, thrumming with activity. Hundreds of freighters moved between the gravity points and the planets, or dropped into FTL and rushed into interstellar space. She could see thousands of asteroid settlements and industrial nodes scattered across the system, each one part of a giant industrial base that was—if her communications analysis was correct—being turned into a war machine. She shuddered as she ran the calculations, trying to determine just how much war material the system could produce. The answer was depressingly high. Admiral Teller might have to take the system quickly, or not at all.

And yet, there were signs that all was not well. Reports of police activity, communications blackouts…hints and tips that the planets might be on the verge of revolution. The news reports were dull to the point of threatening to put her to sleep—they didn't even mention the antimatter bombardment—but the low-power channels were much more interesting. It was impossible to determine just how many of the threatened uprisings were real, yet…it was clear trouble was brewing. She found herself studying the planetary rings through long-range sensors. What would happen if the entire system exploded into violence?

Mass slaughter, she told herself, as she steered a course back to the gravity point and readied a drone. She was careful to keep her distance from the battleships. *If we didn't get here in time, we'd have to watch helplessly as billions of people died.*

She composed herself as she launched the drone, hoping the enemy wouldn't detect it before it entered the gravity point and vanished. Mercado's defenders were on alert, their sensors constantly sweeping space…the drone was tiny, but they might just see it before it could escape. And then…she put the thought aside as she prepared for her role in the operation, waiting for the signal that would tell her when to begin. It wasn't easy coordinating an operation across hundreds of light years—there was no way Admiral Teller could send her a detailed message—but they'd planned as carefully as they could. The signal itself would be impossible to miss.

And now I wait, she thought. *And get ready to move.*

• • •

"That's a tough defence," Colin mused, as the drone's report was downloaded into the main display. "But pretty much what we were expecting."

He made a mental note to compliment the analysts. They'd studied the captured files, then put together a picture of what Mercado could do in its own defence. They hadn't been entirely right—Mercado could have moved more battlestations to defend the gravity point—but they'd done enough. It was unfortunate that the enemy fleet was keeping its distance, yet...he shrugged. They'd assumed as much, when they'd drawn up the plan. The enemy was unlikely to put his own head on the block. What sort of idiot would commit suicide on demand?

Unless they're desperate, he reminded himself. *If they lose this system, they're going to lose direct contact with large swathes of territory. It'll take them years to rebuild even if we all drop dead tomorrow.*

He glanced at Karan's back. "Commander. Are the assault pods ready to go?"

"Aye, Admiral." Karan didn't look up as her fingers danced over the console. "I've updated their targeting systems. The fortresses won't know what hit them."

"I think the survivors probably will," Colin said, dryly. He took a long breath, feeling the weight of command falling around his shoulders. "You may fire when ready."

"Yes, sir."

CHAPTER SIXTEEN

Governor-Admiral Pentode hadn't expected much from his posting to Mercado. A hundred years or so as the governor, wearing his admiral's hat as little as possible, followed by a return to Tokomak Prime and the resumption of a steady climb to the very top of the heights of power. His life had been mapped out for him right from birth, his family and clan resting their hope in his career as they struggled for influence on Tokomak Prime and power in the galaxy itself. None of them had *ever* envisaged their great hope suddenly finding himself on the front lines of a war... of course, he told himself from time to time, a great deal had happened that his parents and ancestors had never expected. The Empress sending his grandparents and great-grandparents to a retirement home, for example.

He would have smiled at the thought of being *free*, for the first time in his life, if he hadn't known the risks. The Empress had made it brutally clear to him, when she passed through the system for the first time, that she wouldn't hesitate to relieve him if he failed to come up to her exacting standards. And, the second time she'd come through the system, she'd ordered him to defend his system and fight to the last... or he'd wish he'd been killed by the human barbarians. Pentode had taken the threat seriously. The Empress might have lost most of her power, but she was still formidable. And none of her 'advisors' would lift a single hand to help *him* if she decided to kill him.

The display glowed, showing where the enemy antimatter pods had detonated, setting off a chain reaction that had devastated his minefields. Pentode hadn't expected the antimatter mines to do more than slow the enemy for a few seconds, but as the time ticked on and no enemy ships materialised, it had become amazingly clear that the enemy had merely intended to harass him. Pentode cursed the humans savagely as he watched his ships and personnel wear themselves to the bone, struggling to hold the line. There was no way any of them would be ready for combat when the humans finally showed their hand.

He allowed his expression to darken as he studied—again—the reports from the last engagement. Raw data was lacking. What little had been forwarded to him was almost completely useless. The humans had taken out an entire squadron, giving the ships and crews no time to either return fire or surrender, but how? They shouldn't have been able to target their missiles so accurately. Pentode had heard the increasingly nasty rumours, but he hadn't believed them. Not until now. The humans were revoltingly ingenious and they were going to get a lot of his people killed.

And yet, he *had* to hold. The system was vitally important. It could *not* be abandoned or...he tried to think of the consequences, only to find himself caught in a trap. The consequences were unthinkable. He'd go down in history as the single worst failure his people had ever produced, even if...no, it was unthinkable. The humans had to be stopped. And he'd do it, or die trying.

Still, he told himself. *They have to come through the gravity point.*

The thought calmed him, as well it might. There were *hundreds* of light years between the two gravity points, a distance that could be crossed in an instant if a ship jumped *through* the points, but one that would take *months* in FTL. The humans would *want* to surprise him, he was sure, yet...how could they *do* it? He knew where they'd appear, unless they wanted to spend months crawling from N-Gann to Mercado. He rather hoped they would. If he had a few months, he could make the system impregnable.

An icon appeared in front of him, right on top of the gravity point. A missile-sized object...he swore as a gunboat swooped towards it, only to be obliterated when the antimatter containment field was switched off and matter met antimatter, the resulting blast destroying all traces of the gunboat. His bulging eyes twitched as he studied the sensor feed, wondering just what the humans were doing. They'd already done all they could with antimatter pods. He had no intention of *stopping* them if they wanted to waste their antimatter on targets that were already dust and less than dust, but it was odd. The humans could hardly afford to waste their resources.

His confusion grew as the last traces of the blast died away. There was no sustained bombardment, no horde of missile pods looking for targets...had the antimatter pod been launched by accident? He was well aware of how scavenger races could kill themselves—and others—by experimenting with technology they didn't understand, but the humans weren't that stupid. They couldn't improve upon their technology if they didn't understand it. And yet...maybe it had been an accident. No other explanation seemed to fit...

Red icons appeared, *behind* him. For a moment, Pentode refused to believe what his eyes were seeing. The humans *couldn't* have sneaked a fleet behind him, not unless they'd designed and built FTL drives an order of magnitude faster even than courier boats! It was impossible! And yet, the icons were falling into attack formation, readying themselves to take him from the rear and punch through to the gravity point. He'd drawn up his plans on the assumption the enemy would come through the gravity point...

He got control of himself with an effort, pushing the sense of gibbering panic out of his mind. "Rotate the fleet," he ordered. The enemy had caught him by surprise, but they hadn't won. Not yet. Not ever. "And prepare to engage!"

A low shudder ran through the battleship as she slowly rotated on her axis, bringing her weapons to bear on the human targets. Pentode felt an ugly sense of glee burning away the last of his shock as he realised the humans had made a serious mistake. They could have slipped closer, right into sprint-mode engagement range, if they'd had the nerve. Instead, they'd given him time to prepare. He felt his jaws open wide as the range started to shorten rapidly. He'd give them a beating they wouldn't forget; he'd stop them dead...

"Close the range," he ordered. Another shudder ran through the deck. "And fire on my command."

His eyes narrowed still further as the human ships slowed. That was odd. They should be picking up speed, trying to engage him before he was fully ready. He had nearly four times as many ships... they had their technical innovations, but numbers like that would be telling even if the humans had *far* superior weapons. Instead, they seemed intent on prolonging the engagement. Did they want him to win? Doubt assailed him as he realised things were looking *really* odd. Was he being drawn *out* of position instead?

And then the tactical display changed again.

• • •

Seven hundred assault pods made transit in a single heartbeat, thirty-nine of them interpenetrating and vanishing in eye-tearing flashes of light. The remainder orientated themselves and opened fire, using the targeting data they'd uploaded from the stealth drone. Six thousand missiles lanced through space, rocketing towards the fortresses. The enemy point defence picked off several dozen, but the remainder kept coming, crashing into the fortresses with terrifying force. One by one, their shields collapsed and missiles struck their bare hulls, tearing them to shreds.

Five minutes after the assault pods arrived, none of the fortresses remained intact.

• • •

Hameeda almost laughed as the entire enemy fleet seemed to flinch. A cooler commander might have feared she *was* luring them out of position, while a less imaginative commander might have stood her ground and waited for her to come to him ... instead, she noted calmly, the enemy battleships had been caught between two fires. And, to add insult to injury, one of the fires was nothing more than ECM drones and sensor ghosts.

And now you probably suspect the truth, she thought. The enemy ships were still following her, like ducklings following their mother, but she was pretty sure that was just inertia. They might be able to snatch a victory if they destroyed a *real* fleet, yet ... the *real* fleet was behind them, just starting to make transit now. What would they do when the penny finally dropped? They could take out Hameeda and the LinkShip and they'd still be fucked when Admiral Teller deployed his fleet. *What are you planning to do?*

She was tempted, as the enemy ships opened fire on sensor ghosts, to simply turn the drones off and laugh in their collective face as they realised they'd been screwed. It wouldn't be long before they realised their missiles weren't doing anything, or that her ships weren't shooting back. They'd pretty much *have* to draw the correct conclusion and then ... she saw the first hints of confusion amongst the enemy position, the first discreet suggestions the enemy commander was hopelessly out of it. She guessed there was an angry argument going on, in or out of the commander's brain. What should he do?

No, she corrected herself. *What would he do?*

• • •

Pentode found it hard, so very hard, to muster any sort of coherent response to the disaster unfolding behind him. Nineteen fortresses, enough firepower to stand off any reasonable threat, had been smashed to atoms, buried under enough missiles to destroy a force two or three times their size. He tried to take hope in the thought of just how *many* missiles the humans had expended, but it wasn't enough. His ships were out of place; the second human fleet was making transit and the first was...

His thoughts felt sluggish, as if he'd been using direct brain stimulation, but one thing was clear. The first human fleet wasn't firing back. Why?

The answer jolted him out of his stupor. The first enemy fleet wasn't firing because it *couldn't* fire. He'd been tricked, lured out of place by enemy *drones*. And that meant he wasn't in *quite* as bad a mess as he'd thought. There were still options.

"Rotate the fleet," he ordered. "Reverse course. Immediately."

He ignored the gasps of shock as he studied the reports from the gravity point. No commander in his right mind would present the enemy with his rear, in the certain knowledge that it would be easy for the enemy to shoot a missile up his fundament, but if there were no enemy ships behind him...he snapped out orders as the fleet moved, retreating back the gravity point at sublight speeds. The humans had timed it well, damn them. He didn't have the time to drop into FTL before it was too late.

"They're not firing," an operator said. "I..."

"They're not *real*," Pentode snarled. The deception was good, an order of magnitude better than anything in *his* arsenal, but they couldn't fake missiles. They couldn't even fake ships being *struck* with missiles. "They tricked us!"

He forced himself to watch as the humans expanded their grip, sending their ships through in a steady stream of dangerously-close transits. He'd seen something like it before, but only when the ships were crewed by expendable servitors. Here...it was a minor miracle that none of the human ships collided with another. He would have been impressed if it hadn't been so damn dangerous. His only hope—now—was to bull his way to the gravity point and sit on it, shooting anything that poked its way through the twist in time and space. And even *that* was risky. The humans could fire more missile pods through the gravity point and blow hell out of him.

"Admiral," a subordinate said. "I'm picking up a request for orders from the planet."

"Tell them to wait," Pentode snapped. He didn't have *time* to deal with petty little requests from his staffers, not now. If he didn't secure the gravity point, the system was doomed. He forced himself to consider other options, perhaps a simple retreat back to the next system, but...he knew it would lead to his immediate execution. "I..."

"Admiral, the planet is revolting," the subordinate said. "The entire planet has risen against us."

Pentode blanched. The servitors had been dissatisfied ever since they'd heard of a barbarian race that had dared raise a hand to its masters. They'd never realised that everything the Tokomak did was for their own good. They'd never realised...a few months ago, everyone with half a brain had *known* that rebellion was futile. But now...everyone had seen the remnants of the Empress's fleet as she'd crawled back to Tokomak Prime. They knew the Tokomak could be beaten. And even if the revolt was put down, it would do one hell of a lot of damage.

He forced himself to think. The human fleet was getting stronger and stronger as more ships arrived. He still had an edge, but it was shrinking rapidly. What would happen if he *lost*? What would happen if...his brain ran in circles as more and more reports flowed into the datanet. There were riots in all the major cities, uprisings and coups and mass slaughters and...he was almost tempted to surrender, except the humans might not be able to save his people. Every single Tokomak in the system itself was doomed.

The humans opened fire, their missiles streaking into the teeth of his point defence. They were good, very good. His point defence stopped some of them, but the remainder kept coming. They were targeting his battleships, trying to cripple or destroy them. His ships returned fire, but the human ships were heavily protected. Their point defence stopped nearly three-fourths of the missiles aimed at them.

He silently evaluated his chances as four battleships were blown to hell, a fifth shooting lifepods in all directions before following its comrades into death. He *might* bull through the human ships, at the cost of losing most of his fleet. And then the humans would just keep coming. He'd seen the reports. He was facing only a small fraction of their fleet. The remainder would keep coming and push him right out of the system, if he survived long enough. And, in the meantime, the rioters would tear the entire system to pieces.

"Power up the stardrives," he ordered, shortly. Shock ran around the compartment. "We have to fall back."

He ignored a handful of protests, protests that would have made him explode with rage if they'd been fighting a normal battle, then ordered his ships to drop into FTL. The humans could have stopped them, if they'd thought to power up their gravity wells in time...he breathed a sigh of relief as they passed through the danger zone and plunged into interstellar space. The humans would track them, of course, but they'd have trouble bringing his fleet to battle. He'd have time to lick his wounds and decide what to do next. If nothing else, his fleet wasn't *weak*. He'd be a lurking threat the humans would have to confront.

"Dispatch a courier boat to Tokomak Prime," he ordered. "The Empress must be informed."

And even if she wants me dead, she has to know what's happened here, he told himself, stiffly. *Maybe she can put a fleet together in time to save us.*

"Aye, Admiral," one of his subordinates said. "What about the planet?"

Pentode said nothing for a long moment, then spoke. "The planet will have to take care of itself," he said. He'd thought he'd prepared for anything. In hindsight, it was clear his foresight had been nowhere near enough. "We can't help them."

• • •

"The enemy fleet has broken off," Karan reported. "The remainder of the minefield has been cleared."

Colin nodded, stiffly. The plan had worked, but not well enough. He'd hoped to convince the enemy fleet to fight a missile duel, giving him the chance to smash it before it could withdraw or be reinforced. Instead, the enemy had fallen back and run for interstellar space. It wouldn't last long, not without supplies and a secure base, but...he shook his head. It would have to be handled, somehow. He just wasn't sure how.

"Force One is to proceed to the planet," he ordered. They were picking up hundreds of pleas for help, pleas he had to answer. "Force Two is to maintain position on the gravity point. Force Three is to build up, then proceed to Point One when ready. The other two gravity points will have to wait."

Which may work in our favour, he told himself. The fleeing freighters would tell everyone what they'd seen. *Word will spread faster than the Tokomak can stop it.*

He allowed his imagination to fill in the blanks as the squadron slipped into FTL, racing to the planet itself. Word would be spreading fast, heading straight to Tokomak Prime. His most optimistic estimates suggested the Tokomak Empress would hear of their advance in a couple of weeks, depending on factors outside his control. And then? She'd have to stop him before he reached the Twins or…or what? She couldn't simply write off the Twins, or all hell would break loose.

But numbers are her only advantage, he thought. It was harsh, but true. *She'd be a fool to throw them away too quickly.*

"And order the LinkShip pilot to contact me, when she returns to the fleet," he added. "I have an idea I want to discuss with her."

"Aye, Admiral," Karan said.

CHAPTER SEVENTEEN

"You know," Butler remarked, "I'm feeling very naked out here."

"You're not naked," Martin commented, dryly. "For which, I assure you, we are all very grateful."

Butler snorted. "I'll have you know I won the Mr. Great Butt competition on Syndrome Asteroid five years ago."

"I thought it was the Mr. Big Ass competition," Martin said. "And you had to bribe the judges."

"It was no hardship," Butler said. "And that judge was a real..."

Piece snorted, rudely. "Do you *always* banter like this?"

Martin indicated the display. "What would you suggest we do?"

The display shifted, revealing a line of starships slowly making their way towards the gravity point. Someone had been busy. The files insisted the gravity point was unguarded, but there were a cluster of fortresses sitting on top of the point and a squadron of starships floating nearby. Martin was no expert on deep space combat, but he was fairly sure the fortresses should be on the *other* side of the gravity point. There was no point in fortifying a position where the enemy could stand off and batter you to death from long-range. They might as well throw the fortresses into the nearest star.

"The codes will work," Piece said. "There's no need to be nervous."

"I don't feel nervous." Butler elbowed him, gently. "I feel like getting naked."

"I thought you were supposed to set a good example for the troops," Martin teased. "It's written in the manual."

Butler adopted a look of darkest suspicion. "Who told you those manuals existed? Was it Porter? Or Rouge? Or..."

"I *did* read them for myself," Martin said. "Sergeants are meant to wear red so the blood doesn't show and discourage the troops. You're out of uniform."

"I changed into my brown pants," Butler countered, snidely. He indicated the icons on the display. "You know what'll happen if those monsters open fire."

"Yeah." Martin felt a chill that no amount of banter could dispel. "We'll be dead before we know what hit us."

Piece looked from one to the other. "You're both insane," he said. "How did you manage to qualify with attitudes like that?"

Martin shrugged. "We know what we're doing," he assured the operative. "Every last man on this ship"—*except for you*, he carefully didn't say—"has over ten years of experience, in everything from line infantry to SF. They know the score. They can put up with a little clowning around without diminishing their respect for senior officers."

"My respect for you, sir, has never been higher," Butler said, archly.

"You see?" Martin pretended to miss the joke. "He respects me more already."

Piece opened his mouth to say something, but the console bleeped before he could get a single word out. Instead, he bent over the console and activated the conversational overlay once again. Martin watched, feeling more nervous—and naked—than he cared to admit. If they were caught... he shook his head. The Tokomak had to deal with thousands of ships passing through the gravity point, fleeing a human offensive still hundreds of light years away. There was no reason they should pick *their* ship out of the line for further questioning, particularly not with the Galactic-level codes they were using. But Martin wasn't so sure. *He* wouldn't have been pleased if someone talked to *him* in such a manner. He would have looked for a chance to get his own back, if he could keep his involvement a secret...

The console pinged, again. "We have clearance to proceed," Piece said. "And a new download from the news servers."

"Most of which will be lies," Martin predicted. They'd made sure to get downloads from each system they'd crossed. The stories had grown wilder and wilder the further they'd travelled from N-Gann. The Tokomak seemed torn between branding the human incursion as a minor border skirmish and the end of the universe, as they knew it. "Or do you think they'll start telling their people the truth?"

Piece shrugged. "Why break the habits of a lifetime?"

Martin forced himself to relax as *Hoyden* moved towards the gravity point and jumped. Space *twisted* around them, the display blanking and hastily rebooting as the drives shoved them off the gravity point. Red light washed over the display, nearly giving him a heart attack before he realised they weren't *actually* being targeted. The small armada of fortresses on the gravity point were scanning *everyone* with tactical sensors. Martin felt a flicker of contempt, mingled with concern. Perhaps even fear. A jumpy officer might put a missile or an energy beam through *Hoyden's* hull without ever stopping to think about what he was doing. He might not even have a chance to realise that blowing up a Harmony ship would cause a diplomatic incident...

The Harmonies would be very surprised to hear that they had a ship out here, Martin thought, as they were steered away from the gravity point. *And then the whole story would unravel rather quickly.*

He snorted at the thought. The Tokomak would have problems deciding what to do about it, if they realised that humans—and others—were using Galactic-level codes. It would take *years* to change the codes and make sure *everyone* was updated, which would give the smugglers and others a chance to adjust their own codes. And they couldn't inspect *every* ship passing through the gravity points without bringing interstellar trade to a standstill. It might even be worth tipping them off, he thought. They'd cause more problems for themselves when they tried to stop it.

Perhaps later, he thought. *Right now, we have other problems.*

The Twins unfolded in front of him as they glided further into the system, on a course that would—hopefully—allow them to vanish without causing alarm. There were two stars, each one surrounded by a number of rocky planets and gas giants. The system hummed with activity, hundreds of thousands of energy sources appearing on the passive display as more and more data flooded into the system. It was chillingly evident that the Twins' system was an industrial behemoth, bigger than anything he'd seen in the Solar Union. Given time, and proper specifications, the Twins could outproduce the entire Galactic Alliance. Martin had seen immense systems before, but the Twins' system was simply stunning. The mere sight took his breath away.

He glanced at Piece. "And you think your people can take control of the system?"

"You'd be surprised," Piece said. He tapped his console, altering course and steering towards a cluster of asteroids. "The defence network is run by the Tokomak, but everything else... they're literally *infested* by servitor races. Even most of the defence stations have servitors onboard, doing the shit work no one else wants to do. And we've been putting together a network of cells, ready to take the stations or destroy them when the shit hits the fan."

Butler snorted. "And what about the risk of being uncovered?"

"A lot of cells *have* been broken, over the years," Piece said. "But— thankfully—none of the *really* important leaders were taken alive."

He shrugged. "Even if they guessed just how wide the network had become, over the years, they wouldn't be able to do much about it. They're dependent on servitor labour to maintain just about everything. Oh, they crack down on rebel cells whenever they find them—and reshuffle entire teams every year or so—but the networks are too encompassing to be stopped so easily. There are limits to how much they can do without crippling themselves. And now, with a war on, they can't even do *that*."

"I hope you're right," Martin said. "How did they ever get into such a mess?"

"Arrogance and the simple lack of any *real* threat from outside their empire," Piece said, as he fiddled with the console. "Now, if you'll give me a moment, I need to exchange signs and countersigns."

Martin watched, feeling cold as *Hoyden* approached the asteroids. They *looked* like a regular mining colony that was steadily converting itself into a long-term home, somewhere on the edge of civilised space without ever quite slipping into illegality. It reminded him of the Solar Union, although he knew the laws were tougher here. A group couldn't simply set up an asteroid home and expect to be left alone, not when they might be plotting rebellion. They might be flying straight into a trap. Martin promised himself, quietly, that he'd sell their lives dearly if they were. They couldn't be taken alive. They knew too much.

A low shudder ran through the ship as she docked, the airlocks matching perfectly. Piece stood, brushing down his tunic. "You want to come with me? You might enjoy it."

"Sure." Martin's eyes shifted to Butler. "You know the drill."

"Panic if you don't return within two hours," Butler said. All traces of amusement were gone. "And then do as I see fit."

"Pull back and vanish," Martin said. They didn't have time to locate rebel cells on their own, not if this meeting went sour. "And find a way to hurt them when the system is attacked."

Piece nodded, then led him through the airlock and into the asteroid itself. The air smelled unpleasant, although Martin's implants assured him it was safe to breath. The illusion of being in the Solar Union swiftly vanished as they moved past a series of caverns, each one hosting hundreds of people from a dozen different races. The asteroid looked like a refugee camp. Martin had served on a handful of dorm asteroids, where new immigrants stayed until they got their bearings, but even *they* hadn't been so…vile. It looked more like one of the camps on Earth than anything else.

He followed Piece, grimly aware they were being watched. A pair of young aliens were following them, keeping their distance while always keeping them in sight. Piece showed no reaction, but Martin was sure he'd spotted them too. They stopped in front of an airlock, which opened long enough to admit them before closing with an ominous *thud*. Martin felt trapped as he surveyed the room. Four aliens stood around a table, representing four different races. Martin had to consult his implants to place them. All four races had been primitive when the Tokomak arrived on their worlds. They'd never had the chance to make something of themselves. Instead, they'd simply been enslaved.

"Welcome back," one of the aliens said. He looked like a humanoid octopus, tentacles waving in all directions. Martin couldn't tell if he was male or female or something else, something alien. His voice was whispery yet oddly crude, as if the language he spoke hadn't been designed for his mouth. "Are our comrades with you?"

"They are," Piece confirmed. "And all is well here?"

"There have been no great changes," another alien said. He was humanoid too, but the proportions were all wrong. Martin felt a chill just looking at him. "Our *masters*"—the word was laced with weapons-grade sarcasm—"continue to prepare for your war."

Piece took a step forward. "The war is coming here," he said. "And you have to be ready."

Martin listened quietly as Piece outlined the plan, as he knew it. The operative didn't know that Admiral Teller's thrust was just a diversion, although there *was* a realistic prospect of him reaching the Twins and perhaps even carrying the war to Tokomak Prime itself. It would depend on just what, if anything, the Tokomak *did* when they learnt about the fleet. Martin knew it wouldn't be long before they *had* to make a choice. They practically *had* to know the human fleet was advancing now. The informational wave had long since passed through the Twins and gone on.

He forced himself to pay attention as the debate raged on, his implants recording it for later analysis. It was difficult to tell who supported what, let alone which way they'd jump when the shit hit the fan. Resistance movements built on cells and sub-networks tended to be disorganised, even when they needed to act in unison. And the threat of reprisal was always present. If the resistance rose, and failed to take control of the planet and hold it until Admiral Teller arrived, they were doomed. The Tokomak would slaughter without mercy.

And yet, they'd be burning down a sizable chunk of their industry if they want to kill everyone, he reminded himself. *They'd be insane to lay waste to the entire system.*

The resistance didn't seem to agree. He had trouble reading their body language, but it looked like one of the leaders wanted to wait for Admiral Teller before committing themselves to an uprising and two others were wavering. Martin struggled to think of how they might be talked into moving earlier, but drew a blank. They had every reason to *hope* for a human victory, yet...no reason to think there might *be* a human victory. The Tokomak were gathering their strength. They'd soon have enough power to crush the entire human fleet and move on to turn Earth into a blackened wasteland.

"The fact remains that, if you don't act now, you will not be able to act at all." Piece sounded frustrated, although Martin wasn't sure the aliens knew it. Human body language was alien to them too. "If they destroy Earth, they will move rapidly to eradicate you once and for all."

The debate raged on, each resistance leader insisting on having his say. Martin was tempted to request a time out, or a pause long enough to let everyone catch their breath. Some of the leaders seemed torn between the prospect of *finally* doing something and the certainty of utter destruction if the uprising failed. Martin didn't blame them—he'd studied enough uprisings that had been left to die by their foreign supporters—but it was still frustrating as hell. And if the rebels decided to move against the humans, instead? Martin had few illusions. The handful of marines could be destroyed in an instant if the alien rebels decided they were a liability.

"The problem remains Tokomak One," an alien said. "As long as they control the fortress, they can dominate the system."

Martin wasn't so sure. A lone fortress, no matter how powerful, couldn't dominate the *entire* system. But he saw their point. Tokomak One floated over the ring, its weapons threatening any uprising on the planetary surface. And it was almost completely crewed by Tokomak, isolated from the rest of the system. It couldn't be taken by stealth and yet, if it wasn't taken, it could put the entire uprising in jeopardy. The hell of it was that most of the remaining fortresses had already been towed to the gravity points...

He leaned forward. "We can take out the fortress," he said. The station was heavily defended, but there were options. There were *always* options. "And then you can secure the remainder of the system in peace."

"Until they bring their fleet to bear on us," another alien said. "You'd have to take Tokomak One first, before we jumped."

And we'd be exposed if they didn't *jump*, Martin thought. *But, at the very least, we would have given them a chance.*

Piece shot him a sharp look. "Are you sure?"

"Yes." Martin did his best to project utter confidence, although he knew Piece was probably the only one who'd pick up on it. "We can take the fortress and then secure it."

"Or destroy it," an alien said. The others made what looked to be affirmative gestures. "We don't want to see it falling *back* into enemy hands."

"No." Martin nodded. "We can ensure they never see it again."

"And if we do take out the fortress," Piece said, "will you rise?"

He sounded earnest, very earnest. "There won't be another chance. Either we win the war, and you liberate yourselves, or the Tokomak kill us all. They're desperate. They're panicking. And panicky people do stupid things. They have already announced pogroms on human settlers and clones. It's only a matter of time before they do the same to you. What price the industry here if they don't need it, after all of us are dead?"

The aliens spoke amongst themselves for a few minutes. Martin listened, but they weren't using any of the known Galactic tongues. They had to be using a *native* language, a language that had been declared forbidden long ago. He was astonished they'd managed to keep speaking even *one* native tongue. The Tokomak had worked hard to stamp out all memory of the days when their worlds had been small, when they'd been the only intelligent life form in existence. Entire swathes of history had been lost beyond all hope of recovery. Martin had heard stories about civilisations that had never existed, on Earth; he knew more about them than the aliens knew of their own worlds, before they'd been invaded and assimilated. It chilled him to realise just how much had been lost, over the centuries. The Tokomak hadn't even kept records.

They could have done a lot of good, he mused, as the discussion came to an end. *But instead they chose to grind everyone else in the mud.*

"We agree," the octopus alien said, finally. His voice was flat, almost atonal. The faint accent was gone. "But Tokomak One must be taken first. You must make good on your boast."

"And we will," Piece said, grandly. "It will be done."

"It will," Martin echoed. "We won't let you down."

And now we really have to make good on our boast, Martin thought. He kept his face expressionless as they were shown the door. *Or that will be a promise we won't be able to keep.*

CHAPTER EIGHTEEN

Hameeda wasn't sure, in all honesty, if Admiral Teller had given her the mission because he didn't know how best to use the LinkShip or if he merely wanted to delay the next thrust into enemy territory. She could understand the need to secure their rear, and do everything they could to encourage the formation of a planetary government that would be reasonably friendly to the human race, but time was short. The only way to pose a major threat to the Tokomak was to keep going, to keep smashing through their defences as if they were made of paper. They wouldn't be alarmed if the human force got bogged down only a couple of transits from N-Gann.

And the only problem with that is that their defences are not *made of paper,* she thought, as she kept her wary eye on the convoy. Admiral Teller had fired off a *lot* of assault pods when he'd blasted his way into the system, slowing his advance until he could get replacements shipped from N-Gann. *If we can't replace our assault pods, we'll have to mount conventional assaults and that will cost us.*

She scowled, wishing she wasn't tied to the convoy. The small fleet had passed through the first gravity point without incident, then set course in realspace towards the second gravity point. It screamed *TRAP* to her, even though she knew the convoy consisted of alien designed and crewed freighters that had been pressed into service. There was no *technical* reason why they couldn't go into FTL, except that would make interception impossible. She wondered, darkly, if the Tokomak really knew how many rules they'd made that had been taken for natural laws. If they ever thought better of it, if they ever took a good hard look at their guiding assumptions, they might realise just how thoroughly they'd screwed themselves. And then take steps to correct it.

Time passed, slowly. Hameeda fought boredom by running a series of increasingly complex simulations, exploring the limits of the possible. She fought and refought the war time and time again, trying to deduce what might happen if the Tokomak made one choice and their human enemies made a different choice. It was frustrating, even though she *knew* something had to be left to chance. The aliens were *alien*. Their reasoning might be too alien for her to comprehend. They might do something she wouldn't expect, simply because she couldn't understand their reasoning. And...

She shook her head. They didn't have time to worry about it. The sooner they resumed their advance, the better. But Admiral Teller had too many problems to deal with before he could order the fleet to continue punching its way to Tokomak Prime. The provisional government had to be convinced to start putting assault pods—and everything else—into mass production, even though it would cause unrest...more unrest. And the prisoners had to be protected...there were just too many problems. It was easy to believe they'd been better off before they'd formed alliances outside the human race.

But then we'd be fighting alone, she reminded herself. *Allies. Can't fight with them and can't fight without them.*

Her sensors twitched. She was instantly alert, passive sensors sweeping for cloaked ships. There was *something* up ahead, an energy fluctuation that could be nothing more than a random flicker of cosmic energy or a cloaked ship. The Tokomak cloaking devices were good, even if they weren't up to human standards. And they could have stepped down their drives and sensors, lowering the risk of detection still further. The convoy was making no attempt to hide. The Tokomak shouldn't have had any trouble projecting its course and steering a path to put themselves in its way.

Unless they scented a trap, she thought. *They know they have to be careful.*

She gritted her teeth, wishing she dared run an active sensor sweep. It would blow away all ambiguity in a moment, at the price of revealing her presence. The Tokomak—if there *were* Tokomak—would slip into FTL, escaping on a random vector. It was too soon to spring the trap. She tested her systems quickly, knowing the enemy fleet had to be given time to get cocky. They wanted—they needed—a crushing victory they could use to prove they hadn't been defeated. Not yet. Smashing twenty freighters wasn't much, in the grand scheme of things, but it would be a start. And Admiral Teller would wind up looking like an idiot.

And the provisional government will start edging away from us if they think we're going to lose, she reminded herself. *We cannot afford even a single defeat.*

The faint flickers of energy grew stronger. There was a pattern to them... Hameeda bared her teeth as the pattern grew more visible, a clear sign there *were* a handful of ships lurking ahead of them. Random cosmic fluctuations would be... well, *random*. She reminded herself not to focus on them too much. There might be other ships lurking nearby. The Tokomak had had time to call for reinforcements... long-range sensors hadn't picked up any trace of warships entering the system, but that was meaningless. The Tokomak had used freighters to tow their warships before.

They stole that trick off us, she thought, as she silently placed a bet with herself when the enemy would uncloak and open fire. Too soon and the human ships would have time to react, too late and the human ships would get a clear shot at their hulls. *And they used it well.*

She braced herself. It wouldn't be long now.

• • •

Governor-Admiral Pentode felt nothing but bitter hatred as he sat on his command deck and watched the human freighters and their escorts approach. A week. A week... it had only taken a week for the entire system to not only fall to its human attackers, but to devote itself to *serving* its attackers. The provisional government, flush with victory, had started unlocking fabricators and switching over to mass production of every-thing from assault pods to antimatter mines. Pentode couldn't believe it. He'd spent years trying to increase production, yet—a mere week after the humans had seized the system—production had gone through the roof. It was almost as if his servants—his *former* servants—had been unwilling to work for him.

He cursed under his breath as the range closed, knowing he'd already lost. The engagement didn't matter. He'd done his level best to harass ship-ping and asteroid settlements, but…either he died or he was summarily executed when the Empress heard about his failure. His brave stand had cost the enemy, of that he was sure, but…he shook his head, angrily. The war was going to get worse before it got better, if it ever did. What would happen if the humans managed to seize a handful of other systems and make them *all* more productive?

The balance of power could shift very quickly, he thought. The vast stock-pile of warships, arms and ammunition the Tokomak had built up, over the centuries, might be less of a war-winner than he'd thought. He'd run the projections in private, unwilling to risk sharing them with his analysts. *If they start churning out modern warships here, with human weapons, the balance of power could shift against us.*

He shuddered. In hindsight, he should have blown up the entire system rather than retreating into deep space. He'd assumed the humans couldn't make use of the system, but he'd been wrong. *Catastrophically* wrong. They were actually making *better* use of the system, if only because the wretched provisional government knew it was doomed if the humans didn't win. Pentode shuddered, embracing a thought most Tokomak would have found utterly unthinkable. The ancients had been wrong. They'd imposed order and stagnation on the universe, at the cost of growth and development. And respect for the Tokomak, the oldest of the old. He'd intercepted enough transmissions, all in the clear these days, to understand just how deeply they were hated. There were people in the system—*his* system—who would burn Tokomak Prime to the ground and then sow the ashes with radioactive waste, just to make sure the planet never recovered. And that meant...

"Admiral." The tactical officer looked composed, too composed. Pentode had spent too long worrying about what his subordinates thought of him now, reminding himself that the Empress had been a mutineer herself. "The human ships are within range."

Pentode nodded, stiffly. Blowing up a handful of freighters wouldn't delay the humans for more than a day or two, if that, but it would show the provisional government the war wasn't over. Not yet. And it would force the humans to make a choice between securing their rear and pressing on, giving him a chance to cut their supply lines. He could buy time for the empire to strike back...

"Target their escorts," he ordered. "Open fire on my command."

He braced himself. The humans probably weren't *crewing* those ships. They'd pressed a vast number of freighters into service, freighters configured for races that ranged from near-human to completely alien. Killing them wouldn't be killing humans...it would do. It would make life harder for the enemy and that was all that mattered. If they didn't surrender quickly, he'd blow them away without hesitation.

And maybe even if they do surrender, he thought, darkly. *They're traitors. They deserve nothing more than death.*

"Decloak," he ordered. "And fire!"

The display wavered as the cloaking device powered down, his active sensors going online and sweeping space for potential threats. The human freighters and their escorts, a handful of destroyer-sized ships, appeared to be alone. An entire human fleet could be shadowing them, he knew, but his FTL drives were already spooling up. He'd have time to jump into FTL and vanish if the humans were plotting an ambush. The idea of running from a fight bothered him, but...it wasn't the first time. The longer he kept his fleet alive, the better.

He smiled as his ships opened fire, hurling a wave of missiles directly towards the enemy escorts. It was overkill, but he didn't want to take any risks. He was painfully aware he no longer had access to any shipyards, let alone qualified yard workers. The ungrateful bastards in the local facilities had practically *jumped* at the chance to turn against their masters. He was more concerned about resupply, something *else* that hadn't been a problem until the humans attacked...

The display flickered, faint edges of gravimetric shadows appearing in front of him. Pentode blinked in disbelief. Gravity shadows surrounded stars, planets and *some* gravity points—quite why there were gravity points that didn't project gravity shadows had never been explained—but they didn't appear in empty space. Unless...his mind caught up with what he was seeing as the gravity wells grew stronger, expanding waves of gravity overlapping until he could no longer tell which ships were producing the gravity wells. And his missiles were slipping right *through* their targets.

His hearts skipped a beat as the ships—no, *drones*—exploded. Antimatter. The drones were crammed with antimatter. The blasts were little threat to a shielded warship, but they were powerful enough to wipe out most of his missiles before they could be retargeted. Pentode cursed, savagely, as he realised he'd been lured into another trap. The humans had pinned him in normal space, cutting off his line of retreat. And yet, there didn't seem to be any *warships* waiting for him. They'd baited a trap without teeth? It sounded impossible. The humans weren't mad. Or stupid. And that meant...

"Target the freighters," he snapped. The gravity well projectors *had* to be taken out, quickly, before their mere activation summoned human ships from right across the system. Gravity didn't propagate at FTL speeds, but there was no effective difference. They no longer had time to capture and loot the ships. They had to take them out and run. "Fire!"

•••

Hameeda allowed herself a moment of surprise as the enemy took the bait, firing hundreds of missiles towards the drones. She'd never been entirely convinced the Tokomak would be fooled by a show of weakness, if only because they weren't sure what the humans could and could not do. A harmless waif in a darkened street on Old Earth *might* be packing so many combat implants that she could give a trained marine a very hard time. Indeed, a lot of Earth's problems might be solved if everyone *did* carry concealed weapons at all times. But the Tokomak had taken the bait.

She felt a flash of pain as the antimatter warheads detonated, some of her sensors registering their outrage as they were permanently blinded. She detailed her automatics to handle repairs or replacements, then concentrated as the gravity well projectors came online. A low quiver ran through the ship as the gravity waves washed against her hull, a sensation she found surprisingly disturbing. Anything brushing the ship in deep space was probably very bad news indeed. There were stories about astronomers who went out to study interesting stars from point-blank range and never came home, having travelled a little *too* close to their target star.

They're trapped, she thought, as the Tokomak targeted the freighters. Quick thinking on their part, but not quick enough. *And now the conclusion.*

She sent a simple command to the freighters. The missile pods on their hull opened, then fired as one. She smiled, grimly, as thousands of missiles roared towards the enemy ships. The enemy would normally take one look and jump into FTL, but they couldn't do that as long as the gravity wave projectors remained operational. She was surprised the scheme had worked as well as it had. The Tokomak knew the trick. They'd not only faced it before, during the Second Battle of Earth; they'd used it themselves. And now it was going to kill their entire fleet.

With missiles that even they consider outdated, Hameeda thought. The enemy point defence was already firing, cutting hundreds of missiles out of space. But there were hundreds more. *They're not going to live long enough to regret it.*

She watched, and waited. It wouldn't be long now.

• • •

Pentode heard someone swear behind him as the missiles blazed towards his ships. There were hundreds—no, *thousands*—bearing down on him, an unstoppable mass that would smash his ships to smithereens. He couldn't believe it. He'd flown right into a trap, a trap that would deter his distant subordinates from harassing human shipping themselves. They'd see what had happened to him and take heed, keeping their distance from the humans...

He silently tried to calculate the odds, but he knew it was useless. The humans had caught him with overwhelming force. There was little hope of surviving the first barrage and, even if they did, no hope of surviving the second. The more he thought about it, the more he *knew* he was doomed. And his entire fleet with him. Honour demanded he fight to the last, spiting defiance as he died. Cold logic told him the sacrifice would be pointless.

"Drop shields," he ordered. "And signal surrender."

He heard the gasp as his crew hurried to obey. How many ships had surrendered since the war began? Not many. The news broadcasts claimed that *none* had surrendered, but Pentode knew that for a lie. Once, it would have been unthinkable. Now...now, there was no other choice. It was death or a POW camp, and he didn't want to die. The humans seemed to be treating their prisoners well. It was their only hope.

The missiles came closer, slipping into attack position. They were getting closer and closer...he twisted his hands, knowing the humans might not have *time* to shut down the missiles before it was too late. They might not even have heard his surrender. And then...the missiles powered down, holding position in the middle of his formation. His point defence tracked them automatically, but didn't fire.

"Admiral, we're picking up a message," the communications officer said. "Audio only."

The voice was human, speaking Galactic with a cold, almost metallic accent. "You are to switch to emergency power and wait to be boarded. Any resistance will result in the destruction of your vessels."

"I understand," Pentode said. They were going to call him a traitor. Or worse. But there was no choice. "We will comply."

He sighed in resignation. Yes, there was no choice. Or was that what he was telling himself because he didn't want to die? For nothing? He wondered, as he waited, if he'd ever know.

• • •

Hameeda frowned as she signalled for support, wishing she'd thought to request a marine company or two ... even though she couldn't have *hoped* to accommodate them on the LinkShip. The prospect of surrender hadn't been considered, not really. Given the nature of the trap, it had been deemed unlikely the enemy *would* surrender even if they wanted to. But they had and ... she sighed as she waited. She had no qualms about destroying hostile warships, but firing on ships that were trying to surrender—that she *knew* were trying to surrender—was a war crime. And it was one she had no intention of committing. If the Tokomak found out...

She shook her head. It didn't matter. She'd have to live with whatever she did afterwards. And she knew she couldn't live with cold-blooded slaughter.

And I won, she thought, with a cold smile. It was *her* victory. *We've wasted quite enough time already. But now we can resume the advance.*

CHAPTER NINETEEN

The shipyard was not, technically, a shipyard in any real sense. It was nothing more than a cluster of maintenance and accommodation pods, positioned near a thousand battleships that had rolled off the production lines hundreds of years ago and promptly placed into the naval reserve. The ancients hadn't really been able to put their fears into words, according to the files; they'd built a fleet that, as far as anyone could tell, they hadn't needed. Worse, perhaps, there was no *realistic* prospect of needing. And the construction work had just gone on and on...

Neola allowed herself a tight smile of gratitude at their foresight. The reserve fleet was powered down—and it would take months of work to get this shipyard alone emptied of ships—but it was still a formidable force. Millions of technicians swarmed over the ships, cleaning compartments, replacing components that had decayed over the years and loading magazines with missiles and supplies from Tokomak Prime. Behind there, she knew that millions more were training to crew the ships, readying themselves to go into battle. Her lips twitched again as she contemplated what she'd done. The young were no longer held back by the old. It *was* possible to be ambitious—now—and see that ambition pay off. Her people were girding their loins for war.

And yet, it isn't enough, she thought. *We need more and more recruits.*

She shook her head. She hadn't appreciated the scale of the damage until she'd started trying to fix it. For every recruit who rushed to the recruiting department, there were ten who wanted to stay in their homes and pretend nothing had changed. They lacked the drive to succeed, the drive that had been bred out of them as their lives became a combination of far too easy and, at the same time, stagnant. What was the point of working hard, Neola asked herself, if one never got what one wanted? Or it took so long that one no longer wanted it when it arrived? She thought she understood the humans better than she wanted to admit, even to herself. Their commanders were *children*, by Tokomak standards. They had yet to realise what long life would do to their society.

And they can learn, if they look at us, Neola thought. She needed millions of new recruits, men and women who could man the ships and take them into battle... she knew she'd barely get a fraction of what she needed. *And we can't even force our people to serve.*

Her mouth tightened as she contemplated the manpower figures. She'd had to conscript labour from every system within two hundred light years, regardless of its political reliability. She had no illusions, not any longer. The Tokomak Empire rested on the labour of hundreds of alien races who *hated* it with a passion, who were only kept in line by the threat of overwhelming force. There was no way she could *trust* the aliens to prepare and crew her capital ships, yet she had no choice. She simply didn't have enough technicians she could trust. She looked at the nearest starship, silently wishing she could strangle the ancients who'd allowed their people to go to seed. They'd thought their dominance was a natural law.

They'd been wrong.

She turned, remembering the reports trickling in from all over the empire. Entire planets and star systems in revolt, hundreds of starships vanishing in transit... slow-downs, strikes, even terrorist outrages that, normally, wouldn't merit attention from Tokomak Prime. But now... it was impossible to believe things would go back to normal. So far, the troubles hadn't spread corewards, but that would change. There were billions of servitor races on the core worlds. It would only take a few hundred to cause real trouble.

I could win the war and exterminate the entire human race, she thought. *And I might still lose everything.*

She gritted her sharp teeth as the console beeped, the sound no doubt heralding another set of extremely good excuses why the local bureaucracy couldn't do what she wanted. The war was looming, the situation was urgent...and bureaucrats were still demanding paperwork had to be in order before they did *anything*. It was a headache in peacetime, but in war it was disastrous. The humans would have to be invading Tokomak Prime itself before the system awoke to the peril, and by then it would be too late. The ancients had wanted a finely-tuned system they could control with minimal effort on their part. They'd got it too, at the price of the system being unable to cope with surprises. And the humans had been a surprise.

"Empress, we have received a message from the Council," her aide said. "They request your urgent presence."

"Do they now?" Neola scowled. The Council had picked a bad time, although most of them seemed to understand that the human threat had to be taken seriously. "Set course for the planet. We'll come back later."

She settled into her chair as the tiny starship altered course, dropping into FTL for the brief hop to Tokomak Prime. Getting the rules on banning FTL for interplanetary transport lifted had been a struggle, even when she'd had near-absolute power. She could have shot a thousand bureaucrats and the rest would have continued to mindlessly oppose her. And there wasn't even any *logic* behind the rule. It had just hung around long enough to be accepted practice, utterly unquestionable by mere mortals.

Tokomak Prime came into view as the starship dropped out of FTL. The planet was practically encased in metal, no less than four rings hosting most of the population orbiting the world, linked to the planetary surface through giant orbital towers. And below...she remembered, grimly, just how many aliens lived on the surface, doing the jobs the Tokomak couldn't or wouldn't do for themselves. And they were plotting...Neola was sure of it. She would have been plotting, if she was in their place. The planet looked strong, the defences almost impregnable, but…it was rotting from within. When the war was over, something would have to be done.

And it will be done, Neola promised herself. *I'll cleanse the planet even if my people have to wash their toilets for themselves.*

"We have a clear teleport corridor to the surface," her aide said. "Whenever you're ready…"

"Do it now," Neola said.

She snorted as the teleport field gripped her, the starship dissolving into golden light that faded to reveal the council chamber. The ancients had never liked or trusted the teleporter, even though they'd *invented* it. They'd forced people to take shuttles or *walk* to their chambers, despite the inefficiency. Neola…once, she'd thought her position was based on naked force. Now, she could see the value in tradition even as she detested it. The ancients had had a legitimacy to their government she'd always lacked.

"Empress," Coordinator Hakav said. He and Admiral Kyan were alone. The remainder of the council was nowhere to be seen. "Thank you for joining us."

"It is my pleasure," Neola lied. When the war was over, when the pogroms were under way, she would take *real* pleasure in having Coordinator Hakav killed. He talked to her as if she was a naughty little child, even though there were only a few decades between them. "I trust, however, that it is *important?*"

Admiral Kyan rubbed his chin. "We have received a set of disturbing reports from the rim," he said. "The humans have left N-Gann. The last reports stated that Mercado has fallen."

Neola kept her face expressionless, although she was planning a quite unpleasant posting for the communications officers who hadn't alerted her *first*. They didn't have *time* for political games. Perhaps a century or two assigned to a polluted rock in the middle of nowhere would teach them a lesson, or at least keep them from causing any more trouble. She put that aside for later and schooled her face into calm. Losing Mercado was embarrassing—she couldn't deny it—but hardly *fatal*. The enemy was still hundreds of light years from Tokomak Prime.

"That is unfortunate, but hardly unexpected," she said, evenly. "We knew the system couldn't be held forever when the humans decided to take it."

"The humans are sending their entire fleet, and those of their allies, to Tokomak Prime," Coordinator Hakav said. "To *here*."

"Yes," Neola agreed. "And they will still have to force their way through a dozen bottlenecks, each one stronger than the last, to reach the homeworld itself. And, when they do, they will face layers of defences like they have never seen before, as well as the majority of our fleet. They will be stopped. They will be crushed."

"Perhaps." Coordinator Hakav didn't sound convinced. "However, you appear to have ignored the impression created by losing so many important worlds, however briefly."

"The humans may take the worlds, if only for a short period." Neola allowed herself a confident smile. "They will find it a great deal harder to *hold* the worlds. We will recover them after the human fleet is destroyed."

"We may lose many more," Coordinator Hakav said. "There have already been riots on two of the inner worlds. What happens when the next riot gains control of an entire planet? Or a star system? Or even a *sector?*"

"Coordinating operations across hundreds of light years isn't easy," Neola said, coolly. "One world exploding into anarchy doesn't mean that others will follow."

"It might," Admiral Kyan said. "We have already intercepted shiploads of subversive literature coming *here*, to the very heart of our power. How much did we *miss?*"

Neola gave him a sharp look. It was a question no one could answer, and he knew it. There were literally millions of warships, freighters, interplanetary transports, tramps and worker craft moving in, out and around the system at any given moment. The war had only made it worse, with so many workers being shipped in and put to work. Internal Security was doing a good job, but it could only search a tiny percentage of the ships moving around the system. If they'd found one load of subversive claptrap, it had been through sheer luck...

And we have no way to know how much passed unnoticed, Neola thought. The various rebel cells were fond of using primitive methods to communicate, assuming—often correctly—that they'd be overlooked when their ships were searched. *There could be a brewing explosion right under our feet and we wouldn't know anything about it until it was too late.*

"And the *lack* of a communications network only makes it worse," Coordinator Hakav insisted. "If there's no network, we cannot break it down and wipe out the individual cells. Instead, we are forced to either locate each cell individually or wait for them to come into the open. And... even a rumour of a successful uprising might trigger a whole string of uprisings."

"Then we crush them," Neola said. She sat down, projecting an air of calm confidence. "We still hold most of the cards."

Coordinator Hakav snorted. "Assuming we lose a third of our industrialised worlds, we will face the humans and their allies on even terms. And that would be disastrous."

"The key word there is *assuming*," Neola countered. "The worlds you mention are vital indeed, true, but they're also the ones that are heavily garrisoned and fortified. I have already given orders for the local garrisons to isolate themselves as much as possible from the locals, even servitor troops. They will act with as much force as necessary to crush any riots and revolutions before they become disastrous. A couple of salutary examples will deter any further rebels from raising their heads."

"The reports suggest the humans managed to get N-Gann back into full production within a week," Coordinator Hakav insisted. "They don't *have* to capture a full third of our industrial worlds to make an impact. They just need to take them off us."

"Then we destroy the industry before they can be turned against us," Neola said.

Coordinator Hakav started. "The combines would be appalled."

Neola put rigid controls on her temper. There was no point in losing it, not now. The empire wouldn't be in so much trouble if the combines hadn't been so determined to exploit their servitors in every way possible. They'd gone well beyond cold-hearted efficiency and into open malice, as if they felt *driven* to torment their slaves. Neola was a firm believer in her race's right to rule the galaxy—only a few dissidents thought otherwise and *they* were normally sent into exile if they dared question the way of things—but tormenting people, even lesser races, for the hell of it was stupid. No wonder the lesser races were plotting revolution. *She* would be doing the same if she was in their place...

The thought gnawed at her mind. Was there another way? Could they discuss peace?

She knew it was impossible. The humans alone were pushing the limits of technology far further than any of *her* people had ever dreamed possible. Even if the war ended without further ado, even if peace could be maintained without mass slaughter, her people would rapidly be outclassed and relegated to the dustbin of history. And there wouldn't be peace, not really. The Tokomak had too many enemies. They were locked in a war that they had to win, or face total destruction. In hindsight...

Coordinator Hakav was speaking. She dragged her attention back to him with an effort.

"It is our belief the human offensive must be stopped before it reaches the core," he said. "And we are resolved to stop it."

"I see." Neola couldn't quite hide her irritation. "And where do you suggest we make our stand?"

"Gateway," Coordinator Hakav said. "It is perhaps the best place to bottleneck them."

"Perhaps," Neola said. She had to admit he had a point. Gateway, one jump corewards from the Twins, would be a good bottleneck. The Twins themselves would be better, but the local population was untrustworthy and the astrographics dangerously unstable. Better to force the humans to fight their way through a bottleneck than risk an engagement that maximised human advantages. "They'll be bled white if they hit the Twins anyway."

"The Twins would put your ships too far from the homeworld," Admiral Kyan said. "We don't know for *sure* which route they'll take."

Neola *was* sure. The humans knew time wasn't on their side. If they thought they could batter their way straight up the chain, without any clever tricks and side trips that would add hundreds of light years to the journey, they'd do it. And she was morbidly certain they thought they *could* punch through her defences. They'd taken a handful of worlds everyone had *known* were impregnable. They'd come up with weapons that turned gravity points into death traps.

But they're not gods, she told herself, firmly. *They can be surprised. They can be beaten.*

She looked up at him. "Is this the will of the entire council?"

"Yes." Coordinator Hakav sounded very certain. "We do not intend to let them get any closer to the core than strictly necessary."

And you'll blame me for any failures, Neola thought. She rather suspected she knew how he'd sold it to the rest of the council. She wondered if he realised they'd been clever enough to make sure he took the blame, if things went wrong. *You wretched piece of...*

She felt a hot flash of anger, mingled with grim respect. She could see the outline of his plan now, a piece of low cunning that wouldn't have been out of place amongst the previous governors of the empire. Either she won, in which case they would share the credit, or she'd be dead. They'd come out ahead whatever happened, unless the humans won the war. But they probably thought she'd take enough of a bite out of the human ships to allow the defenders of the homeworld to finish the job. They might even be right.

"It will take at least three weeks to ready the fleet," she said. They didn't have time for political games. "By then, the human advance should be clearer. I can move to intercept where possible."

"We quite understand," Coordinator Hakav said. "We have every faith in you."

"But we also need to tighten the defences here," Neola continued. "And at Gateway itself, even if it means stripping defences from other systems. The humans must not be allowed to gain even a *tiny* foothold here or everything will be lost."

"The defences are immense and impregnable," Coordinator Hakav insisted. He waved a hand at the ceiling. "Aren't they?"

"The humans have shown themselves very capable at battering down defences that were believed to be impregnable," Neola reminded him. "And even if they fail, the mere fact the attack was *made* will destroy our reputation once and for all. This system has *never* been attacked. Not once, not ever. And if that changes..."

She paused to allow her words to sink in. "We have to admit, here if nowhere else, that the universe will never be the same again. Our dominance will not remain unchallenged, even if we win this war. We have to make some hard choices and stick to them, whatever the cost."

"We cannot pay *any* costs," Coordinator Hakav rumbled. "There are limits..."

"And if we don't, the cost we will pay is the complete destruction of our society," Neola said, bluntly. It was high time they realised that they were playing with antimatter, that their entire society had been playing with antimatter for centuries. And now it was catching up with them. The slightest mistake could prove fatal. "Now, if you'll excuse me, I'll get to work."

CHAPTER TWENTY

The star had no name, merely a catalogue number that had been assigned thousands of years ago by alien astronomers who'd surveyed the system and decided it was largely useless. It was effectively alone in space, save for a handful of asteroids, a pair of comets and a single gravity point. The researchers had speculated, during the short period of time they'd searched for a second gravity point, that the first wasn't *really* associated with the star at all. But they'd left the system—and the puzzle—behind when it became clear there wasn't a second gravity point to be found.

Hoshiko stood in the observation blister and gazed towards the star. It was a single dot of light, seemingly identical to the remainder of the sea of stars. She wouldn't have been sure it was the *right* star if the blister's HUD hadn't marked it out for her. It looked completely insignificant, nothing more than a pinprick. She found it hard to believe that even the smallest star was still immense, compared to a human-compatible planet. But she knew it was true.

The hatch hissed open behind her. She didn't turn. She knew who it was.

"Admiral," General Edward Romford said. "The assault force is deployed and ready to go."

Hoshiko nodded, without looking away from the sea of stars. "You'll be making the plan up as you go along," she said, warningly. "Are you sure you're ready?"

"We know the basics," Romford assured her. "And we shouldn't have any problems dealing with any unpleasant surprises."

Hoshiko turned to face him. "And if things go wrong?"

"We have contingency plans," Romford said. "Worst case, they know we're on the move sooner than we'd like."

"I know." Hoshiko had run the simulations time and time again, giving the enemy as many advantages as possible. The operation should still work, assuming the enemy didn't have an unexpected surprise up their sleeve. But she would prefer to delay the moment of truth as long as possible. "Ideally, I want them to know nothing about our advance until it's too late."

Romford snorted. "Why do I have the feeling I'm being given an invitation to Culloden?"

"I dread to imagine," Hoshiko said. She made a show of looking at her wristcom. "The lead squadron will depart in one hour. You and the assault force will come in afterwards."

"And if you fail to secure the gravity point," Romford said, "there won't be any need for us."

Hoshiko scowled. She'd sent a pair of freighters through the system, on the pretext of using the gravity point to cut hundreds of light years off their journey. There was a lone enemy starship sitting on top of the gravity point, a surprisingly large picket for such an unimportant sector, and a fortress on the far side. It bothered her. The Tokomak had no *logical* reason to fortify the gravity point, unless they expected trouble. Maybe they were just being unimaginative. If so, it had—for once—worked out in their favour. The fortress had to be taken out *quickly*, before it could raise the alarm. Or all hell would break loose.

We can take out the fortress easily, she thought. Her ships carried enough assault pods to make short work of a dozen fortresses. Admiral Webster had warned her it was only a matter of time until the enemy devised countermeasures, but...she hoped she was definitely inside the enemy OODA loop. *But if we do something so noticeable, the planet itself might raise the alarm.*

She put her doubts and fears aside and straightened. It was time to make war.

"Good luck, General," she said. "And *don't* get killed out there."

Romford snapped her a jaunty salute. "I'll try my level best, Admiral," he said. "And if I do get killed, you can just dig me up and put me back to work."

Hoshiko snorted as Romford turned and left the blister, the hatch hissing closed behind him. She would have been happier if Romford wasn't leading the mission in person—he was too high-ranking to expose himself to enemy fire—but he'd insisted, pointing out the tactical and morale advantages. Hoshiko wasn't impressed. She would have flown her flag on the first ship through the gravity point if she hadn't *known* the fleet couldn't have afforded confusion over who was actually in command. There were enough horror stories about the *real* commanding officer, the poor bastard who'd succeeded to command after his superiors had been killed, being utterly unaware he *was* in command until it was too late...she shook her head. Her fleet was a well-drilled machine, with both a primary and secondary chain of command. They'd practiced handling confusion in combat...

Except emergency drills regularly leave out the emergency, she reminded herself, sourly. *We really shouldn't try it under combat conditions.*

She put the thought aside as she turned and peered through the blister, trying to pick out the remainder of the fleet in the inky darkness of space. There were no running lights, nothing that might give them away to a prowling picket...as unlikely as it was they'd run into a picket out here. She knew the ships were there, over two thousand of the most powerful warships anyone had ever produced, but she couldn't *see* them. *Defiant* might as well be alone in the universe. On a cosmic scale, she *was*. The entire fleet was little more than a grain of sand compared to the immensity of the universe.

An odd feeling welled up inside her. She suppressed it with an effort as she turned and stepped through the hatch, pacing down to the CIC. Officers moved everywhere with practiced urgency, the display updating rapidly as the fleet readied itself for war. Hoshiko waved down the marine guard's attempt to announce her as she took her chair, casting her eye over the final set of readiness reports. She hadn't wasted the weeks in transit— they'd carried out hundreds of drills, all simulated—but she knew her crew would have lost their edge. Hopefully, they'd have sharpened up by now. They *knew* the next set of missiles flying at them were going to be real.

Yolanda turned to face her. "Admiral. The fleet is ready for deployment."

"Good." Hoshiko studied the display, hoping and praying that none of her officers had done a little creative editing when they'd written their reports. She understood the determination not to let one's fellows down, but she couldn't risk sending an unready starship through the gravity point. "Inform Admiral Hanker that he is to assume command of Force Two. If he doesn't hear from us on schedule, he is to proceed as planned."

And the only reason he won't hear from us is things going spectacularly wrong, she thought, as Yolanda turned to carry out her orders. *And if that happens, he'll have to punch his way through the gravity point and rush to Tokomak Prime.*

She turned her attention to the secondary display. The tethers were in place. They couldn't move any closer to the star without risking detection, but... the enemy wouldn't see anything amiss if they saw a single freighter heading towards the gravity point. It might be in an isolated region of space, but it wasn't *that* isolated. Her lips curved into a smile as she battled the impulse to walk to the bridge and take command personally. But it would be a *serious* breach of custom and etiquette. And yet, she missed being in command of a ship. Perhaps, just perhaps, she could find a way to get herself demoted to captain and assigned to a whole new starship. But anything that would get an *admiral* summarily demoted would probably also get her dishonourably discharged from the navy.

Maybe I can convince the navy that I should be rotated back onto a starship's bridge from time to time, she thought. *Just so I don't forget what's important while I'm resting my ass behind a desk.*

A timer appeared on the display, counting down to FTL. Hoshiko tensed, telling herself that everything had been planned as carefully as possible. The plan didn't *depend* on absolute perfection. There was plenty of leeway for when things went wrong, as they inevitably would... she sucked in her breath, trying not to think about how much rested on her. She dared not lose. She would *not* lose.

"FTL in ten seconds," Yolanda said. "The remainder of the fleet is standing by."

Hoshiko nodded, stiffly. There was no point in issuing orders now. They would only cause confusion at the worst possible time. Everyone knew what to do, when the time came to do it. She felt oddly like a spectator, watching from the sidelines as her subordinates went to work. She reminded herself, sharply, that *she* was still on the ship. If *Defiant* was destroyed, she'd go with it.

"Five seconds," Yolanda said. "Four. Three... two... one..."

A jerk ran through the ship. The display blanked. Hoshiko felt an unpleasant sensation—she couldn't put it into words—as the tiny convoy picked up speed. The freighter was the largest they'd been able to capture and repurpose, but her drives were civilian-grade and her maintenance hadn't been too good. Hoshiko was inclined to wonder if the Tokomak sometimes deliberately mistuned their drives. It might deter their subordinate races from travelling from world to world...

Or maybe they just don't react to FTL, she thought. She'd always had the impression that FTL was universally disturbing, but... perhaps not. The Tokomak were hardly inclined to make *themselves* suffer if it could be avoided. *If they don't see it as a problem, they're not likely to attempt to fix it.*

"We're entering detection range now," Yolanda warned. "They'll see the freighter."

"But not the warships behind it," Hoshiko said. The Tokomak should only see *one* FTL signature. But...she'd heard the researchers were trying to find ways to pin down FTL signatures that were larger and more inefficient than they should be. The Tokomak had to be trying to do the same for themselves. God knew they'd used freighters to sneak warships into attack range themselves. "They shouldn't be on the alert."

The starship shuddered slightly as she struck the star's gravity shadow, dull rumbles rocketing through the hull. Hoshiko tried to keep her unease off her face as the rumbling grew louder, the starship unable to compensate for the gravitational fluctuations without her FTL drive. She felt as if she were no longer in control, no longer able to shape her destiny...it was funny, she'd often felt, that she was as brave as a lion when she was in control, but a coward when someone *else* held the reins. Her childhood had been marred by constant fights over who had the right to take the lead.

And it's all an illusion anyway, she thought, glumly. *If a shuttlecraft hits something* really *dangerous, or gets targeted by an enemy missile system, it doesn't matter who has their hands on the controls.*

"Ten seconds," Yolanda said. "Admiral...?"

"Proceed as planned," Hoshiko ordered. It wasn't as if they could do anything else, now. They'd been committed from the moment they'd entered detection range. "The crew knows what to do."

The last seconds ticked away. *Defiant* slammed back into realspace with a violence that surprised her, as if space itself had crumbled beneath the ship and sent her falling to an impact that was both utterly destructive and completely harmless. The gravity field seemed to flicker, the compensators screaming as they struggled to hold the ship together. She felt sweat prickle on her back as red icons flared on the status display, fading away seconds later as the datanet realised the ship was undamaged. A green icon glowed brightly. The cloaking field hadn't fluctuated. The enemy picket should have no idea they were there.

"One enemy ship detected, as expected," Yolanda said. "She's holding station on the gravity point."

Hoshiko studied the passive sensors—and the live feed from the freighter, which had cut the warships loose and was now gliding towards the gravity point. She'd considered having the freighter take them all the way to the point, but an alert enemy watchman *might* have noticed the freighter was wallowing heavily and asked the right questions. They had to know what *Odyssey* had done, when she'd escaped the Harmonies and fought her way to safety. And here, with so few ships using the gravity point regularly, it *was* practical to search each and every ship that wanted to transit. She had no doubt they'd try, if they thought they had a reason to be suspicious. It was what *she* would have done.

The drives hummed as *Defiant* crept forward, inching towards the gravity point. Hoshiko braced herself, knowing she *was* a spectator. The ball—and tactical command—was in the captain's hands. The enemy ship seemed blind to their presence, but her active sensors were sweeping space with predictable regularity. They might just pick up *something*, no matter how good the cloaking devices were. And then... Hoshiko wasn't sure *what* the Tokomak would do. Jump through the gravity point at once, even though they might be seeing things, or focus their sensors? If the latter, she'd have to fire at once and hope for the best. The lone starship—a cruiser, judging by its sensor emissions—could obliterate her entire squadron, if it caught her without shields.

That would be embarrassing, she thought, sourly. *Admiral Hanker would never know what happened to us.*

"Entering firing range now," Yolanda reported. "They don't *look* to have seen us."

Hoshiko said nothing. Her heartbeat was so loud she had problems believing the enemy couldn't hear it. The closer they got, the greater the chance of complete success... but the greater the chance of being detected and blown away before they could raise their shields. If there was a cool customer over there, tracking her ships through passive sensors, he could be waiting for her to come *just* a little closer. She asked herself, sardonically, who'd come up with the plan. Her, of course. It was funny how much *cleverer* it had seemed when they were running through the simulations...

Defiant lurched as she fired her first barrage at the enemy ship. Hoshiko watched as the cruiser started to power up her drives and weapons, too late. Her point defence lashed out, but she didn't have time to target the weapons properly. She didn't even have time to fire back or jump out before it was too late. Hoshiko watched, coldly, as the alien ship exploded into a ball of expanding plasma. There were no survivors.

"Target destroyed," Yolanda said. "They didn't even get a message out."

"There's no one to hear it," Hoshiko said, although she knew that might not be true. A star system was a vast place to hide a small fleet of starships, if the Tokomak had realised where they were going and why. She shuddered to think of how much could have happened while she'd been in transit. Admiral Teller's fleet could have been wiped out and she wouldn't know about it, not for weeks. "Order the squadron to assume position on the gravity point and send the freighter for the remainder of the fleet. I want the marines to move as soon as possible."

She turned her attention to the system display as the squadron shook itself down. The recon reports were clear. The fortress on the other side was practically a sitting duck, if she was prepared to abandon subtlety and make her presence achingly clear. The files weren't *too* clear on the settled world beyond, but she doubted it didn't have the usual web of passive sensor platforms watching for possible intruders. If they picked up the destruction of the fortress, they'd have a chance to send the alert further up the chain before it was too late.

And we don't care about the planet, as long as it doesn't get in our way, she thought. The small colony was worthless, from her point of view. It couldn't provide any real support for the fleet, if the locals were inclined to help, nor could it pose a threat to their rear. *They can wait until the war is over.*

Yolanda looked up. "Admiral, the remainder of the fleet is inbound."

"Inform General Romford that he can begin the operation immediately, once he arrives," Hoshiko ordered. In hindsight, perhaps she should have kept the general closer. The longer they delayed, the greater the chance of the ship they'd destroyed missing a scheduled check-in. "And ready the fleet for an emergency transit."

"Aye, Admiral," Yolanda said. "How quickly do you want to move?"

"If we get the alert, I want the fleet to start streaming through the gravity point as soon as possible," Hoshiko said. It irked her that she'd been asked, although she knew it was better to make sure that everyone was clear on what they had to do. If things went wrong, they couldn't afford to waste time issuing orders. "We'll stick with the plan. No need to change things. Not yet."

"Aye, Admiral," Yolanda said.

I should have kept the LinkShip, Hoshiko thought, grimly. *Or asked for a second one from Sol.*

She shook her head. She'd made her call. It had seemed like a good idea at the time...it still did, when she put her doubts aside. But it meant she wouldn't be able to call on the ship...she sighed, inwardly. She'd just have to live with the consequences. And so would everyone else.

We can do it, she told herself. *And who knows? If they realise we're here too early, they might just give Admiral Teller a clear path to Tokomak Prime.*

CHAPTER TWENTY-ONE

I'm getting too old for this shit, General Edward Romford thought, as the captured warship made her way towards the gravity point. *I should have left the mission to one of the young bucks.*

He shifted uncomfortably inside his armoured combat suit. He'd never grown *quite* used to the armour, even though it had saved his life a dozen times. He would have sold his soul for the suit in Afghanistan or Iraq, where near-perfect protection combined with environmental control would be worth its weight in whatever precious substance one cared to name. Not, he supposed, that he would have wanted to go *back* to the hellholes. He'd spent too much of his life trying to help the locals, and watching helplessly as his buddies died while politicians fiddled, to want to do it again. The Solar Union was his home now. If people wanted to wallow in the dirt, without embracing the chance for a better life, they could do it somewhere else.

The timer ticked down, each second feeling like an hour. Romford wondered if the ship itself was aware, if she was determined to avoid being turned against her old masters, or if he was just imagining it. The concept sounded like the plot of a bad movie...his lips curved into a smile at the thought. He'd always had a fanciful streak, although he'd never had the time to make something of it. And, after he'd been rejuvenated, he'd chosen to stay in the military rather than build a new life for himself. *Someone* had to fight to defend the society he'd helped to build.

Maybe I'll write the story later, he thought. *Or get one of my grandchildren to turn it into a movie.*

He braced himself as the timer reached zero. The universe seemed to sneeze, the display going white instead of blanking out. It looked *more* alarming to him, but he supposed the Tokomak felt differently. The entire *ship* felt eerie to him, as if the designers hadn't been human. They *hadn't* been human. The proportions were all wrong, the displays were too bright and uncomfortable and the cabins…he shook his head. If they'd had to stay on the ship for longer than a few days, he would have had to order the cabins refurbished. He'd been in worse places, but the alien ship was just…*alien*.

The display dimmed, revealing a conventional planetary defence fortress. The files insisted there were *no* defences on the gravity point and only two fortresses protecting the planet itself, something that had struck him as odd given that there was little on the planet worth stealing. On the other hand, they *were* on the edge of the inner worlds. Perhaps they thought pirates and raiders would hit the system first, devastating the entire planet for shits and giggles. Worse things had happened, over the centuries. The Tokomak themselves had done most of them. Or maybe they were just buying make-work projects for their industrial base. They had to justify its existence *somehow…*

"Engage the AI overlay," he ordered. They were already within missile range of the fortress, but destroying it was very much a last resort. "And get us permission to teleport."

His chest clenched as he watched the overlay go to work, projecting the image of a *very* senior Tokomak demanding immediate permission to teleport. He'd known a few rich kids and dumbass politicians in his day, but they were humbleness incarnate compared to the Tokomak. The demands were so rude that, if anyone had dared address them to his face, he would have put a fist in theirs. And yet, the xenospecialists swore blind it was how the Tokomak addressed their subordinates. Edward couldn't understand why they hadn't faced an endless series of terrorism, revolts and revolutions. *He* would have been plotting an uprising from the very day his world was forcibly incorporated into an alien empire.

Lieutenant Munoz's voice echoed through the command net. "They're powering down the teleport baffles now, sir."

"Stand by." Edward felt his chest clench again, for a very different reason. Teleporting had never sat well with him, for all sorts of reasons. It was disturbingly easy to block a teleport signal with very basic equipment, if one knew how to do it. The Tokomak didn't use mass teleports to spread their power because they *couldn't*. They had to force their targets to turn off the jamming first. "Teleport as soon as the baffles are down."

He braced himself. "And then activate the jamming field," he added. "I don't want a *single* signal getting out."

The world came apart in a shower of golden light, then came back together as an alien command centre. Edward sighted his rifle on a stunned alien, the unreadable face somehow suggesting horror and terror, and pressed down on the trigger, spraying the compartment with stun bolts. They'd been configured for Tokomak…he breathed a sigh of relief as he realised there were no other races within the command centre. The analysts had insisted there would be no others, but he hadn't been so sure. And if they'd been wrong…

He smiled, grimly, as he surveyed the scene. A dozen aliens lay on the deck, stunned. They hadn't had a chance to sound the alert before it was too late. They'd awake in an hour or so with *massive* headaches, by which time they'd be in the brig and waiting to be repatriated after the war. He watched two of his men press their suits against the computer nodes, using their processors to hack the alien systems. Thankfully, they'd had a *lot* of practice with hacking enemy computers. Their computer security wasn't *bad*, but it tended to assume that any attackers would be *outside* the station. They found it a great deal harder to deal with someone who was already inside. But that, he supposed, was true of everyone. The absence of proper AIs didn't help.

"The weapons and communications systems have been knocked down for good," Lieutenant Hendry reported. "But I can't bring the intruder control system online."

"Probably for the best," Edward grunted. "Can you bring up the internal sensors?"

"Aye sir." There was a pause as Hendry worked his magic. "There are two hundred souls on the station, not counting us. I don't know how much they know."

"They know we're here," Edward said, with utter certainty. They'd planned the assault well, targeting the vital sections, but he'd assumed that word *would* get out. "We'll have to deal with them."

He snapped orders, then forced open the hatch and led the first platoon into the darkened passageway outside. The Tokomak didn't see any better in the dark than humans...he smiled grimly as his suit peered through the shadows, watching and waiting for potential threats while the enemy were blind. There were plenty of ways to continue the fight, if one happened to lose control of the station's command systems, but...would the Tokomak have time to think of them? A human installation would ensure that everyone was armed at all times, just in case someone managed to trick their way onboard or simply force their way onto the station the old-fashioned way. But the Tokomak...he cast his mind back to the aliens he'd stunned. None of them had carried any obvious weapons. It didn't mean they didn't exist—he knew, better than most, how much firepower could be implanted into a seemingly-harmless human being—but it was odd. Perhaps the Tokomak didn't trust their own people with weapons. If they constantly talked down to their subordinates, he could see why. Sooner or later, one of them would snap and gun his former superiors down.

A Tokomak fumbled through the darkness, heedless of the human threat. Edward stunned him, the stun bolt blindingly bright in the shadows. Two more Tokomak ran down the corridor, only to be stunned before they could escape. Edward checked their bodies briefly, finding no trace of any weapons. It looked as if they were completely unarmed. He wondered if they'd have the sense to surrender, if he offered...

His intercom bleeped. "General, we have activity on the shuttlebay," Lieutenant Hendry snapped. "I think they're powering up a shuttle!"

Edward swore. That *was* smart. The shuttles were unarmed, he thought, but they had communications systems and teleport baffles. The shuttle-bay probably also had everything from portable flashlights to tools and weapons that weren't connected to the main datanet and couldn't be shut down remotely. If there were any contingency plans for dealing with unex-pected and unwelcome guests, they probably centred on the shuttlebay. He kicked himself for not targeting the shuttlebay during the first invasion, even though he'd only had a limited number of marines. What price the shuttlebay if they failed to take control of the command core?

"Teleport us there," he snapped. "Now."

"No can do, sir," Hendry said. "They've got the baffles up and running."

Edward fell into a sprint, the rest of the platoon following him. The fortress was vast... tiny, compared to a planetary ring or one of the planned megastructures, but still immense by human standards. Normally, he could get from one end of the structure to another within seconds by using an intership car or a teleporter, yet... that wasn't an option. All of a sudden, they were running out of time.

"Get the other teams to meet us at the shuttlebay as well," he ordered. "And ask the enemy to surrender. Promise them good treatment, in line with the laws of war."

"Aye, sir," Hendry said.

He sounded doubtful. Edward didn't blame him. The Tokomak *really* didn't have a reputation for treating prisoners well. It made sense—they'd been the masters of the universe until recently, with no one being will-ing and able to call them out for being bastards to helpless captives—but now... if they thought they'd meet the same fate as people they'd taken prisoner, they wouldn't surrender. Edward himself would sooner go down, biting and kicking and scratching, than surrender in the certain knowledge it would mean torture, brainburning and eventual death. It would take time to establish a reputation for treating prisoners well...

...*And some moron will claim we should abuse their prisoners because they abuse our prisoners*, he thought. He could see the logic, but it revolted him. *And once we get a reputation for treating prisoners like crap, we'll never get rid of it.*

A Tokomak stepped out of the darkness. Edward crashed into the poor bastard's arm, sending him howling to the deck. The arm was broken, at the very least. There was no time to stop and do anything to help, not now. The platoon kept moving, running down corridors and jumping down dark intership car shafts until they reached the shuttlebay. It was firmly closed, the hatch secured and bolted. The entire system was manual. They'd even managed to disconnect the override.

"Blow the door down," Edward snapped.

Two marines stepped forward and attached shaped charges to the hatch, detonating them a second later. The massive chunk of metal shuddered, then fell to the deck in chilling slow motion. Behind it, he saw a pair of aliens in spacesuits levelling weapons at the marines. They opened fire as soon as they had a clear shot, firing so wildly that Edward was sure they didn't have any formal training. Plasma blasts streaked through the air and splashed angrily against bulkhead. The marines returned fire, switching their weapons to the lethal setting as it became clear the spacesuits provided a certain degree of protection. Stun bolts were dangerously unreliable. Even a simple layer of cloth could keep someone from being stunned, if the bolt didn't touch their bare skin.

A shuttle hovered off the deck and rotated, a pair of improvised weapons hanging from its wings and coming to bear on the marines. Edward was almost impressed. The Tokomak had improvised a defence that might just work. He didn't have time to admire it. He unhooked a grenade from his belt and hurled it at the shuttle, sending the detonation command as soon as it touched the shuttle's hull. The explosion shook the entire shuttlebay, sending the shuttle staggering to one side and then crashing to the deck in a shower of angry sparks. Edward told himself he should be grateful the enemy hadn't had time to rig a self-destruct system. They might have managed to do a great deal of damage if they'd deactivated the safety interlocks and powered up a drive field *inside* the shuttlebay.

The outer airlock exploded into utter darkness. Edward's suit activated its magnetic boots automatically as the chamber decompressed, hundreds of pieces of debris—and alien bodies—being yanked out into open space. He shuddered as he glanced back, just in time to see emergency hatches slamming closed. The Tokomak obsession with safety had served them well, for once. If the hatches had failed, the entire station would have decompressed in short order. He waited for the outrush of air to come to an end, then snapped orders to his men to search the compartment. Two Tokomak in spacesuits surrendered, when they were found, but the remainder were dead. They'd practically killed themselves.

They must have been hoping to get the shuttle out, he thought, as they checked the remaining shuttles and powered them down. *Someone might have noticed if they'd started lasing the planet with emergency signals.*

He shook his head as he stepped back through the airlock and into the pressurised compartment. The reinforcements were arriving, taking control of the giant fortress and transporting the prisoners to the captured alien warship. No doubt they'd find it a more comfortable environment than a standard POW camp, although he doubted they'd be left there indefinitely. The prisoner count now stood at four hundred, and they couldn't *all* fit on the warship without pushing the life support to the limits. They'd have to be shipped elsewhere or dropped on the planet or *something*...

An alien lay on the deck, stunned. "For you," Edward said, "the war is over."

He keyed his communicator as he made his way back to the command core. "Did we get away with it?"

"They didn't manage to get a formal message off," Hendry reported. "There's no hint they managed to get a laser or microburst signal off either.

Long-range sensors *might* have spotted the decompression, but it's quite a jump from a decompression to a captured fortress..."

"Perhaps." Edward had heard a story, once, about a cloaked ship that had suffered an emergency decompression when it snuck through an enemy picket line. It had been jumped and destroyed. "I take it we haven't received any demands for answers from the planet?"

"No, sir," Hendry said. "But we're quite some distance from the colony. If they sent a message at the same moment we teleported, sir, it would still be on the way."

Edward nodded, shortly. He wasn't *used* to factoring the speed of light delay into his planning. Marines either had near-instant communications or *no* communications. The planet might have already realised what had happened...no, the planet probably didn't have the slightest idea—yet—what had happened. The speed of light delay cut both ways. The planet wouldn't have picked up any signals yet.

"Order the operational crew to take command as soon as possible," he said. His marines were good, but they weren't trained to operate the station for more than a few short hours. Besides, he needed them elsewhere. "And send a drone back to the fleet. They can start making transit now."

He allowed himself a feeling a satisfaction, although he knew he was going to get his ass chewed—and not in a fun way—when the commandant heard he'd led the mission in person. The commandant would understand, but... Edward shrugged. It wasn't as if he was *essential*. The marines would go on with or without him. They wouldn't even have time to *mourn* until the war was over.

The command core was a hive of activity when he arrived, men in and out of suits hurrying around and fixing datacores to the alien systems. Hendry was talking to a young woman in naval uniform, either explaining what he'd done to the core or bragging about his bravery during the invasion. It was hard to tell. Edward smiled, reminded himself that he'd been young once, too, and perched on the alien command chair. The Tokomak commander had clearly been a plus-size individual. Edward was big and bulky, for a human, and his suit was bigger and bulkier, but he still felt like a child on the chair. It was big enough for three marines...

He allowed himself to relax as the fleet made transit. The mission had worked better than he'd dared hope. They'd taken the station, they'd made sure no one *knew* they'd taken the station...if they were very lucky, they'd made sure the enemy would have to *guess* how and where Admiral Stuart's fleet had entered the gravity point chain. Even if they worked out the truth, they wouldn't *know* unless they sent a mission to investigate. The occupation crew would keep telling the enemy comforting lies until the deception could no longer be sustained.

"General," Hendry said. He left the pretty young officer and walked over to the command chair. "Admiral Stuart's compliments, sir, and she would like to see you on *Defiant*."

And that means she isn't on Defiant, Edward thought, remembering the punchline of a particularly sarcastic joke. *But she's too professional for that, isn't she?*

He stood. "Inform her that I'll be there in a moment," he said. There was no point in delaying things. The mission was complete. It was time to move on. "And inform Colonel Despard that he has command."

"Aye, sir," Hendry said.

CHAPTER TWENTY-TWO

"There's no hint the planet saw us," Steve said, reassuringly. "Or should I be worried?"

Hoshiko smiled as she played with her fork. She hadn't felt like eating. Only the fact she'd agreed to dine with her grandfather had kept her from skipping dinner and going straight to bed. The food was good, if composed of rearranged biological matter rather than grown on a farm and cooked by a professional, but...she just hadn't felt like eating. And she found it hard to put her fears into words.

"They *might* have played dumb while dispatching a ship to warn the nearest star," she said, quietly. The planet *hadn't*, as far as her sensors had been able to tell, but that might well be meaningless. The LinkShip could travel in FTL without being detected. Given time, the Tokomak might be able to deduce how it worked and start churning out their own. "We cannot be *sure*."

"You *could* have invaded the planet," Steve pointed out. "Why *didn't* you?"

"Pointless," Hoshiko said, dryly. Steve had attended the meetings where they'd hashed out the broad strokes of the plan, then passed it to the tactical staff to be converted into something workable. "They don't have any deep space capability. We'd just be making their lives miserable for nothing."

"As opposed to making their lives miserable for *something*," Steve said. His face, his oddly old-young face, darkened in memory. "I've always wondered if the victims appreciated the difference."

"Probably not." Hoshiko shrugged. "The end result is the same, whatever the reasoning."

She forced herself to take a bite. The food tasted good, though nowhere near as good as her mother and grandmother's cooking. Mariko Stuart had blended American and Japanese traditional foods into a fusion that either worked very well or turned out to be largely inedible. Hoshiko remembered asking why her grandmother kept trying, which had earned her younger self a lecture on why it was important to push the limits and see what they could do. She'd also been told something about *defiance*, but the explanation hadn't made sense to her. It wasn't as if her grandfather and great-uncles had ever refused to eat Mariko's food.

Probably an Earther concept, she mused. Her stomach growled, reminding her that it had been a long time since she'd eaten. *And something we left in the mud when we climbed to the stars.*

"You can't control it," Steve pointed out. "All you can do is hope for the best."

"And prepare for the worst," Hoshiko countered. "Which we have done. I suppose."

She glanced at the starchart, floating in the middle of the cabin. There hadn't *been* a second gravity point within the previous system, which explained—she supposed—why it really *wasn't* that economically important. The Tokomak hadn't really bothered to develop the system, even though there *was* a second gravity point only a few short light years away. But it was effectively unreachable without FTL. The Tokomak themselves had speculated, years ago, that there might be a *lot* of gravity points that were unreachable, simply because they didn't link to a populated system. FTL had opened up the entire universe to them.

And what would have happened, she asked herself quietly, *if they'd never solved the mystery?*

She considered it for a moment, then shrugged. A great deal of evil would remain undone, but so would a great deal of good. And Earth would have remained uncontacted for thousands of years...given the way the Earthers had been destroying themselves, the entire planet might have been blown to hell long before the Galactics finally arrived. If they ever did. Absent FTL, a system without gravity points was unlikely to be very interesting. Or remunerative.

And there's no point in worrying about it, she mused. *We have to deal with the world as it is.*

"Your grandmother was asking when you were going to get married," Steve said. "What should I tell her?"

Hoshiko blinked, then realised her grandfather was trying to distract her. "Tell her to mind her own business," she said. Her people were usually very good at minding their own business. It wasn't as if she'd grown up on one of the *outer* cantons. "I haven't found a suitable partner."

She snorted. She'd been devoted to her career ever since she was old enough to realise that starship command was a possibility. There had been a handful of lovers—girls as well as boys—but none had stayed with her. It wasn't that she didn't want children, one day. It was that she was devoted to her career and...she had the time, if she wished, to build a name for herself before she took time out to have and raise kids. And find someone willing to raise them with her.

"I don't understand it," she said. If he could change the subject to something awkward, she could change it right back. "Why does she think she has the right to *ask*?"

"You can move from the planet to the stars, but you can't really get the planet out of you," Steve said, after a moment. "We oldsters"—he used the term without irony—"grew up in a very different world. What we had to do, back then...we had different rules, different social guidelines, different everything. And the limits shaped our society."

"I know," Hoshiko said. She'd studied history. Quite a few boneheaded decisions actually made perfect sense when you looked at them through their eyes. "But that doesn't give you the right to impose your limits on us."

"I never said it did." Steve's voice remained even. "I always knew the changes would be bad as well as good. And that you would take things in ways I wouldn't expect."

Hoshiko finished her meal and pushed the plate to one side. "You should have realised," she said. "Everything changed for the Tokomak when they developed FTL..."

"Yes, it did." Steve shrugged. "Did you ever download *Atlas Shrugged*?"

"No," Hoshiko said. "Why?"

"It used to be my bible, my *second* bible." Steve looked oddly embarrassed. "I thought it made quite a few valid points. It *did* make quite a few valid points. We *were* heading downwards when the Horde rediscovered Earth. But... Rand, the writer, couldn't envisage how technology would change between her time and the future, or what it would do to human civilisation. Us oldsters couldn't predict how things would change, but we feared the past. You, on the other hand, find newer and better ways to do things all the time... without the connection to the past that kept us grounded."

"I thought that was the idea of the outer cantons," Hoshiko said. "To allow people to experiment without dragging everyone else down if the experiment fails."

"It is," Steve said. "But the *real* danger, as always, lies with the people who want to impose their views and behaviours on everyone else."

He stood. "I'm not scared of the *war*, Hoshiko. I'm scared of what comes after."

"The galaxy changes, again," Hoshiko said. "And the human race goes on."

She watched him go, disturbed in a manner she found almost impossible to articulate. The question—her *grandmother's* question—had bothered her more than she thought it should have. Oldsters were always worrying about things like marriage, as if society hadn't changed…as if she couldn't have her biological cycle frozen until she was ready to have kids. The days when women were slaves to their bodies—and men—were long gone. She could have one man or many men or one woman or many women and no one, absolutely no one, could say anything about what she did with consenting adults in private. It was *her* choice. She was a grown woman. She could do whatever she liked with her body.

As long as I don't break regs, she thought. Soldiers and spacers gave up a little freedom to protect the freedoms of others. Her superiors would not be amused if she broke them without a *very* good reason. The rules were flexible, but not *too* flexible. *And if I hurt myself, I'd probably get in trouble for damaging naval property. I belong to the navy until I retire or they kick me out.*

She snorted at the joke, then rose to inspect the starchart. The fleet was racing to its next destination, a lone gravity point that linked directly to a chain that ran nearly all the way to Tokomak Prime. It wasn't perfect—she'd have to make an interstellar hop near the end of the journey—but it would do. And, if she was lucky, the enemy would try to bottleneck her—when they finally realised she was coming—without realising she *could* make the interstellar hop.

Too much to hope for, she told herself, firmly. A plan that *relied* on the enemy being an idiot was proof that whoever had come up with it *was* an idiot. It would be nice to think the enemy would panic and do the wrong thing, but she couldn't rely on it. She'd just have to assume they'd either move to block her earlier or make a stand at Tokomak Prime itself. *And, win or lose, we'll shake the foundations of their empire.*

She walked into her bedroom, undressed rapidly and sank into bed. She didn't have much time to rest before the fleet reached its destination. It was a shame they couldn't keep boarding fortresses as they passed, but…there were just too many fortresses in the next system for them to have a hope of repeating their early success. She ran through the calculations again, telling herself that Admiral Teller would be in position to lure their fleet away from Tokomak Prime. And if she was wrong…

The intercom shrilled. Hoshiko started, only dully aware she'd fallen asleep. She sat upright, one hand feeling for a weapon that wasn't there. She rubbed her forehead, forcing sleep out of her eyes. She'd been dreaming, but the dream hadn't followed her into the waking world. There was just a faint sense of foreboding that refused to clear, no matter what she told herself. Too much was riding on her for her to sleep comfortably.

She touched her terminal. Her voice, when it came, was hard. "Report."

"Admiral," Yolanda said. "You asked to be woken when we reached the final waypoint."

"Yes." Hoshiko couldn't keep the anger out of her voice, even though she *knew* Yolanda was just following orders. For once, it was a perfectly valid excuse. She forced herself to speak calmly, making a mental promise she'd apologise when she had a moment. She'd known too many admirals who saw apologising as a weakness, something to be avoided where possible. "Have the ships tethered, then readied for departure. I'll join you before we depart."

"Aye, Admiral," Yolanda said. "The fleet will be ready."

Hoshiko closed the channel, then stood and walked into the washroom. The shower was large enough for three or four people, if they were prepared to be friendly. Her lips quirked. She'd heard of captains and admirals who pulled strings to ensure their lovers were assigned to their staff, so they would have their company on deployment, but she'd never seen it. There would be advantages—she'd enjoyed being able to talk to her grandfather on deployment—but disadvantages too. She had the feeling it would be a major scandal, at least in the military. A deep-space survey ship might operate by different rules.

She showered herself thoroughly, then dried and dressed herself in a clean tunic. The sense of foreboding faded, although it refused to vanish completely. She glanced at the terminal as she left the washroom, but saw nothing to alarm her. The fleet was hovering on the edge of detection range, steadily tethering the first squadron of warships to freighters. It was the same trick they'd used before, repeated on a far greater scale. *This* gravity point was used to seeing dozens of freighters every week.

And warships to escort them, in these troubled times, Hoshiko thought. She wished there was a way to get around the limits of her technology. She thought she understood, now, the human advantage...and the limitations it brought with it. What was the point of imagining uses for newer and better technologies if they didn't exist? She put the thought aside and considered her options. *If we could sneak everything up on the gravity point...*

She shook her head. The odds of being detected were too high. And that would mean an alert rushing down the chain...she knew it would happen, sooner rather than later, but she wanted to delay it as long as possible. It was a shame the next system was heavily developed, with a considerable space-based presence. The odds of them getting a message out were dangerously high.

And they might already know we're coming, she reminded herself, as she stepped through the hatch and headed for the CIC. She would sooner have *known* than remain unsure, even if knowing meant being *certain* the enemy knew she was coming. *And if they know, they might have time to react.*

The CIC looked strikingly calm. Hoshiko nodded to the marine on duty by the hatch, then inspected the display as the compartment came to attention. The lead squadron was tethered to a cluster of freighters, ready to be towed—again—into the enemy system. A handful of captured warships sat next to them, crewed by volunteers. They knew the danger of plunging blind into a gravity point. She would have preferred to carry out a proper recon mission, but she just didn't have time. The entire system might be on the alert.

"Admiral." Yolanda's voice was crisp, professional. "Force One is ready to depart. Force Two is holding steady on the edge of detection range."

"As planned," Hoshiko said. She took her chair, taking a moment to compose herself. "Are we ready to move?"

"Yes, Admiral," Yolanda said. "Your fleet is at your command."

Hoshiko studied the display for a long moment. It was important to remember that the enemy might have picketed the system. If there was a lone starship lurking in the night halfway between the waypoint and the gravity point, they might already be within detection range. The display showed a number of freighters making their way in or out of the system. It would be very difficult to *tell* they'd been detected until they ran straight into enemy fire.

"Force One is to depart in five minutes," Hoshiko ordered. There was no point in wasting time. "Force Two is to follow us, whatever happens, in twenty."

"Aye, Admiral," Yolanda said.

Hoshiko took her chair. The fleet wouldn't take *long* to reach its destination, but...what would happen then? A dozen suggestions crossed her mind, few of them good. If the aliens *knew* they weren't expecting a convoy, they might sound the alarm. If the aliens realised the convoy's drive signatures were too large and powerful, they might...she shook her head, firmly. They'd covered all the bases. They'd done all they could. And some things had to be left to chance.

They have no way of knowing we're coming, Hoshiko told herself, as the fleet lurched into FTL. The display changed, showing a simulation of the system they were approaching. *And we're about to give them a nasty surprise.*

Yolanda looked up as the ship shivered, very slightly. "We'll drop out of FTL in ten seconds," she said. "Admiral?"

"They know what to do," Hoshiko said. She was a passenger on someone else's ship. It was irritating, but it had to be endured. "Let them get on with it."

The display blanked as the ship dropped back into realspace, then rebooted hurriedly. A pair of fortresses floated beside the gravity point, surrounded by a small cloud of mines and sensor decoys. Hoshiko had expected capital ships to back them up, but there was nothing larger than a gunboat. They'd probably been redirected to join the enemy fleet, the one she'd smashed weeks ago. It was quite possible the fortress crews didn't even *know* the fleet had been smashed.

Defiant shuddered as she launched four hammers, targeted on the lead fortress. It would be expensive, but the fortress had to be taken out as quickly as possible. Her sensors picked up a picket tethered to the nearest fortress, already powering up her drives. If she managed to make it through the gravity point, the advantage of surprise would be lost. Hoshiko leaned forward, watching avidly as the hammers struck their targets and punched right through their defences. A series of explosions blew both structures to hell.

"Good work," she said, as the gunboats launched a desperate attack on the fleet. They were screaming for help, but it didn't matter. Their messages couldn't go through the gravity point and alert anyone who *could* help. She watched, coldly, as they were picked off one by one without even scratching her paint. The operation had been a total success. "Inform Captain Clearwater that he has permission to deploy."

"Aye, Admiral," Yolanda said. She paused. "Shouldn't we wait for Force Two?"

"There's no time," Hoshiko reminded her. It wouldn't take much to reveal their presence. If she'd been in command, she would have made sure the fortresses sent routine updates every hour on the hour. Or something, just to create a pattern that would set off alarms when it was broken. "And if we don't get through the gravity point now, we might lose our chance to win quickly."

And if that happens, she thought as Captain Clearwater's ship inched towards the gravity point, *we may take heavy losses at the worst possible time.*

CHAPTER TWENTY-THREE

Captain Philip Clearwater braced himself for a warm welcome as *Rufus* slipped through the gravity point. It wasn't the ship's real name, of course. The part of him that was just a little superstitious wished he'd kept the ship's original name when she'd been captured from the Tokomak and pressed into service, but her name wasn't easy for humans to pronounce. And the translation was just laughable. He'd heard of naming ships after people or concepts, but statements? It was just absurd.

He allowed himself a moment of relief as the display dimmed, revealing a cluster of fortresses positioned close to the gravity point. There were too many of them, suggesting the Tokomak in command of the system had gone above and beyond the call of duty in towing fortresses from planetary orbit and emplacing them on the gravity point. It was worrying, given the simple fact that the Tokomak—in theory—had no reason to assume they'd be attacked there. Perhaps they'd simply decided to fortify *all* the gravity points. They'd need to expand their tax base in the wake of the war and charging transit fees would be a simple and easy way to do it. It would cause long-term damage to the interstellar economy, but it wasn't as if it could grind to a halt completely. Anyone who refused to pay the tolls would be at an immense disadvantage compared to those who did.

Unless someone manages to find a way to wring more speed out of their stardrives, he thought. The Tokomak had thought they'd hit the speed limit, but humanity had proved them wrong. *And then the gravity points might be cut off completely.*

He put the thought aside as the conversational overlay went to work, spitting fire and arrogance towards the fortresses. *Philip* would have hesitated to insult someone commanding enough firepower to reduce his ship to free-floating atoms before he knew what had hit him, but the xenospecialists insisted it was how the Tokomak behaved. It helped, he supposed, that he was commanding one of *their* warships. They never sold their most advanced ships to their allies, let alone potential enemies. He wondered if they realised just how badly their edge had slipped over the last few years. A lone starship couldn't be a game-changer, but a whole string of technological improvements certainly *could.*

"We have permission to proceed, Captain," Lieutenant Boscobel said. "They're not even *trying* to impede us."

"Be grateful," Philip advised. "And ready the drone."

"Aye, sir," Boscobel said. "The drone is on standby, ready to launch."

Philip nodded as *Rufus* moved further from the gravity point, steadily gliding out of missile range. The fortresses paid them no heed, more concerned with chivvying the stream of freighters preparing to make transit. *They* were in for a surprise, when they jumped and ran straight into Admiral Stuart's fleet. He smirked, knowing the Tokomak would have no choice but to surrender. They could neither fight nor run. Who knew? Perhaps Admiral Stuart would simply blow them away as soon as they materialised on the far side. It was the safest possible approach.

He allowed himself a moment to survey the system as they reached the first waypoint. It was heavily populated, more heavily industrialised than he'd thought. It was increasingly unlikely that they'd be able to keep the locals from sending an alert up the chain, even if the human fleet managed to capture the other gravity point before the planets and asteroid settlements realised the system was under attack. He sighed, calculating—again—just how long it would take for word to reach Tokomak Prime. It should work out in their favour...he shook his head. Admiral Stuart had made it clear they were to assume that word had been sent from their very first engagement. They had to assume the worst.

And if the best happens instead, he told himself, *we can be pleasantly surprised.*

"Captain," Boscobel said. "We have reached our destination."

"Fire the drone," Philip ordered. The drone *should* be undetectable, at least until it made transit. "And then bring up the jammers."

"Aye, Captain."

• • •

Hoshiko wanted to bite her nails, or do *something* to distract herself from her nerves. It had been too long since *Rufus* made transit, too long since they'd taken possession of the gravity point...she had no idea when the defenders were supposed to check in with their superiors, but she was grimly certain it was sooner rather than later. The defenders on the other side might already be sounding the alert, convinced that they were about to be attacked at any moment...even if they *didn't* expect attack, they'd have to assume the worst. The only upside, as far as she could tell, was that there was no hint that anyone had sounded the alert about the fleet's advance. The defenders hadn't been on alert...

"Drone transit," Yolanda snapped. "I'm downloading the datacore now!"

"Put it on the big display," Hoshiko ordered. "Quickly!"

She leaned forward as the display updated, showing nine fortresses—four more than they'd expected—sitting on top of the gravity point. There didn't *seem* to be any capital ships backing them up, something that bothered her. The enemy could have placed an entire fleet only a few million miles from the gravity point, concealing them under cloak. *Rufus* didn't have modern sensors and couldn't have used them if she had. The enemy could have positioned themselves perfectly, ready to barge forward and sit on the gravity point after she expended her assault pods on the fortresses.

200

Good thing I brought thousands of them, she thought, although she knew there were limits she couldn't ignore. The enemy might have *intended* to force her to deplete her pods on a series of gravity point assaults, weakening her when she finally encountered their fleet. *We can keep moving fast enough to keep them off balance even if they know we're coming.*

She glanced at Yolanda. "Launch the pods."

"Aye, Admiral," Yolanda said. "Pods away...now."

Hoshiko let out her breath as the first wave vanished. The second wave were already moving into position, ready to target the surviving fortresses and finish the job. They'd be escorted by ECM jammers and decoys, just in case any survivors had the presence of mind to sweep the gravity point for the second wave of pods. She hoped it would be enough, if only to keep from expending a third wave. There was no way to get replacements quickly enough to keep the offensive from bogging down.

They can trade space for time, she thought, numbly. Her imagination showed her a string of chokepoints, each one defended by fortresses, automated weapons platforms and limitless mines. *And we cannot afford to lose even once.*

• • •

"The pods are making transit," Boscobel snapped. "They're going live, *now!*"

"Activate the jammers," Philip ordered. "I don't want them getting a single message out."

He smiled, coldly. The jamming field would be noticed, but...if they were lucky, it wouldn't be as suspicious as a fortress screaming for help. It was a shame the planet wasn't on the other side of the star...he shook his head, dismissing the thought. There were so many asteroid settlements in the system that *dozens* of them would pick up a cry for help and relay it to the planetary defences. Philip wasn't sure what they could do about it, if they could do *anything,* but he didn't want to find out the hard way. They could have an entire fleet of warships orbiting the planet...

But they'd be better off keeping them on the gravity point, if they had them, he mused, as the display updated. *They'd be able to recall them to the planet at a moment's notice.*

He watched as the assault pods launched their missiles, a tidal wave of destruction raging towards the enemy fortresses. Half of them had kept their shields up, a common tactic even though it placed immense wear and tear on the shield generators. The remainder were scrambling desperately to bring their point defence and shields online, too late to do them any real good. They really *hadn't* expected to be attacked. His smile grew wider as the missiles picked up speed. There were any number of things they could have done, if they'd thought they were going to be attacked, without putting too much pressure on their systems. But they'd done none of them.

The lead fortresses exploded into an expanding ball of plasma. Two more followed in short order as antimatter warheads battered their shields down and slammed against their hulls. A fourth wobbled, seemingly intact despite taking one hell of a hammering. Philip eyed it warily, then decided the fortress had been knocked out of the fight. Lifepods spewed out of the structure as the second wave of pods materialised, orienting themselves before they spat death at the remaining fortresses. The Tokomak hadn't had time to do more than order the fortresses abandoned. One by one, the fortresses died.

He sucked in his breath as the first squadrons appeared on the gravity point, heading out into open space. Their sensors probed for threats, pulses of energy locating *Rufus*…and holding her. Philip hit his console, bringing the IFF online before his ship was taken for an enemy ship and targeted for destruction. The last thing he wanted was to be blown away by his own side. Everything seemed to hang in the balance, just for a second, then the targeting locks moved away from his ships. He breathed a sigh of relief. He had no illusions. His point defence couldn't have stopped a hammer if it had been aimed at his hull.

"Captain, laser message from the flag," Boscobel said, as more ships appeared on the display. "Admiral Stuart's compliments, sir, and we can stop jamming now."

"Good." Philip nodded. "Deactivate the jammer, then take us out of the assault lane."

"Aye, sir."

Philip sat back in his chair and watched as the row of human ships flowed through the gravity point, dropping into FTL as soon as they were clear of the gravity nexus. It was all too revealing—there was no way they could cloak the FTL emissions—but, if they were lucky, the Tokomak wouldn't have time to react. There were just too many variables. The Tokomak might already be alarmed. They might have picked up some trace of the brief, but extremely violent engagement. And if they had...

He forced himself to relax. He'd done his bit. It was in Admiral Stuart's hands now.

• • •

"Admiral, we'll be on top of the gravity point in seven minutes," Yolanda said. "All systems and weapons are ready."

Hoshiko nodded, stiffly. They were racing against time. The Tokomak were unimaginative, but they weren't *slow*. They'd have more than enough time to get a warning through the gravity point, once they saw her fleet bearing down on them. She'd considered trying to sneak the fleet across the system at sublight, relying on the cloaking devices to shield them from detection, but her simulations suggested the tactic would fail. Too much could go wrong, even if the enemy suspected nothing. They *had* to get to the gravity point before it was too late.

And we might be ahead of any message announcing our arrival, she told herself, *but our FTL drives are doing a good job of announcing our arrival for us.*

She braced herself as the timer ticked down to zero. There hadn't been *any* defences on the gravity point the last time the captured files had been updated, but that had been *quite* some time ago. The Tokomak could have put *twenty* fortresses on the gravity point if they'd been willing to strip the planet bare...in some cases, it might even have been a wise move. It struck her as overkill, but the Tokomak were firm believers in overdoing something if they had to do it. She had to admire the degree of redundancy they'd built into their systems. If they'd known when to stop, they might have been *quite* impressive.

Defiant lurched as she dropped back into realspace. Hoshiko leaned forward, watching as the display updated. There were four fortresses on the gravity point, all with shields and defences firmly in place. They'd seen her coming...she snapped commands, despite knowing that her staff knew what to do. The cruiser shuddered as she fired a spread of hammers, aimed right at the fortresses. If they were lucky, they might just take out the fortresses before they could return fire.

The display sparkled with red light. No such luck. The fortresses were alert...whoever was in command had the authority and nerve to bring his fortresses to full alert, despite not knowing *precisely* what was going on. A spread of missiles hurled themselves towards her ships, a smaller spread of missiles closed on her hammers...she swore as they detonated, antimatter blasts wiping the hammers out. It was an ingenious tactic, one she'd seen before. The Tokomak must have been doing everything in their power to update their tactical databases. If they wiped out *all* her hammers...

"Conventional missiles," she ordered. Hammers, by their very nature, couldn't be disguised as anything else. The Tokomak would have no trouble taking them out. "Fire."

"Aye, Admiral," Yolanda said. "Firing...now."

Hoshiko watched, grimly, as the enemy missiles slipped into her point defence envelope. They'd clearly learned a *lot* from the previous battles, more than she'd anticipated. She'd expected to see more of their missiles being picked off, but instead...she gritted her teeth as a handful of enemy missiles slipped through the defences and exploded against her ships. The warheads were conventional—the Tokomak hadn't come up with anything new, not here—but it hardly mattered. They'd do a great deal of damage if they weren't stopped.

"Deploy additional ECM drones," she ordered. The enemy had definitely improved their targeting. It looked as if they weren't quite so fooled by her ECM as she'd hoped. "And modify their counter-targeting programs to match enemy..."

A missile slipped through her defences and struck her hull. She bit off a curse, telling herself the shields could take it. Her cruisers had the strongest shields in the known universe, at least for ships of their size. Tokomak battleships had bigger and better shields, but they did it through cramming more shield generators into their hulls and rotating them to provide additional protection. Human researchers claimed it wasn't as efficient as they thought, but Hoshiko could see the advantages. It would have to be a *very* big power surge to take out *every* shield generator on a battleship.

"Admiral, a freighter made transit," Yolanda snapped. "I..."

"Target her," Hoshiko ordered. If the ship had a chance to cycle her drives and jump out, the secret would be thoroughly blown. "Now..."

The fortress commander was having similar thoughts. He spat out more missiles, moving half of them to shield the freighter as it struggled desperately to jump back through the gravity point. Hoshiko watched, praying to a god she didn't quite believe in, only to recoil in disappointment as the freighter vanished bare seconds before her missiles could kill it. She opened her mouth to order her chased through the gravity point, then changed her mind before she could issue the orders. There was no point, not any longer. The freighter would start screaming the moment she was on the far side...

The secret is blown, she thought. *And...*

"Admiral, the remaining fortresses are signalling surrender," Yolanda said. "They're..."

Hoshiko felt a surge of anger. She was tempted, very tempted, to just keep firing until every last enemy fortress was dead. They'd put a major crimp in her plans, even if they hadn't known it at the time. But... she knew she couldn't afford to waste missiles killing the fortresses if it could be avoided. Her supply lines were so weak, they were practically non-existent.

You knew things would go wrong, she reminded herself. *And you expected to lose the advantage of surprise a great deal earlier.*

She turned to Yolanda. "Order them to stand down," she said. "General Romford and his men can secure the fortresses, then transfer the survivors to the nearest planet. The remainder of the fleet is to secure the gravity point itself."

"Aye, Admiral," Yolanda said. "What about the rest of the system?"

"Broadcast a demand for surrender," Hoshiko ordered. She doubted the Tokomak would surrender in a hurry, at least until she threatened the planets themselves, but it didn't matter. She'd settled for holding the gravity points and leaving the rest of the system to take care of itself. "And then inform them they'll be getting the prisoners."

"Aye, Admiral," Yolanda said.

It wouldn't be a problem, Hoshiko was sure. The planetary governments would have no trouble taking care of a few thousand additional mouths. They'd be surprised the prisoners hadn't been transferred to a POW camp, but she didn't have time. The rest of the POWs could be dropped on the planets too. It wasn't as if she needed them. If she won the war, they could go home; if she lost, she'd have worse problems. She doubted the Tokomak would bargain for the POWs as their fleets closed on Earth.

She sat back in her chair, telling herself she'd won. The enemy had lost far more than herself... she sighed, knowing she'd lost the advantage of surprise. The enemy knew she was coming now. Word would spread with all the speed of bad news... very unwelcome when it arrived, but still important. The enemy would start preparing for her...

Now it's a race, she thought, numbly. *And one we might lose.*

CHAPTER TWENTY-FOUR

Hameeda watched, from a distance, as assault pods slipped through yet another gravity point and unleashed their missiles on the enemy defences. The Tokomak were *definitely* alert now—they'd laid thousands of mines on a gravity point that had been undefended only a few short months ago and backed them up with a dozen fortresses—but it wasn't enough to do more than slow Admiral Teller for a few short minutes. Hell, she reflected, he'd slow himself more than anyone else. The only innovation was a cluster of fortresses positioned some distance from the gravity point, just outside assault pod missile range. It would have been a more serious threat if they hadn't been outside their own range too.

She frowned as a cluster of enemy warships dropped out of FTL and linked up with the fortresses, daring their human enemies to either come to them—at which point they'd have to tangle with the fortresses—or risk exposing their backs when they moved to secure the planet and the other gravity points. Someone on the other side was guilty of *thinking*, she noted sourly. They didn't have the firepower to recover the gravity point and they knew it, but they hadn't let themselves be daunted either. Who knew? They might delay Admiral Teller long enough for the relief fleet to arrive.

Her neural net provided a handful of possible scenarios, each one worse than the last. If the Tokomak had dispatched a relief fleet the moment

Admiral Teller had punched his way out of N-Gann, the fleet might be bearing down on them already. If they'd only just realised the humans were on their way, it would be several more weeks before their fleet arrived...giving Admiral Teller the chance to meet them halfway. A chill ran down her spine as an alert flashed, warning her that a cluster of starships *was* heading towards the gravity point. The only thing that kept her from sending an alert to Admiral Teller was the simple fact that the formation looked too old and too small to be a massive enemy fleet. It was much more likely it was a particularly unfortunate convoy.

She sent the alert anyway, then continued to monitor the enemy positions as Admiral Teller secured the gravity point. He was taking his time, although—for once—she supposed it worked in his favour. He certainly didn't want the enemy to recapture the gravity point, putting them in a position they could use to force him into a disadvantageous environment. It was better to make sure he held the position, even if it cost him. She watched the convoy as it inched closer, wondering if the enemy warships would try to warn it away. The poor bastards were flying straight into a war zone.

I guess they never heard the alert, she mused, as the seconds ticked down to zero. *I wonder if they'll be able to reverse course and get out in time...*

She blinked as the convoy dropped out of FTL, far too close to the enemy fortresses for comfort. It *wasn't* a convoy. It was...she stared in disbelief, silently counting the number of outdated warships towed by freighters and flown by...flown by whom? The Tokomak seemed equally surprised, hastily retargeting their weapons. The ships weren't friendly, not to them. But...Hameeda brought up her own tactical sensors as the newcomers fired, aiming at the fortresses. Their missiles were primitive, but there were a *lot* of them. She launched her hammers, despite the expense. A chance to take out the enemy fortresses could not be missed.

A message blinked up in front of her. The newcomers were begging for help...? She forwarded the message to Admiral Teller as she watched the battle, noting how the newcomers were taking a pounding despite numbering the Tokomak. Their missiles and ECM were good, but they didn't come up to Tokomak standards. They lost four ships for every one the Tokomak lost. They even resorted to ramming the fortresses and starships to even the odds. Thankfully, Admiral Teller managed to come to their aid before it was too late.

Well, Hameeda thought. *Who the hell are you?*

She watched, numbly, as Admiral Teller reorganised his fleet. One squadron raced to the next gravity point, while two more headed to the planets themselves. The radio messages suggested the planets had risen in revolt, savage fighting breaking out on and around the ring. She hoped that meant the Tokomak were going to lose control quickly, but... they might fight to the death if they thought they couldn't surrender. Or that they'd be executed when they went home if they *did.*

They can stay with us, she told herself, as she received orders to recon the planets. *They don't have to go home.*

But she suspected, deep inside, that it wouldn't be enough for the prisoners.

• • •

Admiral Colin Teller knew, without false modesty, that he was no diplomat. The fleet didn't have *many* diplomats and almost all of them had been left behind on N-Gann, where they were helping the provisional government become more than *just* provisional. There hadn't seemed any real *need* to bring diplomats, not when they were on the cusp of total victory or total defeat. It had been a surprise when the Tokomak had started to surrender. And it was even more of a surprise to know there was a rebel fleet capable of putting up a pretty good fight.

Although they would have been slaughtered, if we hadn't come to their aid, he thought, mordantly. He'd watched the battle, then studied the analyst reports. The rebels had fought with a desperation that awed him, but they'd come far too close to being trashed. Only their willingness to use suicide tactics had saved them from a quick and completely one-sided defeat. *They gambled everything on our help.*

He studied the two aliens as they were escorted into his ready room. One was a humanoid octopus, looking faintly uncomfortable in the dry human air; the other was wrapped from head to toe in a shapeless black garment that made it impossible to tell anything about his race beyond the simple fact he was humanoid too. Colin would have been more worried about just *what* had boarded his ship if the bioscanner hadn't assured him that he wasn't facing a Tokomak. Besides, the Tokomak were hardly likely to sacrifice thousands of lives just to make a false flag operation look particularly convincing. It would have been strikingly out of character, with no real guarantee of success.

"Lord Admiral," the octopus said. "We thank you for liberating our star system."

"You're welcome," Colin said. The system hadn't been liberated yet, not completely. There were still Tokomak holdouts on the ring, bombarding rebel positions as they prepared themselves for a final assault. The planet itself wouldn't be free until they were talked into surrender or simply destroyed. "We do have to press on, however. The war won't end until…"

"We quite understand," the octopus said. "But we must ask what you intend to do after the war."

Colin frowned. "It depends on how the war ends," he said. "It is our intention to fight our way to Tokomak Prime and end the war if the Tokomak refuse to discuss peace earlier. It is hard to make any promises prior to actually ending the war…"

"We quite understand," the octopus said, again. "What are your *intentions* towards our worlds?"

We need a diplomat up here, Colin thought. *In hindsight, this development was obvious.*

He silently promised himself that he'd have a sharp discussion with the analysts afterwards. They'd *known* there were thousands of starships and ntire communities, some of them consisting of entire *races*, that existed the books. It wasn't *that* unlikely that they could build up fleets of their , even though they were no match for the Tokomak in a straight fight.

They were the Rebel Alliance, matched against the Galactic Empire. It was a shame no space wizards with laser swords were coming to their aid.

"We have no intentions towards your worlds," Colin said. "Right now, we want—we need—to win the war. The Tokomak will take a horrible revenge if we lose. Afterwards, our sole interest will be in maintaining free navigation and trade."

He wondered, grimly, if that was actually true. The Tokomak were a huge problem, but their successor states might—in time—become an even *worse* problem. They'd be innovating, something the Tokomak had forgotten how to do; they'd be eventually fighting and feuding amongst themselves, setting off an endless series of wars that might consume Earth. He could easily see some people back home arguing that humanity should take control of galactic society, all for the greater good. It was impossible, of course. There just weren't enough humans to even *try*.

The octopus made a set of odd gestures. "And how do we know that is true?"

We could have left you to die, Colin thought. *Your deaths would have soaked up missiles that would otherwise have been aimed at us.*

He tried not to let that thought show on his face as he marshalled his thoughts. "I am not a diplomat," he said, with the private thought that neither were they. "I have certain powers, when it comes to making arrangements with other political factions, but they are always subject to confirmation by my superiors. I could promise you everything you wanted, or nothing, yet there would be no guarantee my superiors would honour the agreement. They wouldn't *have* to confirm it.

"That said, I don't believe we have any particular interest in your worlds. We're a space-dwelling society. We have little interest in anything larger than a moon. We see no point in fighting over worlds we don't want, let alone imposing our values on other civilisations. Our only real interest is the gravity points themselves, which we use for free trade.

"*That* said, there is a war on, a war we have to win. It is in your best interests to help us as much as possible, knowing that you too will bear the brunt of their anger if we lose. If you can't help us, or if you won't help us, I suggest you head back to the shadows and stay out of the way. The Tokomak might not notice that you helped us here."

"A valid point," the octopus said. "And we will do all we can to ensure your victory."

He paused. "However, we intend to remove the Tokomak from our worlds afterwards."

The words hung in the air for a long moment. Colin shuddered. Repatriating millions of Tokomak would be difficult, if not impossible. It would take *years* to transport entire populations back to their home-worlds, back to the colony words that were unquestionably *theirs*... he shuddered, wondering if the resistance intended to do more than *just* deport the Tokomak. The hatred the Tokomak had engendered was terrifying in scope. They might be unceremoniously exterminated if—when—they lost control for good.

He struggled to choose his words. He understood, all too well, why the aliens would want a little revenge. They'd suffered so much, over the past few thousand years. But... the Solar Union had been built on the principle of leaving the past in the past, where it belonged. No one who migrated to space got to keep and brood on old grudges. They had to let them go so they could walk into the future. And there was no guarantee the Tokomak would be crushed beyond all hope of recovery. A series of atrocities could set off another series of atrocities... a cycle of hatred and destruction that wouldn't end until large swathes of the galaxy were rendered uninhabitable. There would be death and destruction on an unimaginable scale.

"We understand," he said, finally. "However, we do not intend to allow helpless civilians to be slaughtered..."

"They are not civilians," the octopus insisted. "They are *oppressors!*"

"The ones who are guilty of war crimes, personally guilty, can be tried 'ter the war," Colin said. "But the ones who are largely innocent should be made to suffer, even if you do want to send them home."

He groaned, inwardly. "If nothing else, we don't want to give them incentive to repay your hatred in kind," he added. "Your worlds are still vulnerable."

The octopus looked displeased, although it was hard to be sure. "We will take whatever decisions we see fit," he insisted. "We want them off our worlds."

"And we can move them, after the war is over," Colin said. "Until then, we have more important things to worry about."

He changed the subject, discussing precisely what the alien resistance could offer. It was more than he'd expected, although—in the absence of a human fleet—it was little more than a minor headache for the Tokomak. There were aliens represented throughout the system, all holding low positions the Tokomak didn't want for themselves. Colin had to smile at just how much trouble a lowly clerk could cause, if he wanted to reroute or misfile paperwork or even refuse it on the grounds it hadn't been filed in triplicate. The intelligence insights alone would be worth their weight in gold, if they could be trusted. He was grimly aware the Tokomak might have broken the cells long ago, putting their own agents in place to lure the rebels into a false sense of security. But, if so, it had bitten them rather sharply.

"We do have a fleet," the octopus said. "But our weapons are weak."

"We can provide more," Colin assured him. They'd captured quite a few Tokomak stockpiles. Their missiles could be fitted onto the older warships in a hurry. "But we need to resume the offensive."

They exchanged a few more pleasantries before the alien rebels were escorted back to their ships. Colin watched them go, then rubbed his forehead as soon as the hatch was firmly closed. He really *wasn't* a diplomat. He thought they respected him for making that clear, and explaining the limits of his power, but it was hard to be sure. If Steve Stuart had remained at N-Gann, Colin would have called him forward. Steve Stuart had enough authority and prestige to convince the Solar Union to accept whatever deal Colin made, unless it was grossly unfavourable to the human race. Perhaps even then... Colin shook his head. Steve Stuart and Admiral Stuart were somewhere on the other side of the inner worlds, hacking their way towards the core. He wondered, idly, if the Tokomak had realised they were coming yet.

He frowned as he checked the latest intelligence download. His staff had discovered reports of enemy fleets mobilising, and a stream of warnings to local commanders, but little hard data. There were alerts concerning *his* fleet, as expected…nothing, as far as they could tell, about Admiral Stuart's fleet. The Tokomak seemed more concerned about an ever-growing series of terrorist attacks, revolts and outright rebellions spreading through their empire, yet…it looked as if they were cutting a number of worlds loose while they concentrated on the invaders. He silently admired their perception, even though it was a major problem. If they won the war, they could recover the lost worlds at leisure; if they lost, it wouldn't matter *what* happened to the rebel worlds. And yet…

The orders to local garrisons were blunt. They were *not* to cede control to the rebels, whatever happened. They were to use whatever force was required to keep the rebellions under control, even if it meant destroying entire cities and depressurising entire sections of the planetary rings. The Tokomak might not be reinforcing quickly, if at all, but it might not matter. And then…he shuddered to think of wave after wave of slaughter spreading across the empire. Millions of people, billions or trillions of people, were going to die. The hatred the Tokomak had earned was coming back to destroy them.

He keyed his terminal, bringing up the holographic starchart. There were four more transits between his fleet and the Twins…and, beyond the Twins, Gateway. It was unlikely the enemy would let them get any closer to Tokomak Prime before intercepting them, if only to ensure the deci-sive battle wasn't fought at Tokomak Prime itself. Indeed, he *wanted* to be intercepted. It would give Admiral Stuart a clear shot at Tokomak Prime.

"And there are supposed to be rebels on the Twins," he mused. He w what the marines were meant to do, but he knew better than to t on it. "And…"

He shook his head. The LinkShip would have to recon as far core-wards as Gateway. If she could make contact with the rebels, so much the better...he sighed. He hated being dependent on something outside his control. But it couldn't be helped. A series of revolutions on alien worlds would help his fleet, even if it got millions of people killed.

And what will become of us, he asked himself, *if we ignore the cost of our war?*

It was an unpleasant thought, but...he told himself, firmly, that it wasn't *his* fault. The Tokomak had ruled the known galaxy for centuries. They'd been stagnating when humanity had been experimenting with fire and inventing the wheel. The hatred had been building up on a galactic scale long before humanity had realised it wasn't alone in the universe. And there would have been an explosion, sooner or later, even without the war. The Tokomak had made their bed for themselves, long before he'd been born. It wasn't his fault.

And yet he knew that he'd think otherwise, deep inside, for the rest of his days.

CHAPTER TWENTY-FIVE

Perhaps I should have invested in that sexbot, Hameeda thought as she followed the fleeing freighter through the gravity point. *It would have provided a very welcome distraction.*

The universe dimmed, then settled back into normality. She opened her sensors as wide as she could, assessing the defences on the far side. The Tokomak didn't seem to value the system very much, as far as she could tell. They were laying a small minefield, backed with automated weapons platforms, but little else. The handful of warships holding station near the gravity point looked ready to flee at any moment.

Which makes a certain kind of sense, Hameeda thought, as she steered away from the enemy freighter. She'd followed it through the gravity point to make certain any watching eyes would miss her transit, despite the risk. The LinkShip wouldn't survive if she accidentally interpenetrated with the freighter. *There isn't much in the system worth fighting for.*

She paused long enough to study the torrent of incoming data. The Tokomak were already pushing mines onto the gravity point itself, hoping to cripple or destroy any starships unlucky enough to interpenetrate when they made transit. They assumed, probably correctly, that the next ships to come through the gravity point would be hostile. They couldn't stop a determined offense, led by a wave of assault pods, but they could tie up the attackers and force them to expend vast amounts of firepower breaking into the system. Or maybe Admiral Teller would just cram a freighter full of antimatter and send it in first. The blast would clear the gravity point and blind sensors for thousands of kilometres around.

The system itself was largely worthless, she decided. There were a handful of colonies on the rocky worlds, but none of them looked particularly large. One of the worlds appeared to be undergoing a very slow terraforming process, as if they'd started work and then decided to abandon the project to random chance a few years later. The others were airless wastelands, with little to recommend them. She glanced at the sensor readings, then decided not to bother investigating them more closely. The follow-up units could do that when the system fell.

She slipped into FTL and raced towards the gravity point, dropping out when she reached the edge of detection range. There were five warships holding station on the point, constantly shifting position in hopes of making it harder for any watching eyes to target them. Hameeda watched them for a moment, deciding there was no pattern to their movements. They were surrounded by a network of sensor platforms, filling space with active sensor pulses. It looked as if they were determined not to have anyone sneak up on them and shove a missile through their shields.

Smart, she thought. *Admiral Teller couldn't get a cloaked ship through that.*

She felt a flicker of alarm as a sixth enemy warship materialised on the gravity point. It glided forwards and took a place amongst the defenders, allowing one of the other ships to move back and jump out of the system. Hameeda nodded in cold understanding. There would be a rota, with the defenders on the other side assuming that something had gone wrong when a starship missed its jump. Clever, she admitted. The enemy would have *some* warning before the human fleet attacked … she glided forward and jumped through the gravity point, bracing herself for anything from sensor sweeps to incoming fire. But there was nothing…

A flicker of fear ran through her as she saw how *much* firepower the enemy had assembled on the gravity point. Twelve fortresses, five of them attached to tugs designed to tow them away from the gravity point when the shit hit the fan, backed up by a minefield so vast she honestly thought she could walk right across it. There were only a handful of actual warships, she noted, but…they were hardly necessary. Admiral Teller could take the system, if he was prepared to pay the price. And it would weaken him for the decisive battle.

She glided away from the point, her passive sensors picking up messages from all over the system. It was a mess. Half the asteroid settlements had declared independence, while there were reports of fighting on the planetary surface…she wished she had time to survey the entire system to determine just how much actual *truth* was in the reports. But she didn't. Instead, she set course for the next gravity point and jumped through. The defences in the third system were even *bigger*.

And then we'd reach the Twins, she mused, as she disconnected from the neural net. *And the defences there are awesome.*

She caught some sleep as the LinkShip headed to the next gravity point, then woke up in time to inspect the defences before transiting. The gravity point wasn't as heavily defended—hundreds of freighters were coming and going at all hours—but she was still wary enough to lurk under cloak and monitor the situation for an hour before jumping through the gravity point. The defences were *staggering*, backed up by three squadrons of warships. She couldn't help wondering just how many starships the Tokomak thought were coming in their direction. A *million*? It was a grim reminder of just how much firepower the Tokomak had built up over the years. She wondered, suddenly, if they'd always *intended* to fortify the gravity points, sooner or later. It might explain why they'd built so many fortresses to defend worlds that had been in no real danger.

Unless they also wanted to deter rebellions, she thought, although she wasn't so sure. The Tokomak didn't *need* million-ton fortresses to deter rebels from coming into the open. A handful of automated weapons platforms would be more than enough, if the rebels had no space-based firepower of their own. *But I suppose the rebels did manage to put together a fleet.*

She laughed as the truth dawned on her. The Tokomak had told the entire galaxy that they were invincible. They even believed it themselves! And they didn't *dare* lose, not even once. A single defeat would be the end of their reputation for being invincible... she had to smile, despite the seriousness of the situation. They could lose a thousand warships in an afternoon without materially affecting the balance of power, but if they lost just *one* ship everyone would start to wonder if they could be beaten. She felt her smile grow wider as she contemplated the thought. If losing one ship would be enough to shake them, how about all the ships they'd lost since the war began?

Her sensors continued to update as she glided away from the gravity point, drawing in information from both sides of the binary system. The Twins were *huge*, unbearably huge. There was enough industry in the system to keep an entire sector supplied and yet... it was small, compared to Tokomak Prime. Seven gravity points were clearly visible, each one linked to a different sector of the empire. No wonder the Tokomak were so keen to keep control of the system. If they lost the Twins, they'd lose contact with a sizable percentage of the known galaxy.

And that means they'd be willing to pay any price to recover it, she thought, as she sent the signal. *They dare not leave us in control for any longer than strictly necessary.*

Ice trickled down her back as she waited, feeling dangerously exposed. The microburst was, in theory, impossible to detect without human-grade equipment, but she had her doubts. And besides, there was so much electronic noise in the system that it was quite possible the burst signal would be lost in the haze. It wouldn't be the end of the universe if she didn't make contact with the deep-cover operatives, but... she had orders to at least *try* before she sneaked through to Gateway. The enemy fleet *had* to be fairly close by now. Admiral Teller might wind up facing a far greater threat than he'd anticipated when the time came to fight his way into the Twins.

Unless they've worked out what we're doing, she mused. *And they've decided to ignore us while they deal with the other threat.*

She smiled as she picked up a response, a coded message giving her a set of coordinates. She altered course, remaining firmly under cloak as she headed to the RV point. The location was inhabited, but seemingly off the beaten track. It looked like a handful of asteroids that had been mined out, without ever being formally converted to settlements or simply melted down completely. She tensed as she circled the settlement, watching for enemy warships. There were thousands of places that were effectively off the books, if Piece had been telling the truth, but it was hard to tell if they were *really* secret. Someone would have known the asteroids had been mined out, wouldn't they?

And there are limits to how far anyone could fiddle the paperwork and the records, she thought. The Tokomak were obsessive bureaucrats. There couldn't be a single incident without it being logged and investigated, even something as insignificant as an additional screw being placed in the repair kits before they were sent out. *And if they start looking for discrepancies in the files, they might just start finding them.*

A lone freighter drifted near the settlement, seemingly dead. She pinged it lightly and received a reply. Her sensors swept over the ship as she drifted closer, picking out the teleport beacon. She had an odd flash of *déjà vu* as she teleported the single human off the ship and straight into a stasis chamber. It couldn't be...could it?

She put the LinkShip on automatic, ready to drop into FTL and run if hostile warships showed up, then walked down to the stasis chambers. Piece floated in a beam of blue light, utterly unmoving. Hameeda felt a hot flush of anticipation, mingled with embarrassment and the grim under-standing that she had a job to do. She didn't have long. She'd have to be on her way to Gateway before the Tokomak realised that Admiral Teller was resuming his advance.

The stasis field snapped out of existence. The tractor fields caught Piece and held him while he steadied himself. His face spread into a broad smile when he saw her, clearly remembering the nights they'd spent together during their first voyage to N-Gann. Hameeda was tempted to drag him into her bedchamber at once, but duty came first. She had no intention of trying to explain her failure to her superiors.

"It's good to see you again," she said, as the tractor field released him. "If you'll come with me...?"

"It's good to see you too." Piece sounded rough, as if he wasn't quite sure how to speak properly. She guessed he'd spent most of the last few weeks speaking one or more of the galactic tongues. "I'm surprised you made it here."

"The fortresses are growing stronger all the time," Hameeda said. She led him into the gallery and produced coffee for both of them. "Next time, I might not be so lucky."

She sat down and took a sip of her drink. "Admiral Teller will be here in two weeks," she said, softly. "I've been asked to ask...can you move by then?"

"Yes." There was no doubt in Piece's voice. "The real difficulty will be holding the cells *back* until Tokomak One has been taken or destroyed."

Hameeda nodded, curtly. She'd spotted the vast installation holding position over the planetary ring. It was immense, big enough to take a hammer without being instantly destroyed...although she suspected the burst of intense radiation would kill anyone who wasn't taken out by the blast itself. And it had had its shields and sensors at full power for as long as she'd been watching it. She hoped Piece had a plan to deal with the massive fortress. If he didn't, the revolt would come to a sharp and thoroughly unpleasant end.

She put the question into words. "Can you take it out?"

"We think so," Piece said. "And if the attack fails, we can draw back...probably."

Hameeda arced her eyebrows. "Probably?"

Piece met her eyes, evenly. "I don't think you grasp just how much naked *hatred* has been repressed over the last few thousand years," he said. "Just how much the resistance wants to take action, even if it means certain destruction. I've spent most of the last week trying to keep them from mounting attacks against civilian targets, everything from schools to hospitals and pleasure dens. If there are any real delays, I think the resistance leaders will lose control."

"And there's no way to guarantee when Admiral Teller will arrive," Hameeda mused. "The defences back there"—she jabbed a finger towards the distant gravity point—"are really quite something."

"So I've been told," Piece said. He produced a datachip. "Copies of our intelligence findings, some more useful than others. They have eyes and ears everywhere. Hopefully, Admiral Teller can make some use of it."

"Hopefully," Hameeda echoed. "Is there anything we can *count* on?"

"No." Piece shook his head. "There *are* plans to fuck around with their command and control networks, when the shit hits the fan, but you know how many redundancies they work into their systems. It's quite possible they'll simply reroute around the blockages and corrupt subsystems and take revenge later, once the battle is over. I have been told there are cells on some of the fortresses, but they may not be able to take direct action. The Tokomak don't trust local labour these days. Rightly so."

"I understand," Hameeda said. "How are *you* coping, here?"

"I survive," Piece said. "Martin and his team are training for war, of course. I have to deal with the planning and negotiate with the rebels...do you realise they're already arguing over who gets what, when the uprising is over and they've won? It wasn't a problem before because victory looked a little unlikely, but now...they're on the verge of falling out."

"And before they've actually won," Hameeda said. "Are you sure they can be trusted? If one or more of them is working for the enemy..."

"I can't," Piece said, flatly. "There's no way we can vet them. And yes, you're right. The Tokomak might have sneaked operatives into the resistance long ago and steered it away from doing anything drastic. But...I don't think so. They just don't have that sort of mindset. And the cell network is *designed* for decentralised command. The Tokomak would probably be happier if the resistance was a single hierarchical organisation with top-down control. That would be easier to keep harmless and eventually destroy, when it became dangerous."

Hameeda winced. "I don't envy you."

"As long as we stay in the shadows, we're relatively safe." Piece smiled at her. "Places like this settlement, and countless others, are ignored. There are whole shipping networks that exist without anyone paying official interest to them. I think there are actually some *Tokomak* who've been quietly encouraging the networks, for reasons of their own. They're normally straight-shooters, by their own standards. But...it stands to reason that there have to be some bad apples in the bunch."

"Interesting," Hameeda said. "You know they've actually started to surrender?"

Piece frowned. "That's odd. They normally fight to the last. Or retreat, if they can break contact."

"Yeah." Hameeda nodded. "They'll surrender to us, but not to the rebels."

"I suppose that makes sense," Piece mused. He stroked his chin. "The rebels want bloody revenge. We just want to put an end to the war before it kills us. I take it POWs aren't being mistreated?"

"Not by any reasonable standard," Hameeda said. She'd scanned the reports. Tokomak POWs were complaining about the lack of luxury accommodations, as if they'd expected every last comfort to be laid on. The only upside, she supposed, was that they weren't trying to escape. Humans would be planning *something*, she was sure. "We've certainly kept them safe from their former subjects."

"Good." Piece shrugged and put his mug on the table. "We'll have to work that into our broadcasts. Let them know they *can* surrender, once Admiral Teller arrives. And then hope enough of them believe it to allow us to take the system reasonably intact."

He frowned. "We know they have plans to destroy the industrial base," he said. "We have counter-plans to head them off, but they might not work."

Hameeda shuddered. "Really?"

"It's the logical thing to do," Piece said. He sounded as if he didn't care, although she knew he must be deeply concerned. "They know just how quickly we can press captured fabricators into service. If they can't keep them out of our hands, they'll destroy them."

"Ouch," Hameeda said. She could see the logic, but…it was sickening. The entire system would be reduced to penury. "Are they that desperate?"

"I think it's starting to sink in that they could lose the war," Piece said. "They've never come close to losing a war since they climbed into space. They haven't even fought a war with a peer power for generations. And now…humanity, an insignificant little race from a system that doesn't even have a gravity point, is kicking them in the ass. They're finally coming out of denial."

"How terrible," Hameeda said, archly.

Piece grinned at her. "How long do you have? Before you have to leave?"

"I can stay a few more hours," Hameeda assured him. She started to undo her tunic. "I don't have a tight schedule. I'm expected to recon Gateway before heading back to the fleet."

"Great," Piece said. He stood and unbuckled his trousers. "I'll give you something to remember me by."

Hameeda laughed. "Ass."

CHAPTER TWENTY-SIX

"We're back on an alien freighter," Butler said, as the team waited in the giant airlock. "I thought I'd sworn off them."

"I thought you'd sworn *at* them," Martin said. "Whose dumb idea was this, again?"

"Yours, sir," Butler said.

"A brilliant idea," Martin said. "Sheer genius. A brilliant idea that cannot possibly go wrong."

"Well, they say self-delusion flourishes in the minds of the deluded," Butler said, dryly. "And, as a sergeant, it is my job to knock it out of you."

"When we get home, I'm taking a look at your job description," Martin said. "And if this goes wrong, I'll be sure to add *scapegoat* to your list of jobs."

He snorted, then sobered as the freighter quivered. They were far too close to Tokomak One for comfort, close enough that a single burst of plasma fire could reduce the freighter to atoms. He would have preferred a more conventional assault, perhaps one with a squadron of starships providing covering fire...if they didn't simply blow the alien fortress to atoms itself. But that wasn't an option. Admiral Teller and his fleet were still too far away, while the Tokomak were cracking down hard. They had to move now.

And is that something we believe to be true, he asked himself, *or simply something we've told ourselves to justify moving now?*

He shook his head. The rebels had hundreds of thousands of cells being prepped for battle…one of them, perhaps only one, would jump the gun or do something *else* stupid, something else that would draw the Tokomak like carrion drew flies. He would have been astonished if the Tokomak *didn't* have some inkling there was trouble afoot, despite the combination of endless false alarms and suborned dispatch officers. They knew Admiral Teller wasn't *that* far away. The rebels would be in a better position to negotiate with the human invaders if they were in control of the planetary system when the humans arrived.

And they're not going to control everything, even then, Martin warned himself. There were only a handful of rebel cells on the gravity point fortresses, nowhere near enough to take the stations by storm. *We have to dig in and prepare for a fight.*

An alert bleeped up in his helmet as the air was steadily pumped out. He tensed, bracing himself as the last few seconds ticked away. They were still alive, thankfully. Personally, if he'd been in command of the defences, he would have kept Tokomak One completely isolated from the rest of the system. It *was* a huge station. It could sustain itself long enough to get resupply direct from Tokomak Prime, if there was no other choice. But the local government was clearly having problems maintaining control. The rebels swore blind that they hadn't reported the full extent of their troubles to their superiors. Martin hoped that was true. It would make it easier to shock the Tokomak if—when—the Twins fell.

The hatch opened, smoothly. Martin felt a flicker of fear, half-expecting the compartment to violently decompress even though he *knew* the air had been pumped out, before he walked to the edge of the hatch and peered into space. They were close enough to the station to pick it out with the naked eye, a mute testament to the sheer *size* of the structure. They weren't *that* close, on a human scale. The planet below looked odd, as if it was half-enclosed by a giant metal sphere. It took him a moment to realise he was seeing the edge of the planetary ring. This close, it dominated the horizon. It was easy to believe it was more than *just* a ring.

He swallowed hard, then threw himself into space and glided towards Tokomak One. His passive sensors updated rapidly, reporting matter-transmission beams and radio signals flickering between the station and the converted starship. The teleports had to be powerful, if there was enough bleed for his sensors to pick them up...unless the signals were already degrading. He grimaced, trying not to think about what would happen to a living being if the signals suffered even the *slightest* degradation. They'd be lucky if the receiving station could put them back together again.

Tokomak One grew larger as they approached, growing larger and larger until it dominated the horizon. His perspective altered—he closed his eyes as he rotated the suit—until it felt as if he was descending towards a planetary surface. His enhanced eyesight picked out a handful of weapons and sensor emplacements, scanning space for threats...he hoped, desperately, that they'd miss something as small as a single human. Even the smallest missile known to exist was much—much—bigger. The Tokomak would hardly risk themselves on such a mission. Why would they expect their human enemies to do the same?

They also consider their servants expendable, Martin reminded himself. *They'd have no qualms about sending them into the fire if they felt they had no choice.*

The ground came up and hit him. There was a thud, running through the suit so loudly he was *sure* they'd heard it on the other side of the armour, followed by silence. Martin waited, half-expecting to be struck dead at any moment. They *thought* the point defence couldn't be brought to bear on targets clinging to the hull, but they couldn't be sure. And the station carried hundreds of gunboats. Any one of them could systematically blast the marines off the hull, if it had reason to look. He counted his men as they landed, using hand signals to get them moving towards the uppermost hatch. They didn't have much time. A single rebel cell jumping ahead of time would put the whole system on alert.

He kept his eyes low as they walked up the station, towards the hatch they'd picked out ahead of time. The Tokomak had been careful, but they hadn't been able to keep copies of the station's plans from leaking to the rebels. Perhaps they'd simply assumed the rebels wouldn't be able to take advantage of them. Martin suspected it was true, if only because they could have smuggled a nuke onboard if they'd wished. But Tokomak One was so heavily armoured—inside as well as outside—that a lone nuke, detonating *inside* the structure, wouldn't take it out. Not completely. The Tokomak would have time to pass control to whichever station was next in line before they abandoned Tokomak One.

The hatch looked innocuous as Corporal Higgins went to work, uncovering the processor box and hacking into it. Martin braced himself, knowing they were embarking on the most dangerous part of the operation. It would be easy, very easy, to open the hatch, but doing it without setting off an alarm would be trickier. The Tokomak might be perfectly aware of the danger of leaving someone trapped outside, yet they were equally aware of the dangers of letting someone enter the station without supervision. His lips quirked as Higgins gave them a thumbs up, then opened the hatch manually. The chamber inside was empty. Martin breathed a sigh of relief as he led the way inside, the hatch closing silently behind him. He felt trapped, again, until the inner hatch rotated open. His suit blinked up a series of alerts as atmosphere rushed into the chamber. The air was poison.

Clever, Martin thought. *What sort of madman would poison his own air?*

It made sense, he decided, as he directed the team forward. The poison—it was really a nerve gas, one that would be hard to detect without military-grade sensors—wasn't species-specific. It would attack almost *any* higher life form known to exist, even the Tokomak themselves, and condemn them to death in screaming agony unless they were already immunised. And then…he realised, suddenly, why the Tokomak weren't so concerned about someone sneaking onto the station. They'd poisoned the air. *That* little detail hadn't been in the files, either. A rebel might take his helmet off and drop dead seconds later. He'd never know what'd hit him.

His heart started to pound as they made their way along the corridor, heading deeper and deeper into the structure. Tokomak One was immense, but—according to the rebels—seriously undermanned. A significant number of trained personnel had been reassigned, either to the alien fleet or the battlestations orbiting the gravity point. It wouldn't have normally mattered, Martin knew. As long as Tokomak One remained isolated from the rest of the universe, they could have dominated the entire system while undermanned. But...he tensed as they reached a closed hatch and started to open it. Who knew what was on the other side?

Butler held up his hands in a simple signal. *Two seconds.*

Martin nodded, lifting his rifle as the hatch opened, revealing a corridor leading towards another hatch. A pair of Tokomak stood on guard outside, looking bored. They had no time to react before Martin opened fire, riddling them both with bullets. He would have preferred to use a stunner, or a plasma weapon, but either one would set off alarms. It was just possible the Tokomak wouldn't tune their sensors to watch for chemically-propelled weapons, something so primitive they were hardly ever used. The Tokomak had derailed many races as they climbed towards the stars by taking them as slaves and introducing them to modern technology.

He smiled, thinly, as the bodies hit the floor. The metal beyond looked undamaged. It was designed to stand off a nuke. A handful of bullets wouldn't even scratch the paint. The people inside probably wouldn't have heard the noise. He glanced back at his men following him, then drew his stunner and keyed the hatch. It hissed open. He felt his smile grow wider as he jumped inside and opened fire, spraying the Tokomak with stun bolts. They never stood a chance.

"You'd think they'd be a little more careful," Higgins observed, as he went to work on the commander's console. "Don't they know there's a war on?"

"They're in the safest place in the system, hundreds of light years from our fleet," Martin reminded him, as he checked the offices. The governor-general was nowhere to be seen, probably somewhere on the planet or the ring. Martin hoped he'd be surprised when his servitors tried to cut his throat. "How were *they* to know they might be boarded at any moment?"

He smiled, remembering some of the stories the old hands had told him when he'd gone through OCS. There had been military guards who'd gotten lax, despite being in the middle of a war zone. They hadn't been allowed to keep a close eye on their local allies, he'd been told, and they'd even banned soldiers from wearing their personal weapons on base. The results had been inevitable, once the enemy had managed realised it wasn't a trap. He supposed the Tokomak hadn't been *that* far wrong. The rebels couldn't have taken Tokomak One without stealth and armoured combat suits. If the enemy had had the slightest hint of warning...

Higgins looked up. "I have control, sir," he said. "They'll probably try to lock me out, if they have time, but..."

Martin took a breath. They were committed... he shook his head. *They* had always been committed. It was the *rebels* who were going to be committed now, who'd have to take up arms and fight in the certain knowledge the entire planet would be scorched if they lost. And yet... he'd seen the rebels, tasted their desperation and hatred and grim determination to fight back even if it meant nothing more than kicking and scratching their way to the gallows. And yet... Piece might be cold-blooded about the vast number of aliens—of *people*—who were about to be killed, but Martin didn't have that luxury. His hometown wouldn't have been such a disaster zone if the people who'd ruled it hadn't thought of the inhabitants as nothing more than *numbers*.

"You know what to do," he said. "Start the program."

He forced himself to sit back and watch, grimly, as the automated defences rotated and started firing at the planet below. The rebels had prepared a targeting list, covering everything from military garrisons and police stations to communications centres and Tokomak-only residences. Martin wasn't so sure *those* were good targets, but the rebels had insisted, pointing out that they were effectively fortresses and communications centres in their own right. Bombarding them was the only way to keep the Tokomak from rallying and organising a counterattack, or a defence that might last long enough for help to arrive. The starships on the gravity point couldn't break through the planetary defences alone, but help was on the way. Martin was morbidly sure of it. The Tokomak would want to fight Admiral Teller well clear of their homeworld.

"Firing pattern complete, sir," Higgins reported. "All targets destroyed."

"Switch to the secondary list of targets," Martin ordered. "And then transmit the message."

"Aye, sir," Higgins said.

Martin sucked in his breath, trying not to think about the death and destruction he'd unleashed across the planetary surface. It was easy to forget that the icons marking destroyed targets actually marked dead bodies and shattered lives, that for every guilty person they'd killed they'd probably also taken out a handful of innocent people who hadn't deserved to die. The rebels hadn't cared—they hated all the Tokomak, guilty and innocent alike—but Martin did. And yet, there was no choice. Half-measures would only doom the uprising before it had truly begun.

And am I telling myself that because it's true, he asked himself, *or because I want to convince myself that I'm not the bad guy?*

He pushed the thought aside, savagely, as the first reports started to trickle in. The rebels had risen, right across the planet. Isolated enemy positions, the handful too close to vital locations to be smashed from orbit, were under savage attack, their defenders being pressed to the limit. Emergency transmissions flooded into Tokomak One, everything from screaming accusations to desperate pleas for help. Martin watched howling mobs chasing the Tokomak and their allies, shuddering at how the Galactics had been transformed into helpless villains. He wanted to look away, but he forced himself to keep watching. He had to bear witness to the disaster he'd unleashed.

The hours ticked by slowly. Reports came in from across the system, noting revolts both successful and unsuccessful. Hundreds of freighters left orbit, gambling they wouldn't be fired upon as they fled for the gravity points or deep space. A handful of Tokomak installations managed to isolate themselves from the datanet, suggesting that whoever was in charge had a working brain. It wasn't enough to save them. The rebels kept pressing against them, capturing hundreds of facilities and industrial nodes. A number even fell without a fight.

But there will be a fight, once they get organised, he thought. The corrupted datanet wouldn't keep the gravity point fortifications from realising what had happened. And then...what? The starships couldn't retake the planets, but they could do a lot of damage if they were willing to run a few risks. *Thankfully, there's nothing incentivising them to try to force the defences now.*

He felt sick. The *reason* there were no incentives for the Tokomak to attack quickly was that just about every Tokomak who'd been on the planet was dead. Or captured...the rebels had promised to *try* to take prisoners, but Martin had little hope they'd keep that promise. He watched the live feeds as they grew stronger, broadcasting scenes of anarchy and horror. The Tokomak were gone and the rebels were turning their attention to the collaborators, slaughtering everyone who'd worked for their oppressors. Martin could understand their anger and rage, the desire to see the bastards dead, but...he shook his head. The rebels were likely to destroy the workforce that made the system *work* if they weren't careful. Piece understood the risks, but did *they*?

"The rebels want to join us," Butler said. "And so does Mr. Piece."

"Clear the atmosphere first," Martin ordered. The rebels wouldn't thank them if their leaders died on the station. "And tell them to wear protection, just in case."

"I imagine getting pregnant now would be a bit of a bother," Butler said, dryly.

Martin snickered. "That is terrible," he said. It wasn't the worst joke he'd heard, but it was definitely in the bottom ten. "That is so terrible that I want to court martial myself for laughing."

"I'll speak in your defence," Butler said. He shot Martin a mischievous look that was strikingly childish. "The worst jokes get the best laughs."

"Hah." Martin snorted. "Tell them to wear spacesuits. And, once they're in command of the station, we'll see where we can make ourselves useful."

He looked at the in-system display and frowned. A cluster of icons hovered around each of the gravity points, seemingly motionless. Starships were moving in and out of the system, the newcomers utterly unaware of what had happened. They were in for a shock, when they arrived. And the gravity point defences would know what had happened, now. They'd be planning *something*, even if it was just keeping the points secure until their reinforcements arrived.

We'll have to get busy preparing our defences, Martin told himself. He tried to think of a way to take the gravity points and failed. The defences were too strong. They'd have to wait for relief, hoping that Admiral Teller got there first. If he didn't... Martin tried not to think about it, but the thought refused to fade. *If Admiral Teller doesn't get here first, this entire system is going to get trashed.*

CHAPTER TWENTY-SEVEN

"Most Illustrious Empress," Neola read. "Long may you reign. Long may you lead us to the path of righteousness..."

She fought down the urge to say something cutting, or to order harsh punishments, as she skimmed through nearly ten thousand words of insane flattery. The humans spoke of ass-kissing, a metaphor Neola found delightfully crude, but the Harmonies had elevated it to an art form. They were practically performing sexual acts on her...her stomach churned in disgust as she finally reached the meat of the message, a simple statement that the allied fleet was ready to fight beside the Tokomak for the good of the galaxy. Even *that* was coached in flowery teams that meant absolutely nothing. She resisted the urge to hurl the datapad across the cabin as she paged through another five thousand words of nonsense to make sure there was no sting in the tail. There didn't seem to be one.

"Bah," she said. She'd hoped to have the fleet underway by now, but a combination of manpower shortages and foot-dragging had made it impossible. She was lucky she'd managed to start assembling the fleet two jumps from Tokomak Prime, on the assumption it would be easier for her allies to join her there. Thankfully, her 'advisors' were too far away to look over her shoulder and offer her useless advice. "Don't they have anything useful to say?"

She summoned an aide and passed the datapad to him. "Read this and boil it down to a single paragraph for me," she ordered. "Not the flattery, just the content."

The aide bowed, not quickly enough to hide his fear. "Yes, Your Eminence."

Neola smiled coldly, then turned her attention back to the display. Thousands of starships hung near the gravity point, a formidable fleet nearly as big as the one she'd hurled against Apsidal a few short months ago. It looked unstoppable, to the untrained eye; it looked big enough to pour through the gravity point and crush any opposition by sheer weight of numbers. But Neola knew better. A good third of the fleet was composed of ships begged and borrowed from her allies, from Galactics who might already be thinking about the advantages of a universe without the Tokomak. She was grimly aware that the *only* thing that had made them send their ships to the fleet was the certain knowledge she'd take an awful revenge if they'd didn't...if she won the war. And if she lost the coming battle...

She rubbed her forehead in frustration. She didn't *need* foot-dragging allies. The fleet had never trained together, let alone gone into *battle* together. The idea of regular drills had been quashed long ago, well before Neola had been born. There had been no reason to believe the Tokomak would ever need help, no reason to think they should keep their allies close...she cursed the former governors savagely as she eyed the display. Right now, she knew she'd be lucky if she managed to get every ship moving in the same direction when she gave the order. Training was a mess, practically non-existent...she promised herself that, when the war was over, that was going to change. The only upside, she supposed, was that her allies hadn't been quietly planning to overthrow the Tokomak. They'd have kept their fleets in better shape if they'd seriously expected a war.

The aide cleared his throat, nervously. "They say they are with us 'til the bitter end, Your Majesty."

235

"How reassuring," Neola commented, dryly. "Put together a response. Tell them we're glad to see them"—*that* wasn't true, even though she knew it *should* be—"and that we look forward to fighting beside them."

The aide bowed, again. Neola snorted as she dismissed him, telling herself she should be grateful. The Harmonies might be hidebound, even by *Tokomak* standards, and snooty enough to put *her* nose out of joint, but at least they weren't plotting trouble. They'd even put their planets at risk to help her with an intelligence operation, one that had come surprisingly close to success. She glared at the other icons, wondering which of the Galactics *were* plotting trouble. She would be surprised if they *weren't*. The prospect of being in control of their lives again, after millennia of submission, had to be very attractive. And if they managed to jump ship in time...

She gritted her teeth in bitter frustration. She would have been happier, a great deal happier, if she'd been able to complete her mobilisation plans as she'd intended. Let the humans exhaust themselves taking system after system, while she readied her fleet to kick them back out of the inner worlds, reclaim control of the galaxy and turn their homeworld into a pile of ash. It would be good to be rid of them, once and for all. And then she could hurl the other servitor races into the fire too. They were just too dangerous to keep around. Let them all die. Let her people learn to fend for themselves again. It wasn't as if they were short of people to do the scutwork. They just had to be convinced to do it.

The paperwork kept on piling up in front of her as the fleet worked its way through a series of basic training exercises. Neola tried to stay calm, even when a pair of battleships almost *rammed* each other...a display of incompetence that would probably have made the humans choke themselves to death laughing. The battleship skippers were too old and doddering to fight a modern war...she would have relieved them at once, if they'd been under her direct command. But they were allies...she'd just have to put up with them and hope they could soak up a handful of human missiles before they died. She rather thought that might be a good idea. Weakening the other Galactics might be quite useful.

And we need to get going, she told herself. The humans were pushing corewards...she wanted to give them time to get closer, but her council was demanding she move as soon as possible. And they thought she was making excuses. She snorted in annoyance. She wished she *was* making excuses. *Maybe, once we're underway, I can find a way to put the doddering fools out of my misery.*

It was a bitter thought, one that mocked her as she sorted through the paperwork. There had been a time, not that long ago, when she could have had an entire fleet of commanding officers shot and no one would have dared say *anything.* She could have lined the allied commanders up and shot them...but now it was impossible. Now, she had to be *diplomatic* to people she *knew* were plotting to stick a knife in her back, while leading them into battle against the most dangerous enemy they'd ever faced. Maybe she could put them in command of the first assault wave, if she had to force her way into another system. They might be too stupid to realise she was practically guaranteeing their deaths.

She smiled, humourlessly. "They can't be that stupid."

Another aide stopped as he passed. "Your Majesty?"

"I'm just planning how to take the offensive," Neola lied. "Carry on."

She sat back in her chair and surveyed the CIC. The compartment was thrumming with activity, but she knew she was dangerously undermanned. She'd always been short of good officers, particularly when the longer-serving bureaucrats had become very imaginative when it came to inventing excuses and citing regulations to explain why they couldn't *possibly* be assigned away from Tokomak Prime. The bastards...they knew she couldn't have them shot, not now. If they'd shown so much imagination a few years ago, she wouldn't have *needed* to launch her coup. Her people would have crushed all their enemies and swept over the entire galaxy.

And I'm risking much by taking so many people away from the homeworld, she thought. *If they get lost...*

An alarm chimed. "Your Majesty, a courier boat just transited the gravity point. It's broadcasting a priority-one signal."

237

"Get me a full download," Neola ordered. A priority-one signal meant bad news. She wondered which system had fallen now and why. The human fleet had held position, according to the last update, but it had been several weeks out of date by the time it had reached her. "And put the fleet on notice. We might be departing sooner than planned."

She leaned forward, feeling her hearts sink as the download appeared in front of her. The Twins had fallen...not to the humans, but to rebels. She shuddered as the full impact gradually started to sink in. The Twins weren't *just* a vital industrial base. There were so many gravity points within the system that losing control was an utter disaster. If the rebels held the system, they'd be able to cut the empire into a number of smaller sections...each one too weak to stand on its own. It might not be a complete disaster—the reports stated the gravity points were still secure—but she couldn't take it for granted. The report was already a week out of date.

And it will take us longer than that to get there in force, she mused. A lone starship could get there relatively quickly, but an entire fleet would take considerably longer. *If the humans get there first...*

She tapped her console, bringing up a starchart. The humans were four jumps from the Twins, assuming they hadn't already advanced. They might not *know* what had happened—Neola had issued orders to seal the gravity points if there was a major uprising—but she didn't dare take it for granted. If they knew, they'd throw caution to the winds and push forward to the Twins. It would give them their best chance of delivering a mortal blow to the empire. The plan to stop them at Gateway would have to be abandoned. She'd have to risk taking the fleet further, to the Twins. And hope she could stop them there, before word spread further. The humans might lose the coming battle and still win the war.

"Contact the fleet," she ordered, keeping her voice calm. "The training exercises are terminated. The fleet is to ready itself for an immediate transit to Gateway, then to the Twins. Upload copies of the reports, then inform all senior officers that I expect them to be ready. We depart in four hours."

She waited, wondering if any of her aides would question her. Four hours... it wasn't very long at all. The protests from the fleet commanders would be long and loud. Normally, the fleet would have several *days* of warning before it began to move. She would be surprised if there weren't any problems as they crawled towards the gravity point and began to jump. They were going to outrun their logistics pretty quickly. There'd been no time to set up additional supply dumps. They *had* to reinforce Gateway and recover the Twins before the humans broke into the system. There was no choice...

And if we get moving quickly, she mused, *the commanders won't have time to start complaining.*

She put the thought aside as she keyed her console. She'd have to forward the report to Tokomak Prime, along with an outline of what she intended to do. Thankfully, she had the authority to act without waiting for orders. The humans were probably already on the move, damn them. If she waited, they'd have punched out Gateway and would be breathing down her neck by the time she received orders she probably couldn't carry out. And yet, some part of her rebelled at sending the fleet so far from Tokomak Prime. Her instincts and training both told her that the homeworld came first.

But we have already taken too many losses, she told herself. *If we lose the Twins, we'll lose a great deal more.*

• • •

Hameeda felt cold.

She'd argued with herself for hours before she'd crossed Gateway and continued to sneak up the gravity point chain to Tokomak Prime. She'd known she had to return to Admiral Teller, and tell him what Piece and his team were planning, yet... Admiral Teller needed to know what awaited him corewards of the Twins. She'd told herself, again and again, that it would take longer for her to inform him and *then* head corewards... she was torn, now, between wishing she hadn't done it and being thankful that she *had*. Admiral Teller would probably not be *pleased* to know a giant alien fleet was heading towards him, but he had to know anyway.

She tried not to be terrified as the massive fleet slowly shook itself down and headed for the gravity point. It was so large that even *her* sensors were having trouble picking out individual ships. There were so many drive signatures that they blurred together into a single ominous haze. Her sensors thought there were somewhere between six to seven *thousand* starships, although it was hard to be sure. She wanted to believe that half of them were just drones, nothing more than sensor ghosts. But she couldn't convince herself it was true.

And a good third of the fleet aren't Tokomak, she thought. The technologies were similar, but the drive signatures were alien. *They assembled their allies for the fight.*

She watched the fleet, torn between an insane urge to laugh and a grim awareness that one didn't *have* to be competent with such an immense fleet under their control. It was painfully clear the fleet wasn't properly trained, not to their usual standards. Their formation was ragged—unless they'd adopted human-style formations, which was possible—and they were broadcasting messages in the clear, rather than using communications lasers and encrypted transmissions. The latter could be broken, she knew, but it took time...time she might not have. The researchers kept *promising* a breakthrough, a new kind of computer that could crack enemy codes quickly enough for the information to be tactically useful, yet so far it had yet to materialise. But the Tokomak were broadcasting in the clear...

To be fair, they have no reason to expect me to be here, she reminded herself. *And they don't have any reason to expect* anyone *to be listening to them.*

She frowned. The system was useless, save for a trio of gravity points. It was the last place she'd expect the Tokomak to assemble a fleet, which might have been why they'd picked it. If they'd stayed away from the gravity point, or used a nearby system, she might have missed them entirely. But the system did have its advantages. The lack of a local population meant there would be no unfriendly eyes following the fleet, no rebels who might pass the word down the chain or relay it via FTL to rebellious star systems. No one would watch and laugh as the rusty crews went through their paces, training for war...

Her neural net provided a handful of possible scenarios. If the Tokomak decided to take a few risks, they could get the fleet to the Twins within two weeks. It would cost them—they'd probably lose a handful of ships to interpenetration—but once they got there, they could sit on the gravity point and hold it forever. They had so many ships they could probably hold the gravity points even without fortifications. And Admiral Teller would have to bleed his fleet white...she shook her head. The only option was to get back to the admiral and warn him to pick up speed. He *had* to get to the Twins first.

And they might even win the war outright if they get there first, she mused. *It's time to go.*

She took one last look at the lumbering enemy fleet. She was experienced enough to see the flaws, ranging from ill-coordinated point defence to a shortage of logistic support, but none of them might matter. The Tokomak were supposed to have supply dumps in *every* major system. If they'd crammed N-Gann with enough missiles to smash a *huge* fleet— something she was sure they regretted, now the human invaders had used the stockpiles to do just that—they were bound to have stuffed more into Gateway. And they could take a leaf out of humanity's book and use the missiles as makeshift mines. *That* would be the end, if they timed it right.

The LinkShip rotated at her command, fleeing the fleet as fast as she could. Hameeda ran through the simulations again and again, telling herself she could be back with Admiral Teller before the alien fleet completed its first transit. Unless it was willing to take any number of risks...she wondered, grimly, if they *would* take the risk. Getting there first was important, but so was getting there in a fit state to fight. There was no way they could risk stringing their ships out as they raced to Gateway and the Twins...

But they control the gravity points, she reminded herself. It seemed an unfair advantage, despite the sheer *scale* of the problem of getting thousands of ships through the gravity points in a timely manner. *And they won't have to fight their way through…*

She shook her head. It didn't matter. Admiral Teller was the one who'd have to worry about it. All *she* had to do was get word to him, then urge him to pick up speed. The time for a slow, but steady advance was over. It was time to start running.

Because we've just started a race, she thought. *And whoever gets there first will win.*

CHAPTER TWENTY-EIGHT

The dull red star cast an eerie light over the scene as the human fleet pushed through the gravity point, passing the cooling wreckage of the lone orbital fortress and a dozen converted freighters that had made a brief, but futile stand against the invaders. Admiral Colin Teller stood in the CIC and watched, dispassionately, as the locals fled. The system wasn't *that* populated, but it hardly mattered. There were already reports of uprisings right across the system.

Which is going to turn into yet another diplomatic nightmare, he thought, as he studied the post-battle reports. He'd seen too many slaughters over the past few days, too many alien civilians—and collaborators—ruthlessly hunted down and exterminated by the rebels. He'd had to issue orders to secure a handful of POW camps, grimly aware that—if he had to pull his men out—the prisoners would be slaughtered. *Why didn't it ever occur to the Tokomak to be a little nicer to their subjects?*

He snorted at the absurd thought. One couldn't build an empire designed to enforce stagnation, an empire built on slavery, while being *nice* to one's subjects. *Someone* had to do the dirty work. And besides, the Tokomak had been convinced they were the rightful rulers of the galaxy. They'd never really considered that they *could* lose, not on more than a very small scale. It had kept them from being *nice* to anyone. Why be nice when you controlled the largest hammer the galaxy had ever seen?

Because, one day, you might wake up and discover that someone has invented a superweapon that could turn your entire fleet into scrap metal, he mused, sardonically. *I suppose that's why you made sure that everyone stagnated. You wanted to make sure no one could or would invent a superweapon.*

"Admiral," Commander Hacker said. "The advance elements are ready to begin their move."

"Order them to begin operations, as planned," Colin said. "And alert me if things change."

He turned his attention to the starchart, wondering—again—just what was happening on the other side of the inner worlds. Where was Admiral Stuart? Did the Tokomak already know she was coming? He'd gone through a hundred simulations, trying to deduce when they'd pretty much *have* to know she was coming, but there was no way to be *sure*. There was so little hard data that all his conclusions were pretty much guesswork. He told himself to stop worrying. He had only a handful of transits until he reached the Twins, whereupon he'd have to fight his way into the system. The reports didn't look good. The system was so heavily defended that they could practically have jammed the gravity point with fortresses...

A *ping* echoed through the compartment. "Admiral, the LinkShip has returned," Hacker said. "Ah...her commander is requesting a private conference."

Colin nodded. "Inform her I'll teleport over when she's within range," he said. In theory, their communications should be private. In practice...better to be safe than very sorry. And besides, he was curious. He'd never had a chance to see a LinkShip. "I'll be in my office until she's here."

"Aye, Admiral," Hacker said. "She'll be here in twenty minutes."

• • •

Colin couldn't help feeling an odd stab of jealousy, mingled with pity, as the LinkShip's interior materialised around him. The LinkShip was elegant, in a manner more befitting a luxury yacht than a warship. The fittings looked nice, the bulkheads were finely decorated and the galley looked like a small office rather than something belonging to a warship that might be going into battle at any moment. It almost made him envious, were it not for the fact the LinkShip's pilot could never leave. The navy *had* to make her comfortable.

Which makes her lucky in some respects, he mused. The Solar Navy was a great believer in not giving too much luxury to its senior officers. Colin had a suite, but it was hardly *that* luxurious. *And very unlucky in others.*

He studied Hameeda—if she had a surname, it had never been written into the files—with some interest. She was a tall woman, with long dark hair that was strictly against regulations...although that probably didn't matter, he thought, given that she would be spending the rest of her life on a starship. She looked oddly uncomfortable in her tunic, as if she would sooner be wearing something else. It clung to her in odd places, suggesting it wasn't really *designed* for her. Colin puzzled over it for a moment, then dismissed the thought. If she wanted something suitable, she could have gotten it from stores. Or simply had it put together in her onboard fabricator.

"Admiral Teller," Hameeda said. Her voice was soft, as if she wasn't quite used to speaking any longer. "Welcome onboard."

"Thank you," Colin said, sincerely. "It's a very interesting ship."

"I'm afraid this is probably the best compartment," Hameeda said. "The bridge is really quite a disappointment."

"So I've been told," Colin said. He took the mug of coffee she offered him and sat. The coffee tasted *real*, not navy-issue. "I'd love to take a tour, but I don't have time. I need to..."

He broke off as Hameeda made a gesture. A holographic image appeared in front of him, floating over the table. It looked real enough to touch, without the faint haze surrounding most military-grade hologram. He wondered, absently, why the military didn't eliminate the haze. He could see the sense, sometimes, but really...who was going to believe a tiny holographic fleet was actually *real*? And...his blood turned to ice as he surveyed the fleet in front of him. The handful of icons suggesting the fleet was nowhere near as powerful as it looked were not reassuring. The fleet would have to be a great deal weaker if it wanted to please him.

"Shit," he said, quietly. "How big is that fleet?"

"The uppermost estimate is seven thousand ships, of which roughly a third belong to their allies," Hameeda said, quietly. "It's possible the figure might be a great deal lower..."

"You mean, they might have used drones to make the fleet look a lot bigger?" Colin was clutching at straws and he knew it. He felt as if he'd been punched in the gut. "I assume you checked the data for...hints the fleet might not be real?"

"Yes, sir." Hameeda didn't look insulted by the question. That, if nothing else, was a pretty clear sign she'd worried about it herself. "I checked and rechecked the data. It's possible there *are* a small number of sensor ghosts amongst the fleet, but the vast majority of the ships are real."

"And they were well behind the lines, where they have no reason to fake an entire fleet," Colin mused. "Unless they caught a sniff of you...?"

"I don't believe so," Hameeda said. She sounded pensive, as if she wasn't quite sure she believed herself. "They made no attempt to keep me from sneaking back through the Twins..."

She broke off. "Sir, the Twins have risen and the Tokomak are sending a fleet to put the rebels down."

Colin listened, grimly, to her report. The Twins were in revolt...a good thing, except it meant the Tokomak might have a good chance to put the revolt down before his fleet could get there. And then...seven thousand ships were more than enough to keep him out of the Twins, if they got there first. Or Gateway, if they got *there* first. On one hand, Admiral Stuart's plan had succeeded. He silently credited her with luring the main body of the alien fleet out of position. But, on the other hand, she'd left him with a problem. Did he continue the steady advance? Or did he throw caution to the winds and rush to liberate the Twins?

He closed his eyes for a long moment. He'd read the reports. The Twins were *important* for all sorts of reasons, from simple location to a vast industrial base and military stockpiles that could be repurposed to serve the human race. If he took the system, he'd have all sorts of possible options…options the enemy would have to take into account even if *he* didn't. *He* needed to punch into Gateway, unless…the enemy ships would already be out of position. They certainly wouldn't be covering their home-world. As long as he was threatening them, they couldn't pull the ships out…

And if they do get to the Twins first, they'll slaughter everyone, he thought. He'd read the reports. The Tokomak were lashing out like wounded beasts, determined to kill their tormentors before they were killed themselves. *There are good and practical reasons to go to their aid.*

He keyed his wristcom. "Commander Hacker, inform the fleet that we will depart for the Twins as soon as possible," he ordered. "Recall the advance elements, tell them we won't attempt to secure anything beyond the gravity point itself. Dispatch recon units to the gravity points. I want to know what's waiting for us."

"Aye, sir," Hacker said. He sounded surprised, too surprised to hide it. "The remainder of the fleet should be ready to depart in two hours."

"Shave as much time off that as you can," Colin ordered, although he knew they'd be running up against some pretty hard limits. "And call a staff conference for one hour. All captains and commodores to attend. I'll be back by then."

"Yes, sir," Hacker said.

Colin shut off the wristcom and looked at Hameeda. She looked surprised too…fitting, he supposed. Colin would have preferred to recon the system thoroughly before pushing onwards, just to make sure there were no nasty surprises lurking in the shadows, ready to stick a knife in him when he turned his back. A single enemy squadron behind the lines could cause a great deal of trouble, if it didn't manage to cut his supply lines completely. At worst, he'd be cut off and forced to retrace his steps, cutting his way through enemy defences that had been thrown up in his rear.

Admiral Stuart would take the risk without hesitation. Colin didn't like the thought of it, but he knew he'd have to take the risk too.

"I have downloads on all the gravity point defences," Hameeda said, quietly. "A full-spectrum report and analysis, one for each of them. They can't have changed them *that* quickly."

"Let us hope so," Colin said. He frowned, forcing himself to think. He'd have to rotate his squadrons, sending one set into battle while the other set rearmed. It would be another gamble, one he'd prefer not to take. "How long do we have?"

"I don't know," Hameeda said. "It depends on what assumptions we make…"

"Not enough time, then," Colin said. He had an uneasy sense he was starting a race he might already have lost. "But we will do our level best to get there first."

He scowled. If he could get into the system first and take control of the gravity point leading to Gateway, he could stand off the entire enemy fleet…unless they'd finally started deploying assault pods of their own. If that happened…he considered his options for a long moment, then dismissed the thought. He'd just have to fight a conventional battle and hope his technological advantages would trump sheer numbers. Or that the enemy tired of staggering losses.

Who knows? His thoughts mocked him. *Perhaps the horse will learn to sing.*

Hameeda looked at the table. "What do you want me to do?"

Colin considered it. "I want you to join the staff conference," he said. "After that, I want you to be ready to support the fleet. We're going to have to cut our way through a set of enemy defences and I think we're going to need you."

"Yes, sir." Hameeda looked a little disappointed. Perhaps she'd been hoping to get back to the Twins. "I'm at your service."

"Good." Colin understood her feelings, but he needed the LinkShip. Besides, the planetary defences might have been tightened to the point they'd spot her making transit and kill her before her systems stabilised.

The Tokomak *must* have figured out the human race had *some* way of sneaking through the gravity points by now. "I'm counting on you."

He stood. "If you don't mind, I'll teleport back now," he said. He keyed his wristcom, requesting a window in the teleport baffles. "And I'll see you at the conference."

"Yes, sir," Hameeda said. She didn't sound pleased. He didn't blame her. Command conferences were boring, even if the CO was a sensible man. "I'll be there."

• • •

Hameeda rubbed her forehead as Admiral Teller vanished in a beam of shimmering light, a handful of protests from her security systems blinking up in front of her eyes. It *was* a security risk to lower the teleport baffles long enough for one person to teleport, although she saw no harm in it. Not here, at least. There were no enemy ships for millions of kilometres, if any remained in the system itself. The Tokomak hadn't bothered to make a *real* fight for the system. Hameeda suspected that boded ill for the future. They'd presumably pulled ships and men out to make a stand somewhere else.

Like the Twins, she thought. She hadn't really had *time* to do more than snatch a brief update from the rebels as she passed through the system. She'd *wanted* to stop long enough to invite Piece to join her, but neither of them had the time. The entire system had been in flames. She'd intercepted enough broadcasts to know that chaos reigned, that everyone was panicking if they weren't already under attack. *They must know the Twins have risen by now.*

A diagram appeared in her mind, utterly uninvited. A message would have been sent through the gravity points as soon as the rebellion began. By now, assuming the courier stayed in FTL, it would have reached Tokomak Prime itself. The fleet had probably been alerted shortly before she'd spotted it, which meant … she ran through the calculations time and time again, wishing for harder data. Guesswork. It was all guesswork. One fleet might get there before the other or they might arrive at the same time, causing all *sorts* of interesting confrontations. There was just no way to know, until they actually reached the Twins.

And hope they can hold out until we get there, she mused. It was possible, if her projections were accurate. The gravity point defences didn't have the mobile firepower they'd need to retake the high orbitals. They would have to wait for reinforcements before they made their move. Humanity would have a window of opportunity, a chance to act. *And that we keep the enemy from realising the threat heading towards their homeworld.*

Hameeda stood, brushing down her tunic. She hadn't expected Admiral Teller to insist on beaming onboard and she'd barely had any time to dress. Her lips twitched in amusement. She could hardly appear naked in front of a senior officer. She made a mental note to activate the holographic filter when she attended the command conference. They wouldn't know she was naked as long as she *looked* like she was wearing a uniform...

She strode back to the bridge, silently reviewing the human fleet. It had grown in the last week, with the addition of hundreds of alien-crewed vessels. Cold logic told her that most of them would be completely ineffective against modern warships, or even Tokomak designs, but they had to be there. On one hand, it would be important—later—for the aliens to say they played a role in the war. And, on the other, they might soak up missiles aimed at human ships. She hated having to think like that, but she knew there was no way around it. The sheer size of the fleet bearing down on them made point defence and sensor drones seem pointless. The Tokomak could simply smother them in missiles.

And then proceed to lay waste to our worlds, she thought. She activated the starchart as she sat in the chair, without donning the helmet. It was easy to trace the planned routes leading into enemy territory. *Except... they don't know about Admiral Stuart... do they?*

She shook her head. There was no way to *know*. And that meant the engagement might be completely unnecessary... or pointless... or utterly disastrous. The sheer size of the Tokomak reserves were daunting. If they had time to bring them online, they'd punch their way to Earth before humanity had time to come up with something new, something that would level the playing field or tip it in humanity's favour. The Tokomak could lose the entire fleet bearing down on the Twins and still come out ahead, if they inflicted serious damage on Admiral Teller's fleet. And... they didn't *have* to do much more than force him to empty his magazines. The fleet would be useless without weapons to fire at their enemies.

We're not completely short of options, she told herself, firmly. It was hard to believe Admiral Stuart had been stopped, even if the enemy *did* know she was coming. They would hardly have sent so many warships away from Tokomak Prime if they knew she was out there. *And we have to be giving them a very hard time indeed.*

Her eyes narrowed. *And we've encouraged so many of their slaves to rise up against them*, she thought. She'd seen signs of trouble right across the empire, from messages warning of unrest to starships vanishing in transit or entire planets rising against their oppressors. *Win or lose, their empire will never be the same again.*

CHAPTER TWENTY-NINE

"Launch the assault pods," Hoshiko ordered.

She braced herself as the icons vanished, plunging through the gravity point and into the next system. The Tokomak knew they were coming. They'd harassed her fleet with light units as it punched its way further down the chain, stalling for time while they waited for reinforcements. A handful of gravity points had been covered with hastily-replaced fortresses, but little else. She was grimly aware the Tokomak *had* to be recalling their starships and plotting to make a stand somewhere short of Tokomak Prime itself.

"The second wave of assault pods are ready," Yolanda said. "Recon units are transiting the gravity point now."

Hoshiko nodded, curtly. She didn't have to issue any further orders. They'd carried out enough gravity point assaults over the last year to know the drill, particularly since the Tokomak defenders hadn't realised—yet—just how great an advantage the missile pods gave her. Or, perhaps, they *had* realised...and they were deliberately trying to force her to expend her supply. The kind of mindset that would rate fortresses and even *starships* as expendable was beyond her, even though she could see the logic. If she bogged down, tangled up in a web of fortresses and minefields, the Tokomak would have all the time they needed to gather the forces to rip her apart and go on to smash the Solar Union into rubble. And the Tokomak had enough forces to make such costly tactics practical...

Yolanda cleared her throat. "Admiral, the recon units have returned. The gravity point is clear."

"Take us through," Hoshiko ordered.

She smiled, grimly, as the fleet advanced into another star system. Graviton had been settled thousands of years ago, although—for reasons the files didn't make clear—it hadn't received anything like as much attention from the Galactics until well after they'd discovered the stardrive. She stroked her chin as the display lit up, displaying a mid-sized industrial base spread over three planets and uncounted numbers of asteroids. They were already picking up radio transmissions suggesting there was trouble on the surface, revolts and strikes steadily turning to outright rebellion. Word of their advance had *definitely* reached the planet. The defenders would have too much else to concern them to worry about her fleet.

And it's time to give them another surprise, she mused. She didn't *think* the plan would work perfectly—it was unlikely they'd get the advantage of surprise—but it would concentrate a few minds. *And see just how far we've managed to lead them by the nose.*

"Inform the fleet," she ordered. "We'll light out for Crux as soon as the remainder of the fleet has crossed the gravity point."

"Aye, Admiral." There was a tremor in Yolanda's voice. "We'll be ready."

Hoshiko nodded, watching as the display continued to update. The Tokomak would—she hoped—expect her to keep punching through the gravity points. Perhaps she would have done so, if she hadn't had access to their files. They were still quite some distance from Tokomak Prime, but not far enough to make voyaging through FTL impractical. And they would have a clear shot at Crux along the way. Hoshiko doubted it would make much difference, in the long run, but it was worth *trying* to lure whatever defenders remained at Tokomak Prime out of position. She had no illusions. Tokomak Prime would be defended to the last.

And if Admiral Teller hasn't managed to lure their fleet out of place, she mused, *they'll have enough ships to give us an even fight.*

She shuddered at the thought, then turned her attention to the reports as they continued to flow into her console. Factions on Graviton were begging for help, swearing everything from alliance to outright servitude if she came to their aid, but she didn't have time. They couldn't win Graviton if it cost them everything. Tokomak Prime might know—now—that she was on the way. If they realised she didn't *have* to use the gravity points...

They must know, Hoshiko told herself. *They invented the* fucking *stardrive.*

"Admiral," Yolanda said. "The remainder of the fleet has made transit."

Hoshiko nodded. "Order the fleet to enter FTL," she said. "And take us out on a vague course for Crux. We'll rig up the lines once we're out of detection range."

"Aye, Admiral," Yolanda said. "FTL in three, two, one..."

Defiant lurched as she jumped into FTL, the display blanking as she raced out of the system. The remainder of the fleet followed her, pulsing their drives to ensure they remained in communications range. Hoshiko smiled, appreciating the formation. Her crews had drilled together, and fought together, to the point they could fly in a formation that would have made the Tokomak balk. The enemy might be tracking them, but they'd have problems telling just how many ships were in the fleet. The thousands of drive signatures would blur together into an unreadable mass.

And then we'll start attaching tow cables, she told herself, as she stood. *The defenders won't know for sure what's coming our way until it's too late.*

She smiled, rather grimly. Her fleet wasn't the fastest thing in space—courier boats were faster—but it was pretty damn close. The planetary defenders would have sent warnings in all directions, yet... they might not have had time to see what she intended to do before they dispatched their ships. She wanted to believe they'd have the advantage of surprise, when they reached Crux. But she knew it might not work out so well. The Tokomak might just get an alert up the chain, even without courier boats, in time to organise a defence and dispatch reinforcements.

"I'll be in my cabin," she said. "Pass the word to all hands. Well done."

"Aye, Admiral," Yolanda said.

Hoshiko nodded and left the compartment. Her crews *had* done well. Hopefully, the alpha crews would have plenty of time to get some sleep before they reached their target. Crux wouldn't be an easy target, not by any reasonable standard. The files insisted that it was the most heavily-defended star system short of Tokomak Prime itself.

Her wristcom bleeped as she entered her cabin. "Yes?"

"Your steward seems to think I should join you for dinner," Steve said. "Should I?"

Hoshiko had to laugh. "I suppose," she said. The steward *was* charged with ensuring her mental health, even if it meant ensuring she wouldn't eat alone. "You'd be welcome."

She shook her head as she removed her jacket and checked the live feed from the fleet. There'd been surprisingly little damage, thankfully. She'd assumed—feared—that they'd lose more ships, particularly as the Tokomak adjusted their tactics. But then, if she was right about them deliberately forcing her to expand her supplies…she scowled in frustration. It was never easy to guess which way an alien mindset might jump, not when it might be working from very different assumptions of how the universe worked. The Tokomak might be humanoid, but they weren't *human*. She could understand how *humans* made bad decisions—the decisions were often only *bad* in hindsight—yet alien mentalities were a closed book. The people who claimed that, one day, everyone would be united in a giant collective brain were probably wrong.

Or it might just be a very long time before we achieve full man-machine integration, she thought, as the hatch opened and her grandfather stepped through. *Even LinkShip pilots cannot remain hooked up indefinitely.*

"Congratulations on the battle," Steve said. "You kicked ass."

"I blew up a number of fortresses that could neither evade nor fight back," Hoshiko said, crossly. If *she'd* been defending the gravity point, *she* would have positioned her fortresses some distance from the point itself

255

and used minefields to seal the gap. It would have given her crews time to react, rather than plunging them into a race they couldn't possibly win. "At some point, it starts feeling grossly unfair."

Steve shrugged. "I never had that feeling," he said. "The people we fought were so horrible that I never felt any sympathy for them. I preferred to mourn their victims."

"I'm not going soft on them," Hoshiko said, a little sharper than she'd intended. "I'm just not feeling that heroic."

"I know." Steve gave her a reassuring look. "And I do understand."

Hoshiko sat, rubbing her forehead. It was a display of weakness she would never have allowed herself in front of anyone else, but her grandfather was special. He understood. And he wasn't—technically—one of her subordinates. She wondered, morbidly, just what would happen if she ordered him off her ship. It would be within her legal rights, as supreme commander of the fleet, but… it would be an interesting case. The military authorities might not take her side. It was probably a good thing she didn't *want* to order him off her ship.

She looked up as the steward rolled a trolley into the compartment. Her stomach growled as she smelt the food, stew with mashed potatoes and peas. The steward laid the table with practiced ease, placed two plates on either side and withdrew as silently as he'd come. Hoshiko stood and motioned for Steve to take his seat. Her stomach was still growling, reminding her that it had been a long time since she'd eaten. Ration bars could only take one so far.

"You eat well," Steve commented. "And it has all the right things too."

He smiled. "Do you know how much of a blessing that was, when we had kids?"

"I don't want to think about it," Hoshiko said. She knew her grandfather must have had sex at least once, and her parents too, but… she didn't want to think about it. Really. "It's just a way to get people to eat."

"Precisely," Steve said. "Kids don't want to eat things that are good for them. The things they *want* to eat are—were, in my day—often bad for them. But now, we can produce sweet-tasting things that are actually very *good* for them."

"And naval crewmen," Hoshiko muttered. She cleared her throat. "Is that your way of saying I should eat more?"

"Perish the thought." Steve grinned at her. "I dare say you'd take it about as calmly as I did, when I was your age."

"When dinosaurs ruled the planet, then," Hoshiko needled. It was an old joke. "How old *are* you?"

"Your grasp of basic history is appalling," Steve told her. "I'm not *that* old."

"It all tends to blur together after a while," Hoshiko said. She smiled at his expression. "Are you *sure* you didn't hunt dinosaurs when you were a kid?"

"I hunted terrorists." Steve looked into the distance, his eyes grim. "And your war, for all that will happen if we lose, is far cleaner."

He took a bite of his food. "You should learn to cook," he added. "It's a useful skill."

"I'm aware," Hoshiko said, dryly. "Is there a point?"

"A couple of writers I used to know—they died before I could get them rejuvenated, like Keith—had a character who used cooking as a way to illustrate political thought." Steve smiled at her. "Cooking isn't a matter of throwing things into the pot and seeing what happens. It's more of an art, when you put precisely the right things together and do precisely the right things to them. I took it up myself because it *was* a good insight."

He smiled in happy memory. "Though there was one time I misread the instructions and added cloves—real cloves—instead of garlic cloves. It gave the food a certain...I don't know what."

Hoshiko frowned. "Pardon?"

Steve shrugged. "Something we left behind, a little," he said. "Maybe it doesn't matter. We'll see."

Hoshiko frowned. Her grandfather wasn't *known* for rambling, unlike some of the oldsters who'd been slipping into senility before they'd been rejuvenated. He always had a point, even though she hadn't always been able to see it. She'd always enjoyed talking with him, when she'd been a child, but now...she was in command of the fleet. She didn't have time to engage in discussions...

Or maybe I do, she thought. *It isn't as if I can do anything until we reach the first waypoint.*

She met his eyes. "What do you intend to do, when we win?"

"It depends on the outcome," Steve said, dryly. "We discussed it pretty extensively, back home, before I was dispatched to join you. There are a set of rough guidelines for what we want from any peace talks, but...a lot depends on what happens. It would probably be a mistake to kill the people who can surrender."

"Assuming we can force them to surrender," Hoshiko pointed out. "They might battle us to a draw."

"Yeah." Steve looked pensive. "Or they might defeat us in a straight fight. The cousins across the pond used to say they lost every battle, but the last. I wonder if the Tokomak feel the same way too."

"They told everyone they were utterly invincible," Hoshiko reminded him. "And now, as they suffer defeat after defeat, their claims are starting to look a little hollow."

"Quite." Steve chewed a piece of meat thoughtfully. "It was probably unwise of them to overpromise. Or oversell themselves, for that matter. Nothing they can reasonably accomplish, nothing at all, can live up to their grand claims. They had to have known they could have lost a battle, even a small skirmish between two tiny warships. Did they not know...?"

"There have been plenty of humans who made the mistake of assuming they couldn't possibly lose," Hoshiko commented. "And the Tokomak had thousands of years of unchallenged supremacy before we came along."

"And they could have overwhelmed Earth in an instant if they'd decided to take us seriously, back when I was a boy." Steve laughed, humourlessly. "You know what happened when I was your age?"

"I take no interest in boring pieces of history," Hoshiko said, deadpan.

Steve snorted, clearly realising he was being teased. "There were people who claimed that Earth was being visited regularly by flying saucers.

There were stories about humans being abducted by little gray men and anally probed, then being dumped back on the planet after a whole series of humiliating sexual experiments. And...there were people who made a living using hypnotic regression to bring back buried memories of alien abduction and suchlike, people who claimed the entire government was secretly being run by aliens..."

"You mean it *wasn't*?" Hoshiko smiled. "You're the one who kept saying they came up with insane decisions, following logic no mere mortal could understand."

Steve shrugged. "Point is, back then we didn't know *anything* about galactic civilisation. It never occurred to us that the galaxy would *know* about us and simply not give a damn. Sure, there *were* people abducted by aliens. But they never came home and they never told their stories. It wasn't until the Horde tried to abduct me that we realised the truth. We were *tiny* on an interstellar scale. Why the hell should the Galactics care about us?"

"It was a crazy time," Hoshiko said.

"Yes, exactly." Steve smiled. "The stories probably said more about us than any aliens who might have visited the world. Back then, it was easier to believe that we were being tricked or something rather than accept that *we* were responsible for ourselves. The whole world was going crazy."

"But you survived," Hoshiko said.

"Barely," Steve countered. "It really *was* a crazy time."

Hoshiko met his eyes. "And what's your point?"

Steve looked back at her, evenly. "The Tokomak might not realise that the time has come to negotiate with us," he said. "We're nothing more than upstarts in their view, a child-like race that has somehow gained control of Galactic-level technology and improved upon it. And if that's the case, they may keep talking down to us until it's too late."

"For them or for us?" Hoshiko leaned forward. "They have to realise..."

"They don't." Steve sighed. "There was a time, a hundred or so years before I was born—an eyeblink, to the Galactics—when Europe viewed China as the font of all civilisation. The Chinese had a higher civilisation than Europe…or so they thought. The Chinese thought the same. They thought they could crush the Europeans at any point. It took far too long for both sides to realise that the balance of power had shifted. And by the time it did, it was too late. The handful of Chinese who realised the truth were defeated by their own people, far more than any Europeans. China couldn't reform and so China tore itself apart."

He shrugged. "Maybe they would have made it, if they hadn't been invaded and fought over," he said. "Or maybe they would just have sunk into stagnation. Point is, the people in charge might not realise they've lost even if you're pointing a gun at them. If you're *that* ossified, it may take you years to realise you're no longer in charge."

"Like Great-Uncle Roper," Hoshiko said. The old man in a young man's body had been disturbingly senile. There had been times when she thought it would have been kinder to let him die. "He still thinks he's in Vietnam."

"Worse than that," Steve said. "Your uncle isn't leading an entire country into the fire."

"Or a star system," Hoshiko said. "Or an interstellar empire…"

Her terminal bleeped. She keyed it. "Go ahead."

"Admiral, we're coming up on the first waypoint," Yolanda said. "We'll start attaching the tethers as soon as we drop out of FTL."

"Very good," Hoshiko said. "Inform me when all the tethers are attached."

"Aye, Admiral."

CHAPTER THIRTY

"Duck!"

Martin hit the deck as a spray of plasma fire shot over his head and stuck the far bulkhead, splashes of superhot light flaring wildly. He glanced at Butler, then unhooked a grenade from his belt, shouted a warning and hurled it down the corridor. An alien shape threw itself forward, landing on top of the grenade. Martin had a moment to feel a flicker of respect—and pity—for the alien, before the grenade exploded. The blast vaporised the alien's body and tore the strongpoint apart.

He threw a second grenade down the corridor, then led the charge forward as it detonated. The defenders—Tokomak and their allies, or collaborators who dared not be taken alive—had dug in, sealing off all possible angles of attack as they waited for rescue. Martin knew they couldn't be allowed to die on the vine, not when they were constantly screaming for help from the gravity point defences. He felt the metal vibrate under his feet as another explosion, bigger this time, detonated in the distance. It had to have been a big one. The ring was normally as solid as any planetside structure.

Déjà vu all over again, he thought. The ring was just *too* large for his peace of mind. They couldn't isolate the enemy-held sectors completely and they couldn't destroy the entire structure. The debris falling on the planet below would make the Endor Holocaust look like a child's tea party. *And if we don't get them out, who knows what will happen?*

He glanced up as he heard something above him, a second before a trio of small aliens dropped out of a hatch. They lashed out with makeshift weapons, trying to hurt or kill a human before they were gunned down. Martin didn't hesitate. He shot them down before they could hurt anyone, then kept pushing down the corridor. The little aliens were servitors…he wondered, darkly, why they hadn't simply joined the rebel forces. Surely, they would have been welcome. Or maybe they'd never realised it was a possibility. There was enough horror being openly broadcast over the airwaves for any surviving enemy forces and their collaborators to have grave doubts about their chances if they surrendered.

"We have reinforcements on the way," Butler said. "Rebel troops."

"Surprise, surprise," Martin muttered. He would have preferred *human* troops. "Are they armed and ready?"

"They *say* they're armed and ready," Butler said. "And they're coming."

Martin nodded, then glanced into a large room. A handful of bodies lay on the ground. He frowned, wondering how they'd died. They didn't *look* to have been shot, or caught in one of the explosions…it took him a moment to realise they'd poisoned themselves. They were older children, or young adults…his gorge rose as it dawned on him they'd killed themselves, or had been killed, to keep themselves from falling into rebel hands. He swallowed hard to keep from throwing up, feeling disturbed in a manner he found almost impossible to articulate. The slaughter just kept growing worse.

He put it out of his mind as he forced himself on, searching room after room for the enemy. The compartments were empty, hardly any movement in the tubes or shafts that kept the complex alive. The enemy must be retreating, falling back in hopes of surviving just for a few minutes longer…he let himself wonder if they were already dead, if they had *all* killed themselves, but he didn't believe it. Surely, they wouldn't *all* have killed themselves. He thought he tasted despair as he kept inching forwards. What would *he* have done, if the barbarians were at the gates? Would he have shot Yolanda, and any kids they might have had, to save them from being raped or worse? Or...

A movement caught his eye. A humanoid shape stood in the darkness, peering at him. He tensed, bringing his rifle to bear on the alien. It took a step forward, into the light. A Tokomak, naked save for a belt. Martin wasn't reassured. The Tokomak had been messing around with implanted weapons while humans were still bashing each other's heads in with rocks. The alien could be enhanced to the point where it—he, judging by the genitals—would be a fair match for the entire platoon. It was impossible to be *sure*. He felt his finger tighten on the trigger. One false move and the alien would be blasted to pieces.

"Halt," he barked.

The alien raised his hands, palm outwards. "We wish to surrender and throw ourselves on your protection," he said. The voice was raspy, oddly unnerving. "Please, will you protect us?"

"Come out with your hands up, leaving all your weapons behind," Martin ordered. His mouth was suddenly dry. The vast majority of the ring's population wanted the Tokomak dead. *All* the Tokomak dead. He swore, inwardly, as the aliens appeared. There were kids amongst them, kids who looked to be in their first decade. It was never easy to be *sure* with aliens, but... he gritted his teeth. It wasn't going to be easy to get them to a POW camp without trouble. "This way."

He studied them as they inched forwards. Up close, they looked surprisingly human as long as they didn't *move*. It seemed almost a betrayal when they *did* move, their too-long arms and legs jerking in ways only a contortionist could match. They appeared so close to humanity that he found it hard to even *look* at them, as if he could be tricked into believing them human if he didn't take care. It was hard to be sure, again, but he thought they looked terrified. He didn't blame them. Mobs were stupid and dangerous. They'd tear the prisoners limb from limb if they got a chance.

Butler nudged him. "You sure about this, sir?"

"Yes," Martin said, curtly. "It has to be done."

He detailed two men to inspect the alien positions, and try to determine if there were any more inside, then motioned for the aliens to keep moving. If they were lucky...he keyed his throatmike, reporting on the prisoners and asking the rebel command to clear a path to the FOB. There were already a handful of prisoners in the base, aliens who'd been stunned or managed to surrender before it was too late. Martin told himself, firmly, that the POWs could speak to hold-outs, reassuring them that it was safe to surrender. But, in truth, he wasn't sure that was actually true.

His heart started to pound as they made their way along the main corridor. It was massive by human standards, easily the size of an interstate, but he still felt confined. The ring was really too big. He would have preferred something smaller, something more...*personal*. The ring was an impressive piece of work...his thoughts slammed to a halt as he saw the mob, looming in the distance. He heard a cry of dismay from behind him and bit his lip. It wasn't going to look good, if they had to open fire on the mob to save the prisoners. And yet, he wasn't going to send them to be killed either.

A rebel leader, marked by a red armband, strode forward. "Thank you for capturing these people for us," he said. "You can hand them over now."

"We're going to take them back to the FOB, where they will be treated as prisoners," Martin said. He kept his voice calm. Mobs could scent fear. "You can take your team to secure the rear."

The leader looked worried. Martin winced, inwardly. The great problem with rebel cells—with any sort of insurgency, really—was that the chain of command was nothing more than fiction. A leader who lost face would often lose control, once his position was damaged beyond repair. His people might turn on him, or worse. Martin kicked himself, silently, for forgetting the lessons of the streets. He'd grown too used to law and order, to a clear chain of command...

"We want them," the leader said. "Justice!"

"Justice," the mob echoed. "Justice!"

"There will be justice," Martin said. "But they have to have fair trials."

"Give them to us," the leader ordered. "Now."

Martin leaned forward, lowering his voice. "We promised we would protect them, if they surrendered. We meant it. If you try to take them by force, we'll open fire. Your people will be killed. And afterwards, when the fleet arrives, there will be no help for your planet and it will be *your* fault. Take your people and go."

The words hung on the air, just for a second. Martin tensed. The marines would kill hundreds of people, if it came down to a fight, but…in the end, they would be overwhelmed and killed themselves. God alone knew what would happen when word reached the higher leadership—and Piece—on Tokomak One. They'd be unable to decide between punishing whatever remained of the mob, to please their human allies, or letting the mob go unpunished to please their population. It wouldn't be an easy choice…

"Fine," the leader said. "But there will be justice!"

He turned and walked away, speaking to his people as he led them around the marines and further into the ring. They hissed and spat at the prisoners, but nothing worse. Martin breathed a sigh of relief as they resumed their march, hoping and praying they'd reach the FOB before something else happened. Sweat trickled down his back. He'd fled one set of rough streets to build a career for himself in the marines. He didn't want to die on another set of streets.

The FOB was a large complex that had been a school, before it had been taken over by the provisional government and placed in the care of their most reliable troops. Martin handed the prisoners over to the guards, with clear instructions for their care and dire threats of what would happen if they were mistreated in any way. He hoped they'd listen, now that they were building a new world for themselves. The desire for revenge ran deep, but so did the desire for something new…

You're thinking like a Solarian, he reminded himself. *You should be thinking like an Earther.*

His intercom chimed. "Captain," Piece said. "We need to talk."

"I suppose we do," Martin said. He motioned for Butler to take command. "You can teleport me, can't you?"

265

He closed his eyes, a moment before the teleport field gripped him. The tingle ran up and down his body, seemingly timeless even though he *knew* it was a bare second or two. There were no shortage of horror stories about ghosts in the matter stream, of entities that existed in the never-never land of teleport space... stories that wouldn't go away, no matter how extensively they were debunked. He opened his eyes and breathed a sigh of relief as he looked around Tokomak One. Relaying the teleport signal through a pair of booster stations was always a risk. It wouldn't be taken if things weren't urgent.

"They're planning to rename the station something else," Piece said. He stood by the control pad, watching Martin with grim eyes. "Freedom One, perhaps."

"I think the name's already taken," Martin said. He didn't try to hide his irritation. "Why did you recall me so quickly?"

Piece met his eyes. "The rebel commanders have already lodged complaints about you taking prisoners," he said. "Did you have to...?"

"Yes." Martin looked back at him, refusing to even *think* about backing down. "I'm not going to preside over a slaughter. Sir."

"Our allies want to take control of the ring," Piece pointed out. "They say..."

"It will be a great deal easier to take control, without the enemy kicking and screaming and ruining as much as possible before they get rounded up and killed, if the Tokomak think they *can* surrender," Martin countered. "If they think they'll be killed anyway, *sir*, why in the umpteen billion names of God would they surrender? They might as well do what they can to hurt us before we wipe them out."

"I understand your point," Piece said. "But..."

"Understand this," Martin said. "I will not be responsible, directly or indirectly, for a slaughter. If enemy combatants surrender to me, they will be treated in line with official procedures for handling POWs and their dependents. We will treat them well as long as they behave themselves."

Piece cocked an eyebrow. "Do you understand just how many slaughters you kicked off when you captured Tokomak One?"

Martin felt the urge to slam his fist into the deep-cover agent's face. "Yes. I do. I also know we *had* to take the station. And yes, I know there *were* slaughters. I *do* have blood on my hands. But I won't slaughter helpless prisoners, sir. Is that understood?"

"I've communicated as much to our allies," Piece said. "They may insist on securing the remainder of the ring themselves."

"And much joy I wish them of it," Martin said. The ring was staggeringly huge. It would take *years* for the entire structure to be searched from top to bottom. "Now, was there a reason you called me beyond chewing my ass about prisoners?"

Piece shrugged. "You'll be pleased to know the latest raid was turned back," he said, as he led the way out the chamber and down the corridor. "The gravity point defenders aren't interested in doing more than sniping at us."

"For the moment," Martin said. He'd seen the LinkShip's report. An alien fleet—an unimaginably huge alien fleet—was bearing down on the Twins. Admiral Teller was on his way, if the last update they'd received was accurate, but he might not get to the Twins first. "What happens when their fleet arrives?"

"We get our asses kicked," Piece said. "There's no way we can stand off even a fraction of that fleet."

Martin nodded, curtly, as they entered the command centre. A dozen aliens sat at consoles, working frantically to get the defences on line and build up a datanet before the Tokomak arrived to knock it down again. They'd taken control of the fixed defences, but they had very little mobile firepower. A handful of freighters, crammed with missiles, would delay the Tokomak for a few seconds before they were blown away. The gunboats would pose a tougher threat, but the Tokomak could afford to simply ignore them and concentrate on the orbital defences. They'd know the gunboats wouldn't pose a long-term threat.

Unless they decide Admiral Teller is a more important target, he told himself. *They might just let us live long enough to delay them for a minute, if they concentrate on Admiral Teller.*

"So," he said. "Is there any update from the Admiral?"

"None." Piece indicated the screen. "Our best-case estimate is that he gets here first, whereupon he can make a stand on the gravity point. Our worst-case is that he gets here too late, after the aliens have had a chance to deploy themselves. That's pretty much guaranteed disaster."

"For us," Martin said. "They *might* move their fleet too close to the gravity point."

"They've got enough point defence that it probably won't matter," Piece said. "And, in any case, they're not likely to repeat their old mistakes. They'll keep the fleet at a distance and smash Admiral Teller's ships, one by one, as they try to make transit. It may not be a *complete* disaster, but…"

"It will be," Martin predicted. He knew Admiral Stuart was doing *something*, but… it didn't matter. They had to hold the Twins or everything they'd done would be for nothing. "Can we not find a way to weaken them?"

"So far, no." Piece tapped the display. Large clusters of red icons orbited the gravity points. "They can't get to us, right now, but we can't get to them either. But once they get reinforcements, all those calculations will go out the airlock."

Martin nodded. "I know the score."

"I know," Piece echoed. "We see no way to change it."

"And there's no point in trying to talk to them," Martin said. The Tokomak hadn't answered any of their hails, even the ones offering to organise a local truce until the war was over. "Or have the rebel leaders changed their calculations?"

"They can't." Piece shrugged. "If they surrender, they'll be slaughtered. They knew it before the uprising began."

Martin glanced at the console, wondering—not for the first time—if Piece really cared. An uprising on the Twins, particularly one that took out the planetary infrastructure and the trained workforce, would help humanity even if the Tokomak fought their way back into the system and regained control. It would make a certain kind of sense to let the Tokomak and rebels fight it out, while humanity waited for the right moment to push through the gravity point. He rebelled, instinctively, against the logic ... but he understood it. God, he understood it. He just thought it was revolting.

In more senses than one, he thought. *What happens to the galaxy if the rebel forces are gravely weakened?*

"Then we should start making plans for the coming battle," he said. It went against the grain to just *wait* to be attacked, even though he knew there were times when there was no other way to proceed. "We do have all those missiles stockpiled, don't we?"

"Not enough," Piece said. A set of red icons appeared on the display. Urgent commands echoed around the compartment as the operators struggled to deal with the new threat. "I'm afraid we're dependent on Admiral Teller. If he doesn't get here soon, we're screwed."

CHAPTER THIRTY-ONE

"Admiral," Yolanda said. "We'll drop out of FTL in twenty seconds."

"Understood," Hoshiko said. The fleet was already at red alert, just in case the Tokomak had had enough warning to set up a gravity net and yank them out of FTL ahead of time. "Be ready to engage if necessary..."

She silently counted down the last few seconds, bracing herself as the fleet shuddered back into normal space. They'd used the tethers to convince the locals that *only* a relative handful of ships were bearing down on Crux, but there was no way to be sure the defenders would fall for it. The Tokomak had used the trick themselves, time and time again. She leaned forward as the display rapidly updated, revealing a system frantically scrambling to defend itself. Crux had an immense industrial base, with enough natural resources to keep a spacefaring civilisation going for hundreds of thousands of years. The only downside, as far as the Tokomak were concerned, was that it lacked a gravity point. They'd surveyed the system extensively, according to the files, but found none. It had to have been a disappointment.

Her lips quirked as the fleet shook itself down, heading straight towards the shipyards. Crux was *important* to the Tokomak, both as an industrial centre *and* as the first system they'd settled after they'd invented the stardrive. The massive settlements on the system's planets were completely dominated by the Tokomak, with only a relative handful of other races...according to the census. There was a permanent underclass of undocumented workers, the files stated, but they simply didn't have any legal rights. If they stayed quiet, they were ignored; if they caused trouble, they were summarily shot or deported. Hoshiko was fairly sure there wouldn't be any revolutions or insurgencies *here*. Crux just didn't have the population to make them practical.

Which means we have to take the system the old-fashioned way, she thought. *Or, at least, to lay waste to its industrial base.*

She glanced at Yolanda. "Send the surrender demand," she ordered. "We'll see if they reply."

"Aye, Admiral," Yolanda said.

Hoshiko waited as the fleet closed on the enemy shipyards. They were staggeringly huge, each and every slip filled with starships in varying stages of construction. Other structures—free-floating structures—held position near starships that were clearly being pulled out of long-term storage and readied for dispatch to the front. Her smile grew colder as she spotted the immense reserve fleet, hundreds of starships that were dead and cold and little more than sitting ducks. She'd destroy them without a second thought, if the locals refused to surrender unconditionally. There was no way she could take the risk of leaving them intact. They were just too dangerous.

And if they don't surrender soon, she mused, *we'll enter engagement range.*

She watched the massive defences as they girded themselves for battle. There were fewer starships than she'd expected—they must have been redeployed to the front—but there were dozens of orbital fortresses and literally *thousands* of automated weapons platforms. No minefields, unsurprisingly. There was little point in trying to mine space when the enemy could simply move around them or blow them away from a safe distance. But enough firepower to protect the planets and the shipyards...she gritted her teeth. She didn't have time to take the facilities intact. She wanted—she needed—to destroy them.

"Weapons range in ten seconds," Yolanda said. "Request permission to deploy targeting probes."

"Do so," Hoshiko ordered. "And fire as soon as we enter range."

The last few seconds ticked down. *Defiant* opened fire, the remainder of the fleet following suit a second later. The enemy defences fired at the same moment, clearly calculating that Hoshiko would sooner impale herself on their missiles than risk a jump into FTL so close to the planet itself. She allowed herself a cold smile as her ships fired a second barrage, then a third. They'd have just enough time, if they were lucky, to fire a fourth before it was time to run.

"Launch stealth missiles," she ordered. The enemy missiles were growing closer, the red icons on the display blurring into a single mass, a hammer aimed at her ships. "And jump as soon as the enemy missiles enter engagement range."

"Aye, Admiral." Yolanda counted down the seconds. "FTL in five, four, three..."

Hoshiko felt *Defiant* scream in protest as her stardrive came online, catapulting her backwards at FTL speeds. The gravity field twitched, making her head spin; behind her, she heard someone throwing up violently. She tried to ignore it as the ship crashed back out of FTL, only a few million kilometres from the planet. But, as far as the enemy missiles were concerned, they were *far* out of range. They might as well be on the other side of the galaxy.

You should have set up gravity wells to trap us, she thought, coldly. There was no *technological* reason why ships couldn't use FTL so close to a planet's gravity well. It was simply law and custom, something she'd chosen to ignore. *Instead, you fired your missiles for nothing.*

"*Yorktown* and *Ladysmith* have been destroyed," Yolanda reported. "Preliminary analysis suggests they collided as they came out of FTL. A number of other ships are reporting varying levels of damage to their drives, plus crewmen rendered useless by the mass jump..."

"Reorganise the fleet," Hoshiko ordered, when Yolanda had finished. "And close the range again."

She smiled as she assessed the damage. The enemy had used their ECM to its fullest extent, but they hadn't realised just how badly they'd been exposed by Admiral Webster's targeting drones. Thousands of her missiles had been swatted out of space, but the remainder had all found their targets and they'd *all* carried antimatter warheads. A dozen fortresses had been blown out of space, while seven more were badly damaged. The enemy starships were altering position, trying to plug the hole in their defences, but it was too late. The stealth missiles had slipped through the gap and slammed into a handful of targets, smashing them effortlessly. It looked as though the shipyard was on the verge of total destruction.

"Alpha units, target the remaining fortresses and enemy starships," Hoshiko ordered. "Beta units, target the reserve ships."

She watched, grimly, as a line of enemy gunboats lunged towards her ships, shooting plasma bursts and tiny missiles as they came into range. There was nothing wrong with their bravery, she noted, but they were designed more to intimidate freighters than take on warships. There was a *reason* the starfighter concept had never got off the ground, despite Admiral Glass and his science-fiction writers trying their level best to make it work. The gunboats were just too large to make difficult targets and too slow to make good missiles. They fought desperately, a handful even ramming her ships, but one by one they were picked off with casual ease. They would have been better employed, part of her mind noted, as mobile point defence platforms. But that would have meant floating around and waiting to be hit.

Perhaps they should have crammed their gunboats with antimatter before they threw them at us, she mused. *It would have been much more effective.*

The enemy fire grew more desperate as her ships directed their missiles towards the free-floating reserve fleet. They had no drive fields or shields to protect their hulls, not even point defence weapons ... they were ruthlessly blown out of space, destroyed one by one to keep them from ever becoming a threat. She hoped, despite herself, that they'd killed the workforce as well as the ships themselves. The Tokomak had hundreds of thousands of ships in reserve. They could redirect the crews to other ships if they weren't dead already.

"They're bringing more and more fire to bear on us," Yolanda warned. "The remaining fortresses are holding their own."

Hoshiko scowled. She'd hoped to avoid using hammers. They would be impossible to replace, at least until the fleet linked up with Admiral Teller…if the fleet ever *did* link up with Admiral Teller. She weighed the situation for a moment, then reluctantly gave the order to fire the hammers. They had to win as quickly as possible, in hopes of forcing the Tokomak into a hasty reaction. Ideally, their fleet would be in transit to Crux while *she* was attacking Tokomak Prime.

She watched, resting her hands on her lap, as four fortresses exploded into plasma. A fifth took a glancing blow and survived, although it was clearly damaged beyond repair. Lifepods exploded in all directions, a hand-ful of surviving gunboats moving to pick them up before they could be mistaken for mines or weapons and blown out of space. Hoshiko tapped her console, ordering her ships to ignore the gunboats as long as they were engaged in SAR duties. There was no need to commit mass slaughter, par-ticularly if there was nothing to be gained by doing it.

And what will this war make us, she asked herself, *if there comes a time when we must commit slaughter for tactical advantage?*

She put the thought aside as her fleet punched its way into the shipyard, its weapons rapidly tearing through the remaining defences and into the shipyards themselves. They tried to avoid targeting the fabricators and the dorms, but everything else was fair game. Her lips hardened as she saw a giant battleship, her sides open to space, explode into plasma as a missile strike consumed the construction yard. Alien shuttles flew everywhere, trying to evacuate the complex or distract her missiles from tearing it apart. She cursed the defenders under her breath as one of the shuttles strayed into a missile's path and exploded, wiped out before the pilot knew what had happened to him. The bastards *had* to know they'd lost the battle...why the hell didn't they just surrender?

They're forcing me to expend my missiles, she thought, numbly. *And they're succeeding.*

She closed her eyes for a long moment as the last of the construction ships exploded, taking three half-built cruisers with it. The tactic might work, damn it. She'd brought her fleet train along, but she knew all too well that she only had enough supplies left for one final full-sized battle. She could devastate Crux and lose the battle at Tokomak Prime, the battle she had to win. And that meant...

"Recall the fleet." Hoshiko opened her eyes. "Pull back to overwatch position and hold there. Transmit another demand for planetary surrender, then prime the marines to capture the remaining fabricators. If they refuse to surrender...we'll do what we see fit."

She studied the ring for a long moment, wondering if she dared open fire on it. The giant megastructure would do immense damage if it exploded, pieces of debris falling on the planet below. The impacts would probably render the entire planet uninhabitable. She considered, briefly, trying to take out the orbital towers and shoving the ring into open space, but it would be dangerously unpredictable. The damage would be beyond calculation if things went wrong. She tapped her console, trying to work out the risks, then decided it was pointless. It was the sort of procedure that should only be carried out in peacetime, not when the missiles were flying and it would be all too easy for something to go wrong.

"There's been no response," Yolanda reported. "They've sent out a fleet of courier boats, all heading to Tokomak Prime, but...no response to us."

"Keep disengaging the fleet," Hoshiko ordered. She'd destroyed a sizable chunk of the Tokomak's infrastructure. Surely—now—they'd realise they weren't going to be able to resume business as usual once the war came to an end. The remainder of the system was at her mercy. It wouldn't take *that* long to hunt down the remaining fabricators and destroy them. The mining stations were useless without an industrial base to supply. "And keep repeating the demand for surrender."

She shrugged. She'd smashed the shipyards and a sizeable chunk of the system's infrastructure. She could hit the ring—or the planet itself—at any moment. And they had to know it. She considered, briefly, targeting power stations or other important positions on the planet herself, then dismissed the thought. It would make millions of people miserable, for nothing. Tokomak Prime wouldn't surrender, at least until she managed to hold a knife to their throats. There was nothing to be gained by bombarding an innocent civilian population.

"Call the fleet train," she ordered. "They are to begin reloading the fleet."

"Aye, Admiral," Yolanda said. "Captain Hawkins proposes obliterating the asteroid settlements."

"Tell him to hold his fire," Hoshiko ordered. She understood the younger man's frustration—the Tokomak were surviving because of human scruples, not because they'd fought the invaders to a standstill—but there was no point in expending any more weapons. They'd dealt a mighty blow to their enemies. There was no point in pushing matters to the point where they turned victory into defeat. "And I want his ships ready to depart as planned."

She leaned back in her chair. By any standards, she'd won a great victory. She'd smashed a sizable chunk of one of the largest industrial bases known to exist and rendered the remainder useless, at least for the moment. And she'd carried the war—finally—into territory that was indisputably Tokomak. The Tokomak couldn't make excuses any longer; they couldn't tell themselves they hadn't lost anything important. They knew her fleet was far too close to their homeworld for their peace of mind.

And once the rearming is complete, we'll launch the final offensive, she told herself. *One way or the other, we will make the war end.*

"Admiral, we're picking up a signal," Yolanda said. "It's the planet."

Hoshiko straightened. "Put them through."

She kept her face impassive as an enemy face—a *Tokomak* face—materialised in front of her. It was a face that had haunted her nightmares for years, ever since the sheer power of their enemies had dawned on her. Disturbingly human, arrogant, aristocratic… she told herself, firmly, that she was reading too much into an alien face. There were aliens that looked truly monstrous. The Tokomak might well be a strikingly ugly human.

"You have profaned our space," the Tokomak said. "And you will leave. Now."

Hoshiko had to fight to keep her face blank, although she had the feeling the Tokomak couldn't read her expressions any more than she could read theirs. Less, perhaps. Their servants had had to learn to read their modes out of sheer desperation. The Tokomak had never needed to do the same themselves. It crossed her mind that, if the war ended on reasonably decent terms, the Tokomak would have to adapt or die. There'd be old alien matrons writing to the media about the uppitiness of their former slaves and complaining, bitterly, about the servant problem…

"I shall be blunt," she said, throwing diplomacy to the wolves. "I control the system. I can force my way into the high orbitals at any moment I wish. If I choose, I can lay waste to what remains of the system, including the planet and its ring. Are we clear on that point?"

The Tokomak looked as if she'd socked him in the face. "I…"

"And nothing can excuse your rudeness," Hoshiko continued. The Tokomak were obsessed with good manners, amongst themselves at least. "I am Admiral Stuart"—she was tempted to give herself a whole string of titles, secure in the belief the Tokomak wouldn't know she was lying—"commanding officer of this fleet. To whom do I have the honour of speaking?"

"I…" The Tokomak jerked—for a moment, Hoshiko thought he'd been shot—and then steadied himself. "I am Governor-General Ripen. I must request that you leave this system at once."

So now it's a request, Hoshiko thought. *Oh, how the mighty do fall.*

She allowed herself a cold smile. "No. I have taken this system and I have no intention of letting it go. Not yet. I will not touch the planet, Governor-General, as long as it doesn't impede me in any way. Your ultimate fate will be decided by the peace talks after the war. I strongly suggest that you and your people stay out of my way."

The Governor-General looked even more astonished. She reminded herself that he wasn't human, and his expressions might mean something altogether different, but... she shrugged, inwardly. It didn't matter. As long as he understood the situation, as long as he was prepared to refrain from doing anything stupid, he could do whatever he liked. Besides, he might just realise there was no guarantee Hoshiko would return from Tokomak Prime. The war didn't *have* to end with a human victory.

"If you make trouble for me, I will destroy the ring," she stated, coldly. She wouldn't give him terms to accept or reject. It would give him a chance to convince himself that she wasn't in as strong a position as she was. She would just tell him how things would be. "And that will be the end."

She tapped her console, closing the channel. "Yolanda, alert me if they try to contact us, but do not open a channel," she ordered. "Let them wait for us to go."

"Aye, Admiral," Yolanda said.

Hoshiko nodded as she checked the reports. A couple of days to resupply... she cursed under her breath. The timing was going to be a pain. She made a mental note to dispatch a recon mission, wishing—again—for a LinkShip. It would have made the next stage of the mission so much easier.

But we're on the verge of victory or defeat, she told herself. *Next stop, Tokomak Prime.*

CHAPTER THIRTY-TWO

Hameeda gritted her teeth as she transited the gravity point, nearly ramming a mine as she sneaked through the field and slipped into open space. The defenders had been busy, *very* busy. She tried not to shake as her onboard simulators calculated the odds of survival. It had been sheer goddamned luck she hadn't stuck a mine when she'd jumped into the system. A few microns to one side or the other and she'd have been dead. She skimmed through the defences, heading straight for clear space on the other side of the fortresses. The defenders had built one hell of a strongpoint. They'd positioned half their fortresses at quite some distance from the gravity point, giving them a chance to snipe anyone coming through without being blown away by assault pods.

Good thinking, Hameeda thought, sourly. She frowned as more and more data flowed into her sensors, warning her of fighting across the entire system. It looked small-scale, but alarmingly persistent. *But it won't be enough to stop us.*

She uploaded the data to a pair of drones, then launched them both on ballistic trajectories. They were completely silent, almost invisible even to her sensors—and she had the advantage of knowing where they were going to be—but she wasn't sure they were undetectable. The enemy was flooding the gravity point in sensor emissions, to the point she knew she'd been damn lucky not to be scanned, targeted and destroyed when she made transit. The mines alone might have put an end to her...she told herself, firmly, to stop worrying. She'd just have to hope Admiral Glass and his fellows worked the bugs out of the recon probe concept before it was too late. The Tokomak would realise just what she could do, if they hadn't already, and all hell would be out for noon.

The drones vanished, faint flickers of gravimetric energies reaching her sensors as they made transit. The enemy gunboats stirred, rushing forward to the gravity point. Hameeda gritted her teeth as the countdown began, knowing that she might have helped and hindered the offensive at the same time. The enemy had no way to tell the drones had transited *out* of the system, instead of jumping *into* the system, but...it might work out for them anyway. Admiral Teller would begin the first assault as soon as his staffers had downloaded the data from the drones and updated their targeting locks. And then...

Unless he gets cold feet when he sees the sheer size of the defences, Hameeda thought. *And it would be very hard to blame him.*

She felt a little intimidated herself. This time, the defenders couldn't be smashed from relative safety. She wondered, grimly, if some of the mines were actually Tokomak-designed assault pods. They could start firing back through the gravity point, once the assault confirmed to them that the human ships were in place. She made a mental note of it as the countdown ticked down to zero. It was an idea humanity might want to try if the Tokomak pushed them back out of the system. Who knew? It might give them an edge when the shit *really* hit the fan.

The gravity point exploded with energy as the first antimatter pods made transit, setting off a series of explosions that devastated the mine-fields. Hameeda wanted to whoop and cheer as chain reactions rushed through the mines, blowing hundreds of thousands into atoms before they could react. A second wave of antimatter pods warped into existence a moment later, setting off *another* series of explosions. She smiled, coldly, as one of the gunboats blasted an antimatter pod before its onboard systems could switch off the containment chambers. The resulting explosion vaporised the gunboat as well as its fellows.

But we announced our coming, she thought, as the first assault pods started to materialise on the gravity point. *And they're getting their defences online.*

She watched as successive waves of enemy gunboats fell on the pods, trying to take them out before they confirmed their position, located their targets and opened fire. It was a good tactic, she had to admit as pods started to vanish. Admiral Teller would have no way to know how many pods had been destroyed, and how many enemy fortresses remained intact, before he started to send warships through the gravity point. The remaining pods opened fire, unleashing a wave of devastation that roared towards the nearest fortresses. The Tokomak returned fire, launching missiles towards the gravity point. Hameeda frowned, then cursed as she realised what they were doing. The antimatter-tipped missiles were blowing hell out of the human missiles, trying to reduce the damage they could do. They'd taken the antimatter minesweeping concept and improved upon it.

Bastards, she thought, coldly.

A second wave of assault pods materialised as the first set of missiles found their targets. Four fortresses were blown into rubble, two more heavily damaged ... Hameeda knew, all too well, that it wasn't enough. The Tokomak *knew* they couldn't let the humans get into the Twins, knew they couldn't surrender the system without giving up hope of recovering chunks of their empire in the near future. She eyed their starships, holding position near the outer fortresses, considering her options. She *did* have a handful of hammers. She *could* make an impact, if she picked the right moment.

She held back as the battle raged on, as more and more assault pods flickered into existence and discharged their contents towards the enemy fortresses. A handful—no, nearly half of them—held back long enough for their automatic systems to update their targeting, although that exposed them to enemy gunboats. Hameeda wished *she* could slip them targeting data, even though she knew it would be useless. There was just too much electronic distortion around the gravity point. She couldn't update them without risking detection. Instead, she could only watch as the gunboats blew hell out of the pods before they launched.

A small fleet of starships appeared on the gravity point. Hameeda stared, utterly shocked as a handful interpenetrated and vanished in eye-tearing balls of light. Madness! She couldn't believe that *Admiral Teller*, of all people, had authorised suicide tactics. And yet…she frowned as her sensors sought harder data, noting that the ships were all captured alien vessels pressed into service. The alien rebels? Or robot ships? Admiral Teller had been vague when he'd told her how he planned to conduct the offensive. Had he had something like it in mind all along?

The captured starships opened fire, unloading their missiles towards the distant fortresses even as they picked off gunboats with point defence. Hameeda felt reassured—slightly—as her analysis subroutines calculated that most, if not all, of the captured starships were relying on automatics. The fleet hadn't had a proper AI with them, but it hardly mattered if the ships were considered expendable. They lumbered away from the gravity point, their point defence lashing out in all directions. And then they exploded as one. Hameeda jumped as alerts flashed up in her mind. There had been so much antimatter loaded into the ships that, for a few vital seconds, every sensor in the area was blinded.

She smiled as the next wave of assault pods appeared on the gravity point. They didn't bother to retarget their weapons before opening fire, unleashing hell towards the remaining fortresses. Admiral Teller had planned the assault well, she conceded. The unmanned ships had to have launched drones the moment they arrived, updating the admiral on the success of his assault. She turned her attention to the distant fortresses as the enemy starships started to move, gliding towards the gravity point. They were going to regret that, she thought, as a stream of mid-sized human ships began to appear. Admiral Teller was cutting the time between transitions down to the minimum possible. It was quite possible that one ship would ram another, even if they didn't interpenetrate. But the admiral clearly believed the reward was worth the risk.

Hameeda smiled as the human ships seemed to multiply. The newcomers weren't *real*, of course. No one would risk jumping cruisers through a gravity point in unison. They were drones, nothing more than sensor ghosts...but, with the enemy sensor network having taken one hell of a beating, they'd have real trouble telling the real ships from the ghosts. And then another wave of ships arrived...she frowned, unsure just what was happening. The ships looked real, but they couldn't be real...

She had to laugh as she realised what had happened. The cruisers had been linked together, their hulls practically touching, before one of them had jumped *both* ships through the gravity point. The cruisers were overdesigned, overpowered for their size...she felt an insane urge to giggle as she realised the Tokomak would be totally surprised. They'd *never* think of hooking two ships together and sending them through the gravity point. A handful of massive bulk freighters appeared on the point, their hulls shattering seconds later to reveal a squadron of destroyers each. Admiral Teller really *had* pulled a fast one. The Tokomak had never thought of designing a starship capable of carrying *other* starships.

Not that they ever built anything smaller than a gunboat, she reminded herself, as the growing human fleet swept the space around the gravity point. *They never* needed *to invent starfighter carriers for themselves.*

She smiled as the steady stream of human ships built up into an overwhelming flood, flushing their external racks towards the remaining fortresses. The Tokomak seemed torn between rushing to their deaths and falling back, even though they *knew* that would mean surrendering much of the system. The battle was so intense it had probably set off alarms across the system. Anyone who was sitting on their hands, unwilling to revolt because they didn't know who'd win, would probably be rethinking their stance. And the rebels had to be taking heart. They knew, now, that it was just a matter of time before the human fleet cleared the gravity points and pushed on...

An alarm ran through her head. *Oh no...*

• • •

Neola had thought, when her ships had first entered the Twins, that she'd won the race. It had been obvious, from reports funnelled up the chain, that the revolt had stalemated, that the rebels couldn't secure the gravity point while the remaining Tokomak couldn't retake the planetary rings. She'd told them to do nothing more than snipe at the enemy until her fleet arrived, then concentrated on getting her fleet to the Twins as quickly as possible. But it was becoming apparent that she hadn't *really* won the race. There hadn't been enough time to get her entire fleet through the gravity point before the humans began *their* arrival.

She paced her command deck in impatience as her fleet shook down, readying itself for the jump into FTL. If only she'd had more time! If only her fleet had drilled together, trained together...right now, she would have settled for them reading and actually *understanding* the same tactical manuals. In hindsight, perhaps it had been a mistake to discourage their allies from actually *studying* war. It would have given them ideas, but...it didn't matter. Right now, every last Galactic was under threat. They *had* to fight together.

But I got there in time to win, she told herself. *If I can take control of the gravity point...*

An aide cleared his throat. "Your Majesty, the fleet is ready to enter FTL."

Neola resisted the urge to tear his head off. If the fleet had trained for longer, they could have jumped into FTL and dropped out right on top of the gravity point. She could have slammed a cork in the bottle, then wiped out whatever human ships had made it through before it was too late. But she didn't dare try anything fancy, not with a fleet that would end up scattered, easy meat for its human enemies, if she took the risk. The gravity fluctuations near a gravity point were bad enough, but compensating for thousands of starships dropping out of FTL in the same general location would be considerably worse. Given time, she could have compensated for it. But she hadn't had the time.

"Order the fleet to open fire as soon as they have targets," she said. "And take us into FTL!"

She felt a quiver running through the starship as she dropped into FTL, racing across the system. The humans would see her coming, of course, but there wouldn't be anything they could do about it. They wouldn't even have time to turn and jump back through the gravity point. She'd hoped to sneak up on the gravity point, but the timing simply hadn't worked out. She told herself, firmly, that it didn't matter. The chance to isolate and destroy a number of human ships could not be wasted. And if she was lucky, she could seal off the system and recapture the planets at leisure.

And then teach the rebels the price of disobedience, she thought. There would be no mercy, not this time. She'd drop rocks until they surrendered and then...she smiled coldly. The useful workers would be saved, but the remainder would be transported to a harsh world and told to develop it. If, of course, they wanted to live. Or perhaps she'd simply bombard the planetary surface to ash. It would be much easier to exploit if no one lived there. *If they're dead, they can't rebel.*

Her hearts clenched as the fleet dropped back into realspace, too far from the gravity point for her peace of mind. The massive defences she'd seen, the last time she'd passed through the gravity point, were completely wrecked. A handful of fortresses were still intact, but judging from their weak fire and weaker shields they'd been heavily damaged. The remainder were nothing more than debris, if that. The squadrons of starships that had once held position on the point were battered beyond easy repair, the minefields and gunboats were gone...and hundreds of hostile icons surrounded the gravity point. Neola felt her hearts sink. She knew a sizable number of those ships had to be fake, but how many? Her display kept updating, suggesting the answer was *very few*. Sensor ghosts couldn't fire missiles at enemy targets.

"Activate the gravity well projectors," she ordered. It was unfortunate the humans could probably keep her from interfering with the gravity point itself, something she would have been reluctant to do in any case, but it didn't matter. All that mattered was that she pinned the human ships in realspace, allowing her to smoother them with missiles and batter them to death. "And open fire."

She allowed herself a tight smile. She hadn't quite won the race, but the humans hadn't won it either. And she had most of her fleet with her, while the humans had only a small percentage of *their* fleet with them. She could afford to take heavy losses, if it meant shutting the gravity point. And then...

A low shudder ran through the giant ship. Neola watched the remainder of the fleet open fire, each battleship hurling hundreds of missiles towards their human enemies. The sheer weight of firepower was terrifying, even to *her*. The humans might have better technology—and *that* was galling beyond words—but... so what? Let them swat ninety percent of her missiles, if they could. She'd *still* deal them a heavy blow.

And then we'll crush their homeworld, she promised herself. *And then, we will make sure this never happens again.*

• • •

"Admiral," Commander Jalil said. "The enemy ships have opened fire."

"I can see that," Colin said. "Retarget the point defence."

He kept his voice even, somehow. The wave of missiles roaring towards his ships was really a *wall*, the icons blurring together into an immense and utterly implacable force threatening to obliterate his entire fleet. It was a tidal wave of destruction, one he couldn't avoid. The timing sucked, worse than he'd thought. He would almost have preferred to discover that the enemy fleet had reached the Twins first and taken up position on the gravity point. Then, at least, he would have had the option of declining battle.

"We'll go with Theta-Three," he said, as the vectors updated. The enemy fleet was pushing towards the gravity point, heedless of the risks. They'd either crush his ships or drive them away from the point, winning either way. "Launch the first drone, then get us underway."

"Aye, Admiral."

Colin nodded to himself. He'd done everything he could—everything his tactical officers could think to try—to get ships through the gravity point as quickly as possible. And it had worked, giving him a force multiplier the Tokomak hadn't seen coming. But it had also made it impossible for him to retreat *back* through the gravity point if things went spectacularly wrong. He couldn't even drop into FTL. The Tokomak had arranged things to trap his fleet and pound them into dust...

Clever, he thought. The Tokomak weren't stupid. It was a lesson some of his tactical officers would need to remember, if they survived the next few minutes. *And, if our plans aren't as good as we think, it may be enough to stop us.*

His ship picked up speed as she moved away from the gravity point. The aliens lumbered towards them, keeping their vectors fixed on the gravity point itself. Colin nodded in understanding. Their target wasn't the fleet, but the point. They wanted—they *needed*—to split the human fleet. They'd make it impossible for him to rearm his ships before he ran out of time.

"Launch the second drone," he ordered, as enemy missiles started to enter his point defence envelope. "And pray that God remembers who's in the right."

CHAPTER THIRTY-THREE

Hameeda wasn't sure what to do.

Admiral Teller's ships were moving away from the gravity point, but even *they* couldn't outrun missiles without dropping into FTL...and the Tokomak had made sure they'd trapped the human ships in real space. She ran through hundreds of possible scenarios in a handful of seconds, trying to think of something—anything—she could do, but the most optimistic of them ended with the entire fleet being wiped out slightly less quickly than the *less* optimistic scenarios. It looked as if she'd be bearing witness to the first *true* Tokomak victory of the war, to the destruction of an entire human fleet in full view of the entire system...

Her heart twisted as enemy missiles roared towards their targets. Admiral Teller's point defence was working overtime, binding the ships into a single entity as they swatted missile after missile, but they just weren't stopping *enough*. The fleet seemed to double, then triple, as highly-classified ECM systems came online, projecting a handful of sensor ghosts for each and every *real* ship in the fleet, yet...the Tokomak already had enough data to sort the fakes from the real ships. And the ghosts would start to vanish as the ships projecting them died.

And then everything changed. Again.

. . .

Neola noted, absently, that the human point defence was better than predicted. They'd clearly improved their ECM since she'd last tangled with a human fleet, to the point she *knew* more of her missiles would have been fooled if she hadn't taken the time to gather such precise targeting data. The fake ships looked *realer* than their real counterparts. She snorted, knowing it didn't matter. If half the missiles went astray, the remainder would still find targets and hammer them into dust.

She turned her attention to the gravity point as the fleet converged on its target. The stream of human warships had abated, leaving her in sole possession of the gravity point. She would block it completely, then hunt down and destroy the remaining human ships. And then…she started as new icons appeared in front of her, thousands of tiny objects transiting the gravity point. They were moving towards her…she cursed in horror as she realised her mistake. She'd occupied the gravity point and the humans had replied by launching hundreds of assault pods at her!

"Take them out," she snapped. The human fleet was taking a battering, but…right now, it was suddenly no longer a priority. They'd timed it well. The assault pods were well within *their* engagement range, but right on the edge of *her* engagement range. Her point defence wasn't going to take out more than a handful of them before they opened fire. "Rotate the fleet! Reverse course!"

Alarms shrilled as the missile pods launched their deadly contents. Neola felt her ship shudder, drives screaming in protest as she struggled to reverse course. She kicked herself, mentally, for deploying the gravity well projectors. She'd locked the human ships out of FTL, but she'd locked *herself* out of FTL too! She snapped orders, knowing it would take far too long for the gravity shadows to fade. They didn't have *time*. She glanced at the human fleet, then turned her attention to the enemy missiles as they zoomed towards her fleet. They seemed to be slower than she'd expected…then she realized they were *her* missiles! Tokomak missiles!

The humans had taken them from N-Gann, loaded them into makeshift assault pods and fired them at her. In hindsight...

We know these missiles, she thought, as the missiles flew into her point defence envelope. If they weren't human designs, with human seeker heads, the fleet might just have a chance to survive. They might even win the battle. *We can stop them.*

She gritted her teeth as the missiles started to strike home. They weren't as well-coordinated as she'd come to expect from human designs, but there were so many of them it hardly mattered. She watched, numbly, as shields were blown down and starships were destroyed, a handful losing power and falling out of formation as lifepods were launched. The humans wouldn't fire on the lifepods deliberately—she admitted that much about them—but in such a confused environment their electronic servants might have other ideas. She tried not to curse openly as hundreds of starships were damaged or destroyed, including too many of her allied ships. Their commanders were not going to be pleased. She ignored the lights on her display as her subordinates tried to call her. If they'd drilled their units better, they might just have stood a chance.

"The human fleet is holding position," her aide informed her. "They're targeting missiles on us."

"Return fire." Neola studied the display for a long moment. The range was increasing, even though the human ships were barely moving. Her fleet was a disorganised mass. "Order the fleet to form up as planned."

She forced herself to think as the display steadily updated. It was hard to be sure, but it looked as though she'd disabled or destroyed a third of the human ships. She'd expected more... the point defence had been better than she'd feared. The human fleet was a well-drilled mass, while her fleet... she promised herself that she'd have the commanders punished for their failure, after she won the battle. They couldn't afford to be complacent any longer. The humans had taught them that, time and time again. It was high time they learnt to listen.

"Detail four squadrons of destroyers to cover the gravity point," she ordered. "And reinforce them with ECM drones."

She nodded to herself as her aides scrambled to obey. The human ships might be more powerful, but anything that came through the gravity point would have their sensors scrambled…just long enough, she hoped, for a destroyer to land a killer blow. The humans would need better targeting data if they wanted to throw another wave of assault pods at her, if indeed they *had* another wave. Her fleet was such a priority target that she couldn't believe they would have held anything back, if they had it. They'd resorted to throwing captured missiles at her. She hoped that meant they didn't have many of their own.

And it's all the more important we crush that fleet, she mused, as the range started to close again. She was grimly aware of unseen eyes following the battle, of civilian ships that could carry word of the outcome well away from the system before she could stop them. *This time, the entire galaxy is watching.*

• • •

Colin toted up the results of the missile duel with a profound feeling of dissatisfaction. The Tokomak had battered the fleet, perhaps more extensively than they'd realised. It didn't help that too many of his ships were on the wrong side of the gravity point, unable to intervene…unable even to *watch*, now they'd shot off the last of their assault pods. The enemy fleet had been caught flatfooted, facing a wave of missiles even bigger than the one they'd hurled at *him* and yet they'd survived. They'd soaked up the losses and kept coming.

He frowned as the display continued to update. The gravity shadows were rising and falling, as if the Tokomak couldn't make up their mind if they wanted to trap the fleet or not. It must have been maddening to them to know they'd trapped *themselves*, along with their human enemies. Colin wouldn't have hesitated to break contact and drop into FTL if they'd given him the chance. He wondered, idly, if they *would*. They'd lose the tactical engagement, but they'd still come out ahead.

And yet, they can't simply let us go, he thought. *Who knows how much trouble we'd cause them before we ran out of supplies?*

"Sir," Commander Jalil said. "The enemy is resuming fire."

"Deploy drones, then start randomly activating and deactivating cloaking devices," Colin ordered. It would keep the enemy guessing, perhaps long enough to force them to expend all their missiles. They certainly weren't sparing the firepower. Colin would have hesitated to fire so many missiles in a single barrage. It helped, he supposed, that the Tokomak had supply dumps and a fleet train a single jump away. "And continue firing."

He gritted his teeth as the enemy fleet picked up speed. They weren't *quite* as fast as his ships in realspace, but he doubted he'd have time to simply outrun them ... not, he supposed, that it would do much for his reputation. He'd be quite happy to have idiots singing songs about an admiral who "bravely" ran away if it preserved his fleet and crew for another day, even if it meant the entire system watched as they ran. And yet ... the enemy fleet seemed to grow faster. They'd removed the safety interlocks on their drives. That was unlike them ...

They know this is for all the marbles, he thought. *If they lose here, they may lose everything.*

The enemy missiles roared into engagement range. The point defence opened fire, their targeting computer well aware—now—of just what the enemy missiles could and couldn't do. Thousands were picked off, hundreds more diverted to expend themselves uselessly against drones and translucent sensor ghosts ... the remainder slammed home, smashing into his ships like hammers wielded by an angry god. He ignored the surge of messages through the datanet, damage control teams being ordered to do what repairs they could while the fleet was underway. A cruiser fell out of formation, her drive field flickering out of existence as she lost main power. Five enemy missiles blew her to bits before she could even *start* launching lifepods. Colin felt his gut churn as she was lost with all hands.

A hammer struck his ship. Colin kept himself composed, knowing it was just a matter of time before the alien fleet wore his defences down and crushed him. The range was still closing, somehow…the Tokomak had boosted their drives. He didn't know how long their drives could take it, but it hardly mattered. They just had to last long enough to keep closing the range. Knowing them, they probably had supply dumps loaded with spare drive units as well as missiles and everything else they needed to wage war.

He frowned as a red light appeared on his display. A courier boat, coming in from the distant gravity point. The enemy-held gravity point. He felt his frown deepen, then shrugged. It didn't matter, not now. All that mattered was staying alive long enough to give Admiral Stuart a shot at Tokomak Prime.

• • •

Hameeda brought her drives and weapons online, then deployed a handful of drones as she roared towards the gravity point. The enemy destroyers seemed to flinch as she raced towards them, accelerating so rapidly that they might well have mistaken her for an oversized missile, then moved to block her as she angled towards the gravity point itself. She launched her final drone, aiming it at the gravity point, then boosted her speed as she rushed right into their defence envelope. Their point defence fire was spotty, as if they couldn't quite believe their sensors. Hameeda had to smile. The LinkShip wasn't a gunboat and it wasn't a warship, but…what *was* it?

She darted from side to side, flying in predictable patterns for as long as she dared—roughly two or three seconds—then dropping into randomised formations that made it look as if she was jerking at one of the alien ships before changing her mind and darting towards a *different* target. They were confused, unable to target her properly as her drone vanished through the gravity point. Hameeda yanked herself away, hoping that whoever was in command on the far side would be ready. Surely, they knew they had to come to Admiral Teller's aid.

A handful of conjoined cruisers appeared on the gravity point. Hameeda opened a communications channel at once, thrusting all the targeting data they could possibly need at them. The cruisers opened fire, their weapons sweeping the gravity point. The enemy destroyers turned, but it was too late. Only one of them managed to get off a shot before they were blown out of space. The cruisers separated and glided forward, one of them launching a drone back through the gravity point. Moments later, the human fleet resumed its advance into the system.

And now you're caught between two fires, Hameeda thought. She eyed the enemy fleet as it closed on Admiral Teller. The Tokomak had to know what had happened, now. *Will you try to reclaim the gravity point? Or will you crush Admiral Teller, knowing you'll cede the gravity point to us?*

• • •

Neola was not *used* to indecision. She always knew what to do, or so she told herself. It helped that she normally had enough ships and firepower to compensate for any hasty missteps... she stared in disbelief as the humans rapidly recaptured the gravity point, their impossibly-advanced starship fading back into cloak as she completed her mission. For a moment, Neola honestly wondered if another alien faction had intervened on humanity's side. It was possible, she supposed. Vast sections of the galaxy remained unexplored, even after thousands of years of galactic civilisation. And yet... she dismissed the thought as she tried to decide what to do. The rules had changed, yet again. If she didn't retake the gravity point, she'd lose the battle, but if she let the human fleet go...

"Your Majesty," an aide said. "A courier boat just hit the edge of the gravity shadow. It's broadcasting a message in clear."

"In clear?" Neola was astonished. The couriers—they belonged to the same race, Galactics with a very high tolerance for boredom—*never* broke protocol. Messages were supposed to be encrypted, always. "What's the message?"

Her aide stared at the console. "They're saying... they're saying that *Crux* has fallen! The humans invaded the system!"

"What?" Neola couldn't believe it. Crux was within a week of Tokomak Prime, thousands of light years from the Twins... or N-Gann. "Crux?"

"Crux," the aide confirmed. He sounded stunned. "The entire fleet heard the message."

"And the humans too," Neola said. Crux? How had the humans—or anyone—reached *Crux*? It was impossible. They would have had to travel thousands of light years...she hesitated, then brought up a star chart. It might just be possible. She'd been ordered to concentrate all her efforts on saving the Twins, while the *real* threat crept towards Tokomak Prime. "And..."

"Your Majesty!" Another aide, so shocked he was breaking protocol. "The Harmonies are leaving formation!"

Neola spun around. "Order them to return to formation at once!"

"And the Boksq," the aide said. He didn't sound as if he'd heard her. She had to suppress the urge to kick him—or worse—as he stammered through his report. "And the..."

Neola glanced at the display. Her fleet was scattering, hundreds of ships—*allied* ships—breaking formation. They were leaving...a lump of ice materialised in her chest as she realised they no longer believed the Tokomak could win the war. Tokomak Prime itself was under threat! It was impossible...she wondered, just for a moment, if the humans had somehow faked the message, but she couldn't convince herself to believe it. There was no way to duplicate the authorisation codes without access to the sealed files and the only way to get *that* would be to invade and occupy Tokomak Prime *anyway*.

They must have had contingency plans for our defeat, she thought, numbly. She wanted to punish them, to lash out with her missiles at ships that were still within range, but everything had changed. There were just too many threats...no, only one of those threats was actually *important*. The remainder would have to be ignored, for the moment. *And now they're going back to defend their homeworlds*.

She stood. "Contact the fleet," she ordered. There was no more time. She'd deal with her shock later, when the fleet was underway. "Cease firing. Break contact with the enemy fleet. Deactivate the gravity well projectors. We will return to the gravity point at once and race back to Tokomak Prime."

Her orders echoed through the compartment, calming nerves as they put her staffers back to work. She projected confidence, even though she knew the empire might be on the verge of defeat. The reports hadn't been clear on how many ships had been advancing on the Twins…she understood, now, why the humans had moved so slowly. They'd sent half their fleet to sneak up on Tokomak Prime, using sensor ghosts to keep her from noticing…

If she'd been younger, she would have whimpered. The humans had done the impossible. They'd coordinated an assault across interstellar distances…had they invented a form of FTL communications? Or had they simply gotten lucky? She hoped it was the latter, no matter how much it galled her to admit it. The former would have spelled certain doom, even if the Tokomak still had a vast numerical advantage.

She sat back down, forcing herself to project calm. It was bad, no point in denying it, but it wasn't complete disaster. Not yet. They could still win. Tokomak Prime was heavily defended, with hundreds of starships and fortresses charged with protecting the system and its gravity points from harm. The humans would find themselves outmatched. She could still win.

And when we do, she promised herself as the fleet dropped into FTL, *we'll teach those false allies of ours a harsh lesson. And none of them will ever dare defy us again.*

CHAPTER THIRTY-FOUR

"Admiral," Yolanda said. "Long-range sensors are detecting a courier boat approaching the system, on a course suggesting it's coming from Tokomak Prime."

Hoshiko looked up, sharply. She was grimly aware that time was in short supply, but rearming her ships and preparing for the final offensive was taking longer than she wished. The Tokomak on Tokomak Prime already knew she was here, unless she was *much* mistaken. She wanted to think that they'd simply refuse to believe the reports—it was something akin to *submarines at Tunbridge Wells*, as far as they were concerned—but she didn't dare let herself believe it. They might *just* take the risk of sending their fleet to Crux.

And if they did, we'd see them coming and set off to Tokomak Prime itself, she thought, coldly. *What price the jewel in the crown if the crown itself is lost?*

She shrugged. "If they're heading to Crux, warn them off when they drop out of FTL," she ordered. "And if not... we'll see."

"Aye, Admiral," Yolanda said.

She sounded unflappable, for which Hoshiko was grateful. *She* felt on edge, torn between the urge to launch the fleet immediately and the awareness she *had* to stack the deck as much in her favour as possible when she invaded Tokomak Prime. The recon units hadn't returned, but the files had made it clear that the system was practically impregnable. It was so heavily defended that they probably hadn't weakened the planetary defences—much—when they'd shifted fortresses from the high orbitals to the gravity point. And they only had *one* to defend. She supposed that had prompted their interest in trying to find a way to travel in FTL without using the gravity points.

And if they hadn't, Earth might never have reached the stars, she mused, as she turned her attention back to the reports. *Who knows what would have happened to us then?*

She scowled as she read the latest message from Governor-General Ripen. The alien was either an idiot or... simply too dumb to admit, to himself, that he no longer wielded absolute power. His last few messages had threatened legal action against the human race, a concept that would have been laughable even *before* the war had reached his system. She supposed it wasn't *that* dumb—the Tokomak controlled the courts, allowing them to ensure that legal matters were always decided in their favour—but how would they enforce their judgement? If she won, their judgement wouldn't matter; if she lost, the entire human race would be wiped out anyway. There was no justice when people—humans and aliens alike—didn't have reason to believe the judges were impartial. And the Tokomak couldn't be bothered to maintain a *pretence* of being even-handed.

He can worry about what happens after the war, she thought, crossly. *The rest of us will fight and win the war.*

Yolanda broke into her thoughts, thirty minutes later. "Admiral, the courier boat has dropped out of FTL. They're broadcasting a diplomatic ID and requesting permission to board. They claim they're carrying diplomats with full powers to negotiate."

"I see," Hoshiko said. She *had* signalled a willingness to talk, when she'd contacted enemy authorities during the early stages of the war, but there'd been no answer. She'd always assumed the Tokomak had figured they were certain to win the war and therefore saw no point in chatting to their enemies. "And they're willing to come aboard?"

"Yes, Admiral," Yolanda said. "They were clear on that."

Hoshiko frowned. It was rare for the Tokomak to make such a concession. It could be a sign they'd finally accepted they had to deal with humanity as equals or ... she scowled, inwardly. It could also be a droll admission that a cramped courier boat was no place to hold *any* sort of discussion. But then, the Tokomak would probably prefer to be uncomfortable than make any sort of concession. Governor-General Ripen would be watching. So would half the galaxy.

"Inform them that we'll beam them onboard, once they're within range," she ordered. "Put them through a complete biofilter and security scan, then bring them into the main teleport chamber. I'll have Grandpa meet them there."

She keyed her wristcom, updated Steve. He was the sole diplomat—her lips quirked at the thought of her grandfather being diplomatic—on the ship, although she did have wide-ranging powers to talk to the enemy if she had to. *Someone* would have to discuss peace terms, after all. She stood, passing fleet command to her subordinates as she headed for the teleport chamber. It was unlikely it was some kind of trick, but—if it was—*Defiant* would be the only ship affected.

Steve met her in the chamber. "I've given orders to clear a room for the discussions," he said. "It isn't *quite* what they're used to, but it will do."

"I'm sure it will," Hoshiko said. She felt a little underdressed. Technically, she should be wearing her dress uniform and her grandfather should be wearing diplomatic robes. The Tokomak had dictated how *they* should look, along with so much else. But it would do them good to see the humans wearing whatever they liked. Besides, it was unlikely they'd know the difference. "Do you want me to attend the talks?"

"Probably not," Steve said. He gave her a wink. "I may need to sneak out to consult with you at some point."

Hoshiko raised her eyebrows. "You? Consult with me? With *anyone*?"

"It's quite easy to let yourself be pushed towards a certain decision, in a face-to-face meeting," Steve said. "If they think I have a control, if they think the person who makes the decisions is staying back, they won't push me too hard."

Probably, Hoshiko thought. *How long has it been since they've had to treat anyone as equals?*

She watched, grimly, as the teleport pad lit up. Two pillars of sparkling light appeared, rapidly burring into two alien forms. The Tokomak were taller than she'd realised, so tall they were practically looking down on her. They wore long white robes, marking them as senior diplomats; their faces, disturbingly human, twitched in manners that were thoroughly *inhuman.* She reminded herself, once again, that they weren't human. A twitch that meant something to humanity might be completely meaningless to them.

Steve stepped forward. "Welcome onboard," he said, in perfect Galactic One. "We look forward to holding talks with you."

"We are pleased to be here," the lead alien said. She—Hoshiko *thought* she was female—had a high-pitched voice that grated on her ears. "Escort us to the conference room."

"Of course," Steve said. He pretended to pay no attention to Hoshiko as he turned to the hatch. "If you'll follow me, I'll take you right there."

• • •

Steve had never been a *career* diplomat, although he'd never really seen that as a bad thing. In his experience, career diplomats spent more time pleasing their hosts, diluting demands until they became limp-wristed *requests* and generally making concessions that made life harder for the president and the military. It was understandable, he supposed, that one couldn't speak softly and carry a big stick when no one believed the stick was actually going to be used, but not forgivable. A career diplomat would probably have listened to the entire opening babble without interruption. Steve had neither the patience nor the cast-iron bladder to tolerate an endless lecture on the glories of galactic history.

"Let me be blunt," he said, curtly. The two aliens looked shocked. "We are at war. The war has already claimed millions of lives and will claim millions more, if we don't put a stop to it."

"That is why we're here," the smaller alien said. Steve thought he was a male, although it was hard to be sure. The Tokomak could change gender as easily as they changed their clothes. "If you leave our space, we will graciously grant you leave to depart."

Steve had to laugh. He'd seen bare-faced effrontery before—his old comrades had joked, bitterly, that the Iraqis and Afghanis lost all the battles and won all the negotiations—but this one took the cake. The Tokomak couldn't just order them to leave and seriously expect them *to* leave, could they? He was well aware of how easily diplomats could delude themselves, particularly when their hosts found ways to make them comfortable in exchange for cooperating, but there were limits. He was rather glad Hoshiko wasn't in the compartment. *She* would not have taken their remark kindly.

"I told you I'd be blunt," he reminded them. "You started this war. You attacked Earth"—it might be a shithole these days, but it was still home—"you launched a genocidal campaign against the human race, you broke diplomatic immunity and attempted to capture one of our ships and, finally, dispatched an even *larger* fleet to Sol in the hopes of finishing the job. It is clear to the entire galaxy that you intended to exterminate our race and enslave our allies. We have waged war against you in self-defence."

"We chose to wage war in defence of the galactic order," the male said. He showed no visible reaction to Steve's bluntness. "You chose to wage war to upend the galactic order."

Steve was tempted to point out that the galactic order was stacked against everyone unlucky enough not to reach space before they were discovered, and even *they* got the short end of the stick when the Tokomak wanted something they had, but he kept the remark to himself. It probably wouldn't have helped matters. Instead, he leaned forward, trying to convey a sense of reasonableness. The Tokomak might not understand his body language, but the humans who'd watch the recording afterwards *would*.

"Here are our terms," he said. "You will concede our independence and the independence of our allies, including the worlds we liberated during the war. You will concede our control of the gravity point chains leading from Sol to N-Gann, ensuring that you are unable to resume your advance on Earth. Outside those chains, you will permit our traders to use the gravity points freely, with no more tolls and tariffs than you impose on your own ships. You will formally apologise for your attack on Earth, in return for which we will not demand compensation or any other form of retribution. And you will pledge not to undertake any further offensive operations against us."

The male made a hissing sound. "Do you expect us to *agree* to that?"

At least I managed to get under your skin, Steve thought. *And you're not even considering the prospects for altering the deal a few years down the line.*

He scowled, inwardly. There was a great deal to be said for such a deal, if the Tokomak could be trusted to keep it. The Solar Union couldn't liberate the whole galaxy. Indeed, Steve knew—better than most—that it wouldn't be long before the giant enemy fleet was nothing more than scrap metal. He'd seen Admiral Glass's projections, watched as improbable ideas started to leap off the drawing board and into real life. Really, he was irked the war had started so quickly. If they'd had another hundred years of peaceful development, the war would have been over within weeks and the Tokomak would have lost. And the *Pax Humanity* would have spread over the galaxy.

"We are not disposed to let you get away with your aggression," Steve informed him. "And we are not inclined to bow the knee to you"—the concept didn't translate well, but he thought they understood—"and accept you as the masters of the known universe. We can and we will deal with you as equals—we would be willing to trade with you as equals—and even guarantee to let you keep what you currently hold, but not to let you dictate to us. You started this war. You will have to pay a price to end it."

The female smiled, showing sharp pointed teeth. "And if we continue the war until we crush you?"

"Then you can dictate terms to us," Steve said. "But, for the moment, we have the edge. And we're not going to give it up."

"Then we will discuss terms," the female said. "Perhaps we should start with..."

Steve sighed, then braced himself for a round of hard bargaining.

• • •

"They're not serious," Steve said, five hours later. "They're not convinced they've lost. Not yet."

Hoshiko nodded, studying the report from the xenospecialists. The Tokomak hadn't asked for the compartment to be cleared of monitors, they hadn't even swept the room themselves... it suggested, very strongly, that they didn't care about the outcome. They might be happy for the humans to take themselves back to their homeworld, giving up everything they'd captured for a gossamer-thin promise of peace, while planning their revenge fifty years down the line. They didn't look ready to make any concessions that humanity could use to make it difficult for them to resume the offensive. They'd been quite insistent on either recovering the gravity point chains or having the right to move warships through them whenever they pleased. And they'd pressed hard for a blanket ban on fortifying the gravity points.

Which is pretty damn hypocritical, judging by how much effort they *put into fortifying them when there was a real threat,* Hoshiko thought. *And they expect us to give up such an edge?*

Steve shook his head. "There's little of substance in the talks. I'm not sure if they're delusional or simply buying time, but... they're already trying to sidetrack me with plans for a future conference, with diplomats from both sides assembled on neutral ground."

"Is there such a place?" Hoshiko didn't look up from the report. "Every world in the known galaxy belongs to one side or the other."

"Quite." Steve took a sip of his coffee. "Not to put too fine a point on it, I think they're stalling for time. They want diplomats from Earth, with better accreditation, to handle the next round of talks. And they want a total freeze of operations on both sides while we prepare for the talks."

"Out of the question," Hoshiko said. "It will take a year—longer, now—to send a message to Earth and get a reply, let alone diplomats. In that time, they could bring more of their fleet online. No, Grandfather. We have to wage war now or risk total defeat."

"I agree with your logic," Steve said. "And I don't think we could panic them into submission."

"Not unless you told them it was a choice between victory or defeat," Hoshiko said. "And they'd have reason to believe they might win."

She weighed the odds, grimly. The fleet *might* win, particularly if she was prepared to be ruthless, or…the balance was more even than she'd have liked. There was no way to know what had happened to Admiral Teller…her eyes shifted to the alien courier boat, holding station near the fleet. She could send the marines to take possession of the ship and raid its files, but…she rather suspected they'd be wiped of anything beyond navigational data. The Tokomak hadn't known how she'd react to a diplomatic mission. They must have feared she'd blow the courier right out of space.

We still could, she mused. *And yet, what would that do to our reputation?*

"I could win the war in a single day," she said. "Or lose it. That's still true."

"Yes," Steve agreed. "But if you do nothing, they'll have time to adapt to us."

"And crush us, next year," Hoshiko said. She'd seen the projections. Unless humanity came up with a whole new weapons system, they'd be steamrollered by an immense fleet and crushed like bugs. "Put like that, there's really no choice at all."

She glanced at the report, then up at him. "How much authority do they have?"

"They say they have practically unlimited authority, combined with an understanding of what they can and can't promise us," Steve said. He looked as if he wanted to spit. "I don't believe them."

Hoshiko nodded, stiffly. She had authority too, and guidelines that would bite her if she pushed her authority too far. The Tokomak would probably be the same. They'd have some authority, but they'd be disowned if they promised too much. And there was no way to know what might be *too much*. She rather suspected that even their best offer, the one that came with a very nasty sting in the tail, was more than their superiors would care to accept.

"Give them an ultimatum," she said. "They can agree to our terms for a practical end to the war, with everything we want wrapped up in a nice little bow, or the war can resume until one of us emerges victorious. And then send them back home to tell their superiors. We'll follow with the entire fleet. If they agree, with us pushing into their system, the war is over. If not, we fight it out."

Steve nodded. "Good thinking."

"And see if you can stall them a little too." Hoshiko checked the updates. "We'll be ready to leave in a day or two. We may as well cut their warning time as short as possible. You can give them the ultimatum when we're ready to go."

"They'll still have a few days of warning," Steve pointed out. "That could be decisive."

"If that matters, we're completely screwed anyway," Hoshiko countered. Three days wouldn't matter...less than three days, if the diplomats didn't realise she was following them, loaded for bear. It wasn't enough time to matter. "One way or the other, Grandfather, it will all be over soon."

CHAPTER THIRTY-FIVE

Neola was in an absolutely foul mood as she marched towards the council chambers, escorted by two of her aides and a squad of armed—and loyal—soldiers. The flight back from the Twins had been nightmarish, the experience taunting her with visions of her ships, spread out like beads on a string, being jumped and ambushed one by one. She'd watched, helplessly, as word spread ahead of her, the remaining allied ships taking their leave almost as soon as they had a chance to run. There had been no way to stop them. Tokomak Prime was under threat.

And we had to send orders to redeploy all of our remaining ships from the gravity point chain, she thought. She knew, all too well, that the human fleet she'd battered would be able to push its way down the chain once it recuperated from the battle, threatening the homeworld from a different direction. Thankfully, the gravity point fortifications at the far end of the chain were almost impregnable. *Those fools! Those utter fools!*

Her mood didn't improve as she walked into the council chamber itself, leaving her escort watching the doors. The newscasts were normally bland to the point of uselessness, even after she'd taken the helm, but now... she cursed the reporters who dared panic the population with the truth, just as she cursed the 'advisors' who'd stripped her of supreme power and authority. The newscasts should have been shut down by now, but... it was unprecedented. Of *course* it was unprecedented. Normally, the truth was quite good enough to publish. But now...she cast her mind back to the first reports she'd read as she reached the system. The Tokomak homeworld was on the verge of panic.

She glared around the chamber as she took her seat, noting that only two councillors had deigned to attend the meeting they'd called. The others had probably remembered urgent business a few thousand light years away, as if running and hiding would make a difference if Tokomak Prime fell. The empire would fall with it...and if it didn't, she'd regain full power and punish them for their cowardice. They would be sent into permanent exile on a hellworld or maybe just dumped on a human-dominated planet...or what remained of it after she'd completed her grisly task. It had been a mistake to let *any* of the younger races climb into space. If they'd been confined to their planets...

"The humans have rejected our terms," Coordinator Hakav. "They have dared issue us an ultimatum."

"The humans are not stupid." Neola hated the human race with every fibre of her being, but she'd concede that much. And even an intellectually-challenged race would smell a rat after reading the statements from Tokomak Prime. "They knew you weren't serious."

She bit down the urge to remind them it was all their fault. If she'd been allowed to keep her fleet at Tokomak Prime, she could have responded to the human advance before it threatened the homeworld itself. Or she could have made a stand at Tokomak Prime itself, with thousands of warships and the extremely heavy planetary defences backing her up. Now...she still had ships and men, but she was grimly aware she didn't have much time. The human fleet was probably already on its way. They'd never have a better chance to win the war outright.

"But we would have honoured the terms," Coordinator Hakav insisted. "They weren't..."

"They wouldn't have taken our word for *anything*," Neola said, crossly. She picked up a datapad and shoved it at him. "They don't trust us. *No one* trusts us. And now our allies are crawling to the humans for the best terms they can get."

Admiral Kyan started. "They can't *already* be going to the humans."

"Why not?" Neola rounded on him. "What's happened, over the last few years? A series of crushing defeats, defeats that have proved to everyone with *eyes* that we can be beaten! And how many of our *loyal*"—she spat the word—"allies have dreams of regaining their independence, the freedom they enjoyed before we invented the stardrive? And even if they think themselves loyal, they'll want to secure their future if the humans take our place. I'm *sure* they're already bending the knee to the human race."

She thumped the table. "And now a human fleet is bearing down on us!"

"The detectors are clear," Admiral Kyan said. "I think..."

"You *think*?" Neola was tempted to point out that it had been a *long* time since Admiral Kyan had commanded a fleet in battle. He was on the council because of his bureaucratic skills, not because of any tactical acumen. He hadn't even commanded a fleet manoeuvring its way through scripted exercises, with everyone perfectly aware of what the outcome would be well before the manoeuvres were completed. "The human ships would have to be practically on *top* of us before we got the alert. You didn't even think to send out *pickets*!"

She controlled herself with an effort. "We have two choices," she said. "We fight and we win, or we surrender. And, by surrender, I mean we concede effective defeat. We accept the terms the humans offered, knowing that—in the long run—it will condemn us to slow decline and eventual collapse. It will be the end."

"They've promised to respect our space," Coordinator Hakav said.

"It doesn't matter." Neola laughed, humourlessly. "Think about it. The humans don't *need* to wage war on us to crush us. In the short term, we'd lose both a sizable chunk of our empire and our economy, while we'd be deprived of the ability to fund our reconstruction by charging transit fees on the gravity point. In the *long* term, the humans would encourage the rebirth of innovation right across the known universe. We will find ourselves at a permanent disadvantage when competing with the younger races. Our industries will be unable to compete. We'll be unable to offer resistance if—when—they push their way into our space."

She looked from one to the other. "We have no choice. We must win."

"You paint a grim picture," Coordinator Hakav said.

"It's the truth and you know it," Neola said. "How hard is it, even *now*, to get the bureaucracy moving in the right direction? We have been breeding innovation, daring and even ambition out of our people for thousands of years. We have imposed so many barriers to mental development that even I found it hard to think outside the box. How many of us had the wit to think about overthrowing the oldsters and the nerve to carry it out?"

"You," Coordinator Hakav said.

"Just me," Neola confirmed. "And it was laughably easy, once I'd had the idea. But it wasn't easy to get that far."

She shook her head. "I've studied human history, what little they have," she said. "Change is a constant. Even their oldest empires rarely lasted long, by our standards, and they kept changing from birth to death. The pace of change is so rapid that even *they* have concerns about it. We will be unable to complete, on a level playing field. We don't have time to revitalise our own people. Even *trying* is likely to make sure we fail."

"And so the humans will destroy us," Coordinator Hakav said.

"Unless we stop them now." Neola looked up. "I want a *full* state of emergency. We call up everyone, put them to work. The entire planet goes into lockdown—all alien workers are kept under tight control—and all resources are devoted to the coming battle. This battle is for *everything*. Either we win or..."

"We take your point," Coordinator Hakav said.

"Then you have to understand," Neola said. "The time for petty bickering is over. The humans could be here tomorrow. And we have to be ready."

She stood. "Do I have your support? Or will you try to impede me one final time?"

Coordinator Hakav and Admiral Kyan exchanged glances. Neola kept her face impassive, wondering which of them would be the first to speak. Or, perhaps, to draw up contingency plans for a human victory. She didn't mind, even though it smacked of defeatism. If they didn't win the coming battle, they were doomed anyway. And she'd be dead. She was sure of it. Victory or death were the only two options for her, now. She wouldn't survive another defeat.

"You do," Admiral Kyan said. "We'll support you completely."

"Good," Neola said. "Now, here is what we're going to do..."

She started to outline her plan, knowing that it might not be enough. The gargantuan industries of Tokomak Prime were already churning out hundreds of thousands of weapons—and millions of missiles, railgun pellets and mines—but they just didn't have the *time* to deploy them. The orders she'd already issued, when she'd assessed the situation, barely scratched the surface of what needed to be done. And the bureaucrats had tried to get in her way. She scowled, baring her teeth. Any bureaucrat who tried to get in her way *now* wouldn't live to regret it.

And if we don't stop the human fleet, she told herself as her eyes strayed to the blank display, *none of us will live to regret it.*

• • •

Hameeda couldn't help herself. She gave Piece a hug as soon as he and his marine companions materialised onboard the LinkShip, despite amused glances from the marines and a handful of comments she chose not to hear. They'd probably realised what she and Piece had been doing when she'd sneaked into the system...she put the thought aside, firmly. It didn't matter. Her people normally didn't care what other people did, as long as it was between consenting adults in private. Too many of Earth's problems had grown out of idiots minding the business of other idiots.

"Welcome onboard," she said, to the marines. "I'm afraid we're a *little* short of space."

"We've been in worse places," the lead marine said. He was a towering black man with a nasty-looking scar on his face. "When will we be linking up with *Defiant*?"

"*Defiant* is on the way to Tokomak Prime," Hameeda said. The entire system had heard the message that had made the Tokomak break off and flee back to their homeworld. It was just a shame Admiral Teller hadn't had a chance to organise pursuit, in all the chaos. The Galactics deserting their former masters had made it hard to tell who was friendly and who was hostile. "I think we'll be heading there shortly ourselves."

The marine nodded. "Where should we dump our kit?"

"I've opened the hold for you," Hameeda said. She directed the LinkShip to move out of orbit and head to the fleet. "I'm sorry about the facilities."

"Like I said, we've been in worse places," the marine said. "Right now, a cold hard deck with no one shooting at us seems like a great idea."

"And we might get to Tokomak Prime before the shooting stops," Piece said. "You might wind up being the first on the ground."

The marine shot him a sharp look. "Not for a while, I think."

Hameeda directed them down the corridor, then looked at Piece. "What happened?"

Piece sighed. "They're used to nice clean wars, with the good guys and the bad guys clearly differentiated," he said. "They don't like wars where good guys can become bad guys at a moment's notice and the oppressed become the oppressors when they finally get their hands on the whip. They spent the last two days protecting enemy civilians from the mobs and desperately trying to ready a defence if Admiral Teller lost the battle. I think they're a little worn down."

He snorted. "And a little sick of me too."

"I'm sorry to hear that," Hameeda said, as she led him into the gallery. "What now?"

"I don't know," Piece said. "Admiral Teller assigned a representative to handle things here and further our alliances with the locals, but...the provisional government might not last. It was composed of factions that had nothing in common, beyond hating their masters. And now their masters are gone."

"Ah," Hameeda said. "Welcome to the People's Front of Judea! The only people we hate more than the Romans are the fucking Judean People's Front."

"Exactly." Piece smiled, tiredly. "Hopefully, the threat of being hung separately will keep them hanging together long enough to batter out an acceptable compromise. Or at least keep them from starting a civil war before the *real* war is over."

Hameeda considered it. "Is that what *happens* when people live on a planet?"

"It happened on Earth, before the Solar Union," Piece said. "As long as there are limits to resources, or the appearance of limits, people keep scrabbling over them. And when there's nowhere to go to get away from everyone else..."

He laughed, harshly. "I suppose the real lesson of the Solar Union is that we *can* all get along, as long as there are a few hundred thousand kilometres or even a light year or two between us."

Hameeda poured them both coffee, then sat down. The LinkShip was catching up with the fleet, which was securing the gravity point and pouring into Gateway. The defenders on both sides of the gravity point hadn't put up much of a fight, if only because they'd been manned by Galactics who simply wanted to go home. Admiral Teller had been happy to accept their surrender, hoping to save time. The Tokomak fleet—what was left of it—had simply kept running. Hameeda hoped it wouldn't get to Tokomak Prime before Admiral Stuart turned the enemy homeworld into ash.

She ran through the simulations, but drew a blank. There were just too many unknowns. Admiral Stuart could have crossed the gulf between Crux and Tokomak Prime by now, depending on what assumptions she fed into the simulators, or she might still be in transit. It was just *possible* the Tokomak would get there first. They were crossing a far greater distance, but thanks to the gravity points they could jump hundreds of light years in a single bound. It was hard to believe Tokomak Prime would surrender in a hurry. The system was so heavily defended that it would be a very hard nut to crack.

Although if we cut them off from the rest of the universe, she thought, *their empire is doomed anyway.*

A message appeared in front of her, from Admiral Teller. She scanned it rapidly, then ordered the LinkShip to increase speed. Admiral Teller intended to chase the enemy fleet all the way back to Tokomak Prime, to harass the enemy and—hopefully—reinforce Admiral Stuart when she hit the system. Hameeda wasn't sure they'd get there in time, but it hardly mattered. If nothing else, a human fleet rampaging through the oldest known gravity point chain would make it clear the Tokomak had lost control.

"We're going to Tokomak Prime," she said. "Or at least I am. What about you?"

"I haven't had any orders," Piece said. "I'm happy to stay with you, if the Admiral has no objections, or go where he sends me. Right now, I'm pretty much useless."

"Not useless," Hameeda said.

"I might as well be," Piece told her. "Back there"—he jerked a finger towards the bulkhead—"they don't need a covert operative any longer. There's a formal ambassador now, to all intents and purposes. I might just get recalled to Earth. They owe me about a year of decompression time and shore leave before I get reassigned."

Hameeda lifted her eyebrows. "And what will you do afterwards?"

"I have no idea." Piece finished his coffee and put the mug aside. "There'll always be work for people like me. Perhaps I'll be sent back out here, as the post-war government sorts itself out. Perhaps I'll be assigned to a world that remains under Tokomak control, with orders to cause trouble for them. Or … I don't know. People with my sort of skills are rare."

"Not as rare as LinkShip pilots," Hameeda said.

"At least you deal with humans," Piece retorted. "Do you know how easy it is to *really* mess up when you're dealing with *aliens*? It's like walking through a minefield when you know the mines are there, but you don't know where they *are*. What we consider socially acceptable is utterly unacceptable to them, and vice versa. And there are so many alien races that it's impossible to generalise."

He smiled. "The Tokomak didn't care," he added. "But they had enough firepower and arrogance to make sure they didn't *have* to care."

Hameeda finished her coffee. "It can't be *that* bad," she said. "Really?"

"It is." Piece chuckled. "There's a race with an unpronounceable name that has the strongest taboos against eating in public. To eat together is the height of intimacy, to the point that suggesting someone goes to a restaurant is pretty much akin to suggesting someone should visit a brothel. But sex? They'll quite happily have it in public, any way you like."

"There are humans who'd think that sounds like a great idea," Hameeda said.

"And they're not the worst," Piece told her. "There are races that have intelligent males and unintelligent females...and others that are precisely the same, with the roles reversed. Races with three or more genders, races that have rules so strange we can barely grasp they exist and cannot understand them at all...and they're all jammed together, thanks to the Galactics. It isn't easy to keep them all going in the same direction."

He peered into the future. "The Tokomak did it by force," he said. "I wonder what we're going to do."

CHAPTER THIRTY-SIX

There was a sense of quiet desperation in the air.

Neola sat in her CIC, watching her staffers as they scrambled to obey her orders and prepare the fleet for what might be its final battle. Thousands of warships—and hundreds of thousands of civilian ships—held station near the homeworld, millions of crews, dockyard workers and conscripted civilians rushing desperately to get the fleet ready before the human ships arrived. Neola was proud of her people, proud of what they could do when their back was against the wall, yet...she tried hard to keep her doubts to herself. If she lost control of the system, even if she didn't lose the homeworld, she would almost certainly lose everything. The empire would shatter into a thousand pieces as hundreds of different races started pulling it apart.

She glared at the latest set of updates. The Harmonies had formally declared their independence, even though they'd been the most loyal of allies only a few short weeks ago. The others were being a little more circumspect, as if they couldn't quite believe the Tokomak era was over, but she had no trouble reading between the lines. Gravity points were being closed, messages requesting help were going unanswered...they were hedging their bets, ready to make their peace with the humans if they won the war. And as more and more gravity points were lost, communications with the remainder of the empire were lost along with them. She didn't *know* what was happening across the stars, but she could guess. An empire that was hundreds of thousands of years old was finally collapsing under the forces unleashed by the human race.

Perhaps we should never have waged war on them, she thought, grimly. *Or perhaps we should have committed a larger fleet to strike their homeworld when the war began.*

She quietly reviewed all the decisions that had been made, when the humans impinged on their awareness, but found no fault in them. The humans *had* been a threat, yet…they'd thought they could *manage* the human threat. There had been no suggestion, then or ever, that they might have bitten off more than they could chew. There had been no reason to believe that a race that had only been in space for a hundred years, using technology stolen from a bunch of scavengers, could possibly pose a serious threat. But the humans had actually managed to *understand* the technology they'd stolen, something that most primitive races found impossible. And understanding was the key to improving. She looked into the future and saw nothing but darkness. Things were going to change, no matter who won…

An alarm chimed. Red icons appeared in front of her.

"Your Majesty," her aide said, formally. "The enemy fleet has been detected. They'll enter the system in less than an hour."

"Bring the fleet to alert," Neola ordered. The human ships were flying in close formation, accepting the risks in order to confuse her sensors. "And prepare to meet the enemy."

She nodded to herself as the display updated, revealing a second fleet following the first. A fleet train? Or…or what? The humans wouldn't split their fleet, not when it would give her a chance to smash one formation before turning her attention to the other. She eyed it warily, then glanced at the updates from the analysts. There were upwards of four *thousand* human ships bearing down on her.

And that estimate seems a little high, she mused. *But we'll see.*

. . .

Hoshiko felt sweat trickle down her back as the fleet entered the enemy system and advanced towards Tokomak Prime. The system was ancient, so heavily industrialised that the locals were in serious danger of literally running out of asteroids and gas giants to mine, but most of the planets and settlements were unimportant. Tokomak Prime was *the* target, Tokomak Prime and its monstrous defences. She could do a great deal of damage if she hit the remainder of the system, but it wouldn't win the war. She *had* to capture the enemy homeworld.

And they know it as well as we do, she mused. They'd simulated dozens of possibilities, from a deep space ambush to an enemy force that challenged them to come within range of the orbital fortresses, but there was no way to *know* what the enemy would do. *We're attacking a target they must defend.*

She glanced at the timer, then at her staffers. She'd been tempted to make a speech, but Solarians were a practical breed. They wouldn't be impressed if she recited lines from *Henry V* or another movie based on a world few of them had seen. They'd be more impressed if Admiral Teller managed to join them while the attack was underway. Hoshiko would have welcomed it, if there had been a way to make it practical. But there'd been no hope of getting a message to him before it was too late.

"Ten seconds to sublight," Yolanda said. "Admiral?"

"Hold your course," Hoshiko said. She'd wavered between bringing the fleet as close to the alien homeworld and dropping out of FTL some distance from the planet, giving her the chance to organise her fleet before the enemy opened fire. She'd decided on the latter, knowing there was no way to gain the advantage of surprise. "And prepare to engage any targets."

Defiant lurched as she dropped out of FTL. Hoshiko braced herself, half-expecting to see missiles roaring towards her ships. Even with the new FTL baffles, there had been little hope of concealing their approach vector. Given time, *she* would have tried to yank the fleet out of FTL early and batter it to rubble before her crews could react. But the Tokomak hadn't tried anything clever. They'd just lined their fleet in defence of their homeworld and waited.

"Holy God," someone breathed.

Hoshiko was inclined to agree, although she would never have admitted it. There were *hundreds* of fortresses orbiting Tokomak Prime, a degree of overkill that even the Tokomak would have agreed bordered on paranoia. Three giant rings circled the world, as if they were planning to eventually enclose their homeworld in a suit of armour. She sucked in her breath as her display picked up drive signatures, hundreds of thousands of drive signatures. It looked as if every starship the Tokomak possessed had rallied to fight their final battle. Her sensors noted the presence of thousands of civilian ships, holding station with the warships. There were so many ships she honestly doubted the enemy commander could control them all.

Although they have always had that problem, she reminded herself. *They're probably figured out a way to cope, even if they haven't solved the problem completely.*

"Admiral," Yolanda said, slowly. "I count upwards of *nine thousand* warships holding position near the planet."

"Then I shall be most displeased if anyone should happen to *miss*," Hoshiko said, keeping her voice under tight control. The Tokomak intended to throw *everything* at her, up to and including the kitchen sink. "Launch recon probes, then transmit the formal demand for surrender."

She waited, trying to ignore her heart pounding in her chest. Steve and the xenospecialists had concluded that the Tokomak wouldn't surrender, not as long as they thought they could still win, but she liked to think they'd see sense. She hadn't been *joking* about being annoyed if her tactical officers happened to miss. There were so many targets that missing *everything* would be difficult...and, behind them, there was the planet itself. She shuddered at the thought of what would happen if an antimatter warhead hit a planetary surface. The resulting explosion would do immense damage to the entire biosphere.

See sense, you fuckers, she thought. *We're not giving you a bad offer.*

The seconds ticked away. The enemy fleet slowly organised itself, altering position until it was drifting between Hoshiko's fleet and the planet itself. There were thousands of gunboats taking up position, backed up by everything from freighters to worker bees that had been pressed into service. Hoshiko watched as more and more data flooded into her terminal, the recon probes lasting barely long enough to send back a few images before they were detected and destroyed by the enemy defence grid. They'd blanketed the system in so much energy, she noted, that it would be almost impossible to get a stealthed or cloaked starship into the high orbitals. And they probably knew the electronic terrain well enough to tell when something was wrong.

"No answer," Yolanda said. "But their fleet is powering up its weapons."

"No great surprise," Hoshiko noted. "It would be more astonishing if they *weren't* powering up their weapons."

She waited, wondering how long she *should* wait before she opened fire. They had to give the enemy *some* time to respond, but how long? The range was steadily closing. She'd have to fire the ballistic missiles in less than five minutes or she'd sacrifice whatever advantages they'd give her. Hell, she wasn't sure they'd give her *any* advantage. The enemy sensor network was on alert, backed up by enough point defence weapons to give a gunboat pilot nightmares. They didn't *need* solid targeting locks to make life difficult for her. They had enough weapons that they could afford to fill space with plasma bolts, in the certainty they'd probably hit *something*...

"Launch the ballistics in two minutes, if they don't reply," she ordered, curtly. It would mean committing herself to the offensive, but she wasn't going to give the enemy any more time than strictly necessary. "And then we'll move on their heels."

• • •

"No answer," Neola said, as the human message scrolled up in front of her. It sounded reasonable, but it was nothing more than a rehash of terms the council had already moved to reject. "Is Force One ready to jump?"

319

"Yes, Your Majesty," her aide said. "They are ready to move on your command."

Neola nodded, slowly. Force One was crewed with volunteers, crew who *knew* she was asking them for the ultimate sacrifice. She hated the thought of sending *Tokomak* on missions when they would almost certainly die—*that* was for the servitor races—but there was no choice. Their deaths would buy time for her fleet to finish its preparations and move to the attack. And if it damaged the human fleet, so much the better.

She gritted her teeth. *That* wasn't guaranteed. She knew there couldn't be more than four thousand starships facing her, but the human ECM was very good. Her sensors were insisting that the human fleet outnumbered her ten to one, something she *knew* was flat-out impossible. If the humans had such a large fleet, they'd have won the war by now. But merely knowing that the fleet couldn't *possibly* exist didn't help her sort the real ships from the fakes. She wouldn't *know* which ships were real until they opened fire. Until then, she'd have to assume that all the ships were real until proven otherwise.

"Then order them to jump in ten seconds," she said. "And the remainder of the fleet will hold position here."

"Yes, Your Majesty."

Neola sat back and waited. She'd done all she could, although she knew it wasn't enough to guarantee a victory. The days when they could crush an enemy, even a more advanced enemy, by sheer weight of numbers were gone. But...

Maybe we can surprise you one final time, she thought. *And that might just give us an edge.*

• • •

"Ballistic missiles away, Admiral," Yolanda reported. "The enemy hasn't reacted."

Hoshiko nodded. Launching unpowered missiles on ballistic trajectories was risky—their flight paths would be easy to predict, if the enemy saw them coming, making them sitting ducks—but it might just get a few thousand missiles into sprint-mode range before the penny dropped. The alien fleet was sitting right on top of the gravity well, too close to the planetary gravity shadow to jump into FTL without serious risk. They might *just* be caught in the open if her missiles managed to get into range before they were detected...

"Long-range sensors are picking up odd emissions," Yolanda said. "I..."

She broke off as red icons flared into existence on the display. "Contacts! Multiple contacts! Right on top of us!"

"Engage at will," Hoshiko snapped.

She sucked in her breath. A large fleet of enemy ships—warships and converted civilian starships—had appeared right in front of the human fleet, so close they'd practically slid into the forward elements. Two starships had died in colossal explosions, explosions so powerful that nothing short of interpenetration could possibly explain them. But that was impossible...she swore under her breath as she realised she'd underestimated her foe. The alien ships had jumped through FTL, at such short range they'd practically carried out a Picard Manoeuvre, arriving before her FTL sensors had a chance to realise they were coming and sound the alarm. Their coordination was shitty—their ships were so badly scattered that a number had arrived well clear of the fleet—but it hardly mattered. They'd dropped out well inside her defence perimeter.

"They're launching missiles in all directions," Yolanda snapped. "And the civilian ships are moving into attack vectors..."

"Ramming vectors," Hoshiko corrected. A civilian ship couldn't beat a warship, but if two starships collided at a reasonable fraction of the speed of light they'd both be destroyed. It wouldn't *matter* if one of them was a civilian ship or not. "Concentrate all fire on ships intending to ram."

She cursed the enemy commander, again. There was something oddly *mechanical* about the warships—how they moved, how they fired—that suggested, to her, that they were largely running on automatic. The Tokomak had been strongly opposed to developing AI systems, but their automatics could keep a ship flying and fighting with a skeleton crew until it was destroyed. And they'd already smashed her defence plans. They volley-fired missiles into the teeth of her point defences, aiming their courses to take them through the gaps and ram their targets. It was going to cost them, but she had a feeling it was going to cost her more. The Tokomak had their backs pressed firmly against the wall. Of *course* they'd pull out all the stops to keep her from hitting their homeworld.

"*Nelson* is gone, Admiral," Yolanda said. "She was rammed by a liner. I think they must have loaded the ship with antimatter."

"...Shit," Hoshiko said. The blast hadn't been *that* big—she guessed the liner hadn't been *crammed* with antimatter—but it had been big enough to do real damage. If other ships carried more antimatter, the results were going to be explosive. "Order the forward elements to flatten, then bring up the rear. I want those ships taken out."

She frowned as she watched the ballistic missiles start to go live. "And lock hammers on the enemy fortresses," she ordered. "Firing pattern three...fire!"

"Aye, Admiral."

• • •

Neola allowed herself a tight smile as the human force wavered, wondering if the humans would have the sense to retreat and run for their lives. They hadn't expected her to expend upwards of a thousand warships and nearly *three* thousand civilian craft, not in a tactic that would normally have hor-rified a civilised race like hers. They *certainly* hadn't realised that she'd be willing to take the safety interlocks off her drives, even though *they* were the ones who'd first realised that the interlocks weren't as necessary as everyone thought. They should have guessed...

Alarms shrilled. "Your Majesty, they've launched cloaked missiles at us!"

Neola leaned forward, all good humour gone. The humans had sur-prises of their own...she frowned as she saw hundreds—no, *thousands*—of missiles powering up, angling straight towards her fleet. ECM drones accompanied them, confusing or blinding her sensors. Behind them, she saw the tell-tale signs of hammers racing towards their targets. They looked to be targeted on the fortresses, rather than the fleet...

"Deploy point defence, then antimatter countermeasures," she snapped, knowing it was already too late. Thankfully, her crews had clear orders to fire on any close threat. "Angle the antimatter warheads towards the hammers."

She watched, grimly, as the human missiles tore into her formations. She'd massed a *vast* array of point defence weapons, but they'd had very little warning before their targets flashed into range. She felt a moment of admiration for the human who'd launched the missiles, calculating that they'd remain undetected until they powered up their drives, then turned her attention to monitoring the human fleet. It had taken a battering—and a number of sensor ghosts had been revealed—but it was still intact. She wasn't too surprised. The humans were tough.

"Your Majesty, they're starting to close the range," her aide reported. "They're coming in behind the hammers."

And depriving us of the chance to catch them by surprise again, Neola acknowledged. Her fleet was going to be pinned against the planet, unless she acted fast. She would have preferred to make her stand in unison with the planetary defences, but she didn't dare risk a single missile hitting the surface. Or even one of the rings. *They're pushing us to the wall.*

"Your Majesty, we've lost four fortresses," her aide warned. "They were smashed..."

Neola winced. If a hammer hit one of the rings, the devastation would be beyond imagination. She'd seen simulations that suggested even a *glancing* blow would do horrible things to the planet below. The shockwaves would travel down the orbital towers and literally shake the entire world. In hindsight, linking the rings to the orbital towers might not have been a good idea.

She shoved the thought aside. "Order the fleet to power up the gravity projectors, then advance," she said. There was no point in letting the human fleet escape, if the battle went against it. "It's time to put an end to this."

CHAPTER THIRTY-SEVEN

This is war, Hoshiko thought, numbly.

She watched the enemy fleet slowly advancing away from the high orbitals, heading straight towards *her* fleet. It represented so much firepower that even her most fanatical ancestors would have turned tail and run, if they hadn't blinded themselves to the fleet's existence. The culture shock of knowing they weren't alone in the universe, and that they were pretty much at the bottom as far as the Galactics were concerned, would have given them a collective heart attack. Hoshiko had little regard for that side of the family—reading between the lines, she thought her grandmother had moved away because of that sort of thinking—but she understood, now, how they must have felt. *She* had enough firepower and technological tricks to meet the alien fleet on near-equal terms and *she* was intimidated.

"Order the fleet to concentrate fire on the alien battleships, unless a civilian ship attempts to ram," she said. It *looked* as if the civilian ships accompanying the fleet were converted freighters, with missile pods and point defence weapons bolted to their hulls, but it was impossible to be sure. "And continue to target hammers on their orbital fortresses."

She sucked in her breath as the range steadily closed. The aliens *had* to see that, win or lose, their system was going to take one hell of a beating. She reached for her console to resend the surrender demand, then stopped herself. The Tokomak might take it as a sign of weakness. They knew she would lose the war if she lost the battle. They might assume she thought she was on the verge of defeat. She frowned as a hammer struck a fortress, the impact sending pieces of debris flying in all directions. Their entire civilian population was in terrible danger. Surely they *knew* they should come to terms.

"Admiral, their gunboats are pulling ahead," Yolanda warned. "Tactical analysis suggests they're carrying shipkillers."

"Order the point defence to engage as soon as they enter range," Hoshiko said. "Do we have targeting lock on the enemy command ships?"

"Unsure." Yolanda looked up from her console. "They're switching command frequencies every five minutes. We may not have their command ships identified."

"But close enough for government work," Hoshiko said, wryly. The Tokomak practiced top-down control. Their command and control networks had a clearly-defined hierarchy, with one ship in command of an entire squadron. The human networks were far more flexible. "Lock missiles on them, fire when we enter range."

"Aye, Admiral," Yolanda said. "Engagement range in ten seconds..."

Hoshiko silently counted down the seconds until her flagship unleashed her first spread of missiles. It was a shame they'd already expended the external racks—she'd had the missile pods specially designed to launch missiles on ballistic trajectories—but even so, the salvo from her entire fleet was formidable. There were so many missiles that even Admiral Webster's latest control networks were overwhelmed. The Tokomak fired a second later, filling space with a cloud of missiles. She couldn't help wondering just how many human missiles were going to crash into their opposite numbers as the two clouds converged.

The enemy gunboats sputtered fire at the missiles as they passed, then hurled themselves on the human fleet. Hoshiko watched, dispassionately, as they were picked off one by one, only a handful lasting long enough to launch missiles towards their targets. The gunboats caused more damage by distracting her point defence, she noted grimly. The aliens might not have planned it that way—it was impossible to tell—but if they had it was a brilliant move. She'd barely had time to reorganise her positions before the enemy opened fire. The gunboats had knocked all her planning for a loop.

"The enemy gunboats have been obliterated," Yolanda reported. "But they inflicted minor damage on a dozen ships."

"That's not what I'm worried about," Hoshiko said. "The enemy missiles will pose a greater threat."

She glanced at her console, wondering if they dared jump into FTL—again—and leave the missiles eating their dust. But the gravity shadows were already too strong for her to risk the jump. Her fleet would be scattered, if it wasn't left helplessly floating in space with burned-out drives. She tapped orders, slowing their advance in a bid to open the range just a little. The Tokomak couldn't evade, unless they wanted a swarm of unpowered missiles flying towards their homeworld. She felt an ugly sensation in her gut as she calculated the odds. It was wrong to use an entire planet as a shield...

Her eyes narrowed as her missiles lanced into the teeth of the enemy defences, ignoring smaller targets in favour of the giant battleships. The Tokomak point defence was stronger than ever before, although it was clear the fleet wasn't operating as a single coordinated entity. She wondered, idly, why they hadn't bothered to overcome that weakness—it was a serious weakness, if they lost the command ships—and then dismissed the thought as enemy ships started to explode. The command networks fragmented shortly afterwards, although not as much as she'd hoped. Whoever was in command was smart enough to plan for losing a handful of command and coordination ships.

Which is no great surprise, she told herself. *They know they can take heavy losses.*

"Enemy missiles are entering our point defence range now," Yolanda said. "All units are engaging...now."

Hoshiko forced herself to relax as the tidal wave of missiles crashed against her defences. The Tokomak had launched ECM drones of their own, although—thankfully—the technology was well understood and it was easy, by and large, to dismiss most of the illusions as nothing more than sensor ghosts. Hundreds—thousands—of missiles fell to her point defence, the datanet weaving her ships into a single seamless entity. She smiled coldly, wondering if the Tokomak envied her crews. They'd fought a stream of battles against overwhelming odds, while the Tokomak had practiced exercises that might as well be parades. There had been no surprises, no doubts about who would win... her lips quirked. It was no way to prepare for war.

Her humour soured as hundreds of missiles broke through her defences and fell upon her ships. Yolanda started to recite a list of damaged or destroyed vessels, until Hoshiko growled at her to shut up. She didn't need to know how many of her friends had died in the last few moments, how many people she didn't know would never see home again... she saw an icon vanish from the display, the simple image hiding the reality of a starship being torn apart by explosions, of a crew trying desperately to get into the lifepods before it was too late. *Defiant* shuddered as she launched another spread of missiles, intent on hitting the enemy again and again before it was too late. The orbital fortresses were getting in on the act now, hurling missiles towards her fleet even though her ships were out of range. It might not matter. Their missiles would burn out well before they reached her, but they'd stay on the same course until they plunged into her defences or were lost in space...

"Continue firing," she ordered. "Don't give them a moment to relax."

"Aye, Admiral."

• • •

Neola told herself, firmly, that she could take more losses than the humans. She wasn't sure that was true, not any longer, but she wanted—she needed—to believe it. The humans had been devilishly clever, picking off a handful of her command ships and then smashing their isolated charges before they could link into another subnet. It didn't help that she was having to route some of her targeting networks through the nearest fortress, relying on their sensors to help coordinate her ships as human weapons picked off her sensor platforms or blinded her sensor nodes. The civilian ships, damn them, just weren't ready for war. She'd already caught a handful of ungrateful bastards trying to sneak off before they could do something useful like soak up a missile or two. The humans had to run out of ammunition eventually, didn't they?

She cursed as the second wave of human missiles lanced into her formation. Too many of her ships were isolated… the only saving grace was that the humans were concentrating on breaking up her networks and destroying her battleships rather than smashing starships that were suddenly fighting on their own. She saw two more battleships explode in quick succession, one of them taking a command subunit with it. She snapped orders, cursing the idiots who'd designed the command and control system. It had never occurred to them that she might need to bind her whole fleet into a single unit. They hadn't even installed programming to make it possible.

After the war, there will be a reckoning, she told herself. The rings had already taken glancing hits from pieces of debris. Everyone on the ground would see flashes from the battle, pieces of debris burning as they plummeted towards the ground. No one would stand in her way as she purged the bureaucrats, burnt the red tape and revitalised her people, even if she had to make them perform at gunpoint. *We will fix things, once and for all, and then we will impose order on the rest of the galaxy.*

"Continue firing," she ordered. The human fleet was weakening. She was sure of it. "Do *not* let them get away."

• • •

Sub-Level Mop Grash knew, without false modesty, that he was one of the most highly-educated people ever to leave his homeworld. He'd studied for years in the schools, then universities, to graduate with a degree in cosmic studies that *should* have had applications in the real world. But he also knew—he'd learnt the hard way—that the jobs he thought he could seek were only open to Tokomak. The thought of a non-Tokomak claiming one of those jobs was unthinkable, as far as they were concerned. Grash had been given an unspoken choice between menial work on one of the orbital fortresses, doing jobs the Tokomak didn't want to do for themselves, or sinking into the ever-growing underclass of permanent residents who were either ignored or kicked by their Tokomak superiors whenever they happened to meet. Grash hadn't liked either option, but no one had cared when he'd asked to go home. He wasn't even sure why they'd bothered to educate him if they had no use for him afterwards.

He pushed his trolley into the fortress command centre, trying not to look as if he understood the giant holographic displays and illusions flickering in and out of existence. The Tokomak thought he was nothing more than a dumb animal, a creature that had somehow managed to learn to walk upright without mastering the rudiments of civilisation. Grash didn't pretend to understand *that*—he assumed the Tokomak had access to his university transcripts—but he had no qualms about taking advantage. It was astonishing what someone would say in front of you if they thought you were an idiot who couldn't even speak the language. Didn't they remember they'd forced his entire race to speak their tongue?

The human ships were clearly visible on the displays, handing out a pounding to the defenders. Grash hid his amusement as he reached into his trolley, his hand clutching the chemically-propelled weapon he'd built for himself. It hadn't been easy, but the Tokomak were blind to the loopholes in their security network. He couldn't use the fabricators to make something they'd recognise as a weapon, yet...they didn't seem to realise he could produce the components to build the weapon himself. And he'd been quite a worker in his younger days. It had been quite easy to put the weapon together once he'd heard the reports. It was time for a little revenge.

His eyes swept the compartment, picking out five Tokomak operators working their consoles and a lone commanding officer, reclining in a chair. Grash had no doubt he was already planning five volumes of war memoirs, in which he claimed to have won the war single-handedly despite the Empress's meddling. He'd read a couple of books that passed for literature amongst his so-called superiors and he honestly didn't understand how anyone—including the Tokomak themselves—could get through the first chapters. They'd been so boring they could drain the life out of mating season itself.

He smiled at the thought, then pointed the gun at the commander and fired. The gunshot was louder than he'd expected in the compartment, the commander jerking before collapsing to the deck. The operators spun around, gaping at him. They were so surprised that it took them several seconds to realise that he was holding a gun, that he was pointing it at them. He didn't hesitate. He shot them all, one by one, then sealed the hatch. He wasn't sure if the onboard sensors would have noticed the shots or not, but *someone* would be along sooner or later. He didn't have much time.

Pushing the trolley into the middle of the compartment, he poured one container of cleaning fluids into another and then hurried to the main console as the mixture started to bubble. The operators hadn't had a chance to lock the system before he'd shot them. He breathed a prayer of thanks to gods he'd largely forgotten—any sort of pagan worship was strictly forbidden on Tokomak Prime, where it was seen as primitive superstition—and then opened the system. The Tokomak hadn't realised he could experiment with their simulators too. He didn't pretend to understand the system, but he could shut it down. And he did.

Someone banged on the hatch. Grash turned, in time to see white mist rising from the trolley. Anyone who fired a plasma weapon in the compartment wouldn't live to regret it. He smirked, then put his pistol to his head. He'd always known he wouldn't last long enough to be interrogated. Suicide was bad, but falling into the hands of Internal Security was worse. He'd heard the rumours. They'd rip his mind to shreds and then throw whatever was left of him into the sun.

"You bastards," he said. The hammering was growing louder. It wouldn't be long before someone thought to get a cutter. They'd regret *that*, if they lived. "Goodbye."

Quite calmly, he pulled the trigger.

. . .

Neola cursed as a chunk of the datanet simply collapsed. "Report!"

"We lost the connection to Fortress Four," an aide said. "The communications links just collapsed!"

"Reboot them," Neola snapped. Her mind raced. What had happened? Fortress Four had narrowly survived two hammers that would have smashed it to atoms if they'd connected, but…it hadn't taken any damage at all. The fortress was still intact, glowing peacefully on her display. There was no hint of *any* enemy action. "And get a report…"

"Empress!" Another aide, panic in his voice. "There's an uprising on Fortress Nine!"

"An uprising?" Neola swung around to glare at him. "Who's uprising?"

"The servitors," the aide said. "They went mad and attacked their masters! There's fighting on the rings and…"

Neola barely heard him. There was a *huge* population of guest-workers, of servants and slaves and transients who'd somehow made their way to Tokomak Prime and found themselves unable to leave again. The rings were so vast that there was room for millions of unwelcome guests, as long as they stayed out of the way. She had no idea how they survived, but she didn't much care. She'd thought…she hit the console in frustration. She'd *ordered* her subordinates to move all non-Tokomak off the fortresses!

And they probably asked themselves who was going to clean their feet for them, she thought, sourly. *And then they classed all the guests as essential workers.*

"Order Internal Security to deal with them," she said. The intelligence service had failed, if it had missed all signs of a revolt being planned. The bastards could redeem themselves with brutality. It was all they knew how to do. "Reroute all communications and control networks through the fleet. We'll continue to close the range."

She ignored their surprise. The rebellion wasn't important, not now. If she won, she'd crush them; if she lost, she'd be dead. The humans could have the pleasure of dealing with useless pieces of alien flesh that really should have been moved on long ago. Perhaps she'd order the ring depressurised, after the battle. That would deal with the scum once and for all. The bodies could be fed into the recyclers and turned into something useful.

"Aye, Empress."

Neola forced herself to relax as the battleship quivered, launching yet another wave of missiles towards the human fleet. The two fleets were converging rapidly now, losses mounting on both sides. There was no way either of them could retreat, not now. They were so short of manoeuvring room that they *had* to fight the battle to be bitter end. She watched a pair of hammers take out one of the gravity well projectors, smashing it and its carrier beyond all hope of repair. Perhaps the humans wanted to retreat. But they were pressing further into the real gravity shadow, trapping themselves.

And they can't do anything about that, she thought. *Unless they were willing to blow up the entire planet...*

"Empress," an aide shouted. Panic spread as a missile slammed into the battleship's shields. "We just picked up an emergency transmission from the gravity point. It's under attack!"

Neola felt her blood turn to ice. The two human fleets had finally met. And that meant...

"Increase speed," she snarled. She'd lost too much to give up and surrender now. "We'll finish this before their second fleet can arrive."

CHAPTER THIRTY-EIGHT

Hameeda swore as a sensor pulse swept over the LinkShip...and locked on.

"Shit," she said. She was dimly aware of Piece sitting on the bridge, but most of her awareness was elsewhere. "Hold on."

Her awareness expanded with terrifying speed. The gravity point was surrounded by layer after layer of automated weapons platforms and orbital fortresses. There were no mines, as far as she could tell, but they didn't seem to need them. The automated platforms were already targeting the LinkShip, locking energy weapons onto her hull. At such close range, practically *point-blank* range, they could hardly miss.

She rolled over, throwing the LinkShip into a series of evasive patterns as the weapons platforms opened fire. Alerts flashed up in front of her, warning her that only a handful of hits would be required to batter down her shields and blow her to atoms. The LinkShip had strong shields, for a relatively small ship, but they couldn't complete with a battleship's defences. She launched a handful of sensor decoys, flipping her cloaking device on and off as the enemy fire grew closer. The platforms should have trouble, even at such close range, telling which sensor contact was the *real* ship.

Not that it matters, she thought, grimly. *They have enough firepower to target* all *of the possible contacts.*

She prepped and launched the drone, then threw the LinkShip towards the edge of the gravity point and the looming fortresses. The fortresses opened fire, filling space with plasma bolts as they tried to target her. She selected hammers and fired half of her remaining load at the nearest fortresses, trying to deal them a lethal blow before Admiral Teller punched through the gravity point. The fortresses realised the danger and switched their targeting to the hammers instead, creating a problem no one had realised until it was too late. The targeted fortresses couldn't take out the hammers with point defence—the gravity well dragging the hammers forward soaked up all incoming fire—but the nearby fortresses could and did. They didn't have to shoot through a gravity well... she launched another pair of hammers, then evaded yet another round of incoming fire. Behind her, the gravity point exploded with light.

"Magnificent," Piece breathed.

Hameeda barely heard him. The first wave of alien-crewed freighters, crammed to the gunwales with antimatter, barely lasted a second before they destroyed themselves in an eye-tearing series of explosions. The automated weapons platforms were caught in the blast and vaporised, the waves of superhot plasma roaring out and cascading against the fortresses themselves. For a terrible moment, Hameeda thought—as her sensors howled in protest—that they'd literally snuffed out the gravity point itself. It took her longer than it should have done to reboot the sensors and confirm the twist in time and space was still there. Admiral Teller would have had some problems continuing the assault without it.

She sucked in her breath as the second wave of alien rebels punched through the gravity point, their ships jumping in unison. A handful interpenetrated and died, their deaths barely noticeable compared to the earlier explosions; the remainder opened fire without waiting to orientate themselves, launching salvo after salvo of missiles towards the remaining fortresses. The fortresses returned fire, sweeping the gravity point even as the *third* wave of alien rebels appeared, but it was clear they were on the verge of being overwhelmed. Hameeda's lips quirked as she saw a trio of alien ships make a suicide run on the nearest fortress, one surviving long enough to slam into the fortress's shields and trigger an explosion that wiped both the fortress and starship from existence. Admiral Teller hadn't liked the plan, when the alien rebels had brought it to him, but he'd reluctantly agreed to try it. The rebels appeared to have been right. The Tokomak simply weren't prepared for a savage assault, with no regard for losses.

But then, Hameeda asked herself, *what sane person would be?*

She launched her third and final drone, providing the admiral with one last update. He'd scrambled desperately to put together a handful of assault pods—they were lucky the Tokomak hadn't put up much of a fight as they nosed their way towards the final assault—but he hadn't been able to find enough to guarantee success. Now, the final wave of assault pods materialised, launching their missiles into a badly-damaged alien defence network. Hameeda smiled, coldly, as the Tokomak were battered into uselessness. They'd ceded the gravity point now. They'd just have to hope they could rally their fleet before Admiral Teller built up the forces to destroy the remaining fortresses and push onwards to Tokomak Prime itself.

The LinkShip rotated in space, then dropped into FTL, racing towards the planet. There appeared to be a battle going on, although it was hard to tell. The gravity point was unusually close to Tokomak Prime—the majority of gravity points tended to be considerably further from the system primary—but it wasn't close enough for real-time data. She braced herself as the timer ticked down to zero and the LinkShip dropped back into real space, passive sensors reaching out for data. Her head filled with icons, a massive blur of light that threatened to give her a headache before the tactical analysis subroutines started to impose order. Admiral Stuart's fleet was pushing against the planet and the Tokomak were resisting, fighting back on a scale Hameeda would have thought impossible. The entire planet appeared to be fighting back.

Piece coughed. "Who's winning?"

"I can't tell," Hameeda said. Her tactical subroutines ran projections, but it looked as if there was no clear winner. Not yet. The winner might be the one with a handful of starships left, when the loser had been completely obliterated. And, if Admiral Stuart won, she might not be able to punch through what remained of the planetary defences and the entire war would stalemate. "It could go either way."

She opened a channel to Admiral Stuart, to let her know that Admiral Teller had arrived. She'd have to wait for orders, then convey them back to Admiral Teller...she told herself, firmly, that Admiral Teller could arrive in time to make a difference. Even if Admiral Stuart lost, the Tokomak would be so badly weakened that Admiral Teller could smash whatever was left of their defences. But she knew, better than most, just how little ammunition remained. The battle could still go either way.

• • •

Neola cursed under her breath as the reports from courier boats flowed into the display. The humans and their allies had launched a mad assault, trading thousands of ships—mostly old and useless, part of her noted—to take the gravity point. The fortresses simply hadn't been prepared for an assault on such a scale, an assault where the attackers were willing to clamber over their own bodies to get at the defenders. She remembered the history records of similar assaults, mounted back in the era before FTL, and shuddered. It would be hard to find crewmen willing to throw their lives away to clear the way. The humans truly were a barbaric race!

She forced herself to consider the implications as her staffers hastily reorganised the fleet, again. The command links to the fortresses and the rings were down, although that wasn't a major problem. Not now. The real problem lay in her fragmenting command datanet, combined with the humans constantly knocking it down whenever they spotted a command ship. They seemed to have an uncanny gift for deducing which ship was serving as a relay vessel and blowing it out of space...no, she realised coldly, they *didn't* have a gift. They'd simply read the tactical manuals, which dictated how command ships were to be protected, and adapted their tactics to match. The cynical side of her mind noted the humans had probably spent more time studying the tactical manuals than many of her own officers. Who needed tactics when you wielded the biggest stick in the known galaxy?

But we don't any longer, she thought. She still thought she could win, but...there were two human fleets now. And even if she beat both of them, the Tokomak would be so badly weakened that the other Galactics would have no trouble battering them into submission. And...an alert flashed as a stray missile struck an orbital habitat, blasting it and its inhabitants into dust. *We could win this battle and still lose the war.*

"Your Majesty, the second human fleet is deploying around the gravity point," an aide said, grimly. "They're bringing ships through at a terrifying rate..."

"I can see that," Neola snapped. She glared at the unfortunate officer until he looked away, then turned her attention to the display. She *had* to defeat the first fleet before the second could intervene. The humans weren't *gods.* No matter how many risks they were prepared to take, there were hard limits on how many ships they could bring through the gravity point before the battle was over. "Signal the fleet..."

New alerts flashed up on the display. The second ring—the second planetary ring her people had constructed—had taken a hit. A chain of explosions ran through the structure, shattering parts of the ring and sending chunks of debris flying. The orbital defences hastily retargeted themselves, trying to blast the larger pieces before they could fall from the skies and hit the ground. Neola shuddered, trying to comprehend just how many people had been killed. The ring was so large that even a massive explosion hadn't been enough to destroy it, but...there had been *billions* of people on the ring. They might all be dead.

I have to win this battle quickly, she thought. A piece of debris hit the planet, splashing down in the ocean and sending tidal waves washing in all directions. It looked so...harmless on the display. It was impossible to accept, emotionally, that giant waves would drown hundreds of cities and towns, killing millions upon millions of innocent people. *I have to win before they kill us all.*

"Signal the fleet," she ordered. "The battleline will close the range."

"Yes, Your Majesty."

• • •

Hoshiko barely had a second to acknowledge Admiral Teller's arrival, even if he *was* on the gravity point, before the hammer struck the planetary ring. She watched in horror as it threatened to disintegrate, feeling oddly relieved when the explosions stalled before they could march all around the ring...and the planet itself. The ring looked like a donut, one someone had taken a bite from and then put back around the planet, but...pieces of junk fell on the planet below, despite the best efforts of the planetary defences. She tried not to think about how many people—both Tokomak and their slaves—had just been killed. They hadn't stood a chance.

Unless they were in shelters, she told herself. *They won't have been sunning themselves, will they?*

"Admiral," Yolanda said. "The alien fleet is increasing speed."

Hoshiko sucked in her breath as the range started to close. *That* wasn't good. Her FTL sensors had tracked courier boats moving between the planet and the gravity point. The enemy commander knew Admiral Teller had arrived, which meant...Hoshiko guessed the enemy commander had decided to try to take her out before the two fleets could converge into an irresistible force. The update from Admiral Teller suggested he was short on everything from missiles to spare parts, but the Tokomak didn't know it. Or so she hoped.

"Hold us here," she ordered. She was tempted to try to open the range, but she was running short on missiles too. "Let them come to us."

"Aye, Admiral," Yolanda said.

"And send a signal to Admiral Teller," Hoshiko continued. "He's to advance upon the planet as quickly as possible."

"Aye, Admiral."

Hoshiko nodded as the alien fleet rapidly converged on her ships. The Tokomak had taken a beating—she'd destroyed or disabled nearly half their fleet—but they still had thousands of starships left, firing missiles and energy weapons as the range closed sharply. It was a giant monster, a fleet so large that the individual icons seemed to blur into a single deadly entity. She found it hard to comprehend how it could even exist, even though she'd commanded a fleet that was almost as large. The Tokomak seemed perfectly capable of soaking up all the damage she did to them and carrying on, until they were in a position to crush her.

A long-range dual works in our favour, until we run out of missiles, she thought, numbly. *They're forcing us to engage them at point-blank range or not engage them at all.*

She felt grim dismay as both sides switched to rapid fire, hurling missiles into the teeth of enemy defences that had no time to prepare for them. Losses wouldn't be *quite* even—her ECM and decoys were still spoofing hundreds of missiles away from their targets—but the Tokomak might still come out ahead. And, as long as they kept their gravity well projectors online, Hoshiko couldn't even retreat. She was trapped in a deadly embrace, an embrace that would end with one side completely destroyed and the other having no more than one or two ships left. And there was no way out.

Admiral Teller will finish the job, she thought, as the lead elements started to exchange phaser and plasma fire. *And he'll push through and take the planet.*

It wasn't much, she knew. But it was all she had.

• • •

Hameeda watched in awe and horror as the two fleets converged, her sensors barely capable of tracking individual ships amidst the surges of energy as they started to exchange fire. The Tokomak were forcing their way into point-blank range, energy weapon arrays that had never fired a shot in anger powering up and blasting wave after wave of fire at the human ships. She wanted to do something—anything—to help her comrades, but nothing came to mind. The LinkShip had no place in a clash of the titans. She couldn't do anything.

The orders flared up in her mind. She was almost relieved to have an excuse to leave, even though she felt as if she was betraying her fellows by carrying out her orders. She'd tell Admiral Teller what to do, then rush back to the battle. Who knew? Perhaps she'd have a chance to do something, after all.

. . .

Neola braced herself as a spread of missiles struck her ship, the blasts battering away at her shields and threatening to tear them down. The range was closing sharply—she'd already watched a human ship torn apart by massed energy weapons fire—but it wasn't enough. It really wasn't enough. Her formations were being shattered and scattered, hastily put back together in time to have them shattered again. There was no time to insist on new tactics, let alone drill her crews in them. The humans were adaptable and her people were...*not*.

Her display updated, sounding the alert. Human starships were rushing towards the planet in FTL, a steady stream of reinforcements coming from the gravity point. Despair overwhelmed her as she realised she'd lost, that there was no way to keep from losing the fleet and the planet. She struggled to think of something—anything—but she'd run out of tricks. She couldn't even turn off the gravity wells! By the time the shadows faded away, allowing her ships to run, it would be too late.

The refrain haunted her. *Too late, too late, too late...*

She cursed, again, as another missile struck the ship. Laser beams drilled into her hull. Alarms rang through the hull as damage control teams struggled to make hasty repairs, too late. Neola knew, with a certainty she couldn't ignore, that her time was up. There was no way to escape, no way to even get to the lifepods before it was too late. A human cruiser rolled out of formation as her remaining energy weapons pounded its shields, but...it was too late. Two human ships were taking aim, their weapons digging into her hull... she saw more and more alerts flash up as her ship died. It just wasn't enough.

The humans will tear everything apart, she thought, wishing—with a bitterness that surprised her—that she'd killed the oldsters while she had a chance. They'd hung around for too long, ensuring her race could no longer adapt to new challenges. *At least I won't live to see it...*

There was a flash of white light, then nothing.

• • •

"Admiral," Yolanda said. "The enemy fleet is disintegrating."

Hoshiko nodded, slowly. The enemy ships, those that had survived, were scattering, some fleeing in all directions while others were deactivating their shields and trying to surrender. She marked them down for attention, hoping they weren't playing dead. They'd get a lot of people—mainly their *own* people—killed if they were. And beyond them, the planet itself seemed unsure of what to do. She felt a stab of pity, mingled with a grim awareness they had to end the war now. The Tokomak could *not* be allowed to recover their strength.

If there's anything left, she mused. *Between us, we took the war right to the heart of their territory.*

"Signal the planet," she ordered, as the final enemy ships surrendered or ran. "Inform them that it is time to discuss surrender."

She let out a long breath as she slumped into her chair, heedless of who might be watching. The battle was over... the battle was over and she'd won. And, between the two fleets, they had more than enough firepower to bring the planet to heel. It was over.

Yeah, her thoughts mocked her. *Or perhaps it's only just begun.*

CHAPTER THIRTY-NINE

Steve didn't rise as the two Tokomak were shown into the makeshift conference room.

It was hard to tell—it was *always* hard to read emotion on alien faces—but they looked stunned, too stunned to comprehend what had happened. They were clearly not experienced soldiers, or politicians who'd had to fight for their positions. The battle had ended over two *days* ago and yet they seemed unable to understand what had happened to their homeworld. They'd been so astonished that they hadn't raised any real objection to the marines quietly securing the remaining orbital fortresses. Their homeworld was naked under human guns.

"Greetings," he said. He would have preferred to speak Solarian—English, with a number of loanwords from other human and alien languages—but he was fairly sure that neither of the aliens would speak anything other than Galactic One. The advantages of rubbing their noses in their defeat would be lost if they couldn't *understand* him. "Please. Take a seat."

The lead alien eyed him warily. He'd been one-third of a semi-authorised triumvirate, according to the xenospecialists. He'd managed to snatch power—or at least *some* power—from the Empress, who'd died in battle against the human hordes. Steve suspected he should be relieved.

Post-battle analysis suggested the engagement had been terrifyingly *even*, with luck more than good judgement determining who would come out ahead. The Empress hadn't made any technological innovations—even now, Tokomak R&D was deader than their empire—but she'd made more than enough *tactical* innovations to make up for it. Now she was safely dead, Steve could even admire her. Who knew what she could have become if her race had been a little more flexible?

And we shouldn't start feeling pity for the defeated until they really cannot hurt us anymore, he reminded himself. He'd had ancestors who'd fought in the Indian Wars. They'd hated and feared their enemies, savages who scalped, raped and killed their captives. The myth of the noble savage hadn't been born until the Native Americans had been crushed beyond all hope of recovery. *The Tokomak haven't lost anything.*

"I speak for my people," the lead alien said. "I..."

Steve cut him off. "The war is over. You have lost. Your empire is in revolt, your former allies have deserted you and entire sectors have slipped out of contact. All that remains, now, is to wind things up in an orderly manner."

He paused, just long enough for his words to sink in. "If you accept our terms, we will be able to handle the post-war situation and then withdraw back to our homeworld. If you refuse to accept, we will do whatever we have to do to convince you to accept—or, if you refuse to see reason, to ensure that you never pose a threat to us or anyone else ever again. We don't want to see you dead, or reduced to just another race of scavengers, but we do want to make sure you cannot threaten us again.

"Our terms are not negotiable. Take them or we will do whatever we have to do to compel you to take them."

The word hung in the air for a long chilling moment. "First, you will concede that you have lost control of all systems and settlements outside your original core worlds. You will no longer wield any form of political control over those systems and formally acknowledge their independence. You will also cede any industrial nodes, planetary defences or anything else you might have constructed in those systems, as partial compensation for how you exploited them over the course of empire. If those planetary governments chose to expel any of your civilians who currently live on those worlds, you will provide a home for them here."

"We paid for those facilities," the second Tokomak insisted.

Steve ignored him. "Second, you will repatriate the non-Tokomak populations on your core worlds, providing each of them with enough funds to keep them alive long enough to find a proper job on their new homeworlds. Should they wish to remain, you will pay them decent wages and, if they change their minds later, a starship ticket away from your worlds.

"Third, in order that you cannot resume the war at a later date, your mobile fleet will be reduced to one thousand starships for the next hundred years. The ships you choose not to keep will be surrendered to human representatives, within the next two months. You will be permitted to retain what degree of planetary fortifications you regard as suitable, but you will not be permitted to fortify any of the gravity points that remain in your possession. In order to ensure you keep your word, human inspectors will have full access to your worlds, industrial stations, shipyards, naval bases and anywhere else they feel they need to inspect."

He met their eyes. "Failure to allow access will be regarded as an admission of guilt and a cause for war."

"This is *outrageous*," the second Tokomak snapped.

"It's better than the terms you would have offered us," Steve pointed out. "In addition, the Solar Navy will maintain picket forces along the gravity point chain leading from Tokomak Prime to N-Gann and a marine garrison at Tokomak Prime itself. Those ships and their supporting facilities will be funded by the Solar Union and the Galactic Alliance."

He took a breath. "Finally, you are to admit—openly—that you imposed your will on large swathes of the galaxy by force and repeatedly broke your own rules in order to do so. We will not demand reparations, nor will we support others if they wish to do so, but we want you to acknowledge that you treated the remainder of the galaxy very badly. You will not be allowed to continue to delude yourselves, or others, about who was right or wrong in this war. There will be no doubt about what you and your ancestors did."

Or about what you were planning to do, he thought. He'd seen the files. *You were planning to commit genocide in a truly galactic scale.*

"If you accept our terms, the Solar Union will do everything in its power to ensure that this is truly an end," he concluded. "We will do our level best to prevent your former victims from victimising you in turn. We will welcome your admission to the galactic community on even terms and allow you access to our markets, where you can sell your goods on their own merits. These terms are harsh, but not—we feel—unjust. However, as I said, if you refuse to accept these terms we will impose them by force."

The second Tokomak leaned forward. "You will protect our worlds?"

"If there is no other choice," Steve said. Thankfully, most of the races that would want *violent* revenge were in no position to take it. That would change, hopefully after things had calmed down and the galaxy had moved on. Steve had no illusions about how long history could linger and overshadow the contemporary world—he'd grown up in the American South—but the Solar Union worked because it had made a deliberate decision to leave the past in the past. "We can and we will block all attempts to attack your worlds, as long as you're behaving yourselves."

He kept his face as expressionless as possible. The Solar Union might reject the terms. He'd pushed his authority about as far as it would go, if not a little further. And the Tokomak themselves might reject the terms. It would be suicide, but they might prefer to fight it out to the bitter end than accept defeat. He knew—and he thought they did too—that the rest of the galaxy would not have to bomb their worlds to ash to take revenge. Simply unleashing a flood of innovation would do it. The Tokomak would be unable to compete and find themselves, eventually, stagnating beyond all hope of recovery.

Unless the shock of the defeat reshapes their society, he thought, dryly. *Their Empress was very capable. Who knows who else might be lurking in the crowd, ready to reshape the universe once again?*

He kept that thought to himself. The Tokomak would be rendered largely harmless for a hundred years. By then, the galaxy would have moved on. Perhaps they'd try to beat the human race—and the rest of the alliance—but the only way they could do *that* would be to *become* them. Who knew? It was astonishing how old grudges faded away once people realised they didn't *have* to keep carrying them. Even as a young man, Steve wouldn't have picked a fight with someone whose ancestors had fought on the wrong side of the Civil War and he wasn't about to start now. And maybe the horse would learn to sing.

"You have one day," he said, standing. "Either you accept our terms or we will force you to do so. Good day."

"You leave us with very little," the first Tokomak observed.

"You have taken much from the rest of the galaxy," Steve pointed out. "You were planning to exterminate my entire race. I think we're being quite merciful in leaving you with enough to protect yourself, if not to threaten the rest of the galaxy. But, by all means, keep complaining. There is nothing else you can do."

He ignored their splutter of protest as he stepped through the hatch. He couldn't show weakness, he couldn't show doubt...he couldn't allow them to think, for a moment, that they could delude themselves into thinking it wasn't the end. He knew what would happen if they tried to keep fighting. Billions upon billions of innocent people, most of them Tokomak, would die. He didn't want to watch it happen, not if it could be avoided. The Tokomak didn't *have* to die for freedom to ring across the galaxy.

The marines nodded to him as he walked past. Steve had told them what to do before the meeting had even started. They'd escort the Tokomak back to the teleport chamber and send them home. They'd have twenty-four hours to make up their minds...he wished he knew, now, which way they'd jump. He'd seen plenty of governments and corporations make stupid decisions because a small minority had bullied them into making a mistake, because the minority didn't have to pay the price for whatever they forced the government to do. That, at least, had changed. Iran had

347

expected bombardment, when the mullahs had defied the Solar Union. Their leaders had been assassinated instead. It was funny how *reasonable* they'd become when they realised it would be the leaders, not their young servants, who would be killed if they continued to press things. Steve didn't regret it. There were rules and laws that should not be broken without serious consequences.

And we did the Iranians a big favour, he thought. He'd never liked Iran, but his dislike had always been targeted on its government and religious fanatics rather than the people themselves. *Things might even have calmed down permanently if the reformers had managed to take advantage of the sudden power vacuum.*

He made his way through the ship until he reached the observation blister. Hoshiko was already there, staring towards the planet itself. Even from a distance, Tokomak Prime looked odd. The planet was encircled by two and a half rings, the final ring battered and broken by the battle. Both sides had cooperated, when the shooting had finally stopped, to do emergency rescue and recovery work. Steve hoped it was a sign of a more positive future to come.

"Grandfather." Hoshiko didn't look away from the planet. "How did it go?"

Steve stood next to her. "I gave them the demands," he said, feeling slightly uneasy. He'd never shied from dictating to two-bit tyrants, when he'd founded the Solar Union, but he felt slightly dirty laying down the law to the Tokomak. He wasn't sure why. Cold logic told him he needed to make sure the Tokomak could never threaten the human race again. "And they have one day to answer."

Hoshiko nodded, slowly. "And if they refuse?"

"You'll have to smash their defences," Steve said. The Solar Union couldn't occupy the planetary surface permanently, but it *could* seize or destroy the remaining industrial base and claim the system itself. And then Tokomak Prime itself would almost certainly starve. "And that will be the end."

"It seems wasteful, somehow," Hoshiko said. "Grandfather, is it *normal* to feel at a such a loose end?"

"When you think you've won and it's all over and you don't know what to do with yourself?" Steve laughed. "I've been there. Believe me, I've been there."

He shrugged. "There will always be work to do as we wrap up the war. You'll have to assign ships and crew to remain on station, here and along the chain. You'll have to help me batter out alliances, or at least agreements, with the remainder of the Galactics. And then you'll have to go home and see what our people think of the outcome. They might tell us to go back and do a proper job of it."

Hoshiko snorted. "And what would *they* do, if they were here?"

"They're not here," Steve said. "Distance may lend enchantment, but it takes away comprehension."

"Yeah." Hoshiko turned back to the display. "I just won the greatest war ever fought, in all of known history. And I feel at a loose end. Can I *exist* without war?"

"Soldiers have been asking themselves that question since time out of mind," Steve said, slowly. "Our family—both sides of the family—have been soldiers, sailors and airmen since our countries were founded. They joined the military when there were wars on and when there were no wars on, because they felt they had a duty. And then some of them came home and asked themselves, deep inside, what they'd *really* been fighting for."

"Like you," Hoshiko said.

"Yes." Steve knew he couldn't deny it. "Back then, I came home to a land that seemed just as insane as the one I'd seen consumed by war. The government was jammed up, infested by ignorant bureaucrats who could be relied upon to make the wrong choice whenever they were confronted by a problem...steered by idiots who claimed to believe the government was inherently racist and sexist and yet wanted to give the government even *more* power. There seemed to be no room for someone who just wanted to be an honest human being, nowhere you could go to get away from the meddlers...wherever you went, they'd simply follow you, daring you to resist. There were a bunch of fools, back when I was in my middle age, talking about armed resistance. I knew they were going to get killed, but I understood. God, I understood.

"But that's not what it's about, not really. We fight to keep our people alive, first and foremost; we fight to maintain our way of life, to protect our right to live our life as we please. If we didn't maintain those freedoms, we...we might have been dominated by foreigners instead of home-grown bureaucratic tyrants."

"I don't think that makes sense," Hoshiko said.

"You've never lived outside the Solar Union," Steve said. He clasped his hands behind his back. "You simply don't have any real perspective."

"We're a *very* long way from the Solar Union," Hoshiko pointed out, dryly.

"You don't have to live here," Steve countered. "You've spent your entire life in the Solar Union or serving on Solarian starships. You could go to one of the outer cantons and live life there, but you've never been anywhere you couldn't leave if you wanted to. Even here"—he waved a hand at the bulkhead—"you volunteered to join the military. People on Earth...they have limits you might understand intellectually, but not emotionally. There were far worse places to live than the United States of America. Some of them bred the most terrible things."

"I'll take your word for it," Hoshiko said.

"You should." Steve favoured her with a smile. "Or you should read the book I wrote about it."

"They made it required reading," Hoshiko teased. "Was it so bad they had to *force* people to read it?"

"No." Steve found himself reddening. "They did that without my consent."

"And you couldn't say no?" Hoshiko arched her eyebrows, looking achingly like her grandmother. "You, *the* Founder?"

"I gave up my formal authority when I stepped down," Steve said. "I thought the Solar Union should develop on its own."

"Yes." Hoshiko met his eyes. "And yet, you're trying to convince us to meddle on Earth."

"It's our homeworld," Steve said.

"One we've outgrown," Hoshiko said. "It's time to reach for the stars."

"I know how you feel," Steve said. "But there's a lot on that planet that shouldn't be allowed to die."

"Yes," Hoshiko agreed. "But how many of us are you prepared to die to protect a heritage we've outgrown?"

Steve's wristcom buzzed before he could answer. "Go ahead."

"Sir, this is Falkner in Communications," a voice said. "We've just picked up word from the planet. They've accepted your terms."

"Thank God," Steve said. He let out a breath he hadn't realised he'd been holding. He hadn't really *wanted* to imagine what would happen if the Tokomak refused to surrender and end the war. The slaughter would be horrific beyond imagination. "Inform them we can hold a formal signing ceremony tomorrow."

He tapped the wristcom to close the channel, then looked at Hoshiko. "It's over. It's really over."

"Yeah," Hoshiko said. She didn't sound convinced. "But history never ends. Does it?"

CHAPTER FORTY

Martin had never really *liked* ceremonial duties, even ones that allowed him to carry loaded weapons and expect attack at any moment. At best, they were boring and tedious; at worst, they tended to dissolve into chaos at random moments, *after* the enemy had had plenty of time to note where the marines were positioned and target them before they started shooting. He'd done enough time on Earth, after he'd joined the Solar Marines, that he'd be happy never to have to carry out any ceremonial duties again.

He kept a wary eye on the Tokomak delegation as they walked into the conference chamber, magnificently ignoring both the marines and the newshounds, and signed the formal surrender accords with a flourish. His CO had warned him to be careful, pointing out that the Tokomak had *invented* most of the microscopic and nanoscopic devices the marines used for covert operations. They might be armed to the teeth, seemingly-harmless enhancements actually designed to unleash death and destruction on unwary targets...they'd teleported through the biofilter and enough security sensors to pick up a nanotech killer lurking in their bloodstream, but that meant nothing. Martin refused to allow himself to relax until the ceremony was complete and the Tokomak were off the ship.

"Well," Major Grafton said. "I guess the war is over. Back to work tomorrow."

Martin nodded. Word had come down from the highest levels, as soon as the Tokomak had accepted humanity's terms. Admiral Stuart was requesting volunteers to stay and man the picket that would remain in the system, keeping an eye on the Tokomak and making sure they didn't try to cheat. Martin was morbidly sure they *would* cheat, once it sank in that they were horrifically vulnerable if someone wanted a little revenge. *He* sure as hell wouldn't trust an outsider to protect his worlds and he was pretty certain the Tokomak would feel the same way. They'd cheat. He was sure they'd cheat. And he'd be there to catch them when they did.

If Yolanda wants to stay, he thought. Being apart from her for a few months was understandable. It was sheer luck they'd been assigned to the same fleet, let alone the same ship. But being separated for at least five years would be sheer hell. *I'll ask her before I make any real plans.*

The crew seemed to explode into party mode as soon as the Tokomak were off the ship. Martin watched in amusement as small parties appeared out of nowhere, senior officers and chiefs letting their hair down and dancing with junior officers and crew in a manner that would have led to courts martial under other circumstances. He pushed his way past a pair of crewmen who were kissing so desperately it looked as if they were going to set each other on fire, then quietly ignored one of his marines who was arm-wrestling a burly crewman. There'd be trouble tomorrow, if things *really* went over the line, but otherwise...he smiled, taking a bottled drink someone slipped him as he made his way into Officer Country. Whoever was brewing alcohol onboard ship would probably *also* be in trouble tomorrow.

He put the thought aside as he reached the CIC. Yolanda was standing by the display, looking lost and alone. Martin wondered, suddenly, why she didn't have many friends apart from himself. It wasn't as if she wasn't personable. And he'd fight the man who dared say she was ugly. On Earth, she had looked a little out of place. Racist policies had made sure of it. But there was nothing unusual about her on a Solarian ship.

"I thought the CIC was supposed to be shut down," Martin said, as she greeted him with a smile. "Are you hoping for extra credit?"

"Someone has to stay on duty," Yolanda said. "And...I didn't feel like joining the party."

Martin sat down and reached for her. "I thought we were safe here."

"We are, in theory." Yolanda sat on his lap. "But it only takes one idiot to restart the war."

Martin let out a breath. "I was wondering..."

He swallowed hard, then started again. "I was wondering if you wanted to stay," he said. "I...I've been asked to stay, but I don't want to stay without you."

"Admiral Teller's volunteered to remain as CO here," Yolanda said. "I'd have to put in for a transfer."

She frowned. "Is there any *reason* to go back?"

Martin shrugged. His family were the marines—and Yolanda. If he had any relatives in the Solar Union, or back on Earth, he didn't know about them. His mother was probably dead by now. There was no one who might be pleased to see him, not now. Yolanda was the only person he *really* knew, outside the marines. It didn't matter to him if he was stationed on Tokomak Prime or the hellhole Earth had become, as long as she was with him.

"I don't think so," he said. "Do you think Admiral Teller would want you?"

"He will need an aide," Yolanda said. "And Admiral Stuart won't. Not back home."

Martin grinned at her. "You'll stay, then?"

Yolanda nodded. "Why not?"

She stood and struck a contemplative pose. "Well, there's the terrible planet with its terrible rings. And there's the terrible population...seriously, do you know how they talked to me? My *teachers* didn't talk like that to me and *they* hated my guts. The Tokomak don't even care enough to hate me. And then there's the lack of shore leave..."

"There *are* holodeck facilities," Martin pointed out.

"And you're with me," Yolanda said. "I *think* that makes up for everything."

"Thanks, I *think*," Martin said. He pulled her back to him. "Should we volunteer first or go to bed?"

Yolanda pretended to consider it. "Volunteer first, I think. We might think better of it tomorrow."

• • •

"So," Hameeda said. "You're going to be staying?"

Piece nodded, stiffly. They lay together on her bed, the LinkShip humming around her as she kept her distance from the planet. Hameeda knew the Tokomak had largely stood down their defences, and that there were marines on the planetary ring to ensure they behaved themselves, but she wasn't too sure they'd keep the peace indefinitely. There were already a handful of 'observation squadrons' from the other Galactics in the system, watching and waiting for something to happen. Admiral Stuart had told them to keep their distance, but no one expected them to obey her orders forever.

"Admiral Teller is going to need me," Piece said. He leaned back, relaxing. "He'll want someone who can deal with the aliens on their own terms. How about yourself?"

"Admiral Stuart wants me to accompany her back to Sol," Hameeda said. "They'll want to run a whole string of checks on me before they start recruiting more pilots. And hear what I have to say about being the only person on the ship."

"Good on their part, I suppose." Piece smiled. "You don't want to stay here?"

"Not forever," Hameeda said. She supposed that meant the end of their relationship. Piece wasn't going to stay as brawn to her brain, even if he wasn't needed on Tokomak Prime. "But I will come back."

"If they let you go," Piece said. "Do you think they'll make you pay for the ship?"

"She's literally priceless," Hameeda said. She shrugged. "Right now, at least. Give us a few years and *every* ship will be a LinkShip."

"I doubt it." Piece looked pensive, just for a moment. "A single ship like yours won't be too big a problem, if she goes rogue, but a battleship would be a *real* headache."

"True." Hameeda conceded the point with a nod. "But the push towards man-machine integration is growing ever stronger."

"And it may come back to bite us," Piece said. "There might have been a reason the Tokomak were *death* on it."

"They didn't want anything to rock the boat," Hameeda said. She sat upright and grinned at him. "This ship is a game-changer. If she packed the same sort of firepower as a cruiser or a battleship, she'd kick their ass. Give us a couple of decades and they'll change the galaxy, for better and worse. The Tokomak *really* didn't want it to happen."

"And it would help if they explained the reasoning behind their decision," Piece mused. "It could be a good reason or ... like you say, something to keep their servants from inventing something that would accidentally rock the boat."

"Or capsize it," Hameeda said. "I'm already as fast as a courier boat. They're saying they might be able to double or even triple my speed, with the advanced neural net controlling the stardrive. What'll happen to the galaxy if someone can travel from Sol to Tokomak Prime in a month? Or less? You'd think they'll appreciate it."

"It would also allow word of revolt to spread before they can put the revolt down." Piece frowned. "*Could* put the revolt down, I suppose. I wonder what will happen when the rest of the galaxy realises things are *not* going to go back to normal."

"I dare say we'll find out." Hameeda pushed him down and straddled him. "And I think we should make use of what little time we have left."

Piece grinned. "Yes, Captain."

• • •

"I'm flattered by your trust," Admiral Teller said. "I wasn't expecting you to suggest me for this role."

"You handled yourself well," Hoshiko told him. She'd read the reports, both the official statements that had been filed in the datacores and unofficial comments that had been passed up the chain by word of mouth. "I wish you'd gotten to the Twins sooner, but there was no way to time it properly."

She shook her head. "I trust you to handle things here, at least until the Admiralty assigns an officer to relieve you," she added. "And I'll try to ensure it happens as quickly as possible."

"Which will be at least eighteen months from today," Admiral Teller said. "I'll do my level best to make you proud, Admiral."

He snapped a salute, then hit a switch. His holographic image vanished, leaving Hoshiko alone. She wasn't *entirely* sure Admiral Teller was a good choice, but she was short of options. She had to go home and face the music, while the other admirals had to command fleet elements assigned to the Twins, N-Gann and Apsidal. They were actually more important than Tokomak Prime, at least for the next few months. Keeping the supply lines open was going to be a major headache.

Particularly if the successor states start fortifying the gravity points, she mused, rubbing her forehead. The Tokomak had managed to enforce a ban on doing anything of the sort, but *she* couldn't. She had a feeling it was just a matter of time before the Galactics started doing just that, if they hadn't already. *It will be one hell of a headache.*

She stared down at the reports, not really seeing them. She had no idea, despite everything, how the Solar Union would react when it heard the news. Her people were a practical breed—they understood that some threats had to be eliminated—but not everyone would accept that she should have carried the war into the heart of the enemy's territory. And, if the waves of chaos made things far worse, they'd blame her for unleashing forces that might destroy the Solar Union itself. There might even come a time when they'd look back on the Tokomak Empire and miss it.

The doorbell chimed. "Come."

Steve stepped into the compartment, looking tired. "How are you?"

"I've been better," Hoshiko said. There were a *lot* of loose ends to tie up, but she felt as if she couldn't muster the energy to tie *any* of them. "Yourself?"

"I just completed discussions with the Harmonies," Steve said. "They've agreed to open trade talks with us, in exchange for us pretending to accept that they acted under outside compulsion. Which may well be true, just..."

"We don't really believe it," Hoshiko said. The Tokomak had given the remaining Galactics special treatment, in exchange for submission and collaboration. She wanted to make the Harmonies pay for the attack on *Odyssey*, even though there probably *had* been some degree of compulsion when the Harmonies had lured the human ship to their homeworld. "Do you think they can be trusted?"

"For the moment." Steve sat, facing her. "And, given time, they'll have to change or die."

"Or just be left behind," Hoshiko said. She glanced at the xenospecialist report. They'd spent the last day on Tokomak Prime, digging into files no human had ever been allowed to see. It would be centuries before they'd seen every file, according to their statement, but they'd seen enough to make a preliminary report. The Tokomak had, quite deliberately, ensured their own stagnation. "If they can still change..."

She sighed. "The Tokomak ensured they couldn't change very quickly, if at all. They were lucky they had *one* officer who could think outside the box."

Steve nodded. "It helped they didn't *need* to, before they met us."

"You don't understand," Hoshiko said. "I read the file. Neola—the Empress—was practically a *child* by their standards. Physically and mentally, she was an adult; socially, she was still a child. She was a bratty teenage daughter as far as her superiors were concerned. They didn't take her seriously because of her extreme youth."

Her eyes met his. "And she was old enough, by human standards, to be *your* grandfather."

Steve frowned. "We knew they rejuvenated themselves," he said. "What's your point?"

"Just this." Hoshiko didn't look away. "Great-Uncle Mongo is *still* the titular commander of the Solar Navy, the senior uniformed officer. His immediate subordinates have been in their jobs for at least the last thirty years. There has been almost no turnover since the Solar Union was established. The Senate has term limits and other rules to keep senators from remaining in power indefinitely, but there are no such limits elsewhere. A bunch of positions are *not* opening up because their occupants are neither retiring nor dying. Admirals, CEOs…everywhere and everyone."

Steve said nothing for a long moment. "And what's your point?"

"I'm ambitious." Hoshiko was honest enough to admit it, at least to her grandfather. "And I'm not the only one. I—we—want chances to shine, to take the helm and see what *we* can do. Right now, the galaxy is big enough for the young and old alike. But what will happen when we literally run out of space? Or of positions we can hold? What happens when our ambitions are frustrated through no fault of our own?"

She waved a hand at the bulkhead, indicating the distant planet. "The Tokomak show us one answer," she said. "Their entire system ossified into stagnation. They couldn't compete with a threat they couldn't meet with overwhelming force. I imagine their younger officers became bitter and jaded, then simply gave up. They couldn't think of a way they could take power for themselves.

"But humans are not Tokomak. And what's going to happen to the young when our ambitions are continually thwarted?"

"I don't know," Steve said. "What do you think will happen?"

"I don't know," Hoshiko echoed. "But I think we'll soon find out."

• • •

End of Book Six
Do You Want More?
Let Me Know.

End of Book Sample
Do You Want More?
LetMeKnow

AFTERWORD

"I am, of course, not a lover of upheavals. I merely want to make sure people do not forget that there are upheavals."
—GENERAL ARITOMO YAMAGATA, IMPERIAL JAPANESE ARMY, 1881

"It's all part of the life-cycle of an economy. First it's lawless capitalism until that starts to impede growth. Next comes regulation, law enforcement, and taxes. After that: public benefits and entitlements. Then, finally, over-expenditure and collapse."
—ANDY WEIR, ARTEMIS

I don't know if anyone noticed, but—in another of my series of books—Neola would be the hero.

Think about it. She's fighting to preserve an empire that, for all its flaws, is far superior to the chaos that would follow its fall. She's fighting to protect a way of life that isn't too bad, at least for her people; she's fighting to protect her people from the inevitable consequences of loosening their grip without taking steps to ensure the people they've abused wouldn't be able to take revenge at some later date. It's easy to say, from the comfort of one's armchair a thousand miles (or light years)

361

from the danger zone, that someone who fights to uphold such values is evil. It isn't so obvious when one happens to be *in* the danger zone. On one hand, an evil system should be destroyed and replaced with something else; on the other, the new regime might be extremely dangerous, perhaps fatal, to the people who didn't create the evil system but are tainted by being its favoured children.

Her tragedy is that the empire has fallen too far to be saved. She might have been better off if she'd fled, leaving the empire to fall, and build a new home somewhere far away. But that wasn't an option for someone like her. She had to fight to preserve it, only to lose when it became apparent that her people could no longer maintain themselves. And so she lost to the barbarians at the gates. *Sic transit Gloria mundi.*

• • •

Let me start this essay with an observation that, at first, appears to be totally unconnected to the theme. Why did the Marvel Cinematic Universe make bank, while the DC Cinematic Universe had a string of failures—their only real success was *Wonder Woman*—and Disney's *Star Wars* start a steady slide towards box office failure?

The answer is not 'toxic fandom' or 'men skipping female-led movies' or 'internet trolls' or one of a hundred excuses that have been trotted out over the past few years, when it became apparent that success had failed to materialise. The answer is not 'sexism' or 'racism' or 'Donald Trump.' The answer is far simpler. Marvel remembered what made its characters popular in the first place, while DC and Disney did not. Marvel remembered what worked and what didn't and built on it. DC and Disney have control of vast amounts of intellectual property and should have been able to use it to make billions of dollars, but lost sight of why their characters became successful in the first place. They had no respect for the past—Kathleen Kennedy recently claimed there was no source material for the Sequel Trilogy, which was a surprise to anyone who read the Expanded Universe (now Legends)—and no real concept of what worked and what didn't. Marvel picked and chose from both the Marvel and Ultimate comic universe to craft the MCU. DC and Disney chose to throw out the baby with the bathwater.

It's fair enough to say that *Star Wars Legends* was not a complete success. The novels ranged from utterly brilliant (*The Thrawn Trilogy*) to great ideas with poor execution (*Jedi Search, Darksaber*) all the way to deeply problematic *(The Courtship of Princess Leia)* and downright weird (*The Crystal Star*). I stopped reading after the brilliant *Hand of Thrawn* books. But there were hundreds of ideas that could and should have been worked into the sequel trilogy. Instead, Disney chose to make new stories out of whole cloth. This might not have been such a problem if the writers had concentrated on writing a good story, then building up the rest around it. Instead, they did immense damage to the *Star Wars* brand.

Now, it doesn't really matter what Disney does with *Star Wars*, not on a global level. It doesn't do any *real* harm to anyone if Disney's movies make so much money that we have to invent new numbers to describe it or flop so badly Disney has to pay people to watch. We don't *have* to have decent *Star Wars* movies to live. We'll always have *The Thrawn Trilogy*.

But what *does* matter is that Disney's mistake is being repeated on a global scale.

An organisation, anything from a simple internet start-up to a full-fledged government, tends to go through three separate phases.

First, the organisation is founded. The founders have a vision and aim to put it into practice. They know what's important. There are few rules, little stratification ... a certain willingness to do something first and get permission later. This can lead to either great success—the organisation makes a killing—or complete disaster, such as happened to Elizabeth Holmes when her ambitions outstripped her talents and/or technological limits. For every organisation that succeeds, there are thousands of failures.

Second, the organisation matures. The founders don't always remain in control. There are a whole new range of departments as the organisation struggles to cope with opening up to the outside world. Budgets and HR (etc) become important. The links between the shop floor (however defined) and management tend to fray. It's not easy to keep the organisation focused when it's expanding and drawing attention from outsiders (rivals, taxmen, etc). An organisation that expands too fast may stumble at this point. If it doesn't, it will stabilise and—hopefully—remain relatively stable.

Third, the organisation starts to die. The founders are gone. Management no longer talks to the shop floor. Beancounters, compliance officers, diversity enforcers (etc) take control. Corners get cut. The bottom line—pleasing the stockholders—becomes more important than doing a good job. The better employees start looking for jobs elsewhere, where they're valued, once they realise that good work and bonuses are no longer linked and there's no path to higher management. Depending on the size of the organisation, it may take some time to realise that it's in serious trouble. (People outside the organisation will notice sooner, then start taking their business elsewhere.) Even if it does, it can be difficult—if not impossible—to fire the useless employees (i.e. everyone who isn't involved with the organisation's core business) and reboot the company. But if the organisation cannot arrest its fall, it will collapse or be destroyed by its more powerful (and younger) competitors.

This is a cycle that repeats itself through history, time and time again. An empire will rise, try to stabilise itself and—eventually—be brought down through a combination of internal problems and outside threats. This tends to happen because the empire's rulers either forgot what was important or were simply unable to maintain the factors that allowed their empire's rise to power. The Romans, for example, faced no peer power...but internal decay weakened their defences to the point barbarians were able to overwhelm them. The French and Germans built their various empires on military force and, when they lost the ability to impose themselves, they lost their empires. The British built their empire on naval power and trading and, when they lost command of the seas, lost their empire. The French, Germans and British understood very well what maintained their power, but were economically unable to pay for their ships and troops.

Indeed, the British Empire's experience provides a foretaste of what America might expect in the coming decades. On paper, the British Empire was the clear winner of the First World War. The British controlled, directly or indirectly, a quarter of the planet's surface. The British army and navy were the most advanced fighting forces in the world. It all looked very impressive, if one didn't look too closely.

The appearance of strength masked a far less stable reality. The British Empire was simply unable to maintain its power, relative to the rest of the world. Maintaining the empire—and the military force that held it—was a colossal drain on British resources. The British invented concepts like aircraft carriers and tanks, but were unable to develop them further; other powers took the concepts and ran with them, developing carriers and tanks that were better than anything the British produced. Britain was, on paper, the strongest power on the planet, but she couldn't concentrate enough force to win a war against a major power without weakening herself fatally elsewhere. And, worst of all, the British public was no longer willing to make the sacrifices required to maintain the empire.

At base, empires—and corporations and suchlike—cannot afford to rest on their laurels. They must continue to develop, to explore newer and better ways of doing things. They must imagine themselves farmers, farmers wise enough to understand the danger of eating their seed corn (thus feeding themselves at the cost of being unable to eat the following year). They must be open to new ideas, ready to allow fresh blood into high places and—at the same time—remove senior figures who are too ossified in their thinking. Done properly, this allows for a steady evolution that combines older ideas and reasoning with newer and better concepts.

Organisations that lose track of the need to evolve start running into problems fairly quickly, as—metaphorically speaking—their arteries start to clog. Bureaucrats cut costs without any real concept of what is actually *important*, ensuring that quality starts to slip and—when purchasers notice—sales start to fall. HR representatives enforce codes of conduct and hiring that are based on abstract notions, not a clear understanding of what the organisation wants and needs. Marketing departments start making promises the organisation can't keep or, worse, get the company entangled in political and social justice issues that cannot help alienating large swathes of the customer base. And, worst of all, the combined effect of all these is to sow distrust and *contempt* for management. A manager who is widely disliked can still be respected for doing a good job, but a manager who is held in contempt will be roundly mocked and ignored as much as possible.

The first signs of looming disaster are easy to see, if you bother to look. On a corporate scale, sales will start to fall. Honest review sites will be filled with acidic comments about your products. Your best employees will start to look elsewhere for better jobs. Your primary departments will start to shrink, while your support departments will begin to grow bigger and more and more intrusive. Your customer base will also shrink, even if you bring out a new product. You've acquired a bad reputation and most of your attempts to fix it are misaimed. And pulling out of a collapsing spiral isn't easy.

On a national scale, there are more significant signs of trouble. The government can no longer afford to maintain its military and police forces. The military and police forces are in trouble because the people promoted to lead are not experienced in actual military and police work. The economy is stumbling, a sizable percentage of the working population is unemployed or underemployed, expenditure on maintaining what one has is so high that money cannot be spared for R&D...once this starts happening, you can rest assured that there will be trouble in the future. And yet, dealing with it is difficult. In some ways, the people who are charged with dealing with the problem are the ones *causing* the problem. They do not, of course, want to give up their power.

If you do not learn from history, you are condemned to repeat it. And if you forget what's important—and how you became powerful in the first place—you are condemned to steadily lose power until you either collapse or get invaded by your more powerful neighbours.

Christopher G. Nuttall
Edinburgh, 2019

PS.
And now you've read the book, I have a favour to ask.
It's getting harder to earn a living through indie writing these days, for a number of reasons (my health is one of them, unfortunately). If you liked this book, please post a review wherever you bought it; the more reviews a book gets, the more promotion.

CGN.

Made in United States
Troutdale, OR
03/05/2024

18216185R00235